THE ECHO BENEATH THE ASHES

RIPLEY LARROW

Brooks Books Publishing

For those who read the first book
and wanted to know what happens next.

Book Two

Trigger Warnings:
Abduction
Alcohol Consumption/Manipulation
Betrayal
Death
Gaslighting
Hunting/ Animal Death
Identity struggles
Imprisonment
Loss of family
Manipulation
Oppression
Religious Persecution
Self-doubt
Supernatural horror and dark magic
Torture
Violence
War

THE ECHO BENEATH THE ASHES

It is a strange thing,
to make peace with the monster in your bones.

Part I:
The Forgotten Name

Chapter One

Three lives had become stagnant in the cave atop the mountain. Keanoff, Edna, and Nemeah watched the sun rise and set over and over again, solemn in their thoughts. Each day that passed after the terrible events in the woods of Nocthrea felt like a failure: a burden of inadequacy weighing heavily on them all. The loss of life also came with the loss of motivation, though they all knew their mission must go on.

Finding the remaining mirrors was bound to come with obstacles. It was only by chance that they had discovered the fourth one hidden within this cavern and guarded by Kallemena's dragon. Its glassy scales clinked faintly in the dim light of their new refuge, each movement sang like wind chimes in a storm.

It was a marvel that the beast had survived five centuries alone, its master imprisoned within the very mirrors it now protected. Nemeah often watched as the massive creature preened its silken feathers like a bird, perched atop a glistening golden nest, the four enchanted mirrors tucked carefully beneath its giant wings. With razor-sharp teeth, it groomed its cerulean and ivory plumage and polished its translucent scales as it watched Nemeah with its icy blue eyes.

A shiver rippled through her as she pulled her thick blanket tighter around her shoulders. Night had fallen, and outside, the wind howled like a living thing, flinging snow across the sky in wild flurries. The moon cast its glow in silver pools across the stone floor, the light drifting in like a ghostly tide. While the world beyond was frozen and stark, the inside of the cave had blossomed into something utterly extraordinary, all thanks to their wonderful Edna.

The days following her husband Jacob's death had been harsh, each one dragging its sorrow behind it like a shadow. The silver-haired widow had now changed. Although grief had dulled her spirit, she still fueled her determination into tasks. Busy hands, she believed, kept the nightmares at bay, at least while the sun was up. She had used her Thorn gifts to transform the cave.

The once barren floor now teemed with vibrant green grass, soft beneath their feet. Tall blades swayed gently, while small flowers with colorful petals broke up the solid green carpet, and clovers sprouted to bring good fortune. Meandering footpaths cut through the growth, leading to various corners, each now dedicated to a purpose.

One nook had become a thriving garden. Trees heavy with figs, apples, and pears arched overhead, their branches low and generous. Pumpkins and squash spilled across the floor in a tangle of thick vines and broad leaves. Tomatoes hung heavily on thick stalks, bright red and inviting. Berries hung in lazy clusters from the stone walls, while grapes clung to the ceiling like drops of ink. Not a single spot in the garden suggested that you were in a cave. Every inch of stone was covered with something to eat. The mingling aromas of basil, thyme, lavender, and sage drifted through the air, filling the space with the scent of a sun-drenched summer meadow.

In the opposite corner, Edna had carefully crafted spaces for sleep with quiet determination. Each of them had a bed of their own, with soft hay and moss rolls wrapped in handwoven cotton blankets. Whenever Edna needed to keep her hands busy, Nemeah would assist in projecting a loom. In just two days, the old woman had woven thick blankets, fluffy pillows, form-fitting dresses, and colorful tunics. It was as if she were preparing to open her own shop. Although Nemeah had offered help many times, Edna always waved her away, engrossed in her silent work. Only the soft sound of her humming suggested she still had a voice.

Since that day in the woods, when the Axis ambushed them and the Morin Zepher took Jacob's life, Nemeah immersed herself in practice. She implored her magic to comply despite her newly formed fear, haunted by Keanoff's warning. He had witnessed what happened when she lost control of her Darra powers: her eyes would blacken, her voice would turn cold and inhuman, and she would strike down her foes without hesitation or remorse. Yes, the Axis had pursued them, but they were still men, made of flesh and blood, obeying orders from those above. The real enemy, the one orchestrating everything, was still a mystery. A figure Nemeah knew she would confront before their journey concluded.

In the days since, she had learned something new: her portals were not born of willpower alone. The compass Kallemena had conjured played an enormous role. When its needle moved, it tugged at her magic, guiding her steps and shaping her doorways, pointing her toward what her heart longed for most. She had returned to the forest once and surveyed the aftermath: the remnants of Edna and Jacob's shattered wagon, dark stains on the ground from the fallen guards, and the place where Jacob had died. But the monstrous undead creations of the Morin Zepher were gone. Had they vanished, or were they still out there? Were their soulless shells waiting for new victims? Nemeah hoped never to see them again. The thought of their dead eyes watching from the shadows made her shudder.

A faint braying pulled her from her thoughts, and she wept as Rhubarb, the old grey donkey, limped out from the trees to greet her. With Keanoff's help, they managed to haul what was left of the wagon and their broken hearts back through the portal to the top of the mountain.

Now they all lived together, waiting for a plan to form, waiting for direction. Nemeah glanced toward the sleeping donkey, whose soft snores mingled with the quiet chime of the dragon's glassy scales. The fire crackled low beside her, its warm light flickering across the cave walls. She stared into it, and in the flames, the image Keanoff had described came alive.

Flashes of a different person shifted through her mind as she saw them from a different perspective. She looked upon this person with disgust and envy, marveling at how easily they dispatched their foes. The words she had spoken echoed in her head again.

"I am the bringer of death. My reign will be eternal." She whispered them aloud, her breath barely stirring the air. "Why did I say that?"

Behind her, the dragon let out a deep, gravelly yawn. It stretched slowly, claws digging into the stone like a cat waking from slumber. With a rustle of feathers and scales, it shook itself and tucked its wings against its sides. Nemeah watched as it stepped carefully through the cave, avoiding Rhubarb and the sleeping bodies with surprising grace. It followed the winding path to the entrance, where it paused to sniff the wind. Then, with a single bound, it glided off into the moonlight, its wings aglow like crystal sails. In a few powerful strokes, it was gone. It would return by morning, as it always did, blood on its teeth and its belly full for another day or two.

A faint rustle stirred from Keanoff's bed before his deep snore returned, steady and unbothered by the dragon's departure. Nemeah's eyes shifted from the cave's mouth to her sleeping companion. Her gaze lingered a moment too long. The white patches he wore in winter had completely faded from his hair, leaving it a deep, walnut-brown. His tribal markings glowed faintly in the firelight as he lay still, one arm outstretched, his chest rising and falling in a slow, peaceful rhythm.

"Will you leave tonight?"

The soft voice startled Nemeah. She sucked in a sharp breath, the lingering scent of charred wood thick in her nostrils. Her gaze shifted to Edna, who was propped on one elbow, her silver hair cascading around her face like fallen threads of moonlight. Nemeah's heart tightened. In the fire's glow, the woman appeared older than ever, her grief worn plainly in every crease and furrow.

Once, Edna had carried herself with a lightness that made her seem untouched by time. But now, her youthful spirit had withered beneath sorrow's weight. Her mouth seemed permanently downturned, her eyes faded, dimmed by burdens too heavy to speak aloud. Nemeah gave a small, guilty nod, like a child caught sneaking out after dark. Her cheeks flushed with heat as she rose, careful not to wake Keanoff or Rhubarb, and folded her blanket over the hay-strewn bedding.

She grabbed the compass and headed toward the cave's entrance, only glancing back once. Edna had already tucked herself beneath her blanket, the covers drawn high over her head. Nemeah clenched the compass in her hand. She had thought this was her secret, this ritual of escape, but she should have known better.

She stepped into the night, exhaling slowly. Her breath spilled out in a stream of white mist, curling like smoke against the cold air. The moon hung high, spilling brilliant light across the mountain's edge. That same ache of uncertainty pressed into her ribs, growing stronger with each passing day. What now? What came next? She did not know. Maybe she did not want to know, because more than anything, she longed for the simplicity of her old life.

The stillness of mornings on the farm, the peace of routine, a world where danger did not lurk behind every shadow. She took a breath and focused. Her hand moved in a slow, practiced arc. Magic gathered from particles in the air, her vision slowly appearing. A portal shimmered into being, its edges flickering like ink bleeding into snow. The shape twisted in the frigid wind, and within it, the old barn took shape: weathered wood, a crooked fence, golden fields just out of sight. Nemeah hesitated for only a second, then stepped forward and disappeared into the dark.

The fields were green with sprouting potatoes and early beans. In the next pasture, hay had already begun to grow tall beneath the warmer breath of Tirnmoor's spring air. The earth shimmered under the moonlight, each water-speckled blade reflecting like stars scattered across the soil, as if the heavens had come to rest on the land she once called home. The distant rumble of thunder told her she had just missed the nightly downpour, and a sense of relief calmed her nerves. The scent of chimney smoke drifted toward her, growing stronger as she descended the familiar slope toward the barn. Its weathered boards had been replaced, and the golden mare inside gave a soft nod of recognition as Nemeah passed the open doorway. The smell of hay and sweet oats filled her chest, drawing forth memories she had not asked for: the morning she left, the way the sun looked slanting through the stable beams, the day after her family saw her gift, the day everything began to unravel.

She stepped slowly toward the stone house. Its door had been mended, and fresh panes glinted in the window frames. Her fingers brushed the cool, wet stones, damp from the recent rain. She traced their familiar shapes until she stood before the kitchen window, the same one she used to peer through while washing dishes or scrubbing potatoes beside her mother. The hearth's flame was low, with only a small flicker stirring among the glowing coals. Silence blanketed the home. The darkened stairwell and closed doors confirmed what she already guessed: everyone had gone to bed. She crept to the front door, testing the latch with her fingers. Secure. Relief unfurled in her chest. Life inside the house carried on undisturbed. Safe and whole, while everyone inside was unaware of the creature that had threatened their lives only weeks ago.

Nemeah circled the house, checking the windows one by one, hoping, aching, for a glimpse of her mother or father. Even a fleeting glint at Orla's small face would have comforted her. She imagined that sweet gap-toothed smile peeking through the glass. But no one stirred. No lights flared. In the quiet pasture, the pigs slept. The cows and donkeys lay nestled together under the night sky. The horse dozed in the barn. Everything was as it should be. Life was continuing without her here. She turned at last and made her way back up the sloped hill behind the barn, her boots sinking softly into the mud. With one last glance at the sleeping house, her house, she raised her hand, the compass warm in her grip, and stepped back through the portal.

That night, her dreams returned to the same shadowy place: a towering black stone building with a golden sun blazing atop its walls. The image had haunted her for days, returning each time she closed her eyes. In every dream, she fought to reach it, struggling through a sea of faceless people crowding the streets. No matter how hard she pushed, the building remained just out of reach. Her fingers grazed the carved door handles but never fully grasped them. The dark wood loomed before her, always slipping away just as she reached for it.

"Move!" she shouted, her voice strained. "Please, move!"

But no one listened. The dream suffocated her; people pressed in close, shoulder to shoulder, unmoving and statuesque. Her heart pounded, breath catching in her chest as fear crept like frost up her spine. She had to reach the door. She had to see what was inside that towering black structure. A sense of urgency, no, doom, pressed down on her. With every second she failed to reach it, something vital slipped away.

Tonight, though, the dream twisted. As she stretched her hand toward the great door, another hand seized her wrist, fingers like iron, pulling her through the crowd, closer and closer to the threshold. A crack appeared in the wood. A sliver of shadowed hallway loomed within. Eyes peered out from the darkness. One blue. One green.

"I am here!" a voice pleaded from beyond the door.

With a sharp tug, the unseen figure yanked Nemeah's arm through the gap. The door slammed onto her wrist with a sickening thud. A scream tore from her throat as pain flared, and she woke up gasping.

"I am here," Keanoff said gently, already at her bedside. His hand encased hers, grounding her as her ragged breaths began to slow. She sat up slowly, her head pounding, sweat clinging to her skin. The fire in the cave had burned low, and a chill now lingered in the dark air. The dragon was now slumbering in its corner, curled in a silent heap of scales and smoke, back from its nightly hunt. Keanoff gently rubbed his thumb over her scar, the one that looked like a snowdrop, grounding her and helping her forget her fear. "Same dream?"

She pulled her hand free and swept the damp strands of hair from her face. "Yes... But different this time. Someone was there. A woman, I think. She pulled me toward the door."

His green eyes searched hers, taking her in completely. She held his gaze. "I think it is real. I think we need to find her."

He did not speak right away. His eyes scanned the cave before settling on his arm. The skin, once bruised and broken from Nemeah's outburst on Nocthrea, was now smooth. It had healed and grown strong, thanks to Edna's medical herbs and his Vira abilities that allowed him to heal faster than others. The memory of that day lingered in his silence. "It is just a dream," he said, voice even.

She shook her head. "No, Keanoff." Her voice begged for him to pay attention. "It is more than that, more than just a dream. I can feel it pulling me in. It seems like something is calling me to her."

He frowned in thought. "Is it like the dream you had about the monster in the woods? When you mentioned he was here?"

A hush settled over them. They recalled the day she had been correct, the day Zepher came for them. After a lengthy silence, Nemeah nodded. "Exactly like that."

Their eyes met. A moment passed between them, filled with understanding and trust. Then, Keanoff's expression shifted. His familiar smirk returned, teasing the corner of his lips. "Well," he said, voice light again, "I could use a change of scenery." With a playful wink, he crawled back to his bedroll and burrowed beneath the thick blanket. "Get some rest. We will need it."

The next morning, they shared their plan with Edna. The old woman shook her head, resolute. No pleading would sway her. "I have lived my adventure," she said, her voice soft but firm. "This cave suits me now. My donkey, and the dragon." She waved towards the creature that stared at the three of them, Edna's jaw set in uncertainty as she faced the beast. "And peace, I have all I need. I am staying here; you two can go."

"Come on, Gran! I will make sure we all come back safe and sound." Keanoff paced beside the fire, hands animated. "Nemeah can whip up a portal, and I will be the guard dog. Or wolf. Or horse. Whatever form you two decide on. And Alban! Oh ho ho, do not forget about that great man! He will be there too, a knight in his shining armor. We will be fine." He was practically begging now, his eyes wide and glistening as he clasped his hands beneath his chin, giving a childlike expression of petition.

She had not said much lately. She had become quieter, slower, and somehow faded. It was not like her. Nemeah noticed it too, how Edna avoided eye contact, drifting between tasks as if she were a ghost of herself. It was not healthy for someone like her to rot away in a cave, even if it was the coziest place in the world. She stepped forward, her voice softening. "It would be a break from the same stone walls, day in and day out. Please, Edna." She wanted to drop to her knees and grovel, even though she did not have the same pathetic look that Keanoff could master.

However, the old woman simply shook her head and continued tending to her kettle, adding herbs to the bubbling water and stitching a thick blanket with practiced hands.

Keanoff sighed. "Looks like it is just the two of us. Well, three with Alban." He shouldered a worn bag and headed for the entrance of the cave. Outside, the sun had just barely crested the jagged mountain peaks. The sky blushed pink and lavender, casting a warm glow against the cold air that swirled in.

"Do you want us to bring anything back?" Nemeah inquired, quickly pulling on her boots and tightening the laces. "A new tea set? Some pots? A few jugs?"

"A chicken," Edna murmured, not looking up.

Nemeah blinked. "A chicken? Is that all?"

The elderly woman gave a quick nod, which marked the conclusion of the entire conversation.

Nemeah chuckled and pulled on her dark blue jacket, the one with the stitched silver stars along the sleeves. "Alright. A chicken it is."

She made her way toward the dragon's nest. Its eye cracked open. The glacial blue iris with its slitted pupil watched her as she reached up and plucked a coin from the pile. A low growl rumbled from its throat.

"You have got thousands," she murmured, patting its scaled side gently. "I just need one."

The dragon huffed, flicked its tail once, and then shut its eye again. Outside, Keanoff was waiting. The wind bit through their layers, but the sun offered a promise of warmth.

Nemeah held up the compass. "Ready?"

He took her hand easily, the movement becoming second nature as Nemeah envisioned her dream. The looming onyx tower and its sun insignia carved deeply into the smooth stone. The heavy wooden doors and the woman with mismatched eyes who now stared back from within.

With a wave of her hand, a shimmering portal blossomed in the air before them. The magic thrummed like a heartbeat, and together, they stepped through. The world shifted and they emerged into a dense forest bathed in dappled sunlight. Vines thick with blossoms coiled around every trunk like serpents, their sweet perfume clinging to the air. The scent was almost overwhelming, like something trying to mask decay. Another flick of Nemeah's fingers, and Alban appeared at her side. His silver armor glinted beneath the green canopy, sword ready at his hip, eyes sharp.

"Which way now?" she murmured, pivoting around. Noise enveloped her. Birds sand and squirrels rustled nearby, while a breeze stirred the leaves overhead.

Keanoff's eyes darted around. "I need to get my bearings." He took a few steps ahead. "I will go scope it out," he started to shift. "Wait here."

Before Nemeah could protest, Keanoff shifted, his form shrinking and reshaping into a hawk midair. Feathers the color of bark and earth burst from his arms, mimicking the wild patterns of his tribal markings and unruly hair. With a few graceful beats of his wings, he soared through the trees and into the open sky above.

He circled high overhead, his eyes scanning the endless green canopy. To the west, he spotted it: a castle rising like a crown above an overcrowded city. Its grey stone walls loomed over the rooftops, regal and unwavering. Beyond that, in the hazy distance, the familiar outline of the mountains anchored the horizon. With a sharp cry, he dove, slicing back through the trees. His form shifted mid-fall, and he landed lightly on his feet, human once more.

"If we head west, we will find a city," he said, brushing leaves from his tunic. "A big one. And I saw our mountains in the distance; we are still close to Edna."

Nemeah had not realized the tightness in her chest until it eased. Just knowing Edna was not far quieted the worry that had gnawed at her all morning. They walked for hours, long enough for the sun to begin its descent. Alban's sword cleared a path as they cut through thick vines and gnarled branches. Down steep slopes and across mossy coves, they trudged until at last the sound of civilization began to hum on the wind.

"Alban, stop here," Nemeah whispered, raising her hand.

She and Keanoff crouched low, pushing through the final stretch of undergrowth until the trees yielded to an open overlook. Below, a city sprawled, vibrant, and loud. Festively dressed people and vendor stalls spilled into cobbled streets, woven between buildings that leaned dangerously, as if precariously stacked against one another like a deck of cards ready to topple at the slightest tremble. In the distance, reaching high above them all, stood the stoic tower.

"Is that a castle?" Nemeah's exclamation resembled that of a child witnessing their first magic trick. "A real-life castle?" She had read about such places, with turrets, moats, and banners fluttering in the wind, but never thought she would see one.

"Aye," Keanoff said, pulling a branch aside for her. "That be a castle."

They stepped onto the road, blinking in the evening light. People flowed past them like a stream, jostling their shoulders and muttering curses under their breath as they navigated around the two newcomers. A sharp crack behind them made Nemeah jump. She turned just as Alban emerged from the brush. With a flick of her hand, she transformed his armor into the rough leathers of a seasoned traveler. He nodded silently and took his place beside them.

Keanoff spun in the middle of the road, arms wide. "So? Where to now, fearless leader? Just point the way."

Nemeah smiled at Keanoff's carefree spin. She had grown accustomed to his brazen approach to life, how he met each moment with unwavering confidence, and had started to mimic it in her own way, even if it did not come naturally. She produced the compass and flipped open its lid. The needle spun once, then again, before settling with certainty, pointing east.

"That way," she said, stepping into the tide of people flowing down the crowded road.

The press of bodies was overwhelming, but Alban's quiet presence just behind her offered comfort. She could sense his vigilance like a silent promise at her back. They wove through the city's winding arteries, each turn drawing them deeper into its tangled heart. The air thickened with a chaotic blend of scents: roasting meat, hot oil, perfume, and the sour tang of refuse baking in the sun. Nemeah could not tell if her stomach rumbled from hunger or protest. The buildings grew taller here, looming overhead like crooked teeth. Their walls blocked out the light, casting long shadows that chilled her skin and stirred something uneasy in her chest.

Still, she pressed on, her fingers tightly gripping the compass. Every corner turned and every fork chosen was guided by the needle's unwavering pull. Finally, she stepped into a narrow, cluttered road flanked by haphazard merchant stalls. Colorful canopies stretched over rusted carts, and trinkets clinked in the breeze. Strange bottles glowed with eerie liquids, and a vendor barked something in a language she did not recognize.

Keanoff wrinkled his nose at the unpleasant odor. "Where in Ardoria have you taken us?"

Nemeah did not answer, for her words were swept away by what she saw. At the far end of the alley, shadowed by the approaching dusk. Sat her dream.

A tall, square structure with walls as black as pitch. They swallowed the light, drinking it in like ink soaking into paper. High above the heavy black doors, a golden sun had been carved, its rays sharp and deliberate. Two guards stood motionless at the entrance, clad in brilliant golden armor that shimmered with an unnatural sheen. It was exactly as she had seen in her dream, and the compass had led her straight to it.

Chapter Two

With every faint breeze, the sickening stench of chickens drifted toward her. Each cage was crammed, feathers and beaks pressing through the bars as the creatures clucked and scratched at the filth-laden floor, desperate for a stray morsel. Nemeah fanned her face just as the sun slipped behind the tall stone buildings of Highspire, casting long shadows over the cluttered street. People moved about; the hustle and bustle was a part of their everyday lives. All moving to the rhythm of the city, and beyond that silent song, the golden sun shone. It seemed to stare down at Nemeah, as if daring her to challenge her courage.

"Think she would want a red one or brown?" Keanoff squinted into the cages, his nose wrinkling and his skin paling at the sight and smell of the squalid conditions.

Nemeah said nothing. Her thoughts were elsewhere, focused on the heavy black doors looming at the far end of the alley. The pull in her chest had only grown stronger since their arrival, an incessant thrumming that refused to be ignored.

"Nemeah?" Keanoff nudged her gently with his elbow. "Still with me?"

She blinked and turned toward the hens, her expression twisting in disgust. "Maybe a red one. Just pick whichever looks furthest from death." Her gaze shifted to the merchant lurking behind his stall. A bloodstained apron hung from his shoulders, speckled with down and bone. His beak-like nose and sunken eyes gave him an unsettling resemblance to the very animals he sold for pennies.

"Excuse me?" Nemeah raised her voice just above the cacophony of clucks. "That building over there, the one with the sun symbol. What is it?"

The merchant shuffled forward and leaned over the cages, his personal stench a noxious wave that hit harder than the coops surrounding him. Nemeah's stomach churned, and she struggled to maintain her composure as the overwhelming reek filled her nostrils.

He glanced at the looming black structure, then back at her with a short, dismissive laugh. "Not from here?" He wiped his hands down the front of his apron, smearing the filth further. "That is the Axis House. Where all the holy fanatics gather to screech about people with powers." He waved his hands around as he said the last part in a higher pitch, mocking the beliefs of the Axis disciples. His gaze lingered on the three, curious now. "Are you one of those crazed lunatics? Believing in unnatural powers?" His eyebrow raised as he took in the group from head to toe.

"Do they keep people there? Like prisoners?" Nemeah asked, voice all too eager for answers. "Have you ever seen them take a woman in there? One with mixed-matched eyes?"

Keanoff let out a harsh cough in response to her inquiry, his own phlegm catching in his throat, turning the fake cough into something real. He sucked in a settling breath, the atrocious stench hitting him full force. He bent over, retching violently onto the dirt. Edna's hearty breakfast now going to waste.

"Ugh! You three are just wasting my time!" He shook his head in frustration. "I am not the town crier; seek your answers somewhere else!" he snapped. "Either purchase a hen or get lost!"

Nemeah reached into her coat pocket and pulled out the gold coin from the dragon's nest. The merchant's demeanor changed only slightly, his eyes gleaming faintly in the fading light.

"How many do you want with that?" he asked as he opened one of the cages. With a quick motion, he lifted a limp black hen marked with dull gold feathers, its body hanging like a rag. It was hardly alive.

"All of them!" Keanoff choked out, wiping his mouth. "We will take the whole miserable lot."

The merchant's smile widened as he reached for his cleaver, clearly looking forward to a long night of plucking and butchering.

"Alive," Nemeah interjected firmly. "We want them all alive."

He paused, shrugged, and began unlatching the cages. As the doors swung open, Nemeah's heart sank. Each cage held more than a dozen birds, crammed into spaces smaller than her bedroll back in the cave. She counted six cages before turning to Keanoff, who was already kneeling and carefully lifting each hen, setting them gently on the ground beside him.

The merchant snorted. "If they run off, I will just catch them again. You wasted your coin, girl." His smug grin made Nemeah's skin prickle as he retrieved his net from the wall behind him.

"How are we supposed to get them back to the," she hesitated, "farm?" She lifted a thin hen from the cage, its light weight unnatural for a fully grown bird.

Keanoff looked up at her, holding a golden-feathered hen in his arms. "They will follow us," he said with complete sincerity, as if it were the most natural thing in the world.

And to Nemeah's astonishment, they did! Aside from a few hens that were a bit too weak to walk, the rest happily fell into formation, creating three neat rows as they trailed behind Keanoff, who strode confidently down the road. Onlookers pressed against the buildings and carts, eyes wide with wonder as the delightful procession passed by: Keanoff leading, clucking, and cooing in what could only be described as fluent chicken. The hens eagerly responded to every sound, both content and curious, as they followed him all the way to a peaceful patch of woods just off the main road. Once there, they scattered joyfully, scratching for bugs, dust-bathing in the loose soil, or simply settling into the grass with little contented clucks of happiness.

Nemeah watched this charming sight with a mix of amusement and disbelief. She laughed when Alban settled onto the ground, the now-hopeful hens refusing to leave his warm embrace. She clutched the compass tightly, thinking fondly of the cave where Edna was. She pictured her bent over her stitching beside the fire, the kettle whistling cheerfully, and the soft chime of the dragon's glassy scales shifting in the warm silence.

"You may want to warn them about what happens next," Nemeah said, arching a brow. "We do not need frenzied chickens running about."

With a playful wink, Keanoff turned to the flock and shared a long, melodic series of clucks and coos that felt like both a cheerful pep talk and a comforting promise of safety. Then, with a graceful sweep of her hand, Nemeah opened the inviting portal. To her delight, the hens did not hesitate at all. One by one, they strolled calmly through the glowing archway and into the cozy cave. Even the injured ones limped forward, as if guided by an unspoken bond of trust. Alban brought up the rear, settling into his usual perch on the stool by the entrance, ready to keep his nightly watch with a sense of calm vigilance.

"I *said a* chicken! Just one!" Edna's voice rang out across the stone chamber, half shrill, half amused. "What in blazes am I supposed to do with all *these*?" Her lighthearted laugh filled Nemeah with joy.

"Gran, you should have seen them," Keanoff said, still clutching his stomach at the memory. "We could not leave them there. It was absolutely terrible."

The dragon stirred, its eyes gleaming as it rose from its nest. With measured steps, it crept closer, sniffing the air, its long neck arching over the newcomers. Every person and chicken froze, watching its every move. Nemeah took a step closer to Keanoff and whispered urgently, "Tell her not to eat them."

He shook his head with a huff. "I have told you before, dragon is a dead language, and we do not even know if it knows how to speak."

Just then, a high, warbling whistle filled the cave. The hens stopped, heads tilted sideways as they stared up at the towering dragon. Slowly, the creature lowered her head, allowing the chickens to approach and inspect her scales and feathers. The whistle dipped in pitch and then rose again, morphing into a series of clicks and soft coos. It sounded like a song from long ago, something the heavens and the earth might once have sung together.

No one spoke as they watched in pure astonishment at how the beast moved easily among the tiny hens. The dragon turned and padded back to her nest. The hens clumsily followed, slipping on gold coins and tumbling across the stone floor. With a sweep of her sturdy tail, the dragon carved a small opening into the side of her treasure trove, which she used for her bed. One by one, the hens crowded inside, tucking themselves beneath her draped wings and against her glass-scaled sides.

"Is that how dragons speak?" Edna questioned, her movements slow as she returned calmly to her cup of tea and the newly sewn quilt.

Keanoff furrowed his brow, shaping his lips thoughtfully. He tested the sound as he blew out, then released a sigh. His mind was fully engaged in discovery mode as he gently pressed his fingers over his mouth and let out a low, steady whistle. The dragon's crystal eyes shifted toward him, and the feathers around her head lifted ever so slightly. He tried again. And again. Each time, adjusting the angle of his hands or the shape of his lips. Slowly and patiently, he refined the sound until, finally, the dragon responded.

A soft whistle echoed back to him, quiet but clear. Nemeah could not help but smile, watching Keanoff in his element. There was something moving about this curious exchange between a man and a creature who had not spoken to anyone in five hundred years. By the time

Keanoff and the dragon established a connection, the sun had dipped low behind the mountains, making way for the rising moon to take its place.

Nemeah kindly lent a hand to Edna in preparing a simple meal while Keanoff continued his playful experimentation with clicks, whistles, and coos. Soon, he bowed his head and settled comfortably beside the fire. The dragon kept a watchful eye on them from her cozy nest, her eyes sparkling in the flickering firelight, until she gently lowered her head and closed her eyes, her wings sheltering the roosting hens lovingly. With a contented sigh, Keanoff slipped off his boots and wiggled his toes toward the warm flames, easing the tension from his temples. Edna gestured gracefully, and a delightful cluster of small white flowers blossomed beside him, their soft yellow centers glowing softly in the dim cave.

"Feverfew," she said, nodding toward the blooms. "For the headache."

Keanoff plucked one and chewed the petals, testing the taste. Then he plucked another. He ate every last flower before glancing over at her with a grateful smile. Edna returned it. Their bond had grown stronger over the past few weeks, and Nemeah felt it. The quiet ache of being the odd one out yet again.

It was not long ago that she had dreamed of traveling with Edna and Jacob, selling herbs in far-off lands and learning the ways of the old world. She could see herself helping Jacob set up the carts, picking flowers and herbs with Edna in flowing fields, and learning the ancestral names of each. But when Jacob died, that dream faded. Still, a small part of her clung to the hope that, after all this, she could still be part of Edna's life, together creating a little family of their own.

Could they be happy? Nemeah looked over at Edna, who stared into the flames of the fire, her thoughts on her life with her late husband. A cold wind entered the cave, raising goosebumps on Nemeah's skin, the feeling of something lost surfacing. Nemeah cleared her throat, forcing the sadness back down. She looked at Keanoff with a questioning expression. "Did you manage to decipher her language?"

Keanoff nodded slowly, as if he questioned his own answer. "It is going to take days, maybe even months, before I can speak it clearly, but I think I have the gist of it." He frowned slightly as he recalled the exchange. "But I think I can translate what she spoke of just now. She said... thank you for the *embari*?" He paused, lips twitching in thought. "She said she will look after them, so I am guessing embari might mean cub? offspring, perhaps. She also needs Edna to grow feed for them."

Edna and Nemeah both smiled at this.

"She knows we are Echoes, then?" Nemeah asked, her gaze drifting toward the now-sleeping dragon.

Keanoff nodded as Edna stirred the stew bubbling in the black pot over the fire. Rabbit, cabbage, and carrots flavored the mix. Spices that smelled faintly of ginger wafted with the steam, and Nemeah's stomach growled at the delicious scent. The old woman ladled generous helpings into bowls while Keanoff continued talking.

"She knows what we are. I think that is the only reason she did not eat us on the first day." He attempted a light-hearted chuckle, but the others did not laugh at the gruesome thought. He straightened and continued. "She said, if I understood her correctly, that she could sense her *myrrakai* on Nemeah. Master or creator, for a term we understand. She knows Kallemena is in the mirror. And others like her are trapped in the others." He took a few bites of his stew before speaking again. "She says she knows who is in the fourth mirror too... but she said it is quite a tale, and she wanted to go back to sleep."

Nemeah felt a flicker of irritation at that. One would think a dragon, lonely for centuries, would welcome conversation, especially with people connected to her "myrrakai." But no, she would rather sleep. "Lazy dragon," Nemeah muttered, scooping a steaming bite into her mouth, regretting the hasty act as her tongue burned and her eyes watered.

"Does she have a name? Something we can call her by?" Edna asked, her eyes a little brighter than before.

Keanoff nodded, swallowing carefully, steam pouring from his nose. "Noa."

That night, Nemeah dreamed of the Axis House again. The great doors loomed just out of reach. Strange eyes stared deep into her soul. The crushing sensation returned, her arm trapped beneath the weight of the closing door. She jolted awake. The world swam in a haze as her vision cleared. The fire had burned out, and the cave was cloaked in the chill of the shadows, save for the faint silver light of the moon beyond the entrance.

The usual sounds, the braying of the donkey, Keanoff's soft snores, the dragon's shifting scales, were gone. The silence was absolute. She slid her feet from the bed, welcoming the cold that rushed up her legs and deep into her bones. Padding forward, she noticed Alban's stool was empty. Had she dismissed him in her sleep? It certainly would not have been the first time. The wind blew through her, chasing away any warmth that had been there. She wrapped her blanket tightly around her shoulders as she stepped out into the night.

Snow fell in slow, heavy clumps. The mountains stood silent, shining like blades of a knife in the night, glimmering in the pale moon's beams. But in the distance, something caught her eye. A glow flickered in the wind. A fire. Enormous and growing. Blazing through the forest, consuming everything in its path. The faint smell of smoke reached her nostrils, acrid and bitter, and she realized then: it was not snow falling from the sky. It was ash. She reached out her thin hand. A flake landed in her palm and dissolved into black dust, staining her fair skin.

"Everyone, come and see this!" she called back. "It is on fire, all of it." She trailed off.

But no one answered. No sounds of movement came from inside the cave. She turned, expecting to see her friends groggily shuffling out behind her, but they were gone. She was no longer in the mountains;

she was in the heart of Highspire. In the midst of a roaring inferno at the city's center, flames tore through the streets. Buildings collapsed under the weight of the flames as smoke and heat reached toward the starry sky. People screamed as they evacuated their homes, children crying in their parents' arms. Animals panicked and fled through the firelit chaos.

"The mountains!" Nemeah cried. "Get to the mountains! You will all be safe there!"

A scream rose behind her. "Help me!" a woman cried out.

Nemeah whirled around to see the Axis House standing before her, its massive black doors blocked by fallen debris. A woman's hand clawed through the gap, reaching for the outside world. "Help me!" she wailed again.

Nemeah rushed to the door, surprised to find she could grip its brass handles. The shock stalled her momentarily. The woman clawed at her arm, her whimpers pitiful under the stress of the night. Nemeah heaved with all her might, but the doors would not budge. She pulled harder, her hands aching, her fingers twitching with the urge to unleash her power. She stepped back, indifferent to whether anyone around her saw her gift. She twisted her hands through the air as if weaving an invisible tapestry. She summoned a great wind, a gale to wrench the door open, but still, it held firm, the large burning beam moving only a few inches.

"Please!" the woman begged. Flames now raced across the roof of the Axis House, roaring louder than the cries within.

"I am trying! Just hang on!" Nemeah pleaded. Calling another wind, she swept everything from the path: the carts, the debris, anything not tied down, except for the heavy beam wedged across the doors.

"No!" she screamed, her voice cracking.

Frustration and panic gripped her chest. She glanced around for help, but the street was empty now. Everyone had left; she was alone, and the woman inside was in trouble. The fire licked at Nemeah's dress, heat curling against her skin and drawing sweat from every pore. She looked back to the doors; the woman was gone, her pleas silenced. The flames consumed the building.

"Someone help her!" she pleaded, throwing herself at the beam, her hands feeling the intense heat of the charred wood sinking deep into her palms and melting her flesh.

The smell of burning skin filled her nose, making her nerves twist as the pain raced up her arms. With a sharp hiss, she pulled away, her hands raw and mutilated from the effort. "No." Her voice was shaky as she knelt down, tears falling to the ground.

"Nemeah!" a man called. "Nemeah, wake up!" A strong hand gripped her shoulder and shook her; her eyes shot open, confused by the sight before her. Keanoff crouched over her, his face taut with concern, as loose strands of his hair brushed against her cheek. Smoke filled her lungs as he scooped her up and carried her out of the cave's mouth.

"What is happening?" she gasped, her lungs burning in the fresh air outside.

The moon had disappeared, and dawn painted the sky with streaks of grey and dark blue; a storm was approaching. She turned back to the cave, and her heart sank. Their home was ablaze. Flames ripped through the trees Edna had tended to. The old merchant wagon was already reduced to smoldering ash. Edna stumbled out of the cave, her face smeared with soot, guiding Rhubarb by the reins while a rattling cough shook her frail form. The chickens rushed out behind her, clucking nervously as they pecked at the ash-dusted snow.

"Are you alright?" Keanoff held Nemeah's arms in his hands, his eyes scanning every inch of her face, searching for any signs of injury. "Are you hurt?"

"No." She managed to say before screaming Keanoff's name.

He had dropped her off in the snow and raced back toward the fire, disappearing into the dense smoke. She staggered to her feet and surged forward, but was scooped up into Alban's arms. Strong and silent, her sentinel held her still, refusing to let her risk her life. Edna and Nemeah watched helplessly as black smoke billowed from the cave and curled toward the sky. Time stretched painfully as Nemeah's eyes searched for any signs of her friend. Then, with a hacking cough filling the silence, Keanoff stumbled from the cave, the four mirrors clutched to his chest. Steam poured from his singed hair, his breath came shallow as if knives pierced his smoke-damaged lungs. Nemeah wiggled free from Alban's grip, falling to the snow beside Keanoff. Her hands hovered over him, unsure how to help.

Edna coughed, clutching her shawl tightly. "How did this happen?"

All three sat together, staring back at the cave. The animals were all accounted for, but their belongings were lost to the fire's hunger. Nemeah's dream pulsed behind her eyes: the fire, the woman trapped, the smoke choking her lungs. She could not help but feel responsible for their burning home. She felt a hand grip her own and jerked away from the pain. The skin on her hands was blistered and raw. Her fingers were swelling, and the burns wept with white fluid. Her wrists were scorched red, her flesh angry and tender.

"My... my hands," she whispered, her voice breaking.

A ringing surged in her ears, the world spinning out from beneath her. Her vision blurred at the edges, her view getting smaller as her breathing quickened. She had never been one for blood or pain, yet she now found herself in a world filled with both. A fainting spell threatened to drag her under as Keanoff steadied her, his hands warm on her frigid arms. Edna gently scooped snow into her nightdress and pressed it against the burns.

"Do not fret. We will get you bandaged up as soon as the fire settles." Edna looked at Keanoff; both of them realized the severity of Nemeah's injuries. They understood that Nemeah's recovery would be long and painful, and the question of her ever using her hands again went unspoken.

Edna turned to Keanoff. "Are you hurt? Any burns?"

Keanoff shook his head, though a deep cough rattled in his chest. Before he could speak, a shadow swept across the snow. The dragon descended, her wings slicing through the air as she landed in a rush of snow and wind. The chickens scattered under her taloned feet. With a low series of clicks and whistles, she ushered them aside before turning toward the smoking cave.

Her large head tilted as she examined the fire's remnants. She let out a rumble and then stepped inside with cautious grace. Her jeweled scales shimmered, chiming softly as she moved. Inside, she stomped out the lingering flames, then fanned her wings, pushing the smoke outward. A gust swept through the cave, leaving only charred wood, blackened stones, and silence. Then she clicked again, sharp and urgent.

Keanoff lifted his head, red-eyed from smoke, his voice barely audible. "I do not know," he rasped, hoarse from coughing.

Noa continued to click, now even faster, repeating a sequence of sounds that demanded a response. Keanoff clicked and whistled back, speaking in the strange tongue he alone understood. The dragon dipped her head and sniffed at the ground, winding her way around the scorched remains. Her path always circled back to where Nemeah's bed once lay. Another whistle and a low growl set Keanoff's patience on edge. She stomped the ground and clicked again. Keanoff responded, a flicker of realization lighting up behind his strained expression.

"She believes it began where Nemeah's bed used to be," he remarked, casting a glance at her. "Perhaps a stray ember or something." He looked down at the four mirrors in his arms, then clicked a final phrase toward Noa before showing the dragon that he held them safely.

Nemeah did not yet know the many faces of the dragon, but she could have sworn she saw relief flicker across Noa's strange features at the sight of the soot-streaked mirrors. All day, they worked to restore their home. Edna was the busiest, coaxing new trees and plants to grow where the old ones had burned, shaping soft beds from roots and moss for everyone.

Keanoff cleaned the mirrors, polishing each one until they shone like new before he set off to hunt. Nemeah took to weaving on the loom, though her hands ached unbearably with every motion. Each flex sent a bolt of pain through her raw palms. An aching stab raced up her elbow and brought tears to her eyes. Edna had wrapped them in a salve of bitter-smelling herbs, the names of which Nemeah could not recall, her head still foggy from smoke and dreams.

She glanced down at the half-finished blanket, the threads running from warp and weft knotted and tangled. She had wanted this one to be perfect, a gift for the man who pulled her to safety that morning. Yet despite her best efforts to ignore her painful appendages, she could not get her magic to guide the loom through the threads evenly. Her face flushed with embarrassment.

She was a terrible weaver even before her hands were injured, but she was still trying, even with trembling fingers and blistered skin. Across the room, Noa watched her. Always watching. The dragon's glacial blue eyes followed her every move, cold and unblinking. A slow churn began in Nemeah's gut, a gnawing feeling of being judged. Of being *measured*.

"What?" she snapped, more sharply than she intended.

The dragon did not blink or flinch. It just kept staring.

Edna looked up, her hands still busy with the new bedding. "You alright, dear?"

Nemeah took a deep breath. "I am fine."

Silence returned to the cave. The two of them worked on their tasks while the quiet exhaustion hung heavily in the air. That night, Keanoff returned with a small turkey that Edna roasted with corn and potatoes. They ate in silence, Alban assisting Nemeah with each bite, her wrapped hands unable to grip even a fork.

Despite their efforts, the scent of the smoke still clung to their clothes, their skin, and the very walls around them. When it was time to sleep, Nemeah crawled onto her fresh bed of moss and hay. Her blanket was unfinished, so she pulled her soot-stained blue jacket around her shoulders. Each time she closed her eyes, the memory of flames leapt behind her lids. She tensed at every crackle of fire in her mind, every phantom scream. She startled when something dropped across her. She shot up to see Keanoff walking back to his own bed, leaving his jacket spread over her.

"What about you?" she whispered.

Keanoff did not reply with words. Instead, a ripple passed through him, and in an instant, a sleek wolf took his place. His green eyes met hers, gentle and steady, before he circled and curled into a ball of fur on his bed. A small smile touched Nemeah's lips as she pulled the jacket tighter around her. But then she felt it again, that piercing stare. She turned; Noa was still watching her.

The dragon sat surrounded by the cooing hens, the four mirrors safely tucked beneath her massive wings once more. Her blue eyes gleamed with quiet intensity. A standoff of silence passed between them, neither one willing to be bested by the other. Eventually, sleep overtook them both, the cave silent except for the soft snores of its occupants.

Chapter Three

The next few days passed in a blur of activity. Together, the trio cleaned what remained of their home and regained their rhythm. Hunting, gathering, tending to the animals, and waiting for their next move was all they really could do. Frustratingly, the mirrors remained silent, with their hidden occupants still withholding themselves from the rest of the world.

Without a clear path and Nemeah's haunting nightmares, she grew impatient with the lives and roles they had fallen into. It only worsened when Edna and Keanoff began taking over her chores before she woke up, or while she was occupied with something else. Their sorrowful glances at her still inoperable hands told her all she needed to know: she was now a burden.

"We have to go there," Nemeah insisted one morning, wrapping her hands in fresh bandages and ointment. The rawness had faded slightly; the blistered skin now peeled in thin strips, and the angry red underneath had calmed. Edna's salve was nothing short of miraculous, eliminating infection and healing her faster than time alone could manage.

"We do not even know if there is someone in there to save," Keanoff said, tugging the last twist of hair into his braid and securing it with a leather cord. "What if you get inside and the place is crawling with Axis dogs just waiting to take your head clean off?" He stood up and stretched, a loud pop cracking from his shoulder as he rolled his neck.

"I will have my powers," she replied, her voice wavering as she looked down at her hands. Her magic had been frail the past few days. Her injuries had taken a toll on what she could conjure and influence. "And Alban, he will be there also." She tried to sound confident, though she knew the others had noticed his absence over the past days as well. "And you, shifting into whatever beast the moment calls for." She tried to smile as she recited the exact phrase he had told Edna days before.

That familiar smirk tugged at Keanoff's lips. He never minded being cast as the heroic type. It suited him far too well, and the idea of a dramatic rescue clearly pleased him.

"Then we watch first," he said, brushing a bit of the morning's breakfast from his tunic. "We study the place. See who comes and goes. It could be days or maybe weeks, but we will at least know what we are walking into. It is a basic war technique. You have to study your enemy. Get into their headspace. Know them like the back of your hand." He clamped his mouth shut as his eyes darted to Nemeah's hands and then to the cave's ceiling, where the grape vines entwined with the stalactites.

Nemeah's heart sank as she looked down at her wrapped hands. Weeks. That was time they did not have. The Eclipse Veil loomed ever closer, its shadow darkening her thoughts each day. And while they waited, Vallorith's plans continued unchecked. Every wasted moment could potentially cost them everything.

"No," she said firmly. "We have already lost time because of the fire. We do not know when Kallemena, or Slek, or Wynna will appear again. They have gone silent. We cannot just sit here and hope for direction. How disappointed would they be to learn we have made absolutely no progress over the past month?" She held up her compass, the bandages around her hand pulling slightly as she lifted it. "What is the point of this, then? Why carry it at all if we will not follow where it leads us?"

Keanoff's smirk faded. He strode over and took the compass from her hand, the needle inside spinning wildly. He stared at it in silence, lost in thoughts of his father and the mirror where he now resided. The needle spun on, as restless as the storm in Nemeah's chest.

He let out a defeated sigh. "It is hard to trust something that seems to only listen to you," he murmured. He handed the compass back without another word and walked toward the cave's mouth.

She held the compass tightly, her heart racing. The spinning did not bother her. If anything, it confirmed what she already knew deep down: the Axis House was their new mission. She was not wrong about this. She could not be mistaken. The time to act was now, not in a week or a month. They could not afford to waste more time just sitting around and watching.

"What about a vote?" Hope jumped through her as she turned toward Edna, who was brushing the coarse fur of the grey donkey. Rhubarb's ears flicked, irritated by a persistent fly. "Should we charge in and save the woman, or sit back while she is locked inside that place, with who knows what is happening to her? Whether she is safe from harm or not."

Desperation leaked through her tone, a feeble attempt to sway the old woman. She had leaned into the imagery on purpose, hoping that Edna would see what she saw when she closed her eyes.

"The woman could be starving. Tortured even." The thought twisted in her chest, but her hope died when she saw Edna's response.

The old woman shook her head slowly and calmly, still focused on her grooming. "It seems rash to rush in there."

Nemeah did not need Edna to complete her thought. She could already sense where this was heading.

"I agree with Keanoff," Edna added. "You two should watch the place for a few days. Talk to the locals. See what you can learn. We certainly do not need a repeat of the last time we encountered the Axis and its disciples." She patted Rhubarb's side and pressed a kiss to his velvety nose.

The donkey let out a bray that echoed faintly through the cave as Edna latched the pen door and made her way toward her garden.

Nemeah exhaled with a hiss, her breath hot with vexation. Without a word, she stormed past Keanoff and out into the cold, brushing off his attempt at comfort as she pushed down the rocky trail. Her mind burned with the same images: fire, smoke, and the woman's scream. Over and over it echoed like a curse she could not shake. It was not until she reached Jacob's grave that she realized someone had followed her.

She dropped to her knees in the snow. Gently brushing the icy flakes from the top of the gravestone, she traced the weathered lines of Jacob's name with her fingers, clearing the dust and grit that had gathered there. Her heart was broken for the old man who had welcomed her. For the short time they had spent together. For the brutal truth that his death had served no purpose but a diversion, a cruel detour during one of her darkest moments. Keanoff sat beside her silently. He slipped his arm around her shoulders and pulled her close. His warmth seeped into her, bringing with it the familiar scent of hay and pine, a smell she had not realized she found comforting until now.

"I know it feels like we are standing still," he said.

She felt his chest expand beside her as he took a long breath of mountain air.

"But without help, last time we would not have made it. Slek, Wynna, and Kallemena; if they had not shown up, we would all be dead. They saved us, Nemeah. But that was pretty much dumb luck, and we may not be so fortunate to gain it in the future."

A single hot tear escaped down her cheek. She swallowed the emotions clogging her throat and pulled away, not wanting him to see her cry. She was strong. She had been and would continue to be. She was an Echo with grand abilities, or had been. She slapped at the tear with her wrapped hand, the thick cloth itching her skin. "Two days," she said at last, voice quiet but steady. "We will watch for two days."

"A week," he countered, raising his hands with palms facing her, silently urging her to listen. "Your hands need time to heal. Edna's medicine is effective, but you are still struggling. It is clear you are still in pain."

Nemeah's eyes fell to her bandages, where pink flesh poked through the once-white fabric. She tested his theory by curling her fingers, and the stiff, shaky movement confirmed that Keanoff was right. She shut her eyes, willing her hands to heal faster.

"One week. And then we will see how you feel." Keanoff extended his hand, palm open between them.

She hesitated, then took it. His touch was soft and gentle as he held her small hand in his. She knew he was right; they could not afford to be reckless, no matter how much she wanted to break down the doors of the Axis house and charge inside.

"One week. But I will be better before then, you will see." Her heart thudded hard in her chest as Keanoff's warm grip melted the chill from her fingers. His forest eyes were watching her, waiting for more rebuttal regarding the time frame they had just agreed upon. Her cheeks flushed, bright red and fully visible as he stood before her, still holding her hand with quiet affection. A smile tugged at his lips before his gaze shifted to the headstone at their feet.

"We have to be careful," Keanoff said gently. "For Edna and Jacob."

"For Edna and Jacob," she agreed.

He gave a small tug on her braid before turning back toward the cave. Together, they walked in silence, her aching hand longing for his calloused fingers to hold them again.

The rest of the day blurred by. Edna seemed more at ease now with more animals to tend, content as she hummed softly to Rhubarb while preparing his meal. Keanoff was making slow progress with Noa. Their shared clicks and whistles filled the cave with strange, melodic bursts, like birdsong filtering through wind chimes. Nemeah worked diligently on a new blanket, one she hoped would not look like the work of a novice. When she finally finished, with only a single knot clumping the fabrics otherwise smooth surface, she gifted it to Keanoff. It felt good to give him something she had created. Something real made by her own two hands.

That night, they laughed over stew and stories from Keanoff's childhood. He recounted tales of his homeland and early struggles with his shifting magic. Of how he had once spent an entire day stuck with antlers and webbed feet. Nemeah chuckled until her sides ached. The moment felt natural, like a missed phase of her life when she belonged among people who appreciated her company. A small family made up of strangers from different parts of the world. She wished for the night to never end.

She did not remember falling asleep. But her dream played on repeat, over and over in her head like an echo urging her to listen. The Axis House. The woman. The Axis House. The woman. Screams. Fire. The Axis House. The woman. As the dream repeated endlessly, Nemeah began to recognize subtle differences. The woman was slowly growing smaller and more fragile, her voice now higher-pitched than before. The eyes, once two different colors, now shone dark blue. The hand gripping her wrist had become shrunken, small, and frail, reaching out in eagerness to grab whatever its tiny fingers could touch. Nemeah grasped the hand and held onto it, feeling the warmth that was familiar and real. She knew this hand.

"Orla!"

She shot upright, her breath heaving and her eyes wide. Silence hung in the air. Then, a groggy rustling as Keanoff rolled over, rubbing his face.

"What is it? What happened?" he muttered, still trapped in the in-between of sleep and wakefulness.

"Orla, they have her!" Nemeah cried, already throwing off her covers and yanking on her boots. "She is in the Axis House. I saw her! She called to me! They have my sister!"

"Wait!" Keanoff scrambled to his feet, hopping as he jammed one foot into his boot, and then the other. "Nemeah, how do you *know* it is her?"

"Because I saw her Keanoff! I saw her, she was there!" She grabbed the compass from her pack, her hands trembling as she fumbled to open the lid, the needle spinning until it pointed her in the right direction.

With a hurried, purposeful wave of her hand, the air before them shimmered. A small portal split open, its borders thin from her wavering strength. Towering trees beyond exuded the scent of damp earth and dense forest. The clatter of wooden wheels on cobbled streets signaled that Highspire was close.

Keanoff grabbed her shoulder before she could step through the portal. "Wait. What if it is not her? What if your mind is playing tricks on you?"

Tears streamed down Nemeah's cheeks as she struggled to free herself from Keanoff's grip. A tremor shook her entire body. He stepped forward, pulling her into his arms, the motion quick and strangely calming in her fragile state. Her arms instinctively wrapped around his waist, and her forehead pressed against his chest.

"Shhh," he murmured, rubbing her back. "Let us go to your farm. Check first, yeah? Just to be sure. For all we know, she is asleep in her bed." He gently pulled back, searching her eyes. Panic. Grief. Fear. All swelled inside her like a bubble about to burst, like a woman teetering on the edge of uncontrolled chaos. "Remember, we cannot afford to be hasty," he added softly. "No rushing in blindly."

Before they could say more, the portal shimmered and shifted. Keanoff blinked as the image resolved. He now saw the backside of a weathered brown barn, thick with thatching and soaked in falling rain. Nemeah did not hesitate; she grabbed his hand with her bandaged mittens and tugged him through. The mud squelched beneath their boots as they landed. Icy rain drenched them instantly, drumming down in fat, relentless drops.

Thunder cracked above, echoing across the hills as Nemeah ran, rounding the barn toward the house. No smoke curled from the chimney, and no firelight glowed in the windows. Her panic intensified her fear as she grew closer to her old house. She stumbled to the window, peering in through the rain-speckled glass. Darkness greeted them. No movement. No life. Her breath caught as she raced to the door. A flash of lightning lit the sky, her shadow stretching deep into the entryway as the door creaked open under her touch.

"It...it was not latched," she whispered as she stepped inside.

Everything was just as she remembered. The table with four chairs was pushed against the wall. The pot hung cold over dead coals. Blankets were folded on the shelves, and the books lay untouched. She rushed to her parents' room. The bed was still made as her mother had done every morning. The wall still housed her father's old gun. The smell of the house was odd and stale, as if no one had been here for a few days. There was no bread in the cupboard, no wash folded in the basket, and no toys scattered across the floor.

"Maeve! Eoghan!" she called, her voice shaking as she rushed back into the main room. She barely registered Keanoff beside her. "They are not here."

"I will check upstairs," he said quickly, then bounded up the stairs.

"Please, please, please be there," Nemeah whispered. Her breath quickened, becoming shallower as her head began to spin and black tendrils fogged her vision.

Above, she listened to the heavy sound of Keanoff's boots pacing back and forth. "Orla? Are you here? Orla!" There was a pause, followed by the hurried sound of footsteps descending. "No one is here," he said, shaking his head. "Maybe they just left? No horse in the barn. Do they travel to see family? Is there any place they usually go?"

"No." Nemeah spat, her emotions taking over. "They are always here unless it is market day." She turned in the small room. "They never spend the night."

Outside, another vicious crack of thunder shook the ground.

"Maybe the storm caught them? Maybe they did stay just this once?" Keanoff's voice quieted as his eyes landed on Nemeah, her presence growing darker in the already dim house.

A flash of lightning outside illuminated the room, revealing Nemeah's features meshing with those that were not her own. Her body stood frozen in the center of the room, eyes wide, pupils consuming every color until hollow portals stared back at Keanoff.

The air thickened around her, rippling with the energy boiling in her chest. Her hands trembled, clenching and releasing at her sides. Then, a cry ripped from her throat as she slashed her arm through the air. A portal erupted before them, spinning wide to reveal the towering black doors of the Axis House.

"Nemeah, no!" Keanoff lunged for her, trying to grab her arm. But he was not fast enough.

Nemeah had already stepped through. The portal's edge shimmered and shrank rapidly. Keanoff felt panic rise in his chest. If he did not move now, he would be trapped on the island of Tirnmoor. With a grunt, he hurled himself forward, barely slipping through as the portal snapped shut behind him. He landed hard on the cold stone roadway, just in time to see Nemeah fling her hand through the air.

Two guards clad in golden armor were tossed like dolls, crashing against the walls with a metallic clatter. Their swords slide from their sheaths. The towering doors to the Axis House were ripped free from their hinges with another swipe of Nemeah's hand. The heavy wood flung aside as if they were made of paper. Beyond them, a stairway plunged into darkness. With another sharp gesture, flames burst to life, snaking along the walls, crawling over stone, and illuminating the path with an eerie orange glow. Alban appeared and descended the steps, felling anyone who stood in his way.

Keanoff stared in disbelief as Nemeah stormed down the steps after him, her movements swift, her figure engulfed by fire and shadow.

"Nemeah!" he shouted, scrambling to his feet. "Nemeah, wait!"

But the flames roared louder, rising like a wall between them. He had no choice but to stagger back from the heat.

"Get him!" The voice came from behind.

Keanoff spun around to see the two guards still conscious, struggling upright, bruised but not beaten. They clutched their swords tightly, their faces contorted in agony and rage. Keanoff raised his hands, desperately searching for an escape, but it was too late. One guard charged at him. Keanoff ducked, the blade slicing the air just above his shoulder. He attempted to flee, but the second guard swung low, grazing his tunic where the leather was almost cut deep enough to expose his stomach.

Instinct took over as he dropped to all fours, a growl emanating from deep within. Fur sprouted from his arms and back. His teeth grew sharp, fingers transforming into claws.

In moments, Keanoff emerged as a massive, snarling beast. The guards hesitated, their eyes wide with disbelief at the sight of a wolf before them. Keanoff attacked before they could regain their composure. Steel clashed against claws. The street resonated with growls and grunts, strikes and parries. Keanoff slashed, narrowly missing one guard's leg. The other guard thrust his sword, but missed as well. They were beginning to tire, their backs heaving and grips weakening.

Suddenly, the fire behind them hissed and extinguished. The abrupt silence enveloped them, leaving their ears deaf to the stillness of the night.

Keanoff turned, spotting the now-open stairwell as five more guards rushed toward him, each clad in polished gold. He was surrounded. The two injured men straightened, emboldened by the arrival of reinforcements. One darted in and slashed his blade across Keanoff's face. Pain flared, and blood poured from his ear. He yelped as he staggered back, knowing this was the end of this fight.

There was no winning; he was outnumbered. With a final growl, Keanoff turned and bolted down the road. His heart ached as he fled, every step pulling him farther from the Axis House, and farther from Nemeah. He leapt, bones shifting midair, fur melting into feathers. With a powerful beat of his wings, he soared into the night as a hawk, racing toward the safety of the mountains they called home.

* * *

Nemeah raced down the stairs, her feet barely skimming the stone steps. Each bound brought her closer to the pull thrumming in her chest. At the bottom, a maze of dark hallways unfurled before her, twisting and splitting like the veins of some sleeping beast. She waved her hand again. Flames crawled along the walls, stretching ahead to light her path.

"Orla!" Her voice echoed off the stone, raw and unfamiliar, sharp with fear and fury. She pushed forward, turning corner after corner, deeper and deeper into the underground, following her silent sentinel. The flames flickered with each hurried step, shadows writhing along the damp walls. "I am here!" she shouted, imagining Orla cold and frightened, trapped behind iron bars. "Where are you?" She yelled again in a voice that was not her own, but still, there was no answer. Only silence.

She spread her hand before her, searching for any life within the winding maze she found herself in. She could sense no one. Hear no one. The halls were empty. Her heart pounded harder, not from the sprint, but from the rising sense that something was very wrong. Her energy, which had surged with blinding force moments ago, was now slipping away. Her limbs felt heavier with every step. A throbbing pain spread through her skull, dull at first, then pounding.

She slowed, her tongue licking her lips and the moisture that collected there. The taste was metallic and bitter as the strange flavor seeped into her taste buds. The air felt damp and suffocating. The walls wept with whatever unknown magic that drifted through the air. She touched the wall, her fingertips coming back wet and slick. She brought them to her nose. An earthy smell filled her nostrils. A smell she was familiar with, thanks to Edna. Realization hit her like a slap to the face. Silvervane had been flooding her system since she entered the Axis house.

Panic clawed at her chest as she turned back, trying to retrace her steps. "Alban, we have to go." The guard scooped her up and ran back the way they had come. They made it only a few feet before she felt herself falling to the ground, her trusted guard vanishing from sight.

She had to escape. She had to find the stairs and Keanoff. She attempted to push herself up, but her legs betrayed her. She collapsed into a crawl, struggling along the ground, her hands throbbing with each movement. Nausea swirled in her gut, and the hallway twisted before her eyes. A dooming realization seized her as she leaned against the wall, still trying to pull herself forward. Every inch was a battle she could not win.

Her body began to feel foreign as her movements became more labored. Her arm gave out, and she sank to the cold stone floor. The flames dimmed. Her skin burned with fever; her vision swam. The last of her strength slipped through her fingers. Then, she heard footsteps and watched as a figure approached, cloaked in crimson. His presence radiated cold malice. Behind him, several guards in gold armor trailed like shadows.

"Go," the man croaked, his voice thick and gravelly, like an old toad. "Search the halls. Make sure she came alone."

Nemeah stirred, her head lifting feebly. Her words emerged slowly and slurred. "Where... is she?"

The man crouched nearby, his face disturbingly calm. His voice was too loud for her pounding head. "You will see her soon."

Chapter Four

Nemeah awoke to the sound of soft humming. A dull ache split her skull, pulsing behind her eyes as she squinted against the gloom. Flickering candlelight danced across black stone walls, casting long, wavering shadows. A groan slipped from her lips as she pushed herself into a seated position. Her battered hands clutched her head, steadying the wave of nausea that rolled through her.

For a moment, she feared her insides might completely revolt. She took slow, measured breaths until the queasiness dulled to a low churn. Then the weight of her current reality slowly crept into her consciousness. She had done the very thing she promised not to. She had acted impetuously, and now, she was paying the price. She was trapped.

Her blurry eyes slowly adjusted to the room, taking in the iron bars that stretched from floor to ceiling. The cold black stone loomed above her, beside her, and beneath her. The cot she sat on, one of two in the cramped cell, spared her from the hard, wet ground. She tapped her foot and flinched; the damp floor welcomed her warm, dry foot.

Her feet were bare. Had she left her boots back in the cave? She would never go anywhere without them. She looked down, her stomach twisting tighter at the sight of her new attire. A white robe clung to her body, unfamiliar and coarse, with a golden sun embroidered over the chest. Her own clothes were missing. The compass was not in her possession. She recoiled as nausea returned like a roaring tide. A frenzied panic surged through every fiber of her being as she clawed at the fabric, desperate to tear it away. Desperate to avoid looking like one of them.

"You should not do that."

Nemeah stiffened. The voice was calm and melodic. It belonged to the woman in the corner, who continued humming as she stood. She moved with unhurried grace toward a bucket by the cell door and crouched beside it. Water sloshed as she pulled out a damp rag. When she stood again, Nemeah could not believe her eyes. She was tall, unnaturally so. Sandy blonde ringlets spilled down her back, past her waist like liquid gold. The flickering candlelight caught the shimmer in her hair as she turned, offering a gentle smile. One eye was blue, the other green.

"You," Nemeah whispered, her voice raspy and her throat raw. "You are the woman I saw in my dream. Your eyes, I recognized you. I saw you trapped in here."

The woman tilted her head, still smiling, and crossed the small space between them. "You must have hit your head pretty hard out there," she said softly, pressing the damp rag to Nemeah's temple.

The sting of contact made Nemeah flinch, but the scent, lavender and jasmine, wrapped around her like a warm blanket in winter. Nemeah took the rag, startled to see a smear of blood when she pulled it away.

She gently prodded her temple, her fingers tracing a scabbed gash and a swollen goose egg that was tender to the touch. How it got there, she could not recall. The last thing she remembered was the man in the crimson robe.

"Are we still in the Axis House?" she asked, dabbing the wound a few more times and assessing her damage.

The woman nodded and settled back onto her cot, her legs folding neatly beneath her as she tucked the hem of her white robe over her feet. The gesture was so familiar that it gripped something in Nemeah's chest. Orla used to sit just like that at the kitchen table.

"Orla!" Nemeah shot to her feet, the world spinning wildly. She grabbed the iron bars for support as her voice tore from her aching throat.

"Where is my sister?" Her fists rattled the bars, but they did not budge. Instead, they stood cold, solid, and unforgiving. "Someone answer me!"

"There are only two of us in here," the woman replied calmly, wincing as she covered her ears.

The sight ignited a wave of irritation in Nemeah. A bitter retort curled on her tongue, but she held it back, swallowing it down with a gulp of frustration.

"They have her," she said, breathless. "They have my sister. Maybe even my mother and father." She collapsed onto the cot, cradling her head in her hands. Her skull throbbed in sync with the frantic beat of her heart.

"Are they Echoes as well?" the woman inquired, her voice high and smooth, like a lullaby wrapped in velvet.

Nemeah lifted her head and examined her cellmate more closely. The woman's features were delicate, almost otherworldly. Her nose was sharp and pointed, her wide eyes mismatched in color. Her lips appeared as though rose petals had been sewn there, impossibly soft and perfectly shaped. Her skin had a warm tone, like hazelnut wood polished in sunlight. She looked angelic, too perfect.

"No," Nemeah murmured, revealing the awful truth. "I am the only one." A bitter thought ran through her. None of this would be happening if she had just been born normal. Powerless like the rest of her family.

"The Axis only takes Echoes," the woman said matter-of-factly, her eyes sweeping over Nemeah. She absorbed every detail. Nemeah's tangled black hair that was streaked with dried blood, the swelling bruise along her temple, and the bandaged hands with peeling skin beneath.

Pale skin, hollow-eyed, trembling. A stark contrast to her own composed calm.

"So what are you?" the woman asked.

Nemeah hesitated. She did not know whether to answer. She was unfamiliar with this woman. For all she knew, she could be an Axis spy. Someone placed here to earn her trust.

"You first," she said coolly, pressing her back against the cold stone wall. The chill bled through the rough cotton robe and into her skin.

The woman smiled, her teeth remarkably white and straight. Nemeah instinctively ran her tongue along her own teeth, self-conscious of their own flaws.

"I am Ismaara," the woman said, standing with graceful poise before dipping into a delicate curtsy. "I am a Freyla. I was captured..." She paused, counting under her breath. "Two months ago? Maybe?" She paused as if lost in her own thoughts before directing her gaze back at Nemeah. "A pleasure to make your acquaintance." She dipped her head, her long curls nearly grazing the floor as she did so.

The way she carried herself, shoulders squared, back rigid, every syllable crisp and deliberate, told Nemeah she had been raised in luxury, perhaps even nobility.

"A Freyla?" Nemeah repeated, raising an eyebrow. "You have the ability to heal?"

Ismaara nodded once and returned to her cot, her movements fluid and practiced.

Nemeah extended her hands, the bandages tightly wrapped around her blistered fingers. "Can you heal these? My hands?" For a brief moment, hope flickered in her chest. Hope that the raw, ugly wounds beneath the cloth might finally disappear.

But Ismaara only frowned. "I could if we were not breathing in the Axis's poison. The root in the air dampens my gift, just as it dulls yours."

Nemeah lowered her hands slowly, careful not to brush the tender skin. "I forgot," she murmured. The stress of everything coming back to her had overshadowed everything.

Ismaara observed her in silence before revisiting her previous question. "So what are you? Cairn? Is that how you ended up burning your hands?" She tilted her head slightly, her brows raised in mild amusement. "You appear to be quite the clumsy Cairn, if I may say. I never thought they could burn themselves."

Nemeah tightened her jaw. "I am not a Cairn," she said, her tone hinting at insult. "I am a Darra." She shifted her gaze toward the hallway, her eyes searching the darkness beyond the bars, looking for anything to steer clear of Ismaara's stare.

But her curious cellmate did not relent. "Then how did you burn them?" she asked, the friendliness drained from her tone. "And do not say 'a fire', obviously. How did you get burned?"

Nemeah could feel her patience slipping away like sand through her fingers. Of course, someone who looked like her would be bold, nosy, and entitled, expecting answers to questions no stranger had a right to ask.

"I am not sure," she muttered. "I was sleeping. When I woke up, my home was burning."

Ismaara's face did not move; she was wholly unbothered. "And no one else in your family is an Echo? That is curious. It is rare for someone to acquire burns that severe," she pointed a slender finger toward Nemeah's wrappings, "and still be able to move their hands. I would know, I have treated plenty." She sighed, raising her arms in an elegant stretch that somehow made the cell feel smaller. "So, how did you get caught? Darras usually slip away unnoticed. Are you even skilled in your abilities?"

Nemeah rubbed the sensitive cut along her temple, wincing as she touched the tender skin. The stream of questions was never-ending, making her head throb worse than before. This woman did not know her and had no right to dig so deep, so quickly. Lying felt safer. But she had already said too much. A half-truth would have to suffice.

"I believed that the Axis had captured my family," she stated, her voice barely above a whisper. "That is why I came here." Her eyes shot Ismaara a glance. "To retrieve them. I was unaware that the air was infused with silvervane." Her heart somersaulted at the memory of Keanoff's voice. *Do not do anything reckless.* She had done exactly that. Her face flushed with guilt as she looked away.

The door's whining creak made her jump as it opened suddenly without warning. A flood of harsh white light spilled into the dim cell, washing away the candlelit gloom and causing both girls to flinch and shield their eyes. Metal clinked and rattled Nemeah's nerves. A guard entered, the weight of his gold armor echoing with each step.

"Ismaara," he grumbled, eyeing the woman who smiled back at him. He turned to the newcomer, her arm still shielding her eyes from the light.

"Good morning, Henry," Ismaara greeted the man with a genuine sense of joy. "Or is it night? Good evening? Midday? Oh well, one can never tell in here." She chuckled softly, eliciting a slight smile from the guard.

A shadow moved behind him. A small woman in a crimson robe followed, her silhouette barely reaching his shoulder. She carried a tray, two silver domes balanced on top. The aroma of roasted chicken and fresh bread wafted through the cell, making Nemeah's stomach come alive with hunger. The woman paused outside as the guard swung open the cell door, the metal creaking on its worn hinges.

Without hesitation, Nemeah sprang to her feet and lunged for the door, her hand slicing through the air to summon her guard, Alban. But nothing happened. No shimmer or sound. Before she could attempt again, a golden-clad arm shot out, seizing her and throwing her backward with brutal strength. She crashed into the wall, the wind knocked from her lungs. A burst of light flashed behind her eyes, and a soft moan escaped her cracked lips as she collapsed to the floor. The woman in red placed the tray inside the cell, careful to keep her distance, as if fearing the two prisoners would tear into her flesh. Her hands trembled as she let go of the tray and quickly scurried back behind the guard.

"If you try that again, I will throw you in the confinement cells," the guard growled, slamming the door.

Nemeah, still winded, blinked through the pain. "Confinement cells?" she rasped, pressing her fingers to the back of her skull.

The guard's helmeted face offered no emotion. "The ones without food or water. Same place we put that no good Vira."

Her skin froze. She rushed to the bars, her fingers wrapping around them, knuckles white as she bared her teeth. "You lie!" Her voice cracked. She swung her arms through the narrow space, striking at nothing as the guard stood just out of reach.

"Enjoy the meal," he said with a dry chuckle before striding away. The woman shuffled behind him, her shadow swallowed by his.

Nemeah slumped forward, her knees buckling under the weight of dread. Keanoff. Was he here? Had he followed her? She pictured him standing in her family's cottage on Tirnmoor, worried and loyal. Had he come through the portal after her? Her fingers trembled as she touched the gash at her temple, blood coating her wrapped fingers once more.

"Better eat before it gets cold," Ismaara said lightly, lifting one of the silver domes. Beneath it sat a meal fit for royalty: roasted meat, golden bread, and diced pears glazed with honey.

Nemeah crawled back to the cot, but the scent now turned her stomach. She could not eat. Not when Keanoff was locked away, probably starving. Not when she was the reason he was there.

"I take it the Vira he mentioned is someone you know?" Ismaara asked, selecting a slice of pear with her fingers. She ate delicately, like a bird picking at seeds, careful to avoid any mess.

Guilt tore at Nemeah. "He is my friend; he must have followed me."

Ismaara tilted her head, studying her as she chewed. Her mismatched eyes did not stray. "So you got yourself caught and dragged your friend down with you. That is more than bad luck."

Nemeah said nothing, forcing down the lump rising in her throat. Shame curled inside her, settling beside the gnawing hunger.

"So," she asked quietly, watching Ismaara's fingers dance around her plate, picking with deliberate precision, "how did *you* get caught?"

"Oh, my brother had the guards throw me in here," Ismaara said casually, as if she were discussing the weather.

Nemeah blinked in disbelief. "What?" she sputtered, leaning forward on her cot. "Your own brother betrayed you?"

Ismaara looked up, a dumbfounded expression on her face. Then her lips curved into a sly smile, and a burst of laughter erupted from her throat. She doubled over in a sudden fit, shaking the cot as her plate nearly toppled to the floor. Tears streamed down her cheeks as she clutched her sides and gasped for breath. *"Betrayed?"* she wheezed between laughs. "Goodness, you are a *riot!*" Still giggling, she shook her head and resumed pecking at her food like a bird, clearly amused by Nemeah's sincerity.

Nemeah just stared, her face plastered with disbelief. Annoyed and confused, she stood up and moved over to her untouched tray. The dome clattered to the floor with a hollow clang as she fumbled with her plate, her hands refusing to obey her commands. She carried the plate back to her cot and sat down, torn between outrage and ravenous hunger.

She ripped a piece of bread from the roll and chewed tentatively. Warmth, salt, and butter flooded her senses. Her body begged for more as she tore off a larger chunk and devoured it in seconds.

"Why would your brother hand you over to the Axis if it *was not* betrayal?" she asked, her voice muffled by the bread. "Does he not realize they will kill you?"

Ismaara looked like she might laugh again, but instead she composed herself and spoke as if the answer were obvious. "The Axis will not kill *me*. You, maybe. But not me."

Nemeah paused mid-chew. "Why just me?" she muttered around a mouthful of chicken. The skin was crispy and perfectly seasoned, the meat infused with rosemary and black pepper, with just enough lemon to brighten it. She hated how good it tasted.

"I *am* an Echo," Ismaara said, "but I am also His Holiness's sister. He would not dare kill *me*."

Nemeah choked. A piece of chicken got caught in her throat as spices shot up her nose. She coughed and gagged, tears brimming in her eyes as a spray of spit and snot followed with every wheezing hack.

"Excuse me?" she rasped hoarsely. "Sister?"

Ismaara tilted her head, lips puckering in mild confusion. "Where are you from," she asked, genuinely curious, "that you do not already know our family's lineage?"

Nemeah finally managed to calm her coughing, her eyes now bloodshot as she stared at the woman. Was she supposed to know her? The name meant nothing, but maybe it should. Was this common knowledge to the people of Highspire? Ismaara's eyes scanned her again, more thoughtfully this time. Her gaze lingered on Nemeah's pale skin, the light freckles, and the tangled mess of dark hair.

"You are from Nocthrea?"

Nemeah sucked in another breath, that same scratchy urge to cough still tickling her throat. "How—"

But Ismaara cut her off, waving a finger as her lips curled into a smug grin. "Darra abilities, let me think." She closed her eyes dramatically, and within seconds, she snapped her fingers with a gleeful "Ah-ha!" Clearly pleased with herself, she opened one eye to look at Nemeah.

"The Axis has not been to Nocthrea in ten years, maybe more. I am guessing that they still do not follow the teachings there?" She nodded to herself without waiting for a response. "It is the furthest province from Verdathos. Too remote. Too wet. Too stubborn. The disciples always complain that the weather there ruins their boots." She scoffed. "Can you imagine? Refusing to spread the 'holy word' because of a little cold rain? Pathetic."

Nemeah arched a brow. "You speak as though you *are one of the disciples?*"

"And then there is your accent," Ismaara continued breezily. "It is subtle, but you drag your vowels, classic southern Nocthrea. The kind of sound you only pick up if you have lived there or paid very close attention."

Nemeah's voice rang sternly in the cramped cell. "How do you know so much about the Axis when they keep you locked up in a cell? And how much is there to even know?"

Ismaara faltered. Her playful smirk faded just a little as she considered the question more seriously. "I know everything. You would die of old age before you fully learned it all."

Nemeah swept her arms wide, gesturing to the confines of the cold stone walls and iron bars. "I am not getting any younger in here, so might as well start talking."

That earned her a smile, a real one this time. "Fine," Ismaara said, settling back on her cot with a sigh. "Let us start at the beginning."

Chapter Five

The cave was still steeped in shadow when Keanoff reached the mountains. His limbs trembled violently with exhaustion as he shifted back into his human form. Each breath tore at his chest, his lungs searing, and his heart hammering with relentless urgency. He stumbled forward, drawn into the darkness until he collapsed beside his bed. His back sank into the moss-laced hay, the earthy scent grounding him as his feet stretched toward the dwindling fire. The embers pulsed faintly, their soft glow casting flickering silhouettes against the stone walls. Across from him, Edna stirred in her sleep, the quiet sounds of distress slipping past her lips, murmurs of a dream woven with grief. Likely of Jacob.

Keanoff reached for his ear, wincing as his fingers brushed against the ragged edge. The spot where the Axis soldier's blade had found its mark. The top was gone. A dry crust of blood had hardened over the wound, and the flesh was stiff with pulsing pain. One ear was now shorter than the other, the symmetry of his animal forms now lost. What would Nemeah say when she saw him like this?

Her emotion-filled eyes flashed through his mind: the way her power had overtaken her during her state of distress, emotions high at the thought of the Axis having her family. The fire that erupted from her palms was uncontrolled, strange, unlike anything he had seen come from a Darra before. He could still feel the blistering heat of it, the scent of burnt hair clinging to his arm as proof.

"Darra cannot create fire," he murmured. Then, more gently, with doubt, "Or can they?"

A soft chime echoed through the cave, the sound of dragon scales brushing against stone. Noa's head lifted, her luminous eyes narrowing as she turned toward the beds. Her gaze swept the room once before fixing on the empty space where Nemeah should have been.

"The moon child did not return with you?" Her clicks were low, tinged with slight concern. She sniffed the air, her nostrils flaring.

Nemeah's usual scent of starlight and smoke was absent. Keanoff did not answer at first. He rubbed his face with both hands, dragging his fingers down to his beard, where they curled tightly in silent frustration.

Finally, he looked up. "The Axis has her," he said hoarsely.

Noa's eyes seemed to bore through him, full of quiet judgment.

"She let her emotions overtake her, and power consumed her. I tried to stop it." His voice broke. "But I failed."

Noa blinked slowly as she pondered his words. "Will you try to retrieve her?"

"I cannot," he whistled, drawing his knees close while resting his arms on them, his posture hunched under the burden of helplessness. "There were several outside with me. Who knows how many are waiting inside the Axis House? I am but just one man."

Silence descended. Even the wind seemed to pause, holding its breath. The fire offered one last pop before extinguishing completely, leaving only a wisp of smoke in its place. Noa rose gracefully, the moonlight glinting off her scales. As she moved, light refracted off her body, scattering tiny arcs of rainbow across the stone floor like shards from a shattered sky.

"I will hunt," she said, her tone calm and assured. "When I return, we will speak of this more. Of the moon child." With that, she unfurled her wings, testing them once before leaping into the night, vanishing into the cold mountain air.

Keanoff's voice chased her into the night sky. "Her name is Nemeah!"

With each powerful sweep of her feathered wings, she soared higher, drawing nearer to the stars, the only place that ever made her feel close to her creator, the one who had given her life. The woman who shaped her from a vision in her mind's eye: from the sheen of her scales to the iridescent tips of her feathers, from the shimmer of her crystal eyes to the frost-tinged breath that left her lips. She had no way of knowing whether she was ordinary for a dragon or something rare and resplendent, for she had never seen another like herself.

Still, she favored the idea that she was magnificent. Wings outstretched, she glided, the wind rushing beneath her, lifting her higher still. Clouds slipped past her body like cool silk, their mist collecting on her scales in fine, glittering beads. She dove sharply, feeling the drop in her stomach, the exhilarating rush of gravity. Up here, she was weightless, untethered, and free.

Five hundred years had passed, and during that time, she had lived and chosen how every moment was spent. She thought of the Darra, the one they called Nemeah. The girl who had brought her master back. The one cloaked in the moon's power and something more, something unfamiliar. Different. There was a pull to her, a thread that tugged at Noa's ancient heart.

Now the air carried a change. The scent of salt permeated the wind. Far below, the ocean roared with a steady rhythm. Noa tilted her wings and tucked them tightly. She plummeted like a spear through the clouds, the wind shrieking past her face until the icy grip of the sea wrapped around her. Cold and crushing, the water swallowed her whole. Bubbles escaped from her scales as she sank deeper, darkness coiling tighter with every foot she descended.

Down here, there was silence. Stillness. She waited, her glowing eyes doing what they always did: luring the prey to the predator. She did not have to wait long this time; she sensed it immediately. A shift in the current. A vibration. The subtle stirring of something large circling in the ominous black water. A curious tentacle broke through the gloom, slow and cautious. It reached toward her glowing eyes, drawn by the glimmer like a moth to a flame.

With the precision of a seasoned hunter, Noa struck. Her jaws clamped down, slicing through slick flesh. The taste of briny squid spread across her tongue, satisfying and familiar. She beat her wings and pulled with her legs, their strength propelling her upward through the crushing depths, water swirling around her. Light began to return. The stars, scattered across the surface, shimmered closer. She broke through the waves, dragging the squid with her.

It thrashed violently, lashing out with its hooked club in a frenzy. But its strikes glanced harmlessly off Noa's thick, glassy scales. Nothing had ever pierced them for as long as she had lived. Within moments, she carried their battle skyward. Higher and higher until the clouds wrapped around them like ghosts. The squid's skin shimmered with desperate camouflage, greens, blacks, and purples flickering across its slick hide, but it was no use. Not here, not in the sky, and not against her.

The dragon opened her jaws, releasing the prey into the open air. The squid tumbled, its limbs flailing. Noa tucked her wings and dove again, a streak of moonlit silver in the sky. She caught the mollusk by its mantle, her fangs sinking deep, piercing through to its soft organs and finally reaching the brain. The creature went limp as death came swiftly.

With a few heavy beats of her wings, Noa turned towards the shore. She flew to the jagged rocks that crowned this remote stretch of coast, where the surf battered the land with wild fury. The shore here was too dangerous for humans or other animals. She knew she could be alone here, able to enjoy her fresh meal in peace. Her talons curled into the stone, and she began her meal, her mind inevitably returning to the Darra. Always the moon child with the dark eyes.

There was something about her. Something that lingered in Noa's mind longer than it should. Every human she had met carried a distinct scent. The plant-grower in the cave reeked of earth; soggy soil and moss, blooming flowers and decay. Keanoff smelled of the forest, with its animal musk, pine needles, bark, and sweat, as well as pheromones. Her master had smelled of skyfire and frostbitten air, free and wild. But the Darra, she was unlike any human Noa had ever known. Her scent was unlike anything found on the ground, in the trees, or by the sea. She smelled of the stars. Like hot and airy flames laced with spice. There was smoke, yes, but not the acrid tang of burning wood. It was brighter, finer. Celestial. It smelled like her.

Noa tore a thick strip from the squid's slick body. The oily meat slid down her throat easily, each bite renewing her strength. She blinked slowly, lost in thought as the fire returned to her, how it had burned and blistered the girl's hands, licking at the cave walls with wild hunger. That fire had not smelled like timber. It had smelled of something timeless. It had smelled of home. She ripped away another piece of flesh, exposing the squid's sweet brain, her favorite part. She devoured it with relish, letting the rest fall where it may. The seabirds would arrive in the morning to fight over the remains, tearing at scraps until only the beak remained.

"Smoke," she considered. "I recall smelling that smoke before."

The moon sagged lower in the sky as she stretched her wings again, her hunger sated and her muscles burning with the memory of flight. She took a deep breath of ocean air before launching herself skyward. By the time she returned to the cave, the one who grew the plants was awake, her face streaked with tears. Keanoff sat beside her, speaking softly of the Darra, his voice thick with sorrow.

Noa padded quietly to her nest, careful not to crush any of the embari Keanoff had gifted her. The little creatures clucked and cooed, pleased at her return. She folded herself into the gold, wings tucked close, belly full, and limbs heavy. Sleep was well within her grasp, but first, she had something to say. She tilted her head and released a nasally whistle, followed by a rhythmic click, then another whistle, sharper this time.

Keanoff answered from beside the old woman, his voice low yet certain, not fearful like the night before. "What smoke?" Keanoff asked, his hand gently rubbing Edna's back in an effort to soothe her trembling shoulders.

"The smoke the moon child carries," Noa replied, her voice tinged with discomfort. "I smelled it when the fire scorched the cave."

"I told you, she has a name."

The dragon let out an irritated roar, sharp and furious. "I have no patience for this small human! Either listen or be blind to the truth!"

She flapped her wings, the wind from their span sweeping through the trees, rustling the branches and sending the donkey into a nervous dance. Silence fell like a stone. Keanoff and Edna stared at her, breath held in fear of what the dragon might do next. Noa folded her wings back slowly and deliberately. The chickens, spooked, scurried to the far side of the cave, unsure whether to flee or faint.

"I have encountered her scent before," she finally said, her voice softer yet still resolute. "A long time ago. It is the same smoke that follows," She grappled with the name, "Neeemahh, it is the same smoke my myrrakai once carried."

Keanoff furrowed his brow. "Kallemena smelled like smoke?"

He rose to his feet, cautiously stepping closer. Edna followed behind, wide-eyed, glancing from beast to man. The dragon's clicks and whistles were like a strange song she would never learn, but she could feel the tension curling in the air.

"What does smoke have to do with Nemeah?" Keanoff asked, his mood becoming tense. His voice was strained, as if he were trying to force logic into the dragon's cryptic words.

"My myrrakai had the same scent," Noa said. "The smell of fire. Not wood fire. Not ash or soot. But the fire of something destined to burn, something meant to wield the flame." Her clicks became more deliberate, her tone slow and labored, as if addressing a child who had just discovered that the sky was not blue after all.

"But Kallemena is a Darra, moon and dream magic," Keanoff pointed out. "Just like Nemeah. Neither of them can make a fire that burns." Frustration bloomed in his chest. "Darra only create, not destroy."

Noa released a long breath, her scales shifting with the motion. "The Darra, no," she responded, maintaining her tone with careful calmness, "But the Cairn, yes."

Keanoff snapped his head up, his eyes searching the dragon for any sign of trickery. He darted a confused look at Edna, disbelief evident on his face.

"You had two masters?" His voice was thick with doubt. "Two myrrakai?"

Edna clutched his hand, her curiosity growing alongside her own questions.

He gently stepped forward, pulling the old woman with him. "Who is the second?"

Noa observed the two humans in her cave, the intruders who had disturbed her peace. They were messy, loud, and emotional. Yet, somehow, they were essential. She had watched them for weeks. Endured their presence. And now, she understood the reason. She lowered her head into her nest. Coins clinked and shifted as she searched carefully, her teeth delicately gripping the handle of a hidden item.

She withdrew it, placing it cautiously on the edge of her golden hoard. A mirror. It shimmered in the dim firelight, loose coins cascading around it like a waterfall of gold. Keanoff leaned forward and gingerly picked it from the pile. It was identical to the one they had carried. Round, smooth, framed in silver. Familiar, except for the crack that split the glass down the center.

"Who is this?" Keanoff's clicks came quicker, nearly tripping over one another. His whistles ended in flustered raspberries. "Who is in this mirror?"

Noa stared out of the cave, her gaze drifting toward the snow-capped peaks where the clouds hung low and heavy. "Ashar. The king of this land."

Keanoff let out a long whistle, then shook his hand as if swatting the sound away. Noa tilted her head, puzzled by the human gesture. He sank to the cave floor, cradling the mirror in his hands and examining the jagged crack that split the glass like a wound, deep and dark.

"How did you get his mirror?" he asked, intrigue filling him.

"I returned for it," Noa said, her voice uncommonly gentle. "I saw my myrrakai drop through the vessel that transported them with the others. The...Ship." She briefly rolled the word on her tongue. "They were lost, but their scent remained. And I detected another. One that misled. The foul odor of decay and death. This person held them."

"Vallorith," Keanoff growled, the name bitter in his mouth. "Or Zepher." He spat, anger flaring as he envisioned the creature that had stolen his father, half man, half feline, all monster.

"I do not know these names," Noa replied. "Only that he took them. I flew back to that place, where the dead had risen, where I was born from my myrrakai's chaos. I dug into the earth until I found a cave. Deep, deeper than light could reach. That is where they were." Her voice dipped lower, darker. "A creature was gathering the mirrors. I tried to use my fire. But it had left me. So I used claws and teeth."

She bared her fangs in memory, white daggers gleaming. "It held my myrrakai's mirror. When I struck, it flung the mirror at me. Though it landed safely, the mirror was already broken. I lunged again, but it fled down into the stone I could not break. So, I took the mirror and flew here, something deep within my heart guiding me to this place." She motioned toward the mirror in Keanoff's hands. "That is my myrrakai. Cairn."

Keanoff translated every word for Edna, both of them now crouched beside the shattered glass. Uncertainty flickered between them.

"If that is Ashar," Edna whispered, "maybe he could help us get Nemeah back? If he is like the others, after five hundred years, he must be powerful. Maybe more than any of them." She clutched Keanoff's arm, her voice heightening with hope. "We could beg him to help us. Beg him to rescue her!"

"But how?" Keanoff asked, looking down at the glass again. "He has not come out, not even with you and me here. And not with his betrothed beside him. Kallemena said she could feel the others trapped in mirrors, yet she had not appeared." His finger traced the fracture line. "I do not think we can rely on him or the others. We may have to get Nemeah ourselves."

"No," Noa interjected with a low whistle. "You should not rescue her."

Keanoff turned slowly. "Excuse me?" He passed the mirror to Edna and strode toward the dragon, fists tight. "She is one of us. She needs our help. They will kill her if we do nothing!" Anger flushed his face, an uncommon and shocking intensity.

"Maybe that is for the best." Noa held his gaze without blinking.

Keanoff scoffed at her irrational suggestion. "I understand you have been alone for centuries and may not grasp what it means to have a family, but you *rescue* family. You do not leave them to die!"

"She is a *mutation*," Noa snapped, her voice like a crack of thunder. "She smells like many different Echoes. She smells like something I have never encountered in five hundred years. She is *dangerous*, and she will get all of you killed. She nearly did already when her power set fire to this cave. *My* home!"

Noa's feathers stood on end, her scales flashing with heat. She bared her teeth in warning. The chickens squawked, scattering toward Rhubarb's pen, pecking nervously at his bedding and alfalfa. With a furious snort, the dragon rose, her movements shaking the floor. Her golden nest collapsed in on itself, a rain of coins clattering like falling hail.

Keanoff instinctively stepped back, shielding Edna. But as Noa shoved past him and spread her wings, preparing to launch, he surged forward, one last question clawing its way out.

"You said she smells like many Echoes." His eyes locked onto hers, unwavering. "How many?"

Noa paused, her gaze drifting toward the mountains. The distant peaks were already blurred by an approaching storm, with lightning streaking across the clouds like veins of fire. Thunder rolled, low and steady, drawing closer with each passing moment. "She smells like them all," she admitted at last, her voice low. "Every single one." With a beat of her wings, she launched into the air just as the first drops of rain began to fall.

***

"Three days now." Ismaara clapped her hands, the sharp sound echoing through the cell. "How have you enjoyed your stay so far?"

Nemeah did not bother to sit up. She rolled her eyes from the hard cot, her body aching and her head still pounding from the constant dose of silvervane in the air. "Trick question?"

Ismaara let out a high-pitched giggle, too perfect, too rehearsed. Nemeah had already pegged it as fake. Each day blended into a dull, repetitive pattern. Silence until late in the cycle, was it morning or night? One meal a day. A generous portion she rarely finished. And them, always them. The guard with the perpetual sneer and the soft-spoken woman in the red robe. Ismaara asked endless questions about her family, her friends growing up, and whether she had ever loved someone back home. It felt like being interrogated by a gossip-starved teenager pretending to be your friend.

"If we fought, would they move me to the cell where my friend is?" The idea had suddenly come to her amidst the ramble of questions. She bolted upright, her heart fluttering at the sudden thought; excitement filled her for the first time in days. "I mean, not really fight, but say we do not get along. You know? Just so I could see my friend. Make sure he is alright."

Ismaara tilted her head, thoughtful. "Hmm. You could try. I mean, they might believe it." She stood and eased herself against the black stone wall. Her hand traced the grooves and texture of the otherwise smooth stone. "But it would be more convincing with proof." She gave a malicious smile as she leaned her head back.

"What are you doing?" Nemeah stood but froze as Ismaara abruptly flung her head forward, her brow smashing into the stone with a gut-wrenching crack.

"What the hell?" Nemeah lunged forward, pulling her away from the wall. A deep purple line had bloomed across Ismaara's brow.

"There. Compelling, is it not?" Ismaara smiled, retaking her seat as if she had not just headbutted the wall.

Nemeah stepped back, horrified. "Are you *crazy?*"

Ismaara's relentless questions resumed as if nothing had happened. Her voice was as cheerful as ever. That evening, when the sound of the door lock announced the guard's presence, Ismaara quickly huddled in the corner of the cell, sobs echoing in the silence. The guard stomped in, eyes widening at the sight of Ismaara's bruised and swollen forehead.

"What happened to you?" he barked.

Ismaara's fingers shook as they examined her bruised face. "She hit me," she murmured, tears glistening on her lashes. "I only wanted to be nice."

The guard spun around, his face twisted in rage. He stormed into the cell, grabbing Nemeah's wrist with a bruising grip and twisting her arm behind her back. "You will be punished for this."

"Wait, that is not how it went!" Nemeah protested, panic rising within her. "She did that to herself. I promise, please tell him!" she urged Ismaara. "Tell him what really happened!"

But Ismaara only looked away. She buried her face in her hands, her body shaking as exaggerated sobs echoed once more. The guard yanked Nemeah forward, dragging her through the doorway. She caught a glimpse of the woman in red, eyes wide with fear as Nemeah passed. The distant scent of food lingered in the air, warm and well-seasoned and now fleeting. She knew it would be her last for a while.

The hallway stretched ahead, paved with the same obsidian stones as the prison walls. They were smooth, cold, and lifeless. The guard did not slow his pace as he marched the prisoner through the halls.

He shoved her onward, half pushing, half dragging her through the church's twisted interior. Door after door blurred past, each one identical to the last. She counted twenty, then lost track after the third or fourth turn. The labyrinth of corridors was impossible to map in her mind. There would be no escaping this place without help.

"Where are you taking me?" she demanded, trying to twist around.

A shove between her shoulder blades was the only answer she received. They turned again, entering another hallway that led to another door. This one looked just like the rest, but the guard paused to unlock it. The room beyond was small and dark, lined with cells built into a curved wall of smooth black stone, six in total. Their barred doors were jagged like teeth. The guard led her to the third cell and shoved her inside. There was no cot and no bucket of water. Just the stone floor and the stale air.

"Are these the cells you spoke of before?" she asked, rubbing her wrists. Her burns throbbed where the guard's hand had gripped her tightly; her skin was cracked and inflamed without Edna's salve to soothe them.

The guard smirked as he locked the cell. His eyes now lingered on the door at the end, his smile fading. When he noticed Nemeah still watching him, waiting for an answer, he turned to leave, but not before calling out. "Brought you a friend, you miserable Vira."

The door slammed shut behind him with a thunderous clang. The echo rippled through the silence like a cruel reminder. Nemeah rushed to the bars, pressing her face as close as possible. The corridor was dim, shadows playing tricks on her perception. She squinted down the row. "Keanoff?" she called out, heart thudding. "Keanoff! Are you there?" Only silence answered her. "Keanoff, answer me!"

"Chains!" the voice snapped. "Keep it down. I am trying to sleep." The voice responded sardonically, and distinctly not Keanoff's.

Nemeah felt her worry ignite as the realization washed over her: the voice was female.

Chapter Six

Nemeah paced her cell. Nine steps from the back wall to the barred door. Turn. Nine steps, then pivot again. Over and over. Her thoughts twisted with each lap, getting captured, Ismaara's relentless questions, her insane stunt of slamming her own head into the wall. Nine steps, turn. The Vira at the end of the hall was not the one she knew. A woman. Who was she? Why was she here?

Nine steps, turn. It had to be for something far more interesting than Nemeah's own story, one that boiled down to her basically walking through the front door like a fool. Nine steps. She winced at the memory and turned again.

"Can you please stop that?" the voice called out, moaning its plea. "I am still trying to sleep."

Nemeah froze mid-stride. Had she been talking out loud? She frowned and placed her finger over her lips, silently scolding herself. Nine steps, turn.

"That. That!" the voice screeched again. "You will drive me mad if you do not stop pacing!"

She glanced down at her bare feet. She had not realized the sound of her steps carried so far. "You can hear me walking?" she asked, pressing her face between the bars, craning to catch a glimpse of the woman at the end.

"Yes. Nine steps, then you turn, then you do it again. It is like a fly buzzing in my skull. Just lie down."

"But there is no bed," Nemeah blurted, too quickly to stop herself.

"There is a floor, is there not? If it is good enough for me, then it is good enough for you! Now, goodnight."

Nemeah glanced around her dim cell. There were no windows, no cracks, and no moonlight or sunbeam to mark the passage of time. "How can you tell it is night?"

"Oh, for the love of gods. It is a Vira thing. Now close your mouth."

Nemeah pressed her lips together. Her wrist still throbbed where the guard had wrenched it, leaving bruises in the shape of his fingers. She crossed to the wall, slid down slowly, and curled into herself. The air felt denser here, the ever-present tang of silvervane coating her tongue like dust. She peered at her hand. The bandages hung loose now, the burns beneath sensitive and peeking through.

Edna's healing salve would make her skin feel better in a heartbeat. She missed Edna. She missed Keanoff. Even the dragon's unnerving, glowing blue eyes. A flicker of comfort washed over her at the thought of Keanoff still free, out there, somewhere. Not locked inside this building filled with people who wanted their kind erased. That thought softened the edge of her fear. She drifted in and out of restless sleep, her head drooping and snapping upright again each time she began to nod off. It took forever for morning to come, or so she guessed. The only indication was her stomach, which rumbled mercilessly. The thought of food only deepened the ache.

Movement outside the cell made her jump, fully awake from her half-dreamy state. She shrank into the corner, trying unsuccessfully to disappear into the shadows. Her ears caught the jingle of keys and the creak of metal. The lock turned with a heavy click, and the door groaned open. A hunched man stepped into the room, bald with brown blotches freckling his waxy skin. When he spoke, his voice scraped like a toad's croak, instantly familiar. He was the one from the night she had arrived. Arrived? No, captured. Captured? Could she even call it that? Had they truly captured her, or had she thrown herself at their feet like some naïve offering? Shame flared up her neck, hot and prickling. She felt like an ignorant child.

"Good morning, ladies," the old man said, more out of formality than courtesy.

"Piss off, old man!" the Vira snapped from her cell.

His deeply lined face crinkled into a broad grin, the insult seeming to amuse him. "Always a pleasure, Yuli," he chuckled, then turned toward Nemeah's cell. "We have a few questions for you, my dear."

A guard appeared behind him, Henry, clad in the same golden armor as always, with iron shackles dangling from his hand. Nemeah's stomach knotted at the sight. She knew what came next.

Henry stepped forward and unlocked the cell, his voice as level as ever. "Do not make this difficult."

But something in his expression made her hesitate. Was that regret showing? Sadness? He gripped her arm and pulled her to her feet, his touch momentarily gentler than she expected. But the hesitation did not last. The cold bite of metal wrapped around her scorched wrists, forcing a sharp breath from her lips. Henry tugged the chain, leading her out.

"We will return with your new companion, Yuli," the old man teased. "Try not to miss her too much."

The door swung shut before Nemeah could hear Yuli's biting retort, though the volume alone promised it was colorful. They walked in silence. Hallway after hallway, turn after turn, the same oppressive maze. The old man muttered to himself as if retracing steps from memory.

Eventually, they stopped before a door that stood out starkly from the rest. Not iron or obsidian like the others, but wood, pale and warmly knotted. Pine? Oak? The difference was jarring.

"Here we are," the old man declared, as if unveiling a royal banquet.

And to Nemeah's surprise, it almost was. Inside was a wide wooden table that matched the door, glossy, light, and richly crafted. Platters of food covered the surface: roasted venison and duck with crisp skin, steaming vegetables and ripe fruits spilling across silver dishes, and tall goblets filled with what smelled like spiced ale. Her mouth watered instantly. Her stomach growled so loudly she knew the others could hear it.

The old man gestured to a chair opposite the spread. "Please. Sit."

Something in his tone was far too cheerful for a member of the Axis. Nemeah hesitated, taking an involuntary step backward right into Henry's chest.

"Do not make this hard," he said again, quieter now. His voice had not changed, but his eyes seemed different. They still held that strange sorrow, which made the air feel heavier.

Her gaze darted between the two men and then back to the feast. The food was fresh, steam still rising from the meats. The scent was almost intoxicating after just one night in confinement. Roasted fats, wild herbs, and sugared fruit. She licked her cracked lips, the brief moisture soothing. What harm could come from a meal? Besides, what choice did she really have? The old man gave her a small wink and reached to pat her shoulder. She flinched away from the contact but did not resist when he ushered her forward. She shuffled to the table and sank into the cushioned chair, her aching body melting into the comfort. For the first time in days, something soft cradled her. Henry stepped aside, taking up a post by the door, his arms folded across his chest, his eyes never leaving her.

"You are a Darra, correct?" the old man asked, producing a thick leather-bound book. A golden sun was carved into its cover, worn at the edges. He sat across from Nemeah, casually gesturing toward the feast before her, as if she were a guest rather than a prisoner.

Nemeah remained silent, watching as he flipped through the text. She did not trust it; it felt too carefully staged, like bait. The old man noticed her hesitation and plucked a grape from a silver bowl, popping it into his mouth. A soft pop echoed as his teeth broke the skin, and he chewed slowly, savoring the fruit. Nemeah reached for the goblet. Her shackles clinked against the empty plate as she brought the drink to her lips. She drank deeply, her body craving the moisture.

The ale's perfumed taste filled her nose, and the cool liquid burned wonderfully down her throat. Her body welcomed it with open desperation. Wiping her mouth with the back of her bandaged hand, she grabbed a warm roll and a slab of venison, tearing into it like a starving wolf. The room remained silent as she devoured bite after bite, consuming more than she should have. Her head buzzed, and her limbs tingled. Warmth crept beneath her skin.

"Let us proceed," the man said, his tone too smooth. "A Darra from Nocthrea?"

Nemeah froze mid-sip. Lowering the goblet, she swallowed hard. Her eyes flicked to the old man and then to Henry. The guard looked away now, shame written plainly on his face.

"We already know," the old man continued. "Ismaara told us everything you discussed. There is no point in hiding it."

Shame scorched her insides like fire. Of course, that witch talked. She had known better. She should have trusted her instincts and stayed guarded. Her jaw tightened as she gave a slow, reluctant nod, the old man's smug gaze never leaving her face.

"And the man with you?" he asked next. "A Vira?"

She said nothing. Her silence was her answer.

"The guards saw him shift," the man added, scribbling something into his book with sharp, swift movements. The scratch of the quill on parchment made Nemeah tense. "And the Cairn? Was that the man who came inside with you?"

Her forehead creased in confusion. "What?"

"The Cairn," he repeated, tapping the page with one bony finger. "The one who held back my men, trapping them inside while your Vira friend fought the soldiers you so rudely tossed into the air. The one dressed in the armor, the fire wielder. Where did he go? You see, we take great care in recording things accurately. History is not built on assumptions and lies."

Nemeah stared at him in genuine confusion. "I do not know any Cairn."

The man studied her, weighing her reaction with a calculating stare. Then, too smoothly, he asked, "What is your mother's name?"

"Maeve." The answer tumbled out before she could stop it. Her eyes widened in horror. Her hands shot to her mouth as if she could push the word back inside.

"And your father? What is his name?"

"Eoghan," she whispered, stricken. She had not meant to speak. Panic crept up her spine like ice, while sweat beaded on her forehead and back. Something was wrong. Her thoughts felt foggy. Her body betrayed her.

"And why did you come here?" another question asked.

"To find my sister. The Axis stole her and my family from their home." Nemeah's voice cracked as tears filled her eyes. The guard beside the door looked down with a flicker of sympathy. "What is this?" she asked, her vision already swimming. "What is happening to me?"

Father Leon laced his fingers under his chin, studying her with unreadable eyes. "How many glasses did she drink?"

The guard cleared his throat. "Four, sir."

The priest said nothing. He just stared at Nemeah, unmoving, like a cat watching its prey. "Who was the Cairn with you the other night? The man in armor."

Nemeah shook her head slowly. "There was no Cairn. The man in armor was my guard, I projected him. I do not know any Cairns."

Father Leon rose, reaching for a nearby pitcher. He poured another goblet of ale, its scent thick and sweet in the air. "Drink," he commanded.

Nemeah's eyes moved from the priest to the cup. Her thoughts now panicked with what the ale signified. "No."

With a swift flick of Father Leon's hand, she heard the loud snap. Henry was on her in an instant. He grabbed her jaw, forcing her head back, his grip like a vice. Her mouth was wrenched open. The ale spilled down her throat, splashing across her chin and into her nose, burning. She sputtered and gagged until every last drop was swallowed. Henry let go, shaking the liquid from his armored hand; droplets scattered across the floor. Nemeah gasped for breath, coughing violently, her eyes red and wet with tears.

Father Leon poured another glass. "Now, either drink it yourself," He nodded toward the guard. "Or Henry will assist you again."

Trembling, Nemeah took the cup. She drank slowly and evenly, each gulp like swallowing treachery. When it was empty, she set it down with fumbled hands. Her skin felt hot, her limbs weak, and her thoughts muddled with a desire for sleep. The two men waited, watching.

"Who was the Cairn?"

"I told you," she rasped. "I do not know any Cairn. It was just the Vira and me. That is all."

The priest said nothing as he sank back into his chair, flipping through his book again with a wet lick of his finger. "And you are Darra?" he murmured, eyes locked on the text.

Nemeah clenched her teeth, desperate not to speak. But her tongue burned. Her whole mouth felt seared by invisible flames. "Yes," she hissed, the word dragged from her against her will. "What is this?" she demanded, horror mounting. "What did you do to me?" Her vision swam. She gripped the edge of the table, trying to hold herself upright, thankful she was not standing.

Father Leon waved a dismissive hand. "It is just the ale. A truth-telling herb mixed in. Not deadly. Just persuasive." He turned another page, something catching his eye. His voice dropped low with awe. "Did you?" He hesitated, as if the thought were absurd. "Did you start the fire?"

Nemeah pressed her lips together, but it was no use. Her tongue burned like a coal in her mouth. "Yes," she gasped. The effort to resist nearly broke her.

Father Leon leaned forward, his age seeming to peel away like old paint. He looked invigorated. Ravenous. "How?" he pressed. "How did you do it?" His eyes fell to her bandaged hands that she now tucked under the table. "Fascinating," he whispered, awe in his voice. "You started the fire and burned your hands?"

She nodded, her head heavy and her eyelids sinking. "Yes," she murmured. "But I burned my hands in a different fire. Not the one I started here." Her words came slowly now, slurred together.

"How? How did you ignite a fire that generated heat? How were your flames able to halt my men?" Father Leon leaned further over the table, his face uncomfortably close to Nemeah's. "Tell me."

"I do not know." Her head lolled back against the high-backed chair, her eyes aching with weariness. Sleep tugged at the edges of her vision.

"You do not know?" he echoed, incredulous. "How can you be unaware of your own power?"

Nemeah gave a slow shrug as a yawn escaped her ale-stained lips.

"What are you?" Father Leon demanded, straightening. He snapped his fingers at Henry again, signaling that it was time for more ale.

Nemeah chuckled, a lazy, hiccup-laced laugh bubbling from her throat. "I am Nemeah." She leaned forward with effort, her head suddenly feeling like it weighed a stone. "I am the harbinger of doom." Her eyes blackened into inky shadows, swallowing the whites. Her voice deepened, unnatural, as her hands spread wide on the table's wooden top. She pushed herself up. "I will be the end of you. And everyone like you. The Axis will *crumble*, and its followers will be consumed by my vengeance. *You will all die!*"

She laughed as she lifted one hand, and smoke poured from her fingertips, snaking through the air in icy tendrils. They shot across the room and wrapped around Father Leon's throat. His body lifted off the ground, flailing, feet kicking helplessly. The pressure on his neck tightened. His vision blurred, breath escaping him in strangled wheezes. The woman's snarled laughter filled his ears. And then, the grip vanished.

Father Leon crumpled to the floor, air rasping back into his lungs. His eyes blinked through the haze just in time to see Henry standing over Nemeah's unconscious form. His dagger gleamed faintly, its hilt darkened by blood. A fresh cut bloomed across Nemeah's temple, re-opening the old wound.

"I warned you," Henry said, sheathing the blade away. "This is the second time she has resisted the silvervane. She poses a threat and must be sent to Verdathos."

The priest nodded, massaging his bruised throat with trembling hands. "Take her back to her cell. I want her dosage doubled. Rations laced into her water and food."

Henry hoisted Nemeah onto his shoulder. Her shackles clinked against his golden armor, her body limp. "The prisoners do not receive food in the confinement cells," he reminded.

"They do now," Father Leon said, still shaken.

Henry carried her back through the twisting corridors and gently laid her on the cold stone floor of her cell. He unlocked the cuffs, slipping them from her damaged wrists. He closed the door, pulling once to test the lock. When he poked his head into the hallway beyond, he was relieved to see it was empty. He let out a slow breath as he eased back into the prison room. He turned and walked softly to the last cell in the row: the Vira's.

"Yuli?" he whispered, his voice barely audible in the darkness.

A shape stirred. Her silhouette approached the bars, golden-brown eyes gleaming faintly in the dark. Her short, wavy hair fell just past her collarbone, swaying gently with each step. She reached through the bars, her hands finding his.

"How are you holding up?" Henry asked, his voice soft. He gently ran his fingers up her arm, the small touch imbued with aching tenderness.

She smiled, her tough demeanor softening at her husband's touch. "I am better now." Her smile was faint, but her eyes sparkled. Just seeing him lifted the weight from her chest. "What did you learn about the new girl?" she asked, nodding toward Nemeah's cell.

Henry hesitated. The image of that dark power, of Nemeah's rage still lingered in his mind. The thought of Yuli locked within the same stones and iron made his skin crawl.

"She is different," he said finally. "She can do things, even with the silvervane in her system. Be careful, my love. Whatever you do, do not make her angry. It is her wrath that seems to set her off."

Yuli nodded solemnly. "So... be her friend?" A grin tugged at her lips, a wide, toothy smile that reached her eyes. The one Henry loved most. The one that made the world outside their predicament fade for just a moment.

He reached through the bars, his fingers grazing her chin. They shifted, navigating the cold iron until their lips met in a kiss. It was brief and tender, definitely too dangerous if caught. When they parted, it was with aching reluctance. If anyone discovered their bond, it would mean death. She pressed a kiss to the pad of his thumb as he withdrew, sealing the moment. He slid his helmet back on, his face once more hidden behind gold and duty. He gave her one last lingering look before turning away.

"Be cautious," he whispered. And then he was gone.

The door shut behind him with a hollow clang, and the silence pressed in again. Yuli's smile faded as she slunk back to her corner, where the driest patch of ground in the cell sat warmed faintly by her body heat. Her lip trembled, but she clenched her jaw. She had not cried since the day she was captured and dragged from the forest while hunting. She did not cry when she was stripped of her powers by the poison in the air and thrown into this damp hole. She would not cry now. Not after everything.

Yuli inhaled deeply, the stale, bitter air of the prison cells filling her lungs. She held it, stilling her body and letting her heartbeat slow beneath her ribs. When she finally exhaled, she felt the sadness loosen its grip. There was no room for despair. Only strategy. Only strength. She would save her tears for the day she escaped. A groggy moan echoed from the other cell.

Yuli tilted her head, her voice soft yet steady. "Welcome back, friend."

Chapter Seven

The door to Father Leon's study flew open, the brass handle slamming against the somber stone wall with a metallic clang. The old priest stumbled in, his nerves fraying like a tight cord that had been cut, the threads fanning out in every direction. Panic gripped his chest with icy fingers and squeezed his heart, the beating growing louder in his ears. What was he supposed to do? Never before had they encountered someone with such defiance, someone who could resist the effects of their most trusted herb.

The Axis was not prepared for this. He made a beeline for the towering bookshelf that stood behind his desk, its shelves packed with sacred volumes and brittle tomes. The knowledge of the Axis and its decrees, laws, rituals, and exhaustive notes on the tarnished ones was all kept there. His trembling fingers slid a leather-bound book from the shelf, the familiar texture grounding him for only a fleeting moment.

He carried it to his immaculate desk, where every quill, scroll, and ink pot was placed with ceremonial precision. With a heavy breath, Father Leon dropped the book. It landed with a muted thud, its spine groaning as it opened. He then retrieved his battered journal. The one he kept closest, the one where he had documented every Echo he had ever encountered. He flipped to the most recent page, his words staring back at him. *What is she?*

Sinking into his chair, the cushion conformed to his body, its arms worn smooth from years of anxious scratching. He reviewed his notes and then turned to the older text. "Nocthrea," he muttered, his eyes scanning the yellowed pages. They whispered as he flipped through them, each one slicing the air like paper blades.

He read without pause. One book became two, then five, then ten. He traced the story of the goddess Caerwen, whose moonlit beauty was corrupted by jealousy, and the mortal men who were never quite fully within her claws. He read how Arvayn, the god of death, lost his heart to the moon goddess and went mad with longing, joining her in the rebellion against the other gods. Their alliance gave birth to a war that spanned millennia, unraveling the fragile seams of the universe itself.

Each clash. Each spell. Each divine wound bled fragments of godhood, echoes that drifted into the world and seeded new powers among mortals. Echoes like the very ones the Axis now hunted. The stories shifted depending on the origin of the text. In Glacia, the war had begun because Lysar demanded worship of the seas. Their land-god, Nuval, rose in defiance to protect mortals. In Kalyra, the goddess Danira wanted her flora to spread unchecked, but the goddess of rebirth, Brynna, refused to yield her people's lands. Every text sang a different beginning, but always the same refrain: a devastating war and the birth of the Echoes.

But in every version, every account, regardless of origin, there was always mention of another. A shadow. A nameless goddess watching from afar. She never asked for adoration, never reveled in the glory of her name or deeds. Always absent from the legends but always present in the background.

Until now, Father Leon had never paid attention to foreign scripture. His life had been shaped by doctrine, and his mission had been clear. Purify the world of abominations. Deeper lore had never seemed necessary. But now it was essential.

Hours slipped by. Hours of relentless searching, scribbling, and cross-referencing. His ink smeared across the parchment, hands stained by the raven-colored liquid, handwriting spiraling into near-illegibility. One phrase repeated again and again, always hidden in the shadow of the pages: The Great Queen. The Mother.

He shot to his feet, nearly toppling his chair as he paced furiously across the study. His hands rubbed over his bald scalp, leaving smudged lines of ink where his hair had long since abandoned him. His thoughts spiraled around one question: "A tenth?" he whispered. "A tenth god?" His hands dragged down his face, creating more marks from his sweat-coated skin. "That would mean."

He turned back to the sea of parchment that filled his desk. The book he had been reading lay buried beneath towering stacks, some nearly as tall as he was. The once-pristine black wood surface was now marred by ink splotches and frantic scribbles. As he reached for his quill, he knocked over the inkwell. The glass shattered on the floor with a sharp crack, sending black droplets splattering onto his robes. His hand trembled as he picked up a fresh scroll, forcing his fingers to steady so his thoughts would not vanish into a tangle of illegible scrawl. Just as he finished signing his name at the bottom of the scroll, a knock rapped on the heavy metal door.

"Father Leon," came Henry's voice. "Some of the men are uneasy about the new prisoner. A good number are requesting transfers to our Axis House in Bristoff. What would you have me tell them?" His eyes focused on the father. The state of the old man's appearance was shocking. Black smudges decorated his skin like a cow in the field, his robe was stained, and the sleeves were pushed up past his elbows, a crazed look in his eye.

Henry stood in the doorway, his helmet tucked in the crook of his arm. His broad, flat nose and solemn demeanor gave him a sculpted, almost statuesque presence. The deep brown of his skin contrasted strikingly with the polished gold of his armor. Father Leon did not respond. He rolled the scroll tight and swept past Henry without a word, a wide grin on his face. The younger man fell into step behind him, his boots echoing down the torch-lit corridor. Night had fallen, though no one could truly tell from the depths of the Axis house. Leon moved faster than expected for a man of his age, his robes fluttering as he climbed three flights of stairs with surprising urgency.

The stench of feathers and feces assaulted them as they entered the message room. Dozens of birds rustled in their cages, their soft coos breaking the stillness. Leon approached one of the cages and chose a lean bird with long wings and a sharp, hooked beak, a definitive sign of a swift courier. With practiced hands, he tied the scroll to the bird's legs and stepped toward the open window. The moment he released it, the bird launched into the wind. It screeched once, then soared into the night, disappearing toward the mother continent of Verdathos. They stood in silence, watching the speck fade into the stars.

Henry cleared his throat, pulling Leon back to the present. "What shall I tell the men, Father?"

Father Leon turned to face him, his strange expression still firmly fixed on his face. His study had been in chaos, the message urgent, yet here he stood, looking oddly at peace. "Tell them all is well," Leon said, his tone calm, almost cheerful. He patted Henry's breastplate and shuffled toward the stairs, his posture slumping back into its usual stoop.

Henry followed, his brow furrowed. "And what about the prisoner? We need to ease their fears if we expect them to stay."

With a dismissive wave of his hand, the old priest replied, "Tell them the echoes will be taken care of tonight."

Henry paused. "Echoes?" he repeated, voice tight. "As in more than one?"

They walked together down the familiar halls, retracing their steps through the winding corridors of the Axis House. The passageways twisted and turned like the inner workings of a great beast, stone arteries pulsing with hushed footsteps and unseen tension. Their descent led them to the kitchen, where a timid woman quietly prepared meals for the prisoners. Descaled fish rested on a bed of fragrant herbs, waiting for the oven's fire to die down, leaving behind glowing embers perfect for slow roasting.

Puddles of dough, tucked beneath linen, rose patiently in the kitchen's warmth, while Sister Agnes stood near the hearth, peeling potatoes and carrots with rhythmic precision. A pie plate sat nearby, already filled with fresh crust and glossy, cooked-down blackberries. Granulated sugar sparkled across the top like frost in the morning light. The air was thick with the briny tang of salted fish, mingling with the earthy aroma of oregano, the bitter scent of thyme, and the sharp, spicy bite of cayenne and chilies. The scent made Henry's stomach growl as the two men paused just inside the threshold.

"Sister Agnes," Father Leon clapped his hands together, startling the woman.

Her knife slipped from her hand, clattering against the stone floor as the potato rolled under the table. Quickly, she wiped her hands on her apron and tucked her short black hair behind her ears, an anxious habit that made her look younger than she was.

"Father Leon," she said, offering a quick nod. "I was just finishing up preparations for the prisoners' supper."

"Very good, Sister." He moved across the room, dipped a finger into the blackberry pie, and tasted it. His eyes fluttered shut briefly as he savored the sweetness. "You always cook the most delicious pies."

Sister Agnes nodded her thanks as she watched the priest stride toward the tall shelving lined with herbs and glass jars. He reached for the very top shelf, the one reserved for medicinal salves and ointments. Both she and Henry watched in uneasy silence as he plucked a small, dusty jar from its place. The label was faded, yet still legible. Father Leon placed the container on the table beside the resting fish.

Agnes's eyes darted from the bottle to Henry, then back to the priest. "That one is not for cooking, sir. It is used for the sick. To ease them into the afterlife." Her voice faltered, and she tentatively stepped back.

Henry stepped forward. Setting his helmet on the table, he read the label, his expression hardening. "Belladonna?" His gaze flicked from the pie to the jar, and horror dawned in his eyes. "We cannot judge them. That decision belongs to His Holiness in Verdathos." His words came in a rush, urgent and desperate. "We cannot poison them like caged animals."

Father Leon looked at him, more amused than offended. "I have already sent word to His Holiness," he said, gesturing toward the hall, referencing the bird he had dispatched only moments before. "I have informed him these echoes are ill and require a swift end. No sense in risking the health of others."

"Ill?" Sister Agnes went pale. "What kind of illness? Is it contagious?"

"They are not sick." Henry's voice was bitter. He caught himself, forced his mouth shut, and swallowed. His outburst had surely revealed a dangerous sympathy. After a breath, he straightened. "No fear, Sister. You will not contract anything." He turned back to Father Leon, adjusting his tone. "I simply would not want my men held responsible if His Holiness were to uncover the truth. We are loyal and devoted to the Axis and our orders." He bowed his head with practiced obedience.

Father Leon's smile returned. "No fear, my friend. All will be well." He dipped a finger into the pie once more, savoring the sweetness, then removed the lid from the jar. He watched with pure fascination as the dried berries fell into the pie, blending perfectly with the filling. With another gleeful clap, he walked out and headed down the hall.

The bell tolled through the Axis House. The guards, changing shifts, marched in synchronized columns through the stone halls, their footsteps thundering like the roar of a distant waterfall. Henry remained frozen and helpless as he watched Sister Agnes unroll the pie crust from her rolling pin, pinching the edges down. The bitter scent of belladonna mixed with the sugary aroma made his stomach turn. He retreated from the kitchen without a word. His heart pounded, and his thoughts raced. He needed a plan, anything to stop what was coming. His stomach grew more nauseous as he neared the heavy double doors leading out of the Axis House. When he slipped outside into the night air, he took a deep, humid breath. The sky was partly clear, the rumble of thunder distant, and thoughts of his wife jumbled his mind. Would he see her again? Alive?

"Commander!" a man shouted behind him.

Henry turned, surprised to see someone speaking to him. Most men reserved conversation for the bunk rooms, where they ate meals and slept until their next shift.

"Where is your helmet?" the man asked, his eyes wide as he took in his commander's face.

Henry brought his hand up, shocked that he had forgotten it in the kitchen. "Chains," he murmured. "Go ahead, I will catch up."

With a salute, the man joined his platoon and marched down the streets. Henry returned to the double doors, guarded by two older soldiers, each nodding as he pulled the heavy door open and slipped inside. The Axis House had gone still. Henry exhaled, barely realizing he had been holding a tense breath, his thoughts still clouded with impending grief.

Then, without wasting a second, he hurried through the halls, taking winding detours to avoid any lingering guards. Every shadow made his pulse race. Every creak of the stone felt like betrayal. He reached the brass door within minutes, his heart pounding at what he was about to do. His hands trembled as he fit the key into the lock. The metallic ping of the latch releasing sounded too loud in his ears. He shoved the door open and rushed inside. The two women fell silent at his presence. Their voices faded, replaced by an eerie stillness. Henry stormed toward the barred cell door, the one containing the dangerous Echo.

"You. Come here," he barked, his voice sharp with panic disguised as anger. "I said, come here!"

Nemeah rose slowly, unsure of what had triggered the outburst. She searched his face, expecting anger, but discovered fear instead. Deep, trembling fear.

"You need to get her out of here." He pointed toward Yuli's cell, words tumbling out in a frantic whisper. "Do that thing! When your eyes go black and the silvervane does not stop your magic."

Nemeah blinked, confused by his question. Was this another Axis trick?

"Do you hear me?" he shouted, gripping the bars and shaking the door hard enough to rattle its hinges.

"Henry?" Yuli called from her cell. Her voice was urgent as she pressed her face between the bars, straining to see her husband. "What is going on? What is wrong?"

Henry quickly left Nemeah and hurried to his wife's cell. "Father Leon knows," he gasped. "He realizes she is different. He is afraid. He will not be sending you to Verdathos. Instead, he intends to kill you both. There will be belladonna in the pie. You will die before sunrise."

Yuli shook her head, feeling confused. "Then we will not eat the pie." She gave a soft smile, trying to ease his worry. "You know I have never liked the pies anyway. Always too sweet."

Henry closed his eyes and gripped the bars. "If you do not eat it, they will know you were warned. Only three of us knew: Father Leon, Sister Agnes, and I. If they suspect anything..." His voice cracked. "I will be executed for treason."

Yuli reached through the bars and grasped his. Tears filled her eyes. "Oh, Henry."

He lifted her hands to his lips, kissing her knuckles, each one marked with the tribal ink of her homeland. The thought of her dying from something so simple, so cowardly, ignited a fire within him. He turned back to Nemeah's cell, his face set with determination. She stood in the same spot, her expression unchanged.

"You need to help her escape," he pleaded. "I beg you." Suddenly, Henry fell to his knees. The action hushed the room.

Nemeah studied the guard before her, the same man who had spoken to her with cruelty and disdain since the day she arrived. Yet now, he knelt at her feet, trembling with fear. Then she heard Yuli's voice: soft and sincere.

"Please, Nemeah. Get us out, and I promise we will repay you somehow. We are not rich, but we will owe you our lives. Forever in your debt. Please."

Nemeah's eyes flicked between the two. She tilted her head, pieces clicking into place. "You two?" A slow, curious smile formed. "You are joined?"

Henry stood up, his expression gentler. "Married. She is my wife."

Nemeah blinked, stunned. "How? An Axis guard and a Vira? That is surely forbidden." She crossed her arms, intrigued despite the urgency. "I want to know how this happened."

"We do not have time for this," Henry muttered, glancing toward the hallway.

But Yuli spoke up, her voice filled with quiet emotion. "We met in the woods. He was cornered by my pack. I asked them to leave him be. Our love grew from there." She was trembling now, the memory delicate yet precious. "It has not been easy, but it is real. And I refuse to lose it now. Please, Nemeah. Will you help us?"

Nemeah's gaze dropped. "I do not even know how. I have no control when my power takes over. It just happens. And even if I could summon it, I have no idea if I would help or hurt you."

Henry did not hesitate. He stepped forward, pulled the ring of keys from his belt, and unlocked Nemeah's cell. The iron door creaked open with a groan. "We are willing to take that chance," he said. "It is better than sitting here and waiting."

Nemeah hesitated at the threshold. "And if I fail? If I cannot get us out?"

"Then we die," Yuli said calmly, before Henry could answer. "But I would rather die free, standing beside him, than wait in a cage like prey."

There was a beat of silence before Nemeah gave a reluctant nod. "Fine. I will try. But I have told you, I do not know how to control it."

Henry was already at his wife's cell, unlocking it. Yuli rushed into his arms, and for a moment, the world quieted around them. The embrace was both desperate and tender, a reunion filled with fear and fierce devotion. Nemeah watched, something softening inside her. She now understood his role, his restraint, and his choices. Her thoughts drifted back to the moment she believed her sister had been taken. That groggy, terrifying haze in the empty house where her family should have been. The helplessness. The fury. That was when the magic surged, wild and raw.

"I think it only happens when I let go," she said, almost to herself. "When my emotions break free." She glanced down at her burned skin. "But I have no idea how to make myself...lose control." She curled her hands, the sting of the damaged skin still piercing.

Henry and Yuli both turned to her. Yuli raised an eyebrow, then crossed her arms. "Chains, you are such a brat."

"What?" Nemeah blinked.

"Oh my powers, oh I am so scared, my poor friends," Yuli mocked, mimicking her tone with dramatic flair. "That is all you have gone on about since getting here."

"Excuse me?" Nemeah spat, bristling.

Yuli rolled her eyes. "The gods know I have heard enough of your moping. Learn to grow up, life is hard on all of Echoes."

"Moping?" Nemeah stepped forward, fists clenched. "I know life is hard as an Echo! Chains, I am one too, and my friends are as well! We have gone through things you could never dream of!"

Yuli arched a brow. "Yeah, sure."

"Yuli," Henry warned.

Yuli tilted her head and scoffed. "You had to leave your family. You had to accept that you would be hunted for life. Tough luck! We have all been through that."

Nemeah felt her powers tingling at her fingertips, the icy embrace creeping just beneath her skin.

Yuli was not done, though. "Woe is me." She pulled the corners of her lips down to make an exaggerated frown. "A little Darra caught by the big bad Axis, with no family or friends who love me." Her voice was taunting, mimicking a small child.

"Yuli," Henry warned one last time, nudging her shoulder. But his gaze was not on his wife; it was fixed on the woman at the far end of the room.

Nemeah's eyes had turned pitch black, the whites swallowed by darkness. Black veins writhed beneath her skin, moving like worms trying to break the surface. Her bandaged fingers twitched. Shadows coiled around her feet like smoke, pulsing with energy. Her lips were now curled into a chilling, too-wide smile. Her voice, when it came, was not her own. It was deeper, layered, something old and unearthly.

"Before I help," she said slowly, "you must do something for me."

Henry positioned himself between her and his wife. "Ask."

Nemeah tilted her head sharply to one side, then to the other. A sickening pop echoed through the room as if something had settled into her bones. Her movements appeared puppet-like and unnatural, as though the thing inside her was adjusting to the fit.

"I need the compass," she insisted. "The one I came here with. The one with the spinning needle."

Henry nodded. "I know where it is." He turned toward the door, pausing only to glance at Yuli. "Wait a few minutes," he said. "I will try to divert everyone from this hall."

Yuli chewed on her cheek, a habit that remained unchanged even under pressure. Her eyes met his with silent understanding.

"She will be safe," came the voice again. "She is with me now, Axis guard."

Henry hesitated, then nodded once before slipping into the corridor. He moved quickly, rounding corners with purpose. Just as he turned into the next hallway, he collided with someone. Sister Agnes. She stood there wide-eyed, clutching his helmet. The scent of burnt pie clung to her like smoke.

"You forgot this," she said, her voice trembling. Her gaze flicked toward the hallway from which he had just emerged, suspicion blooming in her eyes.

* * *

Waves crashed against the stone wall, the ocean swelling halfway up as the first storm of summer tore across the relentless sea. The wind howled, and rain lashed against the windows in heavy sheets. Thunder rolled through the sky, deafening in its intensity, with bright flashes of lightning streaking ever closer, striking the churning waves below. High in the tower, a man stood at the window, watching the storm's approach.

Each arc of lightning sent a prickle across his skin. Behind him, a fire crackled in the hearth, its warmth providing a small comfort against the chaos raging beyond the glass. A knock at the door broke his silence. With a sigh, he acknowledged the intruder.

"Enter," he said, calm despite the irritation threading his voice.

A woman stepped inside. Her brown hair hung in a long braid down her back, and her white robe was damp, faint marks of rain staining the fabric.

"High Priest," she said, bowing low. A letter was clasped in her hand. "This just arrived. From the Axis House in Highspire. From Father Leon."

He waved her forward and took a seat at his desk. "Thank you, sister. You are excused."

With another bow, she backed out and closed the tall doors behind her with a muted clunk. The scroll was water-spotted along its edges, and the wax seal had been slightly softened by the downpour. He was surprised the bird had even made it through the storm.

Breaking the seal, he unrolled the parchment. The writing was hurried, with looping strokes and ink blotches marring the text. His irritation deepened as he read, then again, and again. A strange chill washed over him. He set the scroll on the desk and rose, scanning the dim expanse of the room.

Books lined every wall, their spines marked with silver and gold lettering. A rolling ladder leaned against the far shelves, still and waiting. He moved toward the books, fingers trailing along the aged leather bindings. When he found the title he sought, he pulled it free and returned to the desk, flipping through the worn pages, searching. But the words held no answers, only half-truths and old warnings. He turned back to the window. Lightning danced across the sky, and thunder came hard and fast now, shaking the tower beneath his feet. Clearing his throat, he spoke.

"Vallorith?"

The obsidian mirror on the far wall shimmered, its surface glowing as a figure began to take shape in the room. "You called, High Priest?" came the voice.

The man in the mirror stepped forward, tall, with white-blond hair slicked back from his angular face. Piercing green eyes gleamed beneath heavy brows. Time had not touched him. His skin remained flawless, unmarred by age, thanks to the Freyla he had once trapped within one of the nine mirrors.

"I have received word from Highspire," Isrend said, turning to face the mirror. "They have captured a rather unusual woman."

Vallorith tilted his head, a hint of amusement curling at his lips. "Oh?"

"They claim she is a Darra," Isrend continued, eyes narrowing. "And yet she can produce fire. Real fire. Fire that burns."

Vallorith let out a dry chuckle, his voice laced with dismissal. "My lord, that is quite impossible. No Darra can produce flame. They must be mistaken; she is a Cairn." He gave a shallow, mocking bow. "If that is all, I will take my leave—"

"She resisted the silvervane." The words halted Vallorith mid-step. Isrend leaned on his desk, his mismatched eyes, one blue and one green, fixed on Vallorith. "Father Leon says she overpowered it. And he found something in the holy texts." He shoved an open book across the desk. Vallorith caught it with ease, his eyes scanning the passage:

She remains in the shadows, never to be favored. Never longing to gain power, for she possesses it all, the powers of those who wage war on land and in the sky. Allow her to slumber. Allow her to dream. For if she is ever awakened, her fire will burn. Her winds will change. Her fears will become reality. All hail the one great queen. Mother of the gods.

Vallorith exhaled through his nose. "A bedtime tale lost to time, my lord. Father Leon's age is showing. Trust me, there is no fruit on this tree." He closed the book with a snap and let it drop back onto the desk carelessly.

"And if there is?" Isrend's voice was sharp. "If a woman truly exists who can wield *multiple* Echo powers? An Echo beyond anything we have seen?" He jabbed a finger at the book. "Who is she? Who was this 'one great queen'?"

Vallorith scoffed and turned away, a smirk cutting across his face. "Isrend, it is a fairytale. Put your mind—"

The slam of a hand on the desk stopped him cold. "You will address me by my title," Isrend snapped. "Do not mistake this chamber for familiarity. You are not my friend, Vallorith. You are not my disciple. You are a tool. And tools are only useful as long as they work." The air between them grew razor-sharp. Isrend stepped closer, his voice lower now, but deadlier. "Now. Who is the queen the book speaks of?"

Vallorith's smirk faded as he turned away again, each step toward the bookshelf slow and deliberate, like a prisoner forced to dance to a fool king's tune. He hated this. Hated being reminded of what he had become, of how far he had fallen. From the golden throne of the Axis to whispering secrets behind glass. He slid a black-bound tome from the shelf and returned to the desk. Flipping through brittle pages, he finally stopped. With a thud, he placed the book before Isrend. Drawn in ink was the image of a woman, her eyes filled entirely with black, smoke swirling around her, and fire roaring at her feet. Isrend studied the page in silence, every detail etched into memory.

"They called her Morwyn," Vallorith said, his finger tapping the woman's forehead in the illustration. "Claimed she was the most powerful of all the gods. The creator. The harbinger of life and death." He lingered there for a moment, his eyes narrowed. "A seer. She foresaw the wars. Chose to stay hidden. Saw the rise of the Echoes and how the gods' meddling would unbalance the world. She refused to fight in the god war. Her powers were never splintered like the others." He let out a cold laugh. "It is impossible for anyone to be like her. If someone were... it would mark the rise of a new Echo. One unlike anything we have ever encountered." Vallorith scoffed again. "And I think, as men who have walked this world for five hundred years, we would have come across such a monstrosity by now."

Isrend said nothing. He lifted the rain-splotched parchment again, his tone unreadable as he recited Father Leon's words aloud: "She exhibits unusual traits for an Echo. She can push past the silvervane when her emotions are high. Her eyes turn black. Her magic flows as black smoke and is icy to the touch. She produced a fire that burns. And she called herself the Harbinger of Doom." The letter fluttered from his fingers and landed on the desk. Silence followed.

Vallorith's face, often a mask of amusement or disdain, flickered with unease. He snatched the parchment and read the scribbled report himself. A tight smile tugged at his lips. "My lord, it says right here, she is ill, not expected to make it past the night." He slapped the letter with finality. "She is likely dead already. We have nothing to fear."

Isrend's voice cut through the room like the storm outside. "Send your hound."

Vallorith blinked. "You want me to send—"

"What I want is confirmation!" Isrend glanced from Vallorith to the hourglass on his desk. The golden frame encased the clear glass, and the white sand trickled down slowly, nearing its end. "Ensure she is dead." A moment of silence hung in the air. Then he added, "And instruct him to bring back my sister. She has been gone long enough."

The lightning cracked. The storm was here now, the hurricane howling across the Axis courtyard like an omen.

Chapter Eight

Keanoff pulled at the laces of his boots, tightening each knot and neatly tucking the excess against his leg. His fur-lined tunic was replaced with chainmail, and his pants were reinforced with thicker leather. Next to the fire, he ran a wet stone along the blade's edges, the steel glinting in the orange flame's flicker with every stroke. He was uncertain if he was sharpening the sword properly, having just acquired it the day before in town. He had never needed a weapon before; his claws and teeth typically sufficed.

However, facing the Axis seemed to necessitate additional support. The cave walls echoed with the sound of the stone sliding until Edna's worried mutters drowned it out. Thorns sprouted and withered beneath her feet, manifestations of her nerves, dying just as swiftly. Her anxiety resembled a storm of roots and brambles.

"What if the plan does not work? What if we have not accounted for everything?" she muttered, chewing at her thumbnail, the other hand clutched under her arm. "What if there are more than forty guards? What if they catch you, too?"

Keanoff paused, the grinding of stone against metal falling silent. He inhaled slowly, steadying the fear bubbling in his gut. "Noa will be there," he said. "And if they catch me." His voice faltered before he forced the words through. "Then you and Noa will live here. She said she would bring fresh kills. You will have the chickens and the eggs. You can grow anything else, and the snow will give you all the water you need." He set the blade aside and stood. In one swift motion, he crossed the cave and scooped the old woman into his arms. "We will bring her back, Gran," he whispered. "I promise."

Edna's thin body trembled in his grasp. Her sobs started softly, then shook her shoulders as she clung to him. "I do not want to be alone," she wept into his chest.

Keanoff held her tighter before gently setting her back down. "That is not going to happen."

She wiped her eyes, trying to muster a smile. "Be safe." Her gaze shifted to the dragon waiting near the cave's mouth, its body still and tranquil in the rain. The soft pitter-patter echoed against the stone. "You too," she said.

The dragon lowered her head as if making a solemn promise.

"Back before you know it." Keanoff secured his blade and climbed onto Noa's back. The tension in his limbs did not fade as he settled into place, gripping the ridges of her scales. With a sharp whistle, the dragon launched into the air, wings slicing through the rain. They soared into the night, heading straight to stir up trouble.

* * *

A scream pierced the underground halls. Bodies of Axis soldiers lay strewn across the stone floors. Some groaned in pain, others lay motionless in death. Nemeah moved steadily through the labyrinth, her magic pulling her forward like a tide. Smoke curled at her feet, each step leaving behind the stench of scorched flesh and blood. Yuli trailed close behind, silent but wide-eyed, stepping over corpses one by one. She checked each fallen face, her heart pounding until she confirmed none of them belonged to Henry. Still, she watched in horror as Nemeah's power twisted into new, nightmarish forms.

Smoky tendrils pierced through torsos, limbs snapped with unseen force, and air thickened into water that filled lungs and drowned men where they stood. Yuli was terrified. Utterly petrified that the monster walking ahead might turn on her, that by the end of the night, no one, Axis or otherwise, would be left alive. Alarm bells tolled through the stone corridors, sharp and shrill. They echoed in every direction, a signal alerting every Axis guard in the town to quickly rush back to the epicenter due to danger. Back to the two women fighting to escape.

The sound of heavy boots pounded behind Yuli. She turned just in time to catch a glimpse of the steel rushing toward her chest. A cry caught in her throat, then a burst of black smoke erupted between them, instantly solidifying into jagged ice. The soldier's blade halted inches from her heart. Yuli stumbled back, gasping as the smoke-wrought wall shattered. Shards flew in every direction, burying deep into the soldier's flesh. He collapsed to the floor, twitching, choking, gasping for a breath that would never come. Yuli doubled over, her stomach lurching. Only bile came up; thank the gods she had not eaten in days.

"Come. We are close," Nemeah said. But her voice was no longer her own; it was something deeper. Something old and strict.

Yuli hesitated, still shaking, but she knew the truth: this creature was her only way out. "We have to find Henry," she breathed. "What if they have hurt him? What if they know he helped us?"

Nemeah tilted her head, one hand pressed against the stone wall, searching for the presence of the familiar form. She remained unnaturally still for a moment. "He is alive, headed our way," she said.

Relief washed over Yuli so quickly that she nearly crumpled. Her knees buckled. Her vision blurred. Then came the voices. Shouting. The clang of metal. A woman's scream. And then, "Henry!"

Yuli sprinted forward, turning a corner to discover three soldiers fallen in a heap on the damp floor. Henry leaned against the wall, his armor on his arm dripping with blood. Two women stood behind him, one dressed in white and the other in red. Yuli's protective instincts flared. She bared her teeth and lunged.

"Yuli, no!" Henry's voice was rough yet firm. He caught her with his uninjured arm, halting her suddenly. "They are like us. They are good."

She skidded to a halt, chest heaving as she stared down the two women. The stench of the Axis clung strongly to their robes, forcing her to expel the air from her lungs in a loud huff. Henry coughed, his strength faltering as she quickly ducked beneath his arm and helped him to stand. His weight pressed heavily against her; he was twice the size of the woman he had married. The creature bearing Nemeah's face observed, unreadable.

"We have to move!" Yuli shouted. Anger fueled her, urging her to action. "Now!"

"Nemeah?" Ismaara's soft voice drifted from behind. She stood hand in hand with the cook. Her eyes were wide, flicking from Henry to the girl now cloaked in shadow. "What happened to her?"

Henry coughed, blood on his lips. "Long story."

A more resounding roar echoed through the halls, dozens of boots stomping in unison. The guards were almost on them. Nemeah moved forward, stepping past the reunited group. She stood before the woman in red, her inky eyes boring into hers. A pause. The map of the Axis was seen through the cook's memories. "This way," Nemeah said, her voice low, commanding. "Keep up."

✳✳✳

The towers of Highspire Castle pierced the night sky, silhouetted against the moonlight. From its center, warning bells tolled, loud and unrelenting, as if the city itself had a heartbeat. Below, a tide of shouting voices and hurried footsteps rose from the streets as people fled toward the forest.

"Something is wrong," Keanoff clicked his tongue. "Stay above the clouds until I call for you."

With a leaning tilt of his body, he dropped from Noa's back, plunging through the fog-covered sky towards the pandemonium below. Mid-fall, his form twisted, feathers erupting from his skin as he transformed into a raven. His sleek black wings blended seamlessly into the shadows, allowing him to glide unseen above the turmoil. He surveyed the street leading to the Axis House and froze.

Hundreds of soldiers were packed at the entrance, all pushing and yelling to force their way through the narrow doorway and descend below. Their overwhelming numbers left him in disbelief. There were many more than he had anticipated. Far more than he could handle alone.

As he circled above, shocked, Keanoff landed on a nearby rooftop, the weight of failure heavy on his chest. But before he could retreat, the ground shook. Shouts of "Earthquake!" spread among the guards, followed by others barking orders to brace themselves. Then came the roar, a whirlwind of fire exploded from the doorway, a living cyclone of flames twisting upward. The street ignited. Men scrambled, giving the inferno a wide berth.

Astonishment stayed Keanoff's breath as she stepped through the blaze. Nemeah emerged from the fire like a myth come to life, her form distorted by shimmering heat and moonlight. Her fury rippled off her in dark waves. One by one, the guards charged and fell. Wisps of black smoke sliced through the air, curling around their victims, striking like snakes. Magic moved through her like a storm.

Keanoff dove from the roof, shifting mid-air, landing hard on the scorched cobblestones. He straightened just as Nemeah turned toward him. Recognition flashed in her darkened eyes before they slowly faded back to blue.

"Keanoff?" she whispered.

A smile cracked across her soot-smudged face; soft and fragile, human. It made something prickle and twist inside his chest. The moment shattered all too quickly as new soldiers charged from the street, weapons drawn, armor glinting.

"We have to go!" Keanoff shouted, grabbing her hand.

Nemeah flinched, pain flashing across her face as his grip pressed against her burned skin. She pulled free, her breath ragged. "The others. They are still inside!"

She turned toward the Axis House as smoke billowed from the doorway. Through the haze, she saw Yuli dragging Henry up the last of the stairs, his face pale and his body limp with exhaustion. Ismaara and Agnes followed closely behind, but then came the sound. A deep, shuddering crack. A support beam split and crashed down with a thunderous boom, flames curling around it. Ismaara shoved Agnes forward just in time. The cook tumbled clear, landing hard on the stone outside, but Ismaara remained trapped behind the wreckage. She slid down a few stairs, her leg burned, the fibers of her robe sticking to the gooey flesh.

"Help me!" She screamed as pain overwhelmed her, igniting a wave of panic. Her breaths came in quick, sharp inhales. Desperately, she called for her powers, which were still absent due to the saturation of silvervane in the air. The pain surged through her, a sensation unfamiliar to someone capable of self-healing.

Nemeah froze. "I have seen this," she breathed, staring at her trembling hands. The burned skin cracked and blistered beneath the heat, the memory of her dream flashing behind her eyes. "I dreamed this moment." Her voice rose, urgent. "We have to get her out!"

Keanoff was already locked in battle, his blade clashing in a flurry of sparks as he fought three men at once. He moved like a shadow, his weapon slicing through the air, but he was outnumbered and tiring quickly. In the street, Yuli gripped Henry's sword with trembling hands, standing over her fallen husband. The guards surrounded them now, forming a circle of blades, inching in with each passing second.

Suddenly, a whistle split the air. Shrill and piercing. A shadow passed over them. The thunder of wings crashed through the clouds above. With a roar that shattered glass and heartbeats alike, Noa descended. Her mighty presence pushed the flames higher, fanning them into hungry beasts that devoured whole buildings.

"This is more than the moon child." She hissed, her eyes assessing the strangers. "I cannot carry this many people, Keanoff," Noa growled, her voice rough and crackling like stone. She clamped a soldier in her jaws, bones crunching, before flinging his limp body across the square.

Keanoff whistled and clicked as he cleaved through another man, his blade severing an arm in a spray of blood. "I did not know she was bringing friends," he roared. "How many can you manage?"

"Two," Noa replied with a guttural click. "Three if they are light enough." She swatted a handful of guards away, her claws smoothly cutting through them as if they had been made of clouds.

"Take Henry and Yuli," Nemeah called out, her voice returning to its unfamiliar accent. Her gaze darted between Noa and Keanoff, eyes black, focus unnerving. She whistled again, the sound sharp and instinctual. "Get them to safety, then head back." She waved her hand, a trail of fire soaring through the air. "A gift for you, great dragon."

Noa opened her mouth and caught the flame in her throat, her scales illuminating as bright as the sun. The dragon roared, her loud cry resonating through the world as she drew in a breath and rained fire down on the enemy. The blue light melted everything in its path, the heat forcing steam from the humid air.

With a motion of Nemeah's hand, Henry's limp form rose into the air, suspended effortlessly, and settled onto Noa's back. "Yuli, help Agnes onto the dragon," Nemeah commanded. Her voice had deepened, touched by something unknown. With another annoyed flick of her hand, the two terrified women lifted from the ground and landed beside Henry, their faces pale and stunned. "Go!" she clicked to Noa.

The dragon roared, her tail sweeping through a line of advancing soldiers as if they were nothing more than reeds. She spread her massive wings, the wind catching in a powerful gust, and launched into the sky. Keanoff ducked a swinging blade, narrowly avoiding its edge as he backed toward Nemeah. His hands danced in practiced movements, spinning, cutting, and sidestepping, as if they were moving to an ancient rhythm passed down in blood and instinct.

Then he felt it. The shift. The air grew heavy and damp. The scent of water, rich and storm-born, rolled through the city like a promise. Overhead, storm clouds churned unnaturally, being sucked down toward the earth. Their cottony shapes collapsed, unleashing their contents. Rain fell in waves, crashing into rooftops and streets, dousing the inferno. The heat hissed away as the flames died, screaming.

Nemeah raised her arms, her hands twisting like those of a puppeteer. The wind howled as a vortex formed above them, rain and air spiraling into a wild cyclone. Soldiers were pulled upward, tossed like rag dolls into the sky. Behind them came a groaning, splintering crack. The charred beam that had blocked the Axis House was wrenched from the doorway and hurled behind them, landing too close for comfort. "Get Ismaara," came the voice again, not quite Nemeah's.

Keanoff dashed through the now-open doorway. He found her huddled against the charred wall, coughing. Her leg was severely burned, but at least she was alive.

"You are alright," he muttered, scooping her up with ease. She was small, and his arms were practiced in the weight of a burden. He raced back to Nemeah, water pelting his face, the wind roaring like a god. "Now what?" he called out, shielding Ismaara with his body. All around them was madness, water crashing through alleys like a tsunami, debris flying, soldiers shrieking as they were flung through the air. "How long before Noa returns?"

Nemeah's cold smile did not belong to her. Her lips curled unnaturally, and her sharp, nearly serrated teeth flashed in the growing light.

"She will not be here in time," she said, tapping Keanoff's forehead with two fingers. "You will have to do."

A pulse of energy surged through him like lightning. He cried out, dropping Ismaara as his body buckled forward. A groan, snarling and distorted, tore from his throat as his bones began to crack and re-form. His skin split, falling away like shedding cloth, revealing smooth black scales beneath. Leathery wings erupted from his back, and a tail lengthened, snaking down the broken cobblestone street. He grew, tripling in size, until a towering black dragon stood where Keanoff had been. His eyes narrowed to vertical slits, and a roar ripped through the city, primal and furious. Ismaara screamed; she could not comprehend the sight before her.

The dragon stomped, his claws digging furrows into the stone as if itching for more destruction. His tail thrashed, and his mouth dripped with flaming spittle that melted the stone beneath like acid. The creature coughed, roaring as the flaming liquid erupted from his throat, sizzling a path straight through where the Axis House stood. The building crumbled in on itself, a sight satisfactory to Nemeah's abyss-colored eyes. Nemeah raised her hand, effortlessly lifting Ismaara onto his back. Then she followed, settling herself just behind. With a final commanding click, Keanoff took to the sky, his wings slicing through the clouds as they turned toward the mountains, toward the cave.

The sun rose behind the distant peaks, gilding them in golden shadow. Nemeah swayed in the wind, her breath shallow. The power she had drawn upon, the foreign force surging through her, was fading. She fought to stay conscious, but her grip on reality unraveled thread by thread. Darkness took her. Keanoff felt it the moment she slipped away. The magic tethering them together snapped. His wings faltered, and he roared again, not in rage but in alarm. His form began to change. Bones cracked as he shrank. Scales peeled away, replaced by skin. Wings dispersed into nothing. They were too high, and he knew the cave was too far.

Ismaara screamed again as she slid off his back, tumbling through the open air. The wind howled past them as they fell, muffling every noise and stinging their faces and eyes. Keanoff panicked; he did not know of a form strong enough to carry two full-grown women. He shifted mid-air into a hawk, diving after them, praying for the gods to somehow intervene. A shadow sliced across the sun. Noa. With a gentler touch than expected from a dragon, she caught Ismaara mid-fall, then twisted through the sky to catch Nemeah just in time. With a powerful beat of her wings, she rose above the jagged cliffs, her passengers secure. Keanoff followed behind, his heart pounding and gratitude flooding every part of his being. Together, the four made it safely back to the cave. To their home.

Inside, Edna paced, her face streaked with worry and the marks of age. She had tended to Henry's wound as best as she could, while a fire crackled nearby. A basket of fruit and foraged greens sat beside her, ready for their unexpected guests. Noa landed gracefully, setting Ismaara down with care before carrying Nemeah to her bed of moss and hay.

Keanoff landed hard, the transition from hawk to man hitting him like a mountain. His limbs trembled with exhaustion. Whatever Nemeah had done to him drained every last ounce of energy he had. Edna was by his side in an instant, steadying him as she helped him inside. Once he was seated, she turned her attention to Nemeah, her hands trembling as she searched for a pulse. It was there, but faint.

"You!" Yuli's voice echoed in the cave like thunder, filled with accusation as she pointed a shaking hand at her husband. "You are a Freyla. Heal him!"

Ismaara, still catching her breath, hobbled to the basket of food and began stuffing her mouth with strawberries and slices of orange. "Still got silvervane in my system," she said between bites, cheerful and unconcerned. "I am unable to heal anyone just yet."

Yuli looked ready to explode. Her fists curled, and the muscles in her jaw tightened. She was angered by this woman's disposition. A smile on her face as she stuffed more fruit down her gullet.

"I think I can help with that," Edna said quickly, rising to her feet. With a flick of her hand, flowers and herbs sprouted around her, curling from the earth like obedient pets. She plucked the petals and leaves, twisting them deftly before dropping them into her kettle. Steam rose from the pot within minutes, the scent of earthy tea warming the cold cave air. Edna poured the brew into cups, the liquid rich and golden. She handed one to Ismaara, two to Yuli, and another to Agnes, her hands steady despite the tremble in her soul.

"Oh, I am not an Echo." Agnes began, waving her hands dismissively.

Edna pushed the cup toward her again, firmer this time. "You would refuse a gift in my house?" the old woman stammered. "Cave." She corrected. Her voice had lost its gentle warmth. The kindness of an aged forager was gone, replaced by bitterness, sharp and cold. Her eyes, once soft with a life of leisure, were now hard as flint, glaring at the robed stranger like weeds choking her garden.

They were intruders, and her home had already endured too much. She turned without another word and crossed the cave to Nemeah's bedside, where Keanoff sat quietly, watching over her. Without speaking, Edna handed him a cup. Keanoff nodded his thanks and gently lifted Nemeah's head. Her hair slipped like silk across his arm as he tipped the cup to her lips, allowing the warm liquid to trickle into her mouth. He prayed some would reach her and do something, anything.

Ismaara finally stirred from her spot near the fire, color returning to her face as her magic began to settle. Her fingers glowed faintly as she pressed them to her leg, the burns fading away as if they were merely soot being washed clean. Then, quietly, she turned to Henry and laid her hands upon his arm. The skin knitted slowly beneath her palms, the damage lessening with every breath. She moved to Keanoff next, brushing her magic over the scratches lining his sides and shoulders. However, when she approached Nemeah, her expression shifted, first to confusion, then surprise. She healed the woman's burned hands, but as for the deeper issue, she could not touch that. Her powers had no weight against it. "There is nothing more I can do."

"What do you mean?" Edna snapped. The sharpness in her voice cracked through the cave like dry branches underfoot. She dropped to her knees beside the girl's bed, gripping Nemeah's hand tightly. "Fix her! Wake her up!"

Ismaara placed her hand gently on Nemeah's wrist again. Her touch lingered, as if waiting for something to stir. "There is... nothing to heal," she said at last, her brows drawn. "The burns are gone. Her skin is whole, but I cannot heal whatever is inside her. It feels as if it is a part of her. It is entwined with her very being."

Edna stared at her, wide-eyed and trembling with fury. "Then *why* does she not wake?" Her voice faltered. She pressed Nemeah's hand to her cheek, her voice softening into something broken. "Why does she not wake up?"

Nemeah's skin was warm and vibrant. The sickly pallor had faded, and the veins that once darkened her arms had receded. Her face was serene and seemed untroubled. Her magic no longer flared or flickered, but rested deep within, as quiet as the forest after a storm.

"I do not know," Ismaara said, her voice too chipper for the situation. She shrugged her shoulders like a child. "She will have to wake when she is ready."

Chapter Nine

Edna tended to Nemeah day in and day out. She fed her broth infused with herbs and spices, whispering prayers into each bowl, hoping they would mend what she could not see. With every dawn that passed without awakening, the old woman sank deeper into despair. She feared that the girl she had come to love was slowly slipping beyond her reach, into something else. Keanoff did what he could to ease the growing tension among the newcomers. He explained their mission, spoke of the danger gathering on the horizon, and of the looming Eclipse Veil that threatened them all if the last mirrors were not found and the Echoes freed.

"I have read about that," Agnes said suddenly, her cheeks reddening as all eyes turned to her. "It is part of our early scripture studies back on Verdathos. The legend of the mad Priest who fell during the Battle of the Fire King, five hundred years ago. What you are describing was never confirmed. It was just a fable made up over the years. The facts are that the mad priest went crazy, killed his disciples, and then killed himself."

Without a word, Keanoff crossed the cave and returned with a mirror, which he retrieved from where the dragon guarded it. Noa's luminous eyes did not waver, tracking both the strangers and Nemeah like a sentinel carved from glass. Keanoff held the mirror up to the firelight. Its silver frame shimmered faintly, and the glass pristine. Agnes rose slowly to her feet, drawn to it like a moth to a flame. Her breath caught as she moved closer. She recognized it. She had seen it, its shape and engravings, in old texts at the Axis. The books had been clear: all the mirrors were make-believe. The Echoes inside a figment of childish imagination. A ghost story that she had always believed in.

"This is unbelievable." Her voice was a mix of awe and sorrow. "All the books have lies written within their covers."

A short, humorless laugh cut through the air. "Of course they do," Yuli said, nudging Henry with her elbow as he grimaced. "The Axis lies. Everyone who serves them lies. They have lied since the beginning of time. Brain-dead morons. Lying pants on fire liars!" Yuli felt a hard nudge in her side as she looked at her husband. "No offense." She offered weakly, forgetting that her husband had been a guard for the Axis the day before.

Agnes stood frozen, her lip trembling as every question imaginable came to mind. "But why?" she asked quietly, eyes locked on the mirror. "Why lie about the Echoes, erase their history, and then keep the locations of the mirrors secret?"

A new voice answered, low and ancient. "Ask the one as old as fables. Ask the one as old as lies."

Every head turned at once. Nemeah lay motionless on her bed, her lips barely moving, whispering words no one could decipher. Edna rushed to her side, clutching the girl's cold hand as she leaned in, straining to catch the ghostlike murmurs.

"It sounds like a different language," the old woman murmured, half-questioning, her eyes flicking to Keanoff's.

Edna slowly dabbed sweat from Nemeah's brow with a rag. But the calm shattered as a hand snapped up and latched onto her wrist, ice-cold and lightning-fast. Edna yelped, wrenching free from the girl's iron grip. Nemeah's eyes flew open. That endless black had returned, swallowing all the light in her eyes. She sat up sharply, her gaze sweeping the cave, studying each face with chilling intent. She staggered to her feet, wavering until Edna reached out and steadied her movements. Confusion clouded every feature of her face.

"Where are we?" Her voice, to everyone's surprise, was calm and strangely normal. Even as her shadowed eyes betrayed another presence, her tone sounded like the girl they all knew.

She looked from Edna to Keanoff, then to Noa on her golden nest, chickens frozen in wide-eyed silence. Edna offered her a reassuring pat; her voice was the only anchor in the disorienting darkness. "You are safe, dear," she said gently. "Do you remember Keanoff rescuing you?"

Nemeah turned to the mouth of the cave. Dawn poured in, chasing the shadows across the stone. She rubbed her temples, wincing as a flood of memories and images collided behind her eyes. Her legs buckled, knees slamming to the ground as her breath broke into sharp, panicked gasps. She saw war. Towering beings unleashing raw power, blow after cataclysmic blow. She saw the Axis house, where a timid woman in a red robe was intentionally burning a pie, nervously eyeing the door as smoke curled through the air. Then the images shifted. A room, cloaked in shadows. Two men hunched over a book, its spine split down the center. "Who is the great queen?"
One of them asked the question. He had mismatched eyes, the same eyes as someone she now knew.

Nemeah's head snapped up, her gaze zeroing in on Ismaara, black eyes piercing deep. More images followed: twins laughing in a snow-covered field, a mother standing by the water, watching and waiting for her husband to return. The visions came too quickly, faster than thought, too fast to understand. She cried out, pressing her forehead to the cave floor, hands at her temples as if trying to hold her skull together. Edna dropped beside her, frantic now, unsure how to ease the storm inside the girl. She rubbed Nemeah's back in slow circles, murmuring quiet prayers.

No one moved. No one dared. They had all seen what Nemeah was capable of when she lost control, seen the destruction, and none wanted to be caught in its wake. Then, mercifully, the cries faded. Her breathing steadied, and her hands fell away. She lifted her head. Her eyes were blue again, pale and familiar. But her face looked drawn, hollowed by exhaustion, with bruised shadows pooling beneath her eyes. Edna guided her gently back to the bed. Her movements were sluggish now, as if every ounce of strength had drained from her bones. Sleep was only a breath away.

"What just happened?" Yuli's voice cut through the silence, making everyone flinch. It echoed too loudly in the hushed cave, breaking the uneasy stillness like a baby's cry in the night.

Nemeah turned toward the sound, her eyes recognizing the newcomers, the memory of the escape already fading into a dreamlike fog. "How did we get out?"

"You," Keanoff said sharply, cutting her off.

She blinked at him, startled by the intensity in his tone. Across the cave, he stood stiff and wary, every muscle drawn taut like a bowstring. His fear struck her like a blade, deep and sudden. Was he afraid *of her*? Her gaze dropped to his hand. He was clutching the mirror, knuckles white as bone, gripping the handle like a weapon rather than a relic. More images surged through her mind, unbidden and overwhelming.

A young Kallemena twirling with an older man beneath a canopy of mirrored silver. Their hair the same deep shade of midnight. A crown of glass gleaming on his brow as their reflections spun alongside them. A white-haired woman watched with gentle eyes, her expression filled with quiet joy. Nemeah shook her head, willing the memories to stop, but they only came faster, sharper.

A cage. A woman inside, skeletal and trembling, her black hair falling in curtains around her face. A man, blond, smug, green-eyed, smiling in front of glowing runes etched into a stone wall. And then came understanding. These were not dreams. These were Kallemena's memories. Somehow, she was seeing what the imprisoned princess had lived.

"What is happening to me?" she rasped from her raw throat. The words scraped out like sandpaper.

"That is what *I* want to know." Keanoff's voice held no comfort. Only accusation.

She stared at him, disbelief clouding her already overwhelmed mind. This was Keanoff, the man who stood watch through her nightmares, who traveled with her to her family's vacant home, who willingly followed her into Axis territory. But now? He looked at her as if she were something dangerous. Something *untrustworthy*.

"You conjured fire," he said tightly, his gaze flicking to Noa, who was still silent, still watching. "You spoke in a tongue you have no right to know. And you." His voice rose, fury rising with it. "You turned me into a dragon!"

The words slammed into her like a landslide.

"You had no right to do that to me," he continued, his face dark with anger. "Vira are not supposed to become beasts of destruction. That is not what we are. That is not what we do." He stopped, jaw clenched.

She could feel it, his pain. His confusion. His betrayal.

"Whatever is happening to you is reckless. It is dangerous," he said, his voice breaking as he repeated the exact words *the dragon* had spoken not long ago. "You are different."

Nemeah's heart sank. *A dragon?* She had done that? She stared down at her hands, whole again, the skin smooth and unblemished where once it had blistered and melted. She would need to thank Ismaara for that later. With a breath, she braced herself against Edna's arm and slowly rose. Her legs wobbled beneath her, but she stood, just barely, still trying to make sense of everything she had unleashed.

"I know what I did was foolish, but I thought they had my family." Her voice trembled as she swallowed hard against the burn rising in her throat. She willed the tears back, desperate to keep her composure. "You would all do the same in my situation. You would all charge into danger if you thought they had your family."

Keanoff did not move. "Maybe," he said, voice low and cold. "But I would not put any of you in harm's way, especially if I did not have control over my powers." The words cut deep, blunt, and merciless. "I have seen what you can do, Nemeah. You burned down the city. You summoned tidal waves in the middle of the square. You tore open the sky with a storm that nearly swallowed us." His jaw clenched. "You are no Darra I have ever known."

His gaze swept over her with eerie detachment, the warmth once there now replaced by something frigid. Her face was pale and drawn, her black hair tangled and spilling over the white robe she still wore. Her skin, once kissed with a sun-warmed glow, had gone ghostly. And her eyes, once the soft blue of twilight skies, were deepening again, the color bleeding out as shadow crept in, staining the irises like spilled ink.

"I do not know what is happening to me, but I will figure it out." Nemeah's voice cracked at the edges. She looked at Edna, searching her face for support. "*We will* figure this out. I can ask Kallemena when she emerges, and we will have answers." Her eyes were pleading. "I am still me, Keanoff." She stepped forward, slowly, hand outstretched, an olive branch trembling in midair. She hoped, desperately, that he would meet her halfway. That he would take her hand like he had before. That he still believed in her.

But Keanoff stepped back. "No, you are not," he said, his voice colder than the cave walls. The words struck her like a slap. "And I cannot wait for Kallemena to show herself before we know what to do about it." He turned and strode out, his footsteps echoing through the chamber, a retreat that felt like abandonment.

Yuli and Henry shared a silent glance before following. Outside, the sun glared off the snow-capped peaks, blinding against the white covering the ground. The blinding rays did little to generate heat, but were enough to melt the surface of the snow, leaving the trail slick with slush and churned mud.

"Why are you following me?" Keanoff barked as he stomped down the narrow path, his boots sinking with every step.

"I know a Vira with anger issues when I see one," Yuli called after him. "And I know how fast they spiral when left alone."

Keanoff rolled his eyes. "I do *not* have anger issues."

Henry reached to hold her back, but she shrugged off his hand. "You are angry *right now,*" Yuli said plainly, picking her way through the snow. "And there is definitely an issue back in that cave. I mean..." She hesitated, catching herself as Keanoff shot her a glare sharp enough to silence the wind.

He stopped abruptly. Yuli slid a little on the muddy slope, catching herself. Henry was not so lucky. He slipped and landed hard, the breath whooshing from his lungs in a grunt. Grumbling, Keanoff reached down and yanked him to his feet.

Yuli hurried to brush snow and muck from Henry's back. "Maybe next time, go barefoot." She mused as she looked down at his armored feet, the metal offering little traction.

"Hate being barefoot," Henry muttered.

"I just need some space," Keanoff growled. "Go hunt or something."

Yuli's eyes lit up. "Hunt?" She turned to Henry, then back to Keanoff, the corners of her mouth curling into a grin. "I can help. And before you complain, remember, you have got more mouths to feed now. You could *use* the help."

Keanoff looked to Henry, who gave a weak shrug, still catching his breath.

"Go," he wheezed. "I need meat anyway. If I eat one more bowl of that vegetable stew the old lady makes, I swear I will throw myself off this mountain."

Everyone chuckled. Edna's stews were tasty, but after five straight days of root broth, even the most grateful stomach grew weary. Yuli threw her arms around Henry's thick neck and kissed him with a tenderness only love could conjure. Keanoff turned away, his face reddening from the awkward intimacy of the moment.

"We will be back soon," she said brightly, giving Henry another kiss.

With that, Yuli leapt into the air. Feathers burst from her limbs, a crown of sleek plumes blooming from her head. Her toes curled into talons as her form twisted and grew. A massive harpy eagle soared upward, her wings stretching wide as she caught the wind. Keanoff followed suit. His smaller hawk form emerged, brown and spotted, his wings slicing through the sky. Though dwarfed by Yuli, he flew with practiced grace.

Together, they glided down the mountainside toward the forest blanketing the valley floor, endless pines and oaks teeming with prey. They landed in a quiet clearing, the crisp air still and bright. The sun cast their shadows beneath them as they crouched low, scanning the underbrush for tracks.

"There." Keanoff pointed to a delicate trail in the earth, heart-shaped prints, fresh and narrow. "Deer passed through this morning."

Yuli crouched beside him, studying the direction of the tracks.

"So," Keanoff said, brushing a pine needle from his sleeve, "how did you end up there? The Axis prison. And with an Axis *guard* as a husband?"

Yuli smiled softly, her eyes distant as memory took hold. "Ah. My favorite story." She stepped under a low branch, lowering her voice as they moved deeper into the woods. "My tribe is known as the forest wolves. We live far north of here, near the edge of the Scorvaan desert. Harsh lands. The people beyond us are worse, ruthless, always looking for a reason to fight. Bloodshed is their answer to everything." She shook her head, bitterness flickering across her expression. "They came at night. Burned the village. We left to find a safer place for what was left of the pack."

She paused, tracing a thin finger along the bark of a tree. Slashes showed that deer rubbed the tree with their antlers, marking their territory. "That is when I found Henry. My pack was about to tear into him. He was alone and wounded. I convinced them to leave him;

we did not need more attention while we were looking for a new home." Her face softened. "But I could not stop thinking about him. His golden eyes. That dark skin. The way he looked at me." A shiver ran down her spine, but it was not from the cold. "Infatuated at first sight."

Keanoff grinned. The warmth of their conversation and its lightness helped strip away the weight of everything waiting back at the cave.

"He eventually noticed a black wolf always lurking in the shadows," Yuli continued. "Always following. One day, when I was being less than careful, he trapped me. Net pinned me down, sword drawn." She chuckled. "So I changed right in front of him." She laughed at the memory, her voice rich and full of nostalgia. "The horror on his face was priceless. And that is when I knew I was in love."

Keanoff arched a brow, still grinning. "Why did he not kill you? Axis soldiers are trained to slay any Echo they find, yet he spared you. Why?"

They crouched low in the grass, muscles tensed. Just ahead, a buck grazed in the stillness of the forest, oblivious to the danger just twenty feet away.

Yuli's voice dropped to a whisper. "He did not kill me because in that moment his heart healed."

She shifted into her black wolf form, her sleek body low to the ground, dark brown eyes focused on their prey. Her lips curled back in a silent snarl, fangs glinting in the filtered light. Keanoff followed her lead.

In an instant, his form shrank and morphed into a lean, brown-furred wolf, silent and still. Together, they flanked the stag, circling it in silence. A twig snapped beneath a careless paw, alerting the deer's sensitive ears, and then it was over. Yuli lunged, her jaws clamping down around its neck with deadly precision. Keanoff's claws raked the buck's flank and pinned it, finishing the hunt as the creature collapsed beneath them.

They changed back, breath rising in white puffs against the forest chill. Keanoff knelt, knife in hand, and said a quick prayer before skinning the deer with practiced ease. Yuli handled the gutting, her fingers slick with blood as she worked swiftly.

"You said his heart healed?" Keanoff asked, cutting through the fat with smooth, precise motions. The hide peeled away like a thick blanket.

Yuli nodded as she carefully removed the liver, followed by the heart and lungs. "The Axis killed his mother when he was young. She was a Glade and fell defending their village against them; they like to ambush one person with five."

Kenoff nodded, recalling his own confrontations with the Axis guard.

"He was left to fend for himself. They took him in, raised him in their nursery, and taught him their ways." She shot him a glance. "He grew up believing Echoes were monsters, that his own mother was one. After passing all the tests, he chose to become a soldier. He said the priest's robes were too heavy and itchy to wear for life, so he opted for the shiny armor instead."

A playful smile spread across her face. "And he looks pretty good in it, too." With another laugh, she went on. "When he saw me, memories of his mother flooded back, her kindness and the love only a mother can give. She tried to protect him until her dying breath. In that moment, he realized that the Echoes were not the monsters; the Axis was."

Keanoff was quiet. His knife slowed, the motion faltering.

"She is still good," Yuli said gently.

He stiffened. "I am not sure what you mean."

Yuli reached out, her bloodied hand warm against his wrist. "She got herself thrown into the Axis confinement cells because she heard a Vira was being held there. She thought it was you."

Keanoff's eyes flicked to hers.

"She saved us," Yuli added, pulling her hand back and returning to her task. "We would be dead right now if it were not for her and her... freaky powers."

They finished dressing the carcass and split it in two. Yuli shifted back into her harpy eagle form, her massive talons gripping the shoulder of the buck. With a few powerful flaps, she soared into the clouds. Keanoff transformed into a common brown eagle, his new form capable of carrying the rest of the meat back to the cave. That night, the smell of roasted venison filled the cavern. The meat sizzled, glazed in a tart-sweet berry reduction that Edna and Agnes had thrown together.

The warmth of the fire softened everyone's edges. They shared stories like old friends, tales of distant homes, half-remembered childhoods, and broken beginnings. Slowly, the tension that had thickened the air that morning began to dissipate. Keanoff sat cross-legged, chewing a thick piece of meat as his gaze lingered on Nemeah across the fire.

She laughed, bright and unguarded, as Yuli recounted a story about a thieving squirrel. Her eyes were still blue, and her voice was soft and thoughtful again. That quiet farm girl he had first met, the one who shared her rations with him, thinking he was just a greedy hare. Yet in the flicker of firelight, he still searched for the shadow behind her smile.

"*Ask the one who is old as fables,*" Keanoff repeated her earlier words. "*Ask the one who is as old as lies.*"

Nemeah stared back at him, her eyes slowly darkening to black.

"What did you mean by that?" he asked, his voice low. "Who is that person?"

Her gaze did not waver. The darkness in her eyes sparked his fears. Was this still his friend? Then the moment passed. Nemeah turned her head slowly and looked at Ismaara. "Her."

All eyes followed.

Ismaara blinked, her smile as soft and unreadable as ever. "I do not know what you speak of," she said with a playful smile. "Perhaps you have confused me with someone else."

Nemeah closed her eyes as more unfamiliar memories flooded her mind. The combined scents of fire-cooked meat and icy mountain wind filled her lungs. Flashes of the twins again, a silver chest full of mirrors, and an hourglass pulsed behind her closed eyelids. She hesitated for a moment, gathering the strength to speak through the flood of emotion that now consumed her.

"Ismaara Nyssira Vaelora," she said slowly. "Born to King Orentheon and Queen Kivani. Rulers of Glacia. Sister to His Holiness Isrend of the Axis." She opened her eyes. "You have quite a story to tell."

A hush fell over the cave as Ismaara's face changed, not completely, but enough. Her smile faded. She glanced around at her newfound audience. The silence was thick and expectant. She cleared her throat and gently slid her plate aside. "I guess I do now."

"Wait." Edna leaned forward, her brows raised high. "Orentheon?" Her eyes darted between Nemeah and Ismaara. "As in *Kallemena's* brother? The same Kallemena imprisoned in that mirror, the one Noa now guards?"

"He was my father," Ismaara confirmed, her voice airy and proud.

"How is that even possible? How can she..." Edna's gaze shifted sharply to Ismaara. "*You.* How can you still be alive?"

Ismaara did not answer, but Nemeah did.

"She is a Freyla. One of the rare few who learned how to stretch their own lifespan. It is the same reason Vallorith and the others still live after five hundred years. The same reason Kallemena still clings to this world from within that prison of glass." She turned her focus back to Ismaara, her voice calmer now. "Most Freyla only ever master healing. How did you learn to lengthen life?"

"It is part of the story I am about to tell." Her voice sounded irritated as she let out a huff.

Yuli let out a delighted chuckle. "Oh, this is going to be *such* a good story." She slid into her husband's lap, curling comfortably as the fire crackled nearby.

Ismaara rolled her eyes, clearly annoyed. "It is going to be such a long night."

Part II:
The Fractured Crown

Chapter Ten

The ice-covered plains of Glacia shimmered beneath a fresh veil of snow. The landscape stretched in all directions like a field of scattered diamonds. Tracks from snow hares stitched delicate patterns across the powdery surface, and birds flitted from branch to branch, shaking loose flurries that dusted the trees below. From the harbor came the low moan of horns and the clang of bells as several ships glided into dock, their sails stiff in the frigid breeze. People rushed to the waterfront, men and women, all eager to glimpse their returning princess.

Hundreds disembarked, the docks quickly filling with red and white robes, the familiar uniform of the Echoes who had fled Verdathos. They came with little more than what they carried, their faces drawn with the weight of loss. The fall of the Axis still clung to them like soot; their home was now nothing more than a ruin.

Queen Nyssira pushed through the gathering crowd, her long white hair streaming behind her like a banner of snow. Her sharp eyes scanned the line of passengers descending from the ship ramps, searching every face in a desperate attempt to find one person in particular. At her side, Prince Orentheon appeared, red faced and breathless from running.

"They were not on the other ships," he gasped, his breath steaming in the cold. "They must be on this one."

Nyssira said nothing, her eyes wide as the last few passengers disembarked. Hope drained from her face as she watched her husband, King Thaloren, being helped down the ramp. One of his delicate glass prosthetic legs had shattered, leaving the metal remnants twisted into a useless stump. When their gazes met, she saw the pain in his face, and with it the understanding that his mission had failed.

A keening cry burst from Nyssira's throat. She crumpled to her knees on the icy wharf, her hands clenched against the ground. Her daughter was not aboard. Her sweet girl was still trapped in a world she had not been ready for.

Inside the frosted castle walls, the family huddled together. The absence of the princess was more painful than the first time she had been taken from them. King Thaloren told them of what had happened: the ambush at the gates, where the Axis disciples were forced to fight. How Ashar saved Kallemena's life with his powers.

The story felt happy as he recounted how they were all aboard the ships, sailing for home, with the morning sun rising on a promising day. Victory was well within their hard-earned grasp. But when he saw the dragon fly back to Verdathos, and the elation of his daughter's betrothal die suddenly, he knew something was wrong.

"We returned," Thaloren winced as a healer applied a warm cloth to his wounded leg. His broken prosthetics were replaced with flawless new ones, and his cracked glass armor was traded for silken robes. "There was nothing remaining, only debris. Deserted, everyone safely aboard the ships." He met the eyes of his wife and son, grief swelling in his voice. "We had her."

"You had everyone but our daughter." Nyssira spat, her anger fueled by the helpless feelings that accompanied her anger. Her cries were constant in these last days.

"We will see her again, Mother," Orentheon promised, stepping closer and grasping Nyssira's hand. His tone was resolute, though his fingers shook. "I will find her." Although his vow was not necessary, his parents appreciated the sentiment behind it. He cleared his throat, wary of slipping back into the sadness that lingered with him since his sister's abduction. "There is a person here, someone who claims to have witnessed the events. Claims to have been friends with Kallemena."

Hearing her daughter's name, Nyssira froze. Her sobs turned into ragged gasps. The wound from over a year ago, when Vallorith took Kallemena in the cover of darkness, remained unhealed. Time had only intensified the pain, stabbing deeper and deeper into her core. The hope she had clung to during her husband's absence vanished the moment she realized her daughter had not returned, leaving her a mere shadow of the mother she once was.

"Who is this friend?" Nyssira whispered. Then, with sudden resolve: "Bring her to me. Bring the one who knew my daughter."

A guard bowed low and slipped through the tall glass doors, leaving silence to settle in the chamber once more. The healer finished wrapping and cleansing the king's wounds and packed her things without a word. When she left, the family of three remained behind in heavy stillness. No one dared to speak; there was nothing left to say that had not already been said a hundred times before.

Each one took the events personally, always wondering what they could have done better. Oren curled his fingers, knowing it was his wedding that had brought the priest to Glacia in the first place. He remembered how Kivani looked in her dress, Kallemena's smile, and his parents sitting proudly in the front row. The mad priest standing at the altar, reciting the vows from his little leather book. His slicked-back hair and narrow eyes. Oren slammed his fist on the hearth, the pain bringing him back to reality.

The door creaked open, and the guard returned with two girls in matching robes trailing behind him. It was a welcome interruption from Orentheon's spiraling thoughts. The two girls were nearly identical, except for their age. Both had curls the color of spun gold and bright blue eyes swollen from crying. The older girl clutched a mirror tightly against her chest, the last relic she possessed from a place she had called home for most of her life.

"Sylvie and Poppy Havander, my lord," the guard announced with a gruff voice, then he left, the door closing quietly behind him.

Nyssira examined the girls from head to toe. Both wore white robes embroidered with the feared golden sun, the symbol of the Axis. Her gaze softened as it rested on the younger one, half-hidden behind her sister, peeking out with a shy eye. A memory arose, Kallemena at that age, hiding behind her mother in much the same way when meeting new people. Her daughter's gift not yet revealed, but silently waiting to take hold.

Orentheon stepped forward, his voice direct and urgent. "What news do you have of my sister?"

Sylvie's lip quivered. She stood straight, trying to maintain her composure, but her shoulders trembled. "I..." she began, the word barely a squeak. Her voice was fragile, like the breath of a ghost, and tears welled up in her eyes again. "It all happened so quickly," she said, her voice tight as she nodded toward the king. "We were on the boat... with Kallemena and Ashar. Our other friends, too. And then Ashar..."

"Princess Kallemena and King Ashar," Orentheon admonished firmly. "You will show them respect and address them by their royal titles!"

Sylvie's jaw snapped shut so quickly that she bit her tongue. The metallic taste of blood spread through her mouth. She nodded rapidly, her cheeks flushed and her eyes brimming. Her heart pounded in her chest, certain it would leave bruises behind. How could she explain what had happened in that cursed chamber with Vallorith? It all unraveled so quickly, one blink and they were back in the dark, another blink and she was back on the ship. Just her and all the frightened children from the Axis nursery.

Her trembling hands now gripped the object tighter, the mirror she had found when they returned to search for her friends. Sylvie stared at her reflection, but it hardly felt like herself anymore. "Vallorith pulled us through a portal," she said, her voice brittle. "Zepher was already there waiting. He knocked us out, drained us with his powers. When I came to, Kal... Princess Kallemena was shaking me, yelling that I had to move."

The words came faster now, choked and shaky, tumbling out like a flood that had waited too long behind a dam. "There was fire, everywhere, and she led me to a smaller room. The children were there. All of them from the nursery, scared and panicked." She tightened her grip around Poppy's small shoulders, grounding herself in the warmth of her sister. "She told me she was sorry. Said she could not save Slek. I did not understand her until later."

Sylvie's voice caught as fresh tears stung her wind-battered cheeks. "She opened a portal beneath us, and we all fell onto the deck of the ship. But before I could even catch my breath..." Her body trembled, her knees nearly giving way. "He took her. Zepher. He hit her and dragged her back away as the portal disappeared."

"Who?" Nyssira's tone was alert, her voice taking on the anger of a mother ready to protect her young. The thought of her daughter in that situation sent a fresh pang of frustration through her. Her soul felt crushed knowing she had sat helplessly inside her safe castle walls while her daughter had been treated so poorly.

Sylvie wiped her nose on her sleeve, caring nothing for appearances or mannerisms now. "Zepher," she repeated. "He is a Morin, Vallorith's right-hand man. He does whatever the high priest tells him to."

A deep, cursing sigh escaped Orentheon as he stormed back to the hearth. The fire crackled wildly, flames devouring the stacked logs. He ran a hand through his long white hair, his jaw clenched so tightly that the muscles in his face and neck twitched. "So, we are right back where we started. No trail. No location. Just more smoke and mirrors!" He drew out an aggravated groan before whirling around to face Sylvie, his voice sharp enough to cut through the hardest stone. "If you are lying to us, girl, I swear I will make sure you never see the light of day again. I will lock you in the deepest pit this kingdom—"

"Enough!" Thaloren's voice rang out with a regal command.

The prince froze, his chest heaving. The king turned to the girls, who were now trembling like leaves in a storm, their eyes wide and cheeks streaked with tears. The truth was painted clearly across their faces, raw, frightened, and unfiltered.

"She is not lying," Thaloren said gently. "Look at her. She has no reason to." He rang a small silver bell from the side table. The same guard entered promptly, bowing low. "Take these girls to one of the guest chambers. Ensure they are undisturbed and provided with fresh clothes. Let them rest." His voice softened. "They are guests of the crown. Treat them as such."

The guard offered another respectful nod and gestured toward the hallway. Sylvie and Poppy did not wait to be asked again; they slipped out with quick, grateful strides. Inside the chamber, silence returned. Orentheon resumed pacing, his mind a torment of self-blame and hatred for the priest. Nyssira sat in quiet agony, her hands clasped tightly in her lap. Thaloren rose on his new legs, his shaky steps clinking against the glass floor before he made his way to his wife, taking her hand in his as a silent vow to fix this.

Outside, the mood was softer. Sylvie and Poppy followed the guard through the magnificent halls of Glacia's glass castle. Poppy's eyes widened with each turn. She drank in the arched ceilings, the frosted murals glimmering with crystalline pigment, and the soaring chandeliers that scattered light like stars. The icy walls shimmered faintly, casting prismatic hues on the polished floors. It felt like stepping into a fairytale, one that was perfectly written between the covers of a well-read book.

When they reached their room, Poppy let out a quiet gasp. A fire crackled in the hearth, warm and golden. Two silken gowns rested on the bed; their fabric trimmed with silver thread. Two women were already filling a copper tub with steaming water behind a privacy screen. The staff, two attendants not much older than Sylvie, bowed politely, their smiles genuine and voices kind. It was the first time either girl had encountered anything resembling warmth since fleeing Verdathos. Poppy bounced on her toes as she took everything in, the wonder, the beauty, the magic.

"Your bath, my ladies. Do you need assistance?"

Sylvie's head snapped up, and she shook it with such fervor that a strand of hair flopped in front of her face. "No! No, thank you," she added quickly, her cheeks warming at the very thought of strangers seeing her undressed.

The attendants offered polite bows and glided out of the room, pausing only to remind them that supper would be served in a short while. Once the heavy doors clicked shut, Poppy squealed with joy and dashed toward the bed, flinging herself into the plush comforter with a delighted laugh. "It is three times bigger than my bunk at the Axis!" she giggled. "And ten times fluffier!" She rolled and tucked herself into the covers, her soot-streaked robe leaving behind smudges.

Sylvie wandered the room more slowly. Her fingers brushed against the carved details of the wooden dresser, then trailed along the silk ribbons tied to the posts of the massive bed. Everything gleamed, shimmered, or sparkled. It felt like stepping into a different life. But it also felt wrong.

It was a dream she would rather wake up from. This was not supposed to be her life. Final exams were scheduled for next week, and she had studied hard to ensure she would pass them. Her chest ached in realization that all her efforts were now for nothing. Hours of reading and note-taking, all now done in vain. Her daze broke at the sound of a splash. She blinked and turned to see a robe crumpled on the floor and hear her sister's bubbly laughter drifting over the folding screen.

"It is so warm!" Poppy chirped. "And the soap smells like flowers!"

Sylvie sat on the bed, the noise of the bathwater and childhood joy fading beneath the weight of her thoughts. She held the mirror close, her thumb brushing its polished edge. Her reflection stared back, pale and drawn. "Why would she say that?" she whispered. Kallemena's voice echoed again in her mind: "*I am sorry I could not save Slek...*" Her fingers tightened around the mirror's frame as she tried to remember the details of that moment, the last time she had seen her friends. The room on fire, Ashar fighting with Vallorith, and Zepher's amber eyes. The seriousness of the situation was fresh in her mind as gooseflesh ran up her arms. The terrible memory playing over and over, every detail being categorized and memorized in depth.

A knock tore her from the nightmares. She blinked, surprised to see the sun had disappeared behind the mountains, the moon taking its place. How long had she sat here recalling scenes of the past? She clutched her mirror to her chest and hurried to the tall glass doors. The handles felt cold beneath her hand as she pulled them open. One of the attendants stood on the other side, a patient smile on her face.

"Dinner is prepared, miss. I shall escort you—"

"Thank you," Sylvie replied, forcing a level tone. She glanced behind her, where Poppy's off-key singing of the Axis anthem drifted through the air. "We will be down shortly." Before the woman could protest, Sylvie quickly shut the door, then hissed, "Poppy!"

Her sister emerged from behind the screen, a giant towel wrapped haphazardly around her petite frame. Her hair dripped, and her feet left wet footprints on the glass floor behind her as she padded from the bath. Her blonde hair hung straight, heavy from the water, her face flush with the water's heat.

"They said dinner's ready," Sylvie screeched, already hurrying toward the bath. The water had cooled, but it still felt comforting against her grimy, salt-covered skin. She scrubbed quickly, the lather of the soap rising into thick, scented bubbles that made her feel cleaner than she had in days.

Once hastily dressed, she helped Poppy into her own pale purple gown. With no luck in finding a brush, she braided Poppy's damp curls and then quickly styled her own hair to match. They wandered the vast halls hand in hand, getting lost only twice before a kind servant redirected them toward the dining hall. When they entered, the room fell quiet.

The royals' gazes shifted to them, each forming their own judgments about the girls. Sylvie hesitated. What do you say when entering a room with a king and queen? How did one act? Were their braids too childish? Too informal? Had she tied their ribbons respectably? She really should have asked. Why did she not ask?

"Come and join us." Nyssira rose gracefully and extended a hand toward two open seats beside her.

They obeyed quietly, the long table stretching before them like a scene from a painting. A pair of servants stepped forward, setting down polished plates and silverware, then returned moments later with food that smelled richer and warmer than anything Sylvie had eaten in weeks: roasted meats, spiced vegetables, and soft bread dripping with golden butter. All of it prepared with no silvervane mixed in. Sylvie's gaze drifted around the table.

Orentheon sat across from them, a woman with a poised expression at his side, his wife no doubt. The King occupied the head of the table, with Nyssira beside him in a dress that radiated elegance with its deep blue and silver fabric. Sylvie felt her grip tighten around her fork. She felt as though she did not belong, like a stain on linen. A nick in a marble statue. She scooped up a few peas and placed one on her tongue, savoring the sweet flavor in silence.

"You two were at de Axis? What was it like dere?" The accent was unfamiliar to Sylvie, soft vowels wrapped in a melodic islander lilt. The woman's tight sandy curls were bundled on top of her head, and the green of her gown shimmered against her cedar-brown skin, making her look like something conjured from an exotic land. Her vivid green eyes remained fixed on Sylvie, full of curiosity.

"Excuse my wife," Orentheon said, dabbing the corners of his mouth with his napkin. "She is eager to learn about the place you called *home* before a few weeks ago." His words were tainted with brazen disgust for the Axis.

"It was nice!" Poppy said before Sylvie could stop her. "Sister Tressa would sometimes let us play instead of study, and she taught us songs about the gods of the past. There was a song to remember them by. The song of the nine." She stated proudly before her little voice belted out the tune.

"Life begins with Freyla's grace, Brynna's light, our time, and place. From mountain roots the green trees rise, by Danira's breath beneath the skies. Lysar weeps where rivers wind, And Lirian's sun leaves none behind. The winds of Turan sow the land, spreading seeds with unseen hand. Nuval stands with shield and flame, protector strong, in honor's name. Dathmor speaks to beasts below when Caerwen's moon begins to glow. And when our final breath is drawn, Arvayn waits to guide us on.

Sylvie's eyes widened. "Poppy. I am so sorry, she is just very excited—"

"Kallemena would show us her magic as well," Poppy went on, her voice full of fondness. "She could make butterflies fly in patterns through the air, and her snow owl would let us pet it. Its feathers were so soft. And she said living in a palace was the best, and I have to agree with her." She shoveled a bite into her mouth, still talking with her tiny mouth full, her words muffled. "And she told me about her family, all of you, and how her mother would sing her a song when she felt sad or scared." Poppy started humming as she finished chewing her food and swallowed before her sweet voice began to sing again.

"Hush now, my little light. The stars will guide you through the night. Close your eyes and dream away. Tomorrow brings a brighter day."

Nyssira's hands shook slightly as she twisted her napkin in her lap, needing something to ease the ache growing within her. "I would sing this often to her, even after she was grown," her voice filled with emotion. Tears shimmered in her eyes. "My little snowdrop." The queen was quiet, her thoughts pulling her away to a deep memory as tears silently slid down her cheeks.

Sylvie cleared her throat, attempting to quietly signal her sister to stop her constant chatter.

"I like the song; we would sing it together before we went to sleep. She had to stay in the nursery with us little kids for a whole year. She was slow at learning the stuff about the gods, and she hated the anthem," she giggled, "but she was really good at history and maps. I was sad when she had to leave for the big-kid training, but I knew she would be with my sister. So I was not sad for long."

Thaloren leaned forward, clinging to every word spoken about his daughter. "Were the other children like Kallemena?" he asked softly. "Were they all Echoes?"

Sylvie's voice quickly interjected. "No. Poppy is not an Echo. The rest of the nursery children were not, either. Most were orphaned. They had nowhere else to go. All normal."

Kivani's gaze shifted from Poppy to Sylvie, her expression stern and poised. "Normal? Wut is normal in a world that allows some to hold power and others not? Is this not already normal? What about you?" she asked, her accent making her words sound threatening. "Do you have abilities?"

Sylvie hesitated, then offered a small nod. "I am a Talon," she admitted, her tone cautious.

Across the table, the woman in green beamed. "Sista, you and me are de same!" She held up her hand and summoned water from a nearby pitcher. The liquid lifted and swirled through the air in graceful loops before dancing around Poppy, who squealed with laughter. Then the stream returned cleanly to the jug. "It will be nice to have someone to practice wit," the woman added, her grin radiant. "I look forward to seeing what you can do. Something not normal." She chuckled.

Sylvie shrank slightly. "We are only supposed to use our powers when directed. We were taught never to display them, not unless ordered." She paused. "It is forbidden to use them flippantly."

Kivani's joy vanished as her smile dropped into a scowl. "Nonsense!" She stood abruptly, pressing a hand to the table as she glared between Sylvie and the king. "Dis is wut I will be dealing wit. Restoring the confidence to these people that bad man has weakened. Ridding them of the years of saturated lies he has spoken."

Her voice grew strict, edged in fury as she turned back to Sylvie. "The Axis poisoned your mind. Made you weak." She turned to Poppy with a softer glint in her eyes and winked. "But we will make her strong again. No more fear. No more chains. No more askin' for permission to be wut you are." She looked back at Sylvie, her accent thick. "I am glad that place is in ruins. Good riddance."

Sylvie had never wanted to disappear more in her life. She kept her gaze down, focusing on her plate, praying to the gods that the meal would be over soon. To her dismay, course after course was brought out, each topping the last in flavor and presentation. Sylvie watched her sister eat every bite, enjoying the way the icing on the desserts looked like small flowers and snowflakes. The conversations flowed like a river, first calm and poetic, before reaching white rapids that frothed and churned, before leveling out again. The girl's head was swimming by the time the meal concluded, leaving her tired beyond the fatigue that had already gripped her bones.

That night, back in their chamber, the short-lived silence was a relief before her sisters' chatter returned. She had helped Poppy into a soft nightgown, ruffles lining her sleeves and hem. The entire time, she had to remind her sister to keep still so she could lace up the strings in the front. The small girl bounced with lingering excitement, possibly aided by the sugar now infused with her blood.

Sylvie tucked the unwilling girl into bed and brushed wavy curls from her sister's forehead. It was an act she had not done in many years, yet it came naturally as if she had done it all her life. She leaned over and planted a light kiss on her sister's cheek, startled when the little girl wrapped her arms around her and squeezed tightly.

"I love you, Sylvie." She whispered before her eyelids grew too heavy to fight any longer.

The younger girl fell asleep in minutes, her lips parting as she let out a peaceful snore. The ache in Sylvie's chest was foreign; a feeling of something being done right concerning her sister lingered longer than she would have liked. Sylvie silently crept across the room to the hearth and sat on a padded stool. The fire crackled quietly, its warmth thawing the chill that clung to her.

She held out her hand, turning it over in the firelight, studying the palm as if answers might appear there. The idea of using her abilities freely, of not being punished for it, made something stir deep inside her. Hope? Or danger? She had trained for ten years. Ten years of rituals, obedience, and silence. Years of being shaped into a servant, a weapon to be wielded, a tool.

Her hand curled into a fist. She was unsure if she was clenching it from fear or fury. The idea of being needed by a court or noble house had always provided her comfort, making the hardship feel worthwhile. But now? Now she was merely a guest in a glass castle, a stranger on foreign soil. How long before the king and queen grew tired of feeding her and her sister? Of replaying the same stories about their daughter's final days? What then? She let out a breath, her fingers tightening around the mirror in her hand. The cold glass reflected only questions.

"Why was I drawn to this?" she murmured, lifting it to eye level. Her blue eyes stared back, drawn, hollow, and tired beyond belief. She pressed the glass to her forehead and closed her eyes. Her thoughts churned like storm-tossed waves.

"Sylvie."

Her eyes snapped open. She turned sharply, scanning the room. Poppy still snored, now sprawled sideways beneath the covers. The room was still, only shadows and silence. Sylvie shook her head. "And now I am hearing things." She looked back down at the mirror, noticing for the first time how gaunt her reflection appeared.

Her face was pale, her lips dry, her eyes dark from sleepless nights. The ship's relentless rocking, the creaking wood, the groaning sea. None of it had brought her peace since leaving the Axis. She stood and carefully placed the mirror on the mantle. As she turned toward the bed, a sound stopped her in her tracks. Heavy footsteps padded behind her. A blackened shadow encompassing her own. A cold inhale sent a shiver down her body, her back prickled with dread, and her eyes stung with the threat of tears.

"Sylvie?"

She whirled around and could not breathe. Slek stood there, the firelight casting flickering shadows across his broad frame. He was impossibly large, blocking out the warmth of the hearth. Sylvie did not think; she rushed into his arms, burying herself in the solid comfort of him. His arms folded around her, firm and steady, and she finally let the tears fall, hot and unrelenting. Her chest shook as she clung to him, her face pressed against his chest. The thin fabric of her nightgown did little to stop his warmth from seeping into her skin. Suddenly, she pulled back, her cheeks burning as realization struck. Her arms crossed awkwardly over her chest, her face crimson.

"I-I am sorry, I just," She cleared her throat. "How are you here?" she asked, her voice lowered to a whispered shriek. She glanced at Poppy, grateful the little girl was still asleep.

Slek smiled faintly, clearly entertained by her embarrassment. "I do not know. The last thing I remember was being on the ship with everyone." He rubbed his hand through his hair. "Then I remember falling," His head snapped up to look Sylvie in the face. "I saw Mylo, but his eyes were green, not brown, and he was alive." He looked down at his hands, the fire's glow passing through them. His face changed. "Vallorith." His voice turned cold. "Vallorith did something to me." His gaze darted around until it landed on the mirror. He strode to the mantel and lifted it. The glass reflected the firelight, the room, the shadows behind him, but not Slek. "He trapped us." His voice sounded scared. He turned back to Sylvie. "In here."

Sylvie's heart thudded. She stepped forward and gently took the mirror from his hands. "What do you mean?" she whispered. "How? What is this?"

"I am not sure." Slek's brows furrowed as he closed his eyes. "But I can *feel* them. Fraya. Finn. Wynna. Kallemena... Others, too." He paused. "Ashar." His eyes flew open, terror surging behind them. "And Zepher."

Sylvie gasped, her hand rising to her mouth. A sob slipped from her throat. "Oh, Slek..." Her eyes darted between him and the mirror, her voice trembling. "How do we fix this? How do we *get you out?*"

Slek clutched his head with both hands. His knees buckled, and he collapsed onto the cold floor. His body trembled violently, as though something were pulling him apart from within.

"Sylvie, what is happening to me?" he gasped.

She dropped to her knees beside him, pulling him into her arms. Her hands moved instinctively, stroking his hair, gripping his shoulders, trying to hold him together through sheer force of will. "We will fix this. I promise. We will find a way to get you out. All of you." She pressed his hand to her lips, her tears dripping down onto his ghostly skin. Watching him seize and convulse was unbearable. He was unraveling right before her eyes. Then, he was gone. No sound. No light. No warning. Just gone.

Sylvie collapsed over the empty space where he had been, her sobs shaking her to her core. All that was left was the mirror, still warm where his hands had gripped it. She clutched it to her chest like a lifeline.

Morning could not come fast enough. At the first murmurs of waking servants, Sylvie tore through the castle corridors barefoot, her robe rippling behind her. The mirror tight in her hands, she would never let it go. As she ran, her heart pounded and her breath was short, but she did not stop until she burst into the king's study. King Thaloren turned in surprise. Orentheon and Kivani stood by his side, with maps of distant lands spread across the desk. The guards lunged for her, grabbing her arms and pulling her back toward the hall.

"I know where she is!" Sylvie screamed. Her voice cracked, her desperation raw. "I know what happened to them!"

Thaloren raised a hand, and the guards stopped. His cold, scrutinizing gaze locked onto her. She appeared wild and half-mad as the room fell into a silent standstill.

"Then speak," Orentheon barked. "Where is my sister?"

Sylvie launched into everything: the memories, the mirror, Slek, and the names of the others. Fraya, Finn, Wynna, and Zepher. Her voice was pitchy but never wavered. She had nothing left but truth. When she finished, the room fell into silence once more. The fire was not enough to chase away the chill she had brought through her discovery. Tears tracked silently down her cheeks as she clutched the mirror close, knowing now she would never relinquish it.

"Will he speak to us?" Kivani asked quietly. Her husband gave her a baffled look, as if she were as crazy as the woman before them in her nightdress and rumpled robe.

"I do not know." Sylvie swallowed hard, her throat dry. "But if he does, would you listen?"

Orentheon scoffed. "This is madness. How can we trust a word she says? She was raised by the Axis. They filled her head with lies." He pointed to the object she clung to. "That is nothing more than a damn mirror."

"Orentheon!" Kivani's tone snapped like a whip. "And what else do we have to go on, eh?"

Before he could respond, a loud knock thundered against the door. "Enter," Thaloren commanded, his voice like a blade.

Two guards stepped inside, dragging a man between them. He wore a tattered white priest's robe, and his arms were held tightly by the guards. In his hands, he held tight to a chest.

"My lord," one of the guards said. "We caught him trying to board a merchant ship. He was attempting to smuggle these."

The second guard wrestled the chest from the man's grip and placed it onto the King's desk, opening the lid with a click. Inside lay four mirrors, all identical to Sylvie's, each crafted with ornate scrollwork on the handles, silver gleaming, and the glass perfectly polished.

The prisoner raised his chin defiantly. "I did not steal them. I saved them."

Sylvie's breath caught in her throat. "Rhez?" She turned to the priest in disbelief. "You were one of Vallorith's men. You *know*." She raised her mirror, her voice demanding now. "Tell them. Tell them what these are."

King Thaloren's fingers ran slowly across the edge of one of the mirrors. His eyes narrowed. "Yes, tell us." His eyes fixed on the robed man. "And do not lie."

Rhez looked from Sylvie to the king, and then down at the mirrors.

Chapter Eleven

The man in the white robe sat stiffly across from King Thaloren and his son. Both stood tall, their expressions a storm of confusion, anger, and reluctant curiosity. Beside him, Sylvie sat quietly, the mirror still clutched in her iron grip.

"You must promise," the man said, his voice trying for confidence, "that once I tell you everything, I will be allowed to leave. With those." His thin hand pointed to the mirrors.

Orentheon leaned forward, his voice low and full of venom. "We do not bargain with thieves." His hatred for the Axis clung to every word.

King Thaloren rested a hand on his son's shoulder, steadying him. "You will speak. Then we will decide what sentence fits." His gaze dropped to the man. "That is the best offer you will receive. Decline, and you will freeze in our dungeons, and I assure you, freezing to death is slow and very painful."

Rhez's shoulders twitched. Even the mention of the Glacian cold was enough to unfasten his resolve. Words tumbled from his lips in a rush. "I knew your daughter," he said in a rush. "Well, not personally. I was assigned to bring her food on the ship."

Orentheon exploded. He surged around the desk, seizing Rhez by the collar and hauling him upright. "The ship to Verdathos? Where she was caged like a beast? She is a princess; we should hang you now for how you treated royalty. Our family. My sister!"

Rhez shook furiously. His pleas came fast, sliding from his down-turned lips unchecked.

"We should gut him here," Orentheon growled, drawing a dagger, its tip gleaming as it hovered near the man's stomach.

Sylvie turned away, a soft gasp escaping her lips.

"Orentheon!" King Thaloren's voice halted his son's movements as time seemed to stop. "If you cannot listen without fury, leave this room. You are acting like a child."

With a reluctant snarl, Orentheon let the man go. Rhez crumpled back into his seat, sobbing softly. No shame touched the prince's face, only grim satisfaction.

"Now, continue," Thaloren said, lowering himself into his chair, settling in as if waiting for a storm to pass.

Rhez tugged at his collar, uneasy with the prince now looming behind him. He cleared his throat, a burning scratch begged for moisture, but he dared not ask for a drink. "I brought her meals. Water. As much as I could, before Vallorith would lace it with silvervane…" He trailed off, the memory of the high priest's wrath flashing behind his eyes when he forgot the dreaded herb. He wondered now which he was more afraid of, Vallorith or Orentheon? "When we reached Verdathos, she was handed over to Sister Tressa. Sent to the nursery. I never saw her again after that."

Behind him, Orentheon scoffed. Rhez stiffened in his seat but pressed on, nausea looming under his words. "I worked closely with Vallorith. His ledgers, his appointments. I even transcribed his letters." He sat a little straighter at this; his penmanship was excellent and deserved to be boasted upon. His eyes flitted between the royals, their expressions clearly not caring. "He had a hidden chamber. Deep underground. Only accessible by Darra's portal." He placed a hand to his chest. "I am a Darra. But I lack the ability to make the portals myself."

Another grunt from Orentheon, who returned to his father's side. His glare alone could wither bone.

"B...but..." Rhez stuttered, wringing his hands. "After the fighting stopped, after *you*," he nodded to Thaloren, "and the prince..."

"*King*," Thaloren corrected, without missing a beat. "He is the King of Kalyra."

Rhez nodded quickly, hands fidgeting in his lap. "Yes. You and King Ashar came and left, but I stayed behind. I am no warrior. When the fighting broke out, I was hiding in Vallorith's study, under his desk." His eyes flicked between Thaloren and Orentheon. Both men stared at him with a stony blend of suspicion and mounting anger.

"I was there when Zepher came through a portal," he rushed on. "He was gathering things: books, satchels, scrolls. I assumed he was going on some long journey. I do not know what made me do it, but I slipped through the portal behind him. And it led to the hidden room. Belowground." He pointed to the floor beneath his boots.

"There were nine mirrors mounted on the walls. Each one glowing. Strange. In another chamber, the children from the nursery," his voice cracked, "were there. They were crying and scared. So I did what I do best."

"You hid?" Orentheon interjected, dry as flint.

"Precisely," Rhez said, almost proudly. "I hid. But I *watched*. And what I saw will haunt me until the day I die."

King Thaloren leaned forward, the wooden frame of his chair groaning beneath his weight. "And what did you see?"

Rhez's chin lifted with unearned confidence. "First, I want your word. I will not die in your dungeon."

"You have it," Orentheon answered before his father could speak. "Because if you waste one more second, I will kill you where you sit. Now tell us, *where is my sister?*"

Rhez flinched, body rattling with despair. His confidence shriveled. "He trapped her. In the mirror. All of them. The Vira. The Zeph. The Thorns. Every last one." His wide eyes found Sylvie. "Except you.

You escaped. But Kallemena, she did not. She was pulled into the mirror. A prison of reflections." He held up a shaking finger as Thaloren opened his mouth. "But not before *she* trapped *him*, Vallorith. In a mirror of her own making. This one was different. Black glass, deep as space. It shimmered like stars were burning behind it. It was beautiful."

His eyes took on a dreamy appearance as he paused as if recalling its wonder, then blinked. "Once everyone was imprisoned, only Zepher remained. That is when it happened. A loud crash, and then a claw, *something*, swiped at him. Zepher hurled one of the mirrors at the thing before taking off. The creature grabbed one as well and flew off."

Rhez swallowed hard, his voice faltering again. "I waited. Minutes passed. Then I crept out. I gathered the rest and conjured a box to carry them. To protect them." He nodded toward the chest. "They must be kept safe." His gaze shifted to Sylvie. "How did you get that one?"

Sylvie straightened in her chair, suddenly aware of every eye in the room on her. "We turned around," she said, her voice soft but steady. She met Thaloren's eyes, and he gave a slight nod, remembering the moment he had ordered the fleet back after Kallemena and the others had disappeared. "I found the chamber where Vallorith held us. It was wrecked, claw marks gouged the walls. Furniture was shattered, and there was rubble everywhere."

Her fingers brushed the mirror's edge. Her reflection stared back, a pale girl adrift in a world without her order, without the structure of scrolls and laws. "It was lying under a broken beam. I do not know why, but I *knew* I had to take it. Keep it safe." She looked up, voice catching with emotion. "And I am glad I did. Slek is inside it. Just like the others are inside *those*."

"You said he was trapped as well?" King Thaloren's voice remained measured, though his brow furrowed, heavy with the weight of this new knowledge. He turned to his son. "We must find this," His gaze shifted back to Rhez. "Zepher?"

"He is the Morin I spoke of," Sylvie said quickly. "Vallorith's right hand."

The king nodded, jaw tightening. "Then we will hunt this Morin down. Retrieve the mirrors. From there, we will find a way to free Kallemena and the others from their prisons."

The next few days passed in a blur of preparation. Counsel was held with the kingdom's most trusted advisers. Each offered a different theory, each one pointing in a separate direction, different ports, different continents, scattered rumors of a dark, cloaked figure slipping through shadows. All were heard. All were considered. At last, a course was set.

At dawn, the soldiers would sail. A fleet of glimmering ships would scour the seas, chasing whatever trail might lead to the unraveling of Vallorith's schemes. Down at the docks, warriors in gleaming glass armor marched in formation. Sunlight caught on their polished suits, scattering light in all directions as they boarded the ships one by one.

Back at the palace, Sylvie wandered the gardens with Poppy, her small hand warm in her own. The girl tugged her eagerly through the frost-covered hedges, eager to see the places her friend, now lost in a mirror, had once described. Sylvie followed quietly, her mind lost in thoughts of her past. Statues lined the walkways, masterpieces of enchanted glass that seemed ready to step off their pedestals. Their faces were too perfect, too human. A few made Sylvie shiver.

Poppy danced in the snow ahead of her, her new silken dress spinning around her ankles like petals in the wind. With the palace of crystal rising behind her, she looked like a storybook princess. The sight brought a bittersweet smile to Sylvie's lips. But the warmth did not last. A heavy thought settled in her chest. *What was she supposed to do while they searched for Vallorith?* Wait here? Pretend this place, this shimmering castle and its hollow halls, was her home? Live among

Kallemena's family and people as if the princess's absence was not noticed? The idea felt like a betrayal.

The guilt pressed tighter around her ribs. She had escaped, but why? Why her? The others were trapped in glass prisons, while she walked freely through royal gardens and warm hallways. *For all I know,* she thought bitterly, *I should be inside one of those mirrors too.* The weight of survival bloomed like a bruise inside her, aching, growing, impossible to ignore. Her stare caught on her sister's face, Poppy's smile forever a pure delight. She realized it slowly, that had it not been for her little sister, she too would have been doomed to the mirrors.

***

Kivani watched her husband fasten his chest plate, pulling the leather straps snugly across his torso. His hands moved with practiced precision, though tension lingered in every motion. He still did not fully believe the priest's tale. Rhez's story of mirrors and soul-prisons seemed too fantastical. And yet, if there was even a sliver of truth, Oren would chase it. He would find the mad priest, he would find the Morin, and he would free his sister from whatever fate had claimed her.

In his mind, he saw his mother smiling again. Whole. Holding her daughter in her arms. No longer too grief-stricken to eat, or too broken to speak. No more sleepless nights. No more cries echoing from her chambers. A family whole again, together like it always should have been.

"What weighs so heavily on your mind, dear husband?" Kivani's voice was soft as she crossed the room. She slipped her arms around him, pressing her cheek to his back in a gentle embrace.

Oren did not answer. Everything had already been said a thousand times over. He did not think his heart or his mind could speak of it anymore. Could not relive the pain for another second. He shook his head and continued his work in silence.

"I should come wit you," she said, her voice rising slightly. "I am a strong warrior. A proud Talon." Her island accent curled through each word, melodic and bold. To Oren, it was music.

He turned and pulled her close, kissing her forehead as she ran her fingers through his long white hair. She gave a playful tug, and their lips met in a kiss full of yearning. It was bittersweet, knowing that by this time tomorrow, the sea would stretch between them. He held her tightly, breathing in the scent of coconut and warm sunshine that clung to her skin. He would miss her terribly and silently wished this moment could go on forever.

But Kivani had already slipped from his grasp, hurrying to her wardrobe. She flung open the doors, revealing a suit of armor unlike any worn in Glacia. Its plates were bronze and foreign, its leathers dyed in the rich colors of her homeland.

"Kivani," Oren's voice was gentle, pleading, but she refused to listen.

She was already pulling on her boots, letting the shield clatter to the ground as she fastened the laces firmly around her calf. "I go wit you," she said. "Together, we will find that evil man. We will kill him. We free my sista from her mirror." Tears shimmered in her eyes as Oren stepped forward and gently took the cuff from her hand.

Kivani's body slumped as she tried to suppress her sorrow. Oren cupped her face in both hands, lifting her gaze to his. "I *will* find him. I swear it." His hand lowered, resting against her stomach with quiet reverence. "And we will bring Kallemena home, so she can meet our child."

Tears spilled freely now. She pulled him into another fierce embrace, fingers digging into his back as if she could press them together hard enough to stop time.

Later, when the ships were ready, the women gathered along the icy docks to say their farewells. Nyssira raised her hand to her husband, whispering prayers to the god Nuval for his safety, that no more pieces of him would be lost to war. Beside her, Kivani stood silently, one hand pressed to her stomach as her other waved to Oren.

"May Lysar protect you on the sea, my love," she whispered in her native tongue, the words floating like a song on the cold wind as the ships faded over the horizon.

Chapter Twelve

The storm howled above as wind-driven waves crashed into the hull. It was the third major tempest the prince and his crew had faced, and it would be the last for their trusted vessel. The churning sea concealed jagged rocks beneath its thrashing surface, and when the ship collided with them, there was no hope of saving her. The sea opened wide its sharp jaws and bit down with full force.

Oren and his men had moved quickly when the first signs of water showed through the floorboards. They lash barrels and crates together with the rope from the rigging and float the supplies and themselves toward the beach. Lightning forked across the sky, the only illumination guiding them to an unfamiliar shore. Thunder rolled in around them, deep enough to rattle bones, as the crews' gaze fixed on the half-submerged ship. Its tattered sails flapped in the wind like a final farewell.

"Captain!" Oren shouted above the roar. "Where are we?"

The man stumbled across the sand toward him, each step slowed by the shifting of the soft ground. He gave a quick bow before scanning the wreckage strewn across the beach. He already knew the maps were ruined and the sextant missing, likely swallowed by the sea. He looked up at the blackened sky, thick with rage and rain. Patting down his pockets, he searched for his watch, but it too was gone, lost to the depths of the unforgiving tide.

"No way to chart until morning, and that is if the clouds clear," he muttered to himself grimly. He cleared his throat and shouted over the torrential wind. "My best guess, my lord, is Aetheria. We were tracking her eastern border, but the storm must have pushed us further west. That is likely why we struck the reef." He studied the prince, water streaming from his brow, his white hair undone and whipping in the gale.

"Let us find shelter, then. We will not survive long out here in these elements." Orentheon patted the captain's shoulder before making his way further inland.

The captain turned to his crew, who stood staring at what was left of their battered vessel. "Attention!" he bellowed above the ferocious wind. "Get shelter up, and make it quick! I do not like sleeping in wet socks!"

A collective shout answered him, respectful and strong. The men scattered into motion, chopping down nearby trees and hauling crates to shore. By nightfall, they had stacked enough timber and debris to form a makeshift lodge fit for any beach-dwelling king.

A fire crackled inside. Damp clothes and armor hung along the walls, drying in the rising heat. Most of the men sat in their undergarments, steam rising from their backs, laughter echoing as they swapped ghost stories and tales of lost treasure. But Orentheon sat apart, lost in quieter thoughts. While the others filled the lodge with noise, his mind wandered home to Kivani. Her belly would have rounded by now. The baby would be kicking, twisting within her. He smiled faintly, picturing the life awaiting him.

He missed her terribly. Five months at sea had left a hollow in him. He missed the curve of her smile, the way her island accent made the coldest room feel warmer, like sunlight woven into words. He missed the rich tone of her chestnut-colored skin, the way her long hair spilled down her back like a silken waterfall. She was strength and fire, and somehow, by a miracle, she was his. Oren leaned back, letting the voices of his men fade to a murmur. Outside, thunder grumbled a little softer now. But inside his chest, a different storm raged, one of urgency, hope, and the distant heartbeat of home.

"What say you, my lord?"

The voice pulled him from his thoughts, and his smile faded. "What say me, Captain?" Oren echoed, turning to the man with a beard longer than he thought humanly possible.

The captain's face was one of easy warmth: rounded cheeks, deep dimples at the corners of his mouth. His laugh could fill any chamber, and his grasp of the sea rivaled even the most learned scholars.

"This lot says we will be stuck here for three months. I wager a year," the captain mused, though his gaze sharpened as he studied the prince.

He was not looking at the fire; he was looking through it, through Oren, straight to what weighed behind his eyes. He knew how badly the prince longed for home, for the wife and unborn child waiting there.

"Twenty days," Orentheon answered quietly.

A ripple of laughter broke across the crew as murmurs of doubt arose.

Oren raised a brow, undeterred. "If we are on the eastern coast of Aetheria, we can reach Brimspire in sixteen days on foot. Perhaps fewer, if we press. If we reach the kingdom, I can speak with the king and queen. It has been years since Glacia had any contact with their court, but with luck, they have heard news of the Axis's collapse. Of Vallorith's betrayal."

Someone from the back voiced a question, soft and hesitant. "What if they aid Vallorith? Axis sympathizers?"

A hush followed, and the makeshift shelter overflowed with anxious tension.

Oren's expression hardened. "Then they will have a fight on their hands. Anyone who supports that monster and his church is an enemy to Glacia and to all we defend now."

Silence fell. Outside, thunder gave its last distant groan. The men glanced at one another. No more than forty made up the crew, a rather small number when put up against a whole army. The thought of facing the foreigners on their turf, should it come to that, was not hard to work out. It would mean bloodshed. A quick and brutal end. A massacre. Their shoulders sagged beneath the realization. The unease hung thick.

"Chains, you lot are so serious." Oren let out a sudden, barking laugh. "I know the prince of Brimspire. We were boys together. He will help, regardless of his court's stance."

A few of the crew chuckled, tension loosening from their frames.

"Rest now," Oren said, more gently. "We march at first light."

When morning arrived, the men faced a landscape unlike anything they had anticipated. Where dense forest should have bordered the pale golden sands, only jagged stone spires stood. Some were as wide as walls, others were thin like fingers. Towering statues, carved not by hand but by relentless wind and time. Great canyons wound around them, a maze of chiseled ridges and weathered paths. The sun was barely up, and already the men could feel sweat sliding down their backs and forming along their brows. They all knew what was coming: a very long and tedious walk through hell.

"Bring only food and water," Oren ordered, fastening his sword belt snug around his waist. His glass armor, once gleaming and proud, was left on the beach like a discarded relic for the sea to claim as its treasure.

"Food and water!" The captain shouted to his men. "Every man carries something; leave the rest!" His bark rose above the whispering waves, all heads nodding their compliance.

The ocean had been still since the night before, as if mourning their ship in silence with the crew. No trace of their magnificent vessel remained. Her sails, once a symbol of peace and unity, would never catch wind again. The crew moved swiftly, prying open crates and barrels. Water skins were filled, and sacks of rice and grain were secured. Even Oren took his share, slinging a satchel over his back and strapping water to his chest. He knew every blistering step now was one closer to home. Toward Kivani.

The captain approached, a sextant in hand. He lifted it to the sun overhead, narrowing his eye. After a moment, he stepped forward and gave Oren a sharp nod.

"Then lead the way, Captain," Oren said, and together, they approached the stone labyrinth ahead.

***

Poppy eased out of bed, every creak in her limbs sending a shiver of fear through her tiny frame. Slowly, cautiously, she stretched one foot to the floor, then the other. Once fully lowered, she dropped to her hands and knees, crawling across the cold floor toward the room's towering doors. She cast one last glance at the bed behind her, where her older sister lay still and peacefully asleep.

With a breath held tight in her chest, she gripped the door handle. Inch by inch, she pulled it open, praying the hinges would not squeal, dreading a creak or a footstep echoing from the hall. But none thankfully came, and then, freedom. She slipped into the corridor and gently closed the door behind her. Her heart thudded like a drumbeat, but her face broke into a grin. A small, victorious dance bubbled out of her as she scurried down the hall, bare feet padding fast.

She had been planning this for a month. Quiet whispers with the staff, secret nods from the cooks, even hushed help from the queen and the princess. It was like a mission, one she took great care to keep from Sylvie. The smell hit her as she rounded the corner. She took in deep inhales to fill her lungs completely. Warm, sweet, and magical. This was the magnificent aroma of cake.

Her golden curls bounced behind her as she skipped through the doors. The sounds of the kitchen swept her up in their rhythm: pans clanged like cymbals, spoons tapped bowls in gentle percussion, and the women's voices sang in the native tongue of the land. The language danced like music; soft, round syllables spilling with talk of snow, ice, and the god who gifted them roots strong enough to grow even here.

Poppy twirled between them, greeted with knowing smiles as the women stirred, sliced, and stacked. She made her way to the back of the kitchen, past the steaming ovens, and gasped aloud. There, on the counter, stood a towering four-tier cake. Blue and golden frosting shimmered like sunlight through a cresting wave. Sugar bubbles glistened like glass. Pink flowers, delicate and perfect, crowned every layer.

It was the most majestic birthday cake she had ever seen. In truth, it was the *only* birthday cake she had ever seen. She had heard stories of them from other children in the nursery, whispers of soft sponges and sweet icing, but Poppy had been very young when she was brought to the Axis with her sister. In all her ten years, she had never tasted cake until today.

"This is wonderful," she breathed, eyes wide and reverent.

At the counter, a man finished shaping the final sugar petal before glancing up. When he saw her expression, his whole face lit with pride. He gave her a playful grin, then squeezed a long swirl of frosting onto her finger.

Poppy wasted no time; she licked it clean and let out a squeal of joy. She twirled and leapt, the sugar igniting a burst of excitement in her small frame. "Delicious!" she squeaked, bouncing on her toes. "I love it!"

"Think Miss Sylvie will like it as well?" the chef asked, wiping his hands and beginning to clear his tools.

Poppy rushed forward and threw her arms around him. "Yes, she will love it too! I just know it! Thank you, Delli! It is perfect!"

His eyes glistened, but he cleared his throat quickly, turning away to tend to the bustle of preparations around them. Then a voice called from the hallway.

"Poppy."

The small girl turned and spotted Kivani standing in the hall, her brilliant blue dress shimmering like the ocean tides. In that moment, she looked like a sea goddess who stepped out from myth. Poppy rushed to her, barely able to contain her excitement. She was eager to see the decorations in the ballroom. Though still cautious, she approached her friend with reverence. Kivani had taken a special liking to both Poppy and her sister since their arrival, treating them with a kindness that made the vast, icy halls of the castle feel like home.

Over the past five months, Kivani had called for all orphaned or displaced Echoes to come to Glacia, offering them sanctuary. She had helped the lost find homes, giving them purpose and places in society where they could thrive. Gone were the days when Echoes were bound by duty, forced to serve in places they never chose.

Kivani had even offered Sylvie and Poppy a place within the castle beside her, as family. She envied the girls, in a quiet, aching way, for they had known her sister-in-law longer than she had. But that same connection only deepened her love for them.

Poppy gently reached out, sliding her small hand over Kivani's growing belly. The gentle swell was larger each week, a quiet miracle in motion. She held her palm still, waiting. A few heartbeats later, a soft kick nudged her hand away. Her face broke into a wide, delighted grin.

"Is it all ready?" Poppy asked breathlessly.

"It is," Kivani replied warmly. "Let us go and see it now, yeah?"

Hand in hand, they made their way to the ballroom, where Queen Nyssira was still arranging the tables. If the cake had left Poppy awestruck, the ballroom nearly stole the breath from her lungs. She spun in the center of the room, her curls fanning out as she turned in slow circles. The domed glass ceiling let the golden morning light pour in, illuminating the polished silver lining the walls. Elegant lace streamers, sheer as spider silk, draped gracefully from the high rafters. Floating glass orbs hovered on invisible threads, adorned with pink coral, clamshells, and trailing strands of green seaweed.

It was like stepping into an underwater palace. Poppy cupped her hands over her mouth, stunned into silence. No words could do this place justice.

"Think she gonna like it?" Kivani asked, lowering herself carefully into a chair and rubbing her belly, the extra weight beginning to take its toll on her back.

Poppy turned, ready to nod and beam, but her face crumpled instead. Her lip quivered and tears welled in her eyes. They spilled over before she could stop them, a sniffle to keep her runny nose in check.

"Oh, my dear, whatever is the matter?" Nyssira rushed over, kneeling beside her.

Poppy buried her face in the folds of the queen's gown. Her small shoulders shook as she sobbed, each breath uneven and muffled.

"I am so thankful I got to meet Mena," she said through hiccups. "And I am so thankful we are here. But if she had not disappeared, if the Axis still stood," She pulled back slightly, eyes red and swimming with guilt. "I would never have known this existed. I would still be in the nursery. Still stuck."

Nyssira gently cupped the girl's tear-streaked cheeks. Her voice was soft but steady. "My dear girl. We cannot change the past. And you must not carry guilt for where my daughter is now. I truly believe that one day she will be free. And when she is, she will want to hear everything. All of it. About the day her dear friend celebrated a birthday surrounded by people who love her." She pulled Poppy into a warm embrace, holding her tightly. Her own eyes shimmered, one silent tear trailing down her cheek. The last memory of holding her daughter in her arms pulsed through her heart like a wound.

"Oren will find dat bad man, Poppy," Kivani added firmly. "My husband, he will not stop until his sista is free. And den…" she smiled, placing a hand on her belly, "den we will throw her a party even grander than dis one."

Poppy's tearful eyes brightened just a little at the thought.

"Go and wake your sister," Nyssira said gently, dabbing the girl's face dry with a silk kerchief. "We have an entire day ahead of us."

***

The men trudged on through the night, none willing to be the one to slow the group. Eleven days of constant marching had worn them down. Food was running low. The land offered no edible flora; the rocky terrain was too windswept and barren for even the hardiest roots to take hold. The rivers, though swift and loud, did little to nourish them. White water rushed over jagged rocks and tumbled from cliff faces, turning into mist that vanished on the wind. The sun was relentless during the day, and with no shade to shield them, most of the men were blistered and raw, their skin cracking under the heat.

"My lord." The captain quickened his pace to catch up to the prince, whose long strides never faltered, even on such treacherous footing. "We need to find a place to rest before the sun rises," the captain said, glancing over his shoulder.

The crew that had survived the wreck with confidence now walked like ghosts; sunburned, silent, and starving. A miserable bunch that constantly whispered of home in the frozen tundra.

"They cannot go on much longer. We need rest. *You* need rest, my lord."

Oren came to a stop. His body welcomed the pause with an almost painful relief. His feet throbbed with every step, bruised and swollen from the unyielding stone. Hunger gnawed at his insides, and his limbs trembled with fatigue. Yet whenever the thought of stopping entered his mind, an image of his wife would surface. Her face, her belly; growing each day without him. He turned and studied his men, then raised his gaze to the sky. The stars had faded. Streaks of pink and orange crept across the horizon, promising another cruelly hot day.

"Very well," he relented. "Tell them to stop here. I will go ahead and see if there is a place where we can shelter from the sun." He looked to the captain. "Are we still on course?"

The older man glanced upward. The moon hung low, barely visible against the rising light. "I will check again when the sun is higher. Cannot get much from the sky right now."

Oren's expression tightened, but he did not argue. The answer would have to do. With a respectful nod, the captain returned to the others, helping them shed their packs of what remained of their provisions. Oren wiped sweat from his brow. It left behind a trail of grit, dust, and grime that had been baked into his skin from days without a proper bath.

He followed a winding path through the rocks, where the tall cliffs narrowed into a tight passage just wide enough for a grown man. The heat already felt like it was starting to cook him as he moved forward. The walls pressed inward, and he was forced to unbuckle his sword and toss it through the gap ahead. Grimacing, he squeezed between the stones, his ribs scraping against the rough surface, skin already tender from exposure to the harsh elements. He clenched his teeth against the pain, feeling each small sandy rock grate against his body.

When he had made it through, he stumbled and froze. The point of his own blade hovered at his throat. A masked man held it steady, his posture rigid and unblinking, as if they were a part of their surroundings. Behind him stood five more figures, their spears aimed at Oren's ribs and legs. The weapons were masterfully crafted, glinting in the rising sun, their edges sharp enough to cut the air.

The masks were shockingly vivid against the muted colors of the canyon. A golden bird with a sharp beak hid his captor's identity, while human eyes stayed trained on Oren. Cresting from the mask's edges was a plumage of blue and black feathers, draping down past the men's shoulders and back. A black crown showed who was in charge, and at its center, a red jewel sparkled like the rising sun. Symbols were painted in blue ink on their tanned skins, giving them the appearance of an ethereal brute. They looked like falcons wearing human skin. Fierce, silent, and waiting for their captives' next move.

Oren raised his hands in surrender, taking in the figures before him. "I am Prince Orentheon Vaelora, of the continent Glacia," he said, keeping his voice calm despite the spears at his ribs. "My ship struck the reef during the last storm. My men and I are on foot, trying to reach Brimspire. I know of—"

"Silence!" The command echoed in the cavern they all stood in. The man holding his sword stepped forward, his voice low and rough. His eyes slid down to the hilt, crafted in silver and icy blue metal, with a glass grip and a sash embroidered with a snowflake. "Prince Orentheon?" the man repeated, narrowing his gaze. "Why should I believe you?"

Oren swallowed hard. His mind raced, digging through half-remembered lessons about this harsh land. Had he missed the mention of tribes that lived in seclusion? Clans forgotten by the historians? Or were these bandits, unrecorded and wild? His exhaustion dulled the edge of his thinking, and his head ached from dehydration. Eleven days of marching had left his thoughts slow and his limbs in no condition to fight.

"You do not have to," he replied, his voice rasping from thirst. "But I speak only the truth." He gestured toward the sword. "Keep it, if you must. Take it as payment for my crew's safe passage. It is pure Glacian steel and glasswork; you will not find better anywhere in the world."

The man considered his words, clicking his tongue under his mask. "What would I need of Glacian steel when we have Aetherian stone?"

He sheathed the sword and pulled his own blade from his side. The dark grey rock was polished to perfection, the marbling within it showing its strength. He took a step closer to Oren, his deep brown eyes piercing under the bird mask he wore.

"You could always sell it then." Oren allowed his shoulders to relax. "Maybe buy you and your men some pants." He motioned to their white linen shendyts, a smile breaking across his face.

The man tilted his head, the feathers of his mask rustling in the breeze. "Oren, Oren, Oren," he said, almost to himself. Then, with a slow shake of his head, he reached up and slid the mask away. Beneath it was a slender face, sharp-eyed and familiar. The man smiled before a bout of laughter left his lips. "It has been a very long time," he said with a grin, stepping forward to clasp Oren's forearm.

"Good to see you, too, Malekai." Oren shook the man's hand, his gamble paying off.

The other man's smile widened. "Where is your crew?"

Oren pointed toward the narrow passage behind him. Without hesitation, Malekai gave a quick signal to his men. Before long, Oren and the others were being led out of the canyon and across a dusty wilderness. Just as the crew and Oren felt on the verge of collapse, they saw it. A castle that scraped the clouds.

It looked like it had been carved from the mountain itself, towering on a high plateau whose edges dropped away into deep chasms. Winds howled around it, the noise like a thousand voices speaking a forgotten language. The air was sharp and hot, almost unbearable as the men approached the edges. Deep grooves were carved all around the castle, allowing the strong air currents to make an almost impenetrable barrier between it and the rest of the world.

The men stopped and stared, wide-eyed. The entire structure appeared precarious, built with impossible ambition, as though gravity had been defied. A massive, carved monolith dominated the front, etched with swirling patterns that told the story of both ancient and modern civilizations, woven into a seamless narrative. Malekai raised his hand again, and two of his warriors stepped forward. They moved to the edge of the wind tunnel and began their practiced ritual. With smooth, flowing gestures, they guided the air upward, parting the deadly currents like a curtain. A corridor of calm opened through the roaring winds.

The crew gasped as the ground trembled beneath them. Wind surged into hidden chambers, and stone groaned as stairs slowly rose from the earth, hidden steps revealed by the breath of the Zephs.

"Gentlemen," Malekai said, sweeping his arm toward the gate with a flourish and a grin. "Welcome to Brimspire."

Chapter Thirteen

The castle of Brimspire stood as a pinnacle of inspiration in the vast, untamed wilderness of Aetheria. Its soaring spires rose above jagged plateaus and wind-carved towers. It was said to have been shaped over centuries by the divine breath of the god Turan. Each gust molded the terrain until it looked like a churning ocean frozen in time, with rocky waves and marbled icebergs protruding from the ground, smoothed and twisted by the relentless wind.

The castle itself was a marvel of design. Inside its walls, tunnels and passageways spiraled like a labyrinth, depicting the work of countless sculptors. These hollow corridors reached deep into the earth, where murals lined every surface, telling the ancient stories of the land. The people of this realm had no need for canvas or cloth. They painted directly on the stone, layering their history on the very bones of their kingdom.

Each year, new murals were added. Another tunnel shaped by the powerful command of the Zephs, those gifted with the wind god's powers. The very ones who continue to serve under their king's rule despite the fall of the Axis. It was these people who kept the history alive for the generations that would come after. Brimspire would be known for its endurance, the place that thrived in the windswept barrens.

"You want the continents to take a vote?" King Khareph narrowed his eyes at Orentheon, his voice grating with disbelief. He studied the prince's appearance, noting his skin still red and blistered from the brutal sun that scorched the route to the kingdom. "I see no reason for it. My son, Malekai, is the eldest heir among the seven remaining continents still ruled by monarchs. He should be the one to go to Kalyra in King Ashar's absence."

Oren clenched his jaw, his patience worn thin after eight long days of repetition. Every morning, he was summoned to the throne room. Every evening, he was dismissed without any progress. He was tired of the endless circular debates, each one ending with the same stubborn resistance.

More than anything, he longed to board a ship and go home to his wife, to feel her touch on his skin, to hear her voice once more. But each sunrise pulled him back into this gilded cage, another wasted day away from Glacia.

"King Khareph," he said, his voice tense with exhaustion, "you have never been one to hide your ambitions. All of Ardoria knows you aim to expand westward. And now, with Kalyra without a king, even temporarily, it will seem as though you are laying claim to Ashar's birthright."

He turned to Malekai, searching his friend's face for an ally, a sign of reason. But the young man only sat there, expression unreadable, idly picking at his nails with the edge of a small blade.

The king stood, each movement deliberate. His gaze fixated on Oren, burning with silent defiance. "I grow tired of this game," Khareph said, his voice steady and cold. "Malekai will be sent to Kalyra to act in Ashar's stead." He descended the dais with the slow certainty of a verdict passed, each step ringing with finality. "He will fortify their defenses and act in the continent's best interest, as if it were his own." He gave Malekai a brief nod, and something silent passed between them. An understanding from father to son.

"He will remain there," the king added, "until Ashar returns." A beat passed before he said his final words. "*If* he returns."

The words dropped like a blade into the heart of the room. Oren exhaled sharply, running a hand down his face, and immediately regretted it. His sunburned skin flared with fresh pain, stinging as if to match the anger boiling in his gut. He turned to Malekai, whose knife was still in his hand, casually flipping it between his fingers.

"You were no help," Oren muttered, voice low with irritation.

Malekai gave a casual shrug. "I agree with my father. I am the oldest heir across all seven continents, and the most experienced. Why should I not be the one to help a leaderless land?" His tone was smug, lacking even a trace of concern for the missing king.

"Because the other continents may see it as a threat." Oren's voice rose, edged with frustration. "It could start a war, Malekai." He stepped closer, pleading now. "With your experience, you should have come to that conclusion on your own." He motioned toward the now-empty throne. "You should be helping me convince your father, not fanning the flames."

Malekai did not flinch. He kept tending to his nails with a carved stone knife, his posture as relaxed as if they were discussing what to eat for dinner that evening.

"Orentheon, you and I both know my father is the most unyielding man in all the realms. Once his mind is made up, there is no swaying him." He gestured lazily toward the balcony, where dry, searing wind billowed through the chamber, doing little to ease the sweltering heat. "He would not even allow Thorns to set foot here and make the land fertile. What makes you think we will get him to consider a council vote?"

He rose suddenly and slapped Oren on the back firmly, an almost disciplinary pat. "Enough politics. Come, let us go see your ship."

Together, they walked toward the northern docks, where the plateau dipped into a canyon filled with seawater channeled from the ocean. Beneath the wide, cloudless sky, the sounds of hammers hitting wood and shouted commands reverberated like the rhythm of a living machine.

Rigging lines were threaded and tightened by hand. Great masts stood tall against the wind, their sails were folded and stacked waiting to be hoisted. These ships were different from the heavier vessels of Glacia; they sat lower and sleeker, with a narrow hull built to cut through the sea like a dagger through silk.

"She will fly for you, my friend," Malekai said with admiration, his voice rich with pride. "You will be home before the month is through." He nodded toward a group of men gathered on the deck. Their shendyts matched the canyon's dust in color, while blue ink spiraled across their faces and chests in sacred patterns. "The best Zephs in the kingdom. Five of them. Strongest we have. They will carry you on wind alone if need be, get you there before your child draws their first breath."

He raised an eyebrow, a cheeky grin curving his lips. "And when I have claimed my place in Kalyra, I will come visit. See the little one myself."

A tug pulled at Oren's chest, an ache for home, for Kivani. He longed to be there when his child's first cries broke the air, to hold them, to see the softness of their eyes. But hope was tangled with unease. Responsibility loomed like a shadow. He turned to Malekai. The boy he once knew had become a man, tall and lean. His black hair was tied back, and symbols were painted into his skin like declarations.

"We will be kings soon enough," Oren murmured. He twisted his wedding band, its familiar weight grounding him even as a storm churned in his stomach. "Promise me you will step down when Ashar returns." He extended his hand, firm and expectant.

Malekai looked from the hand to Oren's unreadable face. "And if I do not?" he asked, voice stern and testing. The question lingered between them a little too long. "What if I decide I do not want to leave the land I will be calling home," He waved his hand in the air, "for who knows how long? A land I will defend with my own sweat and blood. A land I may grow to love?"

Oren lowered his hand. "If you do not, you will be stealing a home from a man who has already lost everything. His family, his betrothed, even his freedom." His voice sharpened, the fire in his eyes no longer masked. "You will be stealing joy from my sister. Denying a future to people who only want to live in peace." His gaze did not waver. "And you will be starting a war, one that will make us enemies."

He lifted his hand once more, waiting. Malekai looked out toward the docks where hammers still rang and voices floated like a chorus across the canyon. He smiled, then laughed; loud and forced, echoing too brightly in the dry air. Finally, he reached out and shook Oren's hand.

"I will relinquish control when the time comes," he said smoothly. "Besides, I have heard what your wife is capable of." He winked. "Princess Kivani's already earned a reputation as a formidable Talon warrior."

Oren chuckled, the tension easing between them for a moment. United by memory, duty, and hope, they watched as the ship's sails unfurled, the blue and white fabric catching the wind and snapping like flags of promise.

That night, Brimspire held a farewell banquet. Jugglers spun stones through the air with wild bursts of wind. Paper birds fluttered from guest to guest, trailing ribbon-like tails behind them. Zephs freely shared their talents, creating a rare and beautiful display. Joy radiated from every part of the celebration. Laughter echoed off the walls as stories were shared by firelight. The festivities lasted into the early hours of the morning before exhaustion finally sent everyone to bed.

By noon, Oren and his crew were on the dock, boarding their vessel. Their Zeph guides were already coaxing the winds into place, catching currents, and twisting the air with practiced hands. The ship turned effortlessly, gliding away from the canyon and out into the open sea.

"I will keep my promise!" Malekai called from the cliffs above, his voice nearly lost in the gusts. "If the rightful king ever returns."

The days that followed blurred together. The ship sliced through the ocean like butter with a knife. Unseen and steady, the wind filled the sails with speed and silence. No creaking wood or crashing waves, just smooth momentum. The rhythmic snapping of the sails and the whisper of shifting air was the only proof they were indeed moving.

Each day brought colder winds. By the time Glacia appeared on the horizon, snow fell softly in weightless flurries. The land sparkled with a coat of crystal ice, shimmering in the amber glow of dusk. Lanterns had already been lit, casting a warm, golden light on the shore. The familiar scent of salt and frost stirred a deep longing in Oren's chest. Bells tolled from the harbor, their chimes welcoming the arriving ship.

Then he saw them, two small figures bouncing excitedly on the dock. A woman hurried over to join them, arms waving. His mother with the Havander sisters. Their joy crackled through the icy air as they shouted across the distance.

"Can we go faster?" Oren asked one of the Zephs, his voice unable to hide the urgency.

The man only shook his head, focused on steadying the vessel's glide. Slowly and carefully, they edged toward the dock, the ship easing in like a feather descending to earth. The moment the hull touched the wood, Oren vaulted over the railing. His boots struck hard, a sharp jolt shooting through his knee, but he did not stop. He sprinted down the wharf, breath clouding in the cold, heart hammering in his chest. His mother met him halfway, her arms open, eyes wide.

"What has happened?" he gasped, each word coming with a puff of steam. "Kivani?"

The young girl was the first to speak, her excitement spilling out. "The baby is coming!"

Oren quickly turned toward his mother. Nyssira's eyes shimmered with tears, but her face was lit up with joy. "Go!" she urged. "You might just make it!"

He was running before the words fully left her mouth, snow crunching beneath his boots, the sharp air burning in his lungs as he dashed through the upper corridors. Behind him, he heard the delighted squeals of the girls chasing after him, Poppy's laughter echoing like wind chimes in the frozen air.

Oren pushed open the chamber door just in time to hear the sharp cry of a newborn. His heart thudded so hard it felt as if it might tear from his chest. The heat of emotion rose in his face as he stumbled to the bedside. Kivani looked up at him, her eyes filled with exhaustion and triumph. Her arms cradled a wriggling infant, still red and slick but fiercely alive. Joy and disbelief danced across her face as she reached for him, her hand trembling with relief.

"You have a son, my love," she whispered, her voice breaking with tears. The words hit him like a flood, sweeping away all the distance and time that had separated them.

The baby was cleaned and wrapped in soft linens, then placed into Oren's arms. He stared down at the impossibly small face, a mirror of his own. His thoughts blurred; memories, hopes, promises all collided in his chest. He looked at Kivani, barely able to contain the love swelling inside him. But then her face contorted again, her body arching in pain as another scream tore from her throat.

"What is wrong? Why is she still hurting?" Oren demanded to know, the peace he had just found ripped away in an instant.

The attendants circled around her, their hands moving swiftly, voices rising. "It is another one, my lord," one of them said breathlessly. "A second baby."

"No," Kivani groaned, tossing her head back against the pillow. "Not again."

An attendant gently guided Oren away, his son still held protectively against his chest.

"The second usually comes quicker," she said. "We will have them cleaned up before you know it."

The door shut behind him, leaving him alone in the hallway, too shocked to say anything.

Gasps echoed down the corridor. Oren turned to see his mother and the two blonde girls approaching him, their faces lighting up as they spotted the infant in his arms.

"She," he stammered, still breathless. "She is having another baby."

Nyssira hurried forward and gently took the bundle from him as his knees gave way. He dropped to the floor, overwhelmed by a storm of fear and exhaustion.

"Two babies!" Poppy shrieked with delight, jumping up and down. "Twins!" Her curls bounced with each movement, wild and joyful.

From behind the door, another groan echoed louder this time. The sounds from inside were sharper and more urgent. Oren paced the hallway, nerves twisting in his gut. His hands clenched at his sides as midwives hurried past, calling for more towels, more water, more help. Time slowed to a crawl. Minutes dragged on, stretching into what felt like hours. Still, no word came.

"How is the progress? Can I see her?" he asked, grabbing the sleeve of a passing attendant. "Please. Someone tell me what is going on."

None of them responded. They hurried past, eyes downcast, focused. He looked at his mother. Her mouth was drawn tight, worry etched into every line of her face.

"This is not normal, is it?" Oren asked, his voice low, almost a whisper.

The bile rose in his throat. His chest felt hollow, as if something inside him had caved in. Sylvie had taken Poppy away some time ago, noticing the little girl's growing distress at the blood staining the attendants' aprons. Left behind, Nyssira sat quietly on the floor, the newborn boy resting in her arms. She rocked him gently, humming the lullaby she once sang to Kallemena.

"What will his name be?" she asked softly, tucking the blanket beneath the newborn's chin with careful fingers.

Oren leaned against the wall and slowly slid down until he was sitting on the floor. He pressed his palms over his ears, as if the muffled cries from the chamber might fade if he just blocked them out. "That is for my wife to decide," he muttered.

Nyssira hesitated. "Oren, I know it is hard, but what if?"

"My wife will decide my son's name!" Oren barked.

The hallway fell into complete silence. He immediately turned toward the door. The noise inside had disappeared. No cries. No voices. Not a sound at all. His pulse thundered as he lunged for the handle and yanked the door open. He froze in place.

The room was a mess of blood and rags, the floor stained deep red. Buckets overflowed with soiled cloth. The air was thick, heavy, too hot, and painfully still. The fire in the hearth had long since gone out, but the heat lingered oppressively. All around the room, the attendants stood frozen in place, tears streaking their cheeks as their eyes stayed fixed on the bed.

Oren's breath came in rapid, shallow gulps. His knees felt weak, and his vision was darkening as he moved forward, rounding the large circular bed in the center of the room. He did not want to see. He could not bear what his mind had screamed at him for the past hour. When his eyes landed on his wife, his body barely held itself upright.

Kivani was alive. She leaned back against the pillows, pale and soaked in sweat, her chest rising slowly. A second baby was tightly cradled against her, and although her face was drawn with pain, her eyes met his; tired, glassy, but still alive. She reached out a trembling hand. Blood smeared her fingers, but Oren held them without hesitation. They were alive. Both of them. All three.

"It is a miracle," one of the attendants whispered through her tears. "We thought we had lost her for just for a moment."

The staff moved efficiently, clearing the mess with practiced urgency. Within an hour, the chaos had subsided. The room was cleaned, the linens changed, and fresh firelight flickered once again in the hearth. Kivani had been washed and dressed in a soft gown, and both babies were swaddled and nestled against her as she reclined on the bed, Oren at her side.

"Two babies in one day," Oren murmured, bending to kiss his wife's temple.

"Two babies in two days," a nearby attendant corrected, entering with a tray of warm food.

"Wut?" Kivani arched a weary brow.

The woman chuckled as she crossed the room and threw open the balcony doors. A burst of cool morning air flowed in, fragrant with the scent of snow and cedar. Outside, the first colors of dawn painted the horizon with streaks of lavender and gold.

"One was born yesterday," the woman explained. "The other today. The sun is already rising, my lady." She gestured toward the streaked sky and then checked Kivani's forehead, her touch gentle. "Have you chosen names?"

Oren turned, his face shining with pride. "Isrend Thaloren, for the boy."

"And Ismaara Nyssira, for the girl," Kivani added, her voice soft with sleep.

The names settled into the room like blessings. Kivani pulled the bundles closer to her chest, her eyes drifting between their tiny faces. The warmth of them, the wriggling life in her arms, made the weight of the night feel worth it.

Then came a sudden knock, sharp and urgent. Everyone was startled. Oren stood up instantly, heading toward the door just as it flung open. Nyssira rushed inside, panting, with her eyes wide and full of panic.

"Your father, you must come at once." Nyssira seized her son's hand, urgency lacing her voice as she pulled him from the room.

They sprinted down the corridor together, the chill of the glass hall and the morning light chasing them. They reached the royal chambers, the doors swinging open to reveal a familiar, elegant space.

Like the rest of the palace, the room was round and regal. The large circular bed stood in the center, framed by long curtains that flowed down from its tall posts. A fireplace crackled steadily, warming the room, and a balcony extended outward, offering a sweeping view of the snowy city below. Above them, the domed ceiling of clear glass shimmered with the fading stars, still visible in the early light. A writing desk sat beneath the curve of the wall, letters and books scattered across its surface. His father had been working at it moments before.

But Oren's eyes did not linger long on the furnishings. His gaze landed on an odd sight where two legs with feet were planted on the floor. He watched the toes flexing and curling as if rediscovering their purpose. Slowly, his eyes rose to his father, King Thaloren, standing upright. His posture was strong, and his face was wide-eyed with a mix of disbelief and wonder.

"Father?" Oren whispered, the word fragile in his throat. It did not feel real. None of it did.

Thaloren turned to him, his hand reaching out. Nyssira rushed forward to steady her husband, her arms supporting him as he took a shaky step. But it held. He held. The King of Glacia stood tall once more, restored to his full height. His glass prosthetics lay forgotten on the floor, reflections of a pain that had haunted him for too long.

"My legs," Thaloren breathed, looking down at them as if they belonged to someone else. "They are healed." His voice was hoarse with awe. "The healers said it was impossible. That my nerves were scorched, the flesh too far gone. How am I standing? How is this possible?"

Oren's heart pounded in his chest. His thoughts spun wildly. Then, his eyes settled on the desk. A simple envelope knife rested on it, its silver blade catching a flicker of light. He crossed the room without a word, picked it up, and drew the sharp edge across his palm. A crimson line appeared immediately. Blood welled up to the surface, then retreated. The skin healed before his eyes, and the pain vanished. Even the memory of it slipped away like fog. He looked at his hand, whole again. Untouched.

From the balcony, cheers and shouts erupted in a symphony of happiness as the town below started to celebrate. A sound that had not been heard in quite a long time.

Orentheon thought of his wife, how hours earlier she had been on the verge of boarding the boat to Arvayn's kingdom, the home of the god of death. Then he remembered the words the attendant spoke, *a miracle*. He turned back to his parents, realization spreading across his face like a rising sun.

"It is the Day of Turning," Oren said quietly. He stepped to his father and gently eased his weight from Nyssira's arms. "And your granddaughter is a Freyla."

Chapter Fourteen

Over the years, Glacia had changed just as much as the royal children. A decade had flown by in the blink of an eye. The kingdom, located in the heart of Glacia's largest city, Iskaroth, had become a haven for wayward Echoes. Those who once believed themselves lost, cursed, or without purpose now had a place to call home.

Kivani welcomed each one with open arms alongside Sylvie and Rhez. She helped them find their strengths, guiding them to understand what it meant to be part of something greater. Their powers were no longer seen as burdens to hide but as gifts to be proud of. This lesson was not just for the newcomers; it was for Sylvie as well.

Under Kivani's mentorship, she learned to understand the nature of water, the rhythm of tides, and the steady flow of healing. She realized her power belonged to her alone and should never again be used as a tool by others. Over time, she and Poppy became part of the royal household in all but name. They were invited to every celebration, treated as family, and even welcomed into the king's study while Orentheon and the master architect drafted plans for a new settlement on Verdathos, a permanent home for Echoes still cast out for being different.

Sylvie often watched her younger sister, envious that the life Poppy once dreamed of had slowly become reality. She remembered the time when the two of them first laid eyes on the ice-covered lands, stepping off the ship onto Glacia's frozen docks. The dry air had stung their cheeks, the cold instantly biting into the bone. Guards shouted orders as they herded students and disciples into the southern halls. Blankets were handed out. Bowls of food passed between the starved crowds. Fear hung heavy in the air. Yet even then, Poppy looked around in wonder. A girl of ten, in awe of being inside a real castle.

Now, that same girl hunched over the King's desk, a quill in hand, furiously sketching ideas into the architect's blueprints. The architect wore a comically sour expression, but he let her work without interruption. Sylvie could not help but smile.

Poppy had grown into a bright, determined woman, praised for her efforts to help others despite still being so young herself. She transformed a nursery outside the castle walls into a shining sanctuary. A structure of glass and crystal, inspired by the old nursery churches of her childhood. Children without families found refuge there, just as she once did. They learned not only letters and numbers but also trades and histories from all nine continents, preparing them for futures they never dared to hope for.

In many ways, Poppy was Sylvie's mirror image. Their long blonde curls and sky-colored eyes reflected one another. The only difference was that Poppy carried joy like sunlight, while Sylvie, no matter how much time passed, still carried guilt like a shadow.

Just then, the study door burst open. Two ten-year-olds dashed into the room, arms outstretched like wings, voices rising in high-pitched bird calls as they circled the desk. Ten years had disappeared in a flash. Ten years of healing. Ten years of rebuilding, and yet there was still no sign of Vallorith. Still no key to free the prisoners inside the mirrors. Orentheon dove for his children, catching both in his arms. They giggled as he spun them around before setting them down again, their flapping arms undeterred.

"Father, play with us!" Isrend declared, voice demanding with boyish urgency. "It has been ages!"

Oren ran a hand through the boy's tight curls. Isrend's mismatched eyes, one blue and one green, pleaded for attention.

"We must finish the plans first, then I will," Oren said, ruffling his son's hair before gently steering him out of the room.

Ismaara lingered, twisting a lock of her hair around one finger. "Can Poppy come and play?"

At that, Poppy's head snapped up, her smile immediate and infectious. She shoved the architect's quill into his hand, practically leaping from her seat. "I sure can!" she cried, already crouching like a hunter on the prowl. "And I am starving for two little mice for my supper. Mwahaha!"

She let out a ridiculous, crazed laugh and bounded after the twins, her body curling like a cat about to pounce. Their shrieks of delight and echoing laughter spilled down the corridor, trailing sunlight in their wake. The room, once warm with playfulness, fell quiet.

Sylvie looked up to find Kivani and Orentheon watching her, both serious, their smiles faded. Even the architect had gone still, his quill suspended over his scrolls. The change in atmosphere hit Sylvie like a draft through an open window. Her heart skipped.

"What is it?" she asked, rising slowly. "Has something happened?"

The architect stood abruptly, clutching his papers as if he had only just remembered he had legs. "I will work more on these, my lord," he said, his words rushed. "I should have the final draft by tomorrow."

"Thank you, Brenvek," Orentheon replied distantly.

The man gave a small bow and slipped out of the room. The king turned to Sylvie, his eyes tired yet full of something else: hope, maybe, or pride.

"The new sanctuary on Verdathos can be finished within the year. Brenvek has done the calculations. We have the builders. The Darra and Thorns trained here are ready." Thaloren rubbed his eyes, his body strained from sleepless nights. "This dream started with you and your sister arriving here, Sylvie. And we want you to lead it."

Sylvie blinked. "Me?"

Kivani stepped beside her, taking Sylvie's cold hands in her warm ones. "We want you to run the sanctuary. To be the first face struggling Echoes see. To show dem dat dey can belong somewhere. You and Poppy have grown so much over the years; it is only right dat someone from both worlds, someone who truly knows wut it is like to be lost, guides them." Tears brimmed in Kivani's eyes even as she smiled.

Sylvie glanced between them. They were all smiling now, encouragingly, but the weight of it all pressed into her chest. She wanted to say yes. She wanted to leap forward, accept the role, and *build something* of her own. But a flash of her sister's face stopped her. The girl she had raised and protected. The girl who had become her entire world.

Her voice trembled. "And Poppy?" She looked at Kivani, eyes wide. "And you? All of you?" She swallowed the rising knot of emotion. "This role is important. Surely someone else is better suited?"

It was Oren who answered now. "Kivani will go with you to Verdathos and stay six months, at least. Prince Malekai of Aetheria is sending his Zephs to assist with construction. They will arrive later today, so you will have time to meet." His eyes sparkled with a boyish excitement. "And as for Poppy, well, you saw her with the plans. She has already designed her own nursery on the new grounds. She is eager to follow if you accept."

Kivani rested her hand gently on Sylvie's shoulder, her voice low and steady. "Dere is no one better, Sylv. You gave so much to ya sista. To de Echoes. To dis family. Dis is your time now."

Sylvie turned to her friends and family, not by blood but by every other bond that mattered. "The twins?" Her voice cracked. "You?" A sob escaped before she could stop it. "You will be there too?"

Tears streamed freely now, and Kivani pulled her into a tight, soul-mending hug. "We will be there," she whispered fiercely. "You cannot get rid of me dat easily, sista."

The air in the room grew thick, emotions pulling tight around Sylvie's chest. She felt torn in two. She wanted to go. Verdathos still lived inside her bones, the warmth of its sun, the hush of its forests, the green that made her feel alive. She longed for that place. But the names of her old friends echoed louder. Finn. Freya. Wynna. Milo. Slek. The way things were before Kallemena came to the Axis. Before everything broke. That chapter was closed now, but her heart had not turned the page.

"What about the search for the mad priest?" she asked, her voice low. "What about freeing the others?"

Oren cleared his throat. "We have received word. Zepher was spotted in Morbessa." He glanced at his father. "I am to leave at first light."

All eyes drifted to the silver chest, unmoving in the corner of the study. It had remained untouched since Brother Rhez was caught trying to sneak it from the continent. The metal was still immaculate, scrollwork delicate, corners unblemished, time unable to dull its purpose. Inside it, the mirrors. And within them, the souls.

"We want you to take them." King Thaloren's voice brought her back. "We believe they will be safer in Verdathos. With someone like you. Someone who knew them and still cares."

"With the exception of Kallemena, of course." Queen Nyssira had entered without a sound, her presence ghostlike as she drifted to the chest. Her bony fingers lifted the lid with reverence. She reached in and pulled out one of the mirrors. The glass caught her reflection, soft and silver, worn by memory. "My daughter stays here," she said softly.

"Mother," Oren's tone tried for patience but landed closer to irritation. "She needs to be with the others. When we find Vallorith, it will be easier to release them together."

Nyssira turned sharply, her eyes flashing. "Do not speak that name to me." She spat on the floor, her hands clutched tightly around the cold edge of the mirror. "My daughter stays here. With me."

Silence fell once more. No one argued. They all knew it would be of no use. Nyssira's decline had not been sudden. The early years after Kallemena's imprisonment had been the hardest, but the birth of her grandchildren had offered temporary joy. A distraction. Still, as the twins grew, so too did her grief. She remembered the little girl with raven-black hair, twirling barefoot across the ballroom, humming lullabies into her ear, falling asleep on her shoulder. That child was frozen in glass now, forever unreachable.

Even Kivani's pregnancy, so full of hope, had brought an ache. Would she ever see her own daughter marry? Hold a child of her own? Nyssira held the mirror close as she turned and left the room. Her long white hair trailed behind her like silk unraveling.

By nightfall, the castle was alive with energy. The announcement of the new Sanctuary had spread quickly, and news that Sylvie and Poppy would be at its helm was met with celebration. Laughter echoed down the halls, and crates were already being packed for departure.

"I hear Malekai is quite handsome," Poppy said, pushing with all her weight on the lid of an overstuffed trunk. "And he is not much," she gritted her teeth, repositioning herself until she sat on top of it, "older than you."

The latch finally clicked shut with a triumphant snap.

Sylvie arched an eyebrow. "A prince, Poppy?" She folded another dress into her own trunk with precise movements. "I am not interested, but thank you for your concern."

Poppy's shoulders slumped at the rebuff. Her matchmaking attempts had become routine: first the stable hand, then a string of guards, and now royalty.

Sylvie sighed, guilt twisting in her gut. "How about you find a man for yourself?" she said, instantly regretting her words. The truth was, she did not want Poppy to grow up, leave, marry, or dream of anything without her. She wanted her sister beside her, selfishly, forever.

Poppy's face slowly curled into a smile, her cheeks flushed with a blush as she darted toward her sister and pulled her onto the bed. They plopped onto the soft blankets, the cool air swirling around them while the scent of snow and cedar filled the room. "I have found someone," Poppy whispered, grinning.

"What?" Sylvie's heart skipped a beat. "Who?" She slapped her hand to her forehead. "Please do not tell me it is the guard who calls you Puff Ball?"

Poppy wrinkled her nose. "Eww, no! Loro is like a brother to me," she said, nudging her sister's arm.

"Then who?" Sylvie's stomach fluttered, her pulse thudding with anticipation.

"Brenvek," Poppy said, the name rolling off her tongue like a guilty pleasure.

"The architect?" Sylvie sat upright, bracing for a blow that never came. Relief softened her features. "Oh, he is actually quite good-looking. And very respectable." She remembered that morning, Brenvek's thick black hair tied in a topknot, his Glacian features sharp and statuesque. He towered over Poppy, yet the two looked like they belonged together. Their pale complexions and symmetrical faces made them each striking. "I approve."

Poppy gave a wry laugh. "*You* approve? Did I need your permission?"

Sylvie winced slightly, guilt creeping in. The truth was that part of her approval stemmed from knowing Brenvek would be joining them in Verdathos. If Poppy found purpose there, and this man fell just as hard for her sister, then they would both stay. The thoughts of her sister moving away and leaving her alone disappeared. "No, but as the older sister, I feel like I am entitled to give a blessing or something."

Before Poppy could reply, a token knock sounded, barely a warning, before Ismaara burst through the door. Her dress was dripping all over the floor, and her lips were quivering, almost blue.

"Ismaara!" Poppy cried, springing to the child's side and wrapping her arms around her.

Sylvie hurried over, yanking the comforter from the bed and wrapping it snugly around the shivering girl. Tears streamed down Ismaara's cheeks as distant bells tolled, the harbor's signal of arriving ships.

"I-Isrrennd," Her teeth chattered. "He pushed me into the f-fountain. We were going to see the sh-ships, but I was f-faster, so he pushed m-me."

"Well, *that* was rude of him," Poppy huffed, putting on a comically stern face. "We will have to get him back."

"Poppy," Sylvie warned, already reaching for the silver bell. "Let us not encourage revenge."

An attendant appeared in the doorway before Sylvie even finished speaking. One glance at the soaked princess was all it took for her to bark a flurry of orders in the Glacian language. Moments later, steaming water and fresh garments were being brought in. Within minutes, Ismaara was soaking in a hot bath, her color returning. Poppy sat on a stool beside her, gently brushing out her tangled curls.

Sylvie, meanwhile, dressed in the only gown she had not yet packed, a soft pink dress with flowing sashes of yellow and orange. A gift from Kivani during their visit to Thalasson. The memory warmed her: hot sand beneath her feet, the taste of salt in the air, the fragrance of exotic blooms and tropical trees.

Outside the room, the hall buzzed with activity. Attendants hurried to complete their tasks so they too could catch a glimpse of the arriving visitors, especially the notorious Prince Malekai.

Down at the docks, the long, slender ships eased through the water with practiced grace. Their silent approach mirrored the fall of dusk. The Zephs, ever efficient, loosened the sails' grip on the wind until the vessels coasted effortlessly into place. Five ships had crossed the sea, sleek and empty, ready to carry refugees to their new home. The small crew disembarked, exchanging pleasantries with the awaiting Glacian guards. Word of Kalyra's transformation had preceded them, and its many changes over the past decade sparked wide-eyed reactions.

"Prince Orentheon!" a voice boomed from the ship as the last figure stepped onto the frozen ground. "You have grown old, my friend." Malekai's grin was unmistakable as he strode toward the prince, his sea-worn face sharp and weathered, though still youthful despite nearing forty.

Oren smirked and delivered a friendly jab to Malekai's arm, still as fit and lively as ever. Malekai winced, rubbing the spot, but his smile only grew wider. The two men hugged like brothers reunited after years apart.

"You must be starving after such a journey," Oren said, gesturing toward the looming castle. "Food and ale await. Come, we have much to discuss."

Malekai chuckled knowingly. "I have missed Glacian ale," he said, the thought already warming his chest.

Inside the castle, a grand table stretched the length of the hall, piled high with meats, roasted vegetables, fruit, and steaming loaves of bread. The aroma alone made Malekai's crew practically sink to their knees in gratitude. Oren and Malekai took their seats near the head of the table, deep in conversation. They discussed the lengthy, bitter hunt for Vallorith, the dead ends, and the disappointments. They talked about how the years had changed them. Malekai, ever faithful, still clung to the promise he made long ago.

Proudly, Oren introduced his wife and children. Isrend, his eager, bright-eyed son, recited everything he had learned about Kalyra. The continent Malekai still ruled in waiting, a kingdom held in trust until its true heir returned. Guests and attendants came and went, drawn in by Malekai's stories. He spoke of the beasts he had hunted in his youth, and of the fierce desert tribes of Scorvaan; of their bloodlust, their conquests.

"They would give Father a run for the hills," he laughed, gulping down a generous mouthful of the rich Glacian ale. As his cup lowered, his gaze snagged on a woman across the room.

She was delicately thin, with golden curls flowing over her shoulders. Her eyes mirrored the pale blue of a summer sky, but she was not looking at him. She stood beside Kivani and the Queen, engaged in conversation, her attention completely away from him. Oren's children tugged playfully at the orange and yellow sashes around her dress, yet she did not glance his way.

Malekai blinked. "Who is that?"

Oren turned, following his gaze.

"And why," Malekai added, baffled, "does she not care for my tales?"

The question slipped out before he realized how absurd it sounded. Women always noticed him, the daring and handsome prince from across the sea. But this one, this beautiful maiden, had not even given him a glance.

"Sylvie Havander," Oren answered, setting down his cup. He raised a brow at the look on Malekai's face. "She will be overseeing Verdathos. The queen there in all ways but the title."

Malekai did not blink. "Is she married? Is that why she does not take notice?"

Oren laughed as he stood, a genuine, much-needed smile softening the weight of his duties. "Come," he said, motioning for Malekai to follow, "let me introduce you."

Malekai rose instantly, smoothing his robes while trying to hide his eagerness.

The women did not notice them approach. Their laughter masked the quiet footfalls until Oren cleared his throat. "Excuse the most impolite interruption, dear wife," he said smoothly. "But I thought I would introduce—"

"Prince Malekai of Aetheria," the man finished the introduction himself, stepping forward with an exaggerated sweep of his arm. "Also, overseer of Kalyra." He stood tall and regal, his sun-bronzed skin glowing beneath the room's lights, black hair flowing past his shoulders. He smiled in anticipation, waiting for the admiration he was used to receiving. "I have heard all about the new Sanctuary," he added, gaze locked on Sylvie. "And how you are to be the queen in charge."

Sylvie coughed, the words catching her off guard. "No, not queen, I am not a queen. I will just be helping guide the lost." Her eyes flicked from Malekai to Oren, then to Kivani, a silent plea for rescue.

The prince gently took her hand and brushed his lips across her knuckles. "You could be a queen."

She jerked her hand back so quickly, one would have thought it was on fire. Her cheeks reddened as she struggled to find words. When her mind went blank, she quickly tucked a loose curl behind her ear. "I must finish packing." With a quick, awkward bow, she turned and darted out the doors.

Malekai stood in stunned silence. In all his years, no woman had ever run from him, at least, not seriously. He turned toward the doors she had disappeared through, his expression caught between confusion and something deeper. Was this the pain of heartache?

"She is not so easily impressed," Oren said, clapping him on the back. The jolt brought Malekai out of his daze.

"Yes, well," Malekai straightened, brushing invisible dust from his coat. "I shall have to be more," He paused, coming up empty. "Impressive."

In Sylvie's room, she paced. Never before had someone so boldly taken her hand, kissed it as if it meant something. Her heart still fluttered at the memory. The warmth of his skin, the intensity of his gaze, as if she were the only person in the room. A knock at the door startled her from her crazed thoughts, the guest a most welcome distraction. Before she could answer, Poppy burst in, a tray of food balanced in her hands.

"I grabbed you this," she said, setting it down on the small table beside the window. She snatched a cube of cheese for herself and grinned. "You left so fast, the poor prince looked like someone had knocked the wind out of him." She laughed through her bite.

Sylvie flushed, mortified by her reaction and by how childish she must have looked.

"I think you shocked the wits out of him," Poppy added, popping five more cubes of cheese into her mouth with a satisfied smile.

"Was that food not meant for me?" Sylvie placed her hands on her hips, feigning sternness.

Poppy shrugged innocently, then flopped onto the bed like she had as a child, sinking into the luxurious softness. "He looked upset that you left," she said, voice more serious now. "I think he likes you."

A flutter stirred in Sylvie's stomach, but she forced it away. "I do not care what he likes," she said, adjusting a hairpin. "I care about us starting fresh in Verdathos." She hesitated, then added softly, "Are you really coming with me? Giving up all of this?"

She gestured to the room, with its crystal ceilings, polished floors, and gentle elegance that surrounded them. The new sanctuary would not have such luxuries.

Poppy took in the room, her smile soft but sure. "I will miss it," she admitted. "But this was Kallemena's home. Not ours."

Sylvie looked at her, truly looked. Gone was the gap-toothed girl who dreamed of castles and tiaras. In her place was a woman with purpose. A woman who had chosen to step into something difficult, something unknown, because it mattered. Overcome, Sylvie rushed forward and pulled her into an embrace. Poppy hugged her back tightly.

Guilt swelled in Sylvie's chest. She remembered her younger self, the things she had said, the foolish, heartless words whispered to her friends. How she had once insisted she did not want to be burdened with her little sister. How she had thought Poppy would be better off serving in some noble's house. She could have kicked herself for ever believing that.

"This place was the best thing that ever happened to us," Sylvie whispered, clutching her tighter.

A soft knock interrupted them. The tall glass door creaked open, and Kivani stepped inside, holding another tray. Ismaara peeked in beside her, practically her mother's shadow.

"I was not sure if either of you had eaten," Kivani began, then stopped when she saw the tray on the table and the half-eaten food. She laughed. "Ah, I see I was not de only one with dat concern."

Ismaara darted in and leapt onto the bed just as Poppy had done moments before. The little girl tugged at her curls, wide-eyed. "Can you play with me?" she whispered, glancing at her mother and lowering her voice conspiratorially. "Before she makes me go to bed."

Poppy immediately growled, twisting her body as if it were transforming. "Oh no!" she cried. "I am turning into," She raised her arms like claws. "The bedtime monster!"

Ismaara let out a high-pitched giggle and rolled off the bed, dashing for the hallway with a shriek. Poppy gave chase, stomping and roaring behind her.

Kivani shook her head with a laugh, watching them go. "I will miss de bedtime help," she said fondly, then turned to Sylvie, who was idly picking at the remains of the food from the earlier tray. "Malekai seemed nice," Kivani added as she brought her own tray to the table and slid Poppy's aside to make room.

"I hear he tells great jokes. And Oren says he is an honorable man when he wants to be." Kivani's islander accent, once unfamiliar, had become something Sylvie found comforting. Even at its thickest, she understood every word.

"I do not have time for," Sylvie tugged at a curl. "Honorable men. I will be too busy setting up Verdathos. There is too much to do and not enough time."

Kivani reached over and gently pulled Sylvie into a one-armed hug. She had watched this woman grow during her years on Glacia, seen her shed the chains of the Axis's old teachings and step into her true self. Sylvie had found her voice, her strength, her purpose, and Kivani was proud of every part of who she had become.

"You are an incredible woman," she said softly, her gaze steady. "And I know you will do great dings on Verdathos." She hesitated, then added, "But you should let others get to know you. Let someone see what I see. De world will not stop turning just because you take a breath."

Sylvie felt something crack open inside her, some tight place in her chest that she had been holding shut for too long. She pulled Kivani close and hugged her tight, blinking hard against the sudden sting behind her eyes. When Kivani finally slipped out of the room, the silence that followed was thick and still. Sylvie sat at the edge of the bed, moving food around the tray without really seeing it. Her appetite had vanished, replaced by a fluttering in her stomach she could not quite name.

She rubbed her knuckles, the very ones Malekai had kissed, and sighed. Then, without thinking, she stood and gave a small, spinning twirl. Her dress fanned out around her as she let the warmth of that earlier moment wash over her; the silly, girlish thrill of catching someone's attention. It was foolish, she told herself. Childish. And yet, it felt good to feel something again. She twirled once more, the memory of his gaze still lingering on her skin.

Then her eyes caught on the mirror above the mantle. She froze. The familiar shape of it, the way it had sat there for ten long years, undisturbed. Her breath hitched in her throat. Her fingers dropped to her sides. Her first love was still trapped inside.

Chapter Fifteen

The relocation of all the refugees would take place over a period of three years. First, the builders and staff would sail across the ocean to the long-abandoned continent of Verdathos. There, they would lay the foundations, constructing homes, roads, and gardens from the overgrowth and ruin. Next would come the adults, tasked with establishing schools and shops to support a thriving town. Finally, the orphaned children would be brought over to be raised with dignity, taught with compassion, and offered a life full of possibilities.

It would be a life worth living, a future no one would be denied. Glacia had done its best to accommodate the influx of refugees. But after so many years, the continent had reached its limits. There was no more room.

Sylvie stood at the ship's railing, her eyes scanning the shoreline ahead. Crumbling towers leaned with time's weight, their stone walls blanketed in ivy. Trees pressed forward like curious onlookers, claiming the broken docks. If not for the retaining wall and the battered staircase still barely visible, she would not have recognized the place at all.

A hand touched her arm. Kivani stood beside her, lips set in a tight line as she stared at the ruined sanctuary. "It will be hard work," she murmured, her voice caught between hope and old resentment. A forced smile tugged at her lips. "But we will make it magnificent."

From the third Aetherian ship, six men stepped forward. Without a word, they lifted their hands and began to weave the air, their movements elegant and entwined like climbing vines. A rush of energy pulsed outward. The trees stirred, soil churned, and rocks shifted and sang.

Before the eyes of all who watched, the vegetation pulled back. Leaves unfurled and parted. Stones multiplied and restacked, forming a reinforced wall. Roots snaked over the water and thickened, interlocking to create a sprawling wharf. The stairs reformed beneath the years of abuse from the sea, leveled, smooth, and stripped of seaweed and barnacles.

The first phase had begun. Sylvie's heart beat with long-awaited provocation. Around her, the ships were fastening to the new docks. Excitement burst into the air as passengers spilled forth, some returning after years away, others setting foot on Verdathos for the very first time. But Sylvie could not move. Her boot hovered over the edge of the ship's ramp and stopped.

The memories hit her like crashing waves. This was where it had happened. Where war had shattered lives. Where her friends had been killed or trapped. Where people were torn from their futures simply for being born gifted. The weight of it crushed her. Then, a hand found hers. Warm and familiar. She looked down into Poppy's eyes, already brimming with unshed tears.

"Together?" her sister whispered.

Sylvie's heart clenched. She squeezed Poppy's hand back. "Together."

Step by step, they left the ship and descended the wooden ramp. The new dock held strong beneath their feet, its surface slick with sea spray. The summer sun beat down, the sky cloudless, the air thick with heat and the tang of briny water. Everything was growing here: plants, dreams, and even burdens. At the base of the reformed stairs, they paused.

Sylvie tilted her head back, staring at the height before them. It had not changed. The stone still towered above, just as it had when she stood here as a girl, just after her father died, clutching Poppy in her arms. She recalled the red and white robes of the disciples. Their smiles too wide and eager. Their voices sounded slimy as they said she was special. That she would make a difference. That she had to be strong.

She remembered how her arms had trembled as she handed her baby sister over. How quickly they had whisked Poppy away to the nursery, leaving Sylvie behind. She steadied her breath and placed one foot on the stone stairs.

"Unload the ships. Make stacks. Get the tents ready to be pitched," Malekai barked, his voice slicing through the air like a drawn blade. The crowd shifted to obey, and just like that, all attention turned elsewhere, leaving the sisters to their moment.

Sylvie glanced back. Malekai caught her eye. His expression softened, and she offered a small nod of thanks. The prince's dark gaze lingered on her, a quiet fondness there, unspoken but unmistakable.

Together, the sisters climbed. Behind them, crates were stacked and barrels rolled down the ramps. Kivani held the ocean calm for the Aetherian ships, her hands outstretched in quiet focus. The twins waited impatiently at the bow, their forms silhouetted against the sinking sun.

At the summit of the stairs, Sylvie and Poppy came to a halt. The sanctuary was a shadow of its former self. Twisted trees choked the paths. Thick vines curled around what remained of the blackened walls. The central structure had partially collapsed inward. Where once there had been obedience, now only wild animals claimed the grounds. The ruins stood still, hollow, watching them back.

"It looks so different," Poppy whispered, scanning the remnants for anything familiar.

Sylvie slipped an arm around her shoulders, a smile playing gently on her lips. "It will be different," she said. "We will make it different."

The sound of footsteps broke the moment. The rest of the team had begun the long trek up the stairs, hauling trunks, crates, and supplies vital to their mission. Brenvek appeared at the top, face flushed, sweat glistening down his neck. He dragged his trunk to the side and collapsed onto it, dramatically fanning himself. "Why are there so many stairs?" he groaned.

Poppy was at his side in an instant, teasing his mussed hair and laughing at his disheveled state. Sylvie watched the exchange, warmth rising in her chest at the sight of them. The careful touches, the shy grins, the way their affection lived in silence and glances. She turned away, embarrassed to have lingered too long on their moment. It reminded her too much of another. Of Slek.

She thought of their stolen touches in the halls, of how he had held her during the Axis attack. Of the kiss she had given him, soft and quick, before the world collapsed. Her cheeks flushed at the memory.

A voice pulled her back to the present. "What do you want done with these?" a man asked, balancing two barrels on his shoulders as if they were filled with air.

"Oh, um," she stammered.

"Make camp here," Malekai called out, pointing toward a relatively flat stretch of land. "The Thorns will clear it. Then we will start exploring the grounds."

Sylvie bowed slightly, grateful he had taken command. She watched as the crew slipped into a rhythm that felt almost instinctual. The Thorns worked in sync, clearing brush, gathering kindling, laying out equipment with silent precision.

By nightfall, the campsite had come to life. Canvas tents stood like soft-lit beacons, the fires between them casting a warm glow against the night's creeping darkness. The shelters, gifts from the Aetherian homeland, were made of sandy cloth, marked with swirling foreign symbols. Each held enough space for several beds and a small wash area.

Supplies had been neatly stacked in a ring around the camp, forming a makeshift wall to keep wandering feet from straying too far into the unknown. Verdathos was wild again. But now it would be reclaimed. Not through force but through hopes and ambitions. Sylvie sat by the fire, her eyes fixed on the black wall still standing beyond the tents. There, beneath years of grime, moss, and weathering, the golden sun of the Axis glinted faintly in the firelight. Once, she had gazed upon that symbol with awe, feeling a sense of purpose and belonging. Now all she felt was a bitter ache. Disdain for what it stood for. Grief for what it had cost.

"Is this spot taken?"

She flinched at the sudden voice, drawn from her spiraling thoughts. Malekai stood beside her, not in his usual royal robes, but dressed simply: loose pants, a soft tunic, his hair down, scented faintly of honey and sage.

"No," she mumbled, pulling her skirts closer around her legs.

He sat beside her, their shoulders not quite touching. Together, they stared at the golden sun on the wall, once a mark of order and salvation, now a relic of cruelty and control. Malekai's brow furrowed. His own memories stirred: visits from the high priest Vallorith to his homeland, Zephs brought in red robes to serve beneath his father's rule. He remembered the pride he once felt at the idea of ruling like King Khareph. That pride now felt like a bruise under his ribs.

"My men follow me now because they want to," he said quietly, more to himself than to Sylvie. "Not because they were forced to take an oath like before, when the mad priest controlled them." He let the thought linger, then added, "The fall of the Axis... may be the best thing that has ever happened to this world." His voice was taut and honest. A confession spoken aloud for the first time.

Sylvie looked at him, her gaze soft with curiosity and something deeper. Sadness, maybe. Confusion.

"How are you?" he asked gently. "Being back here after everything?"

Sylvie looked back at the sun on the wall. Her thoughts tangled like overgrown roots. "I thought I would be happy," she said, her voice barely above a whisper. "And I was, at first. But now?"

Her eyes wandered to the twins playing with food in the distance, Kivani and Poppy laughing with Brenvek as they marked where the nursery would go.

"So many memories. And yet they no longer feel like mine. It is like they belong to someone else." She turned back to him and found his gaze already there, tracing the lines of her face. She looked away quickly, warmth rising in her cheeks, silently praying the firelight hid the flush.

"You feel like you are watching your past from the outside?" he asked. "I know the feeling." He picked up a twig and snapped it absently. "I remember looking at Echoes the way my father did, like possessions. Tokens of power." He scoffed, tossing the twig into the flames. "We collected them. As if they were trophies."

The twig curled in the fire, blackening and crumbling into ash.

Sylvie watched the flames flicker. She thought of Slek, of how he had shielded them with nothing but his strength and will. Of his kindness, his resilience, even after years of silvervane dulling his magic. Would he have gone to Aetheria? To serve King Khareph and then the prince?

"You are changing that," she said softly. "I have heard what you are doing in Kalyra. Taking in Echoes the way Glacia did. Rescuing people from Scorvaan raids. Trading years of your life for a kingdom that was not even yours to start with." She turned to him again, and this time, he was smiling.

"It is honorable, yes?" he teased, as if trying to lift the heaviness between them.

She almost smiled back.

"You should visit," he added, looking out toward the dark horizon where the distant mountains slumbered. "When you are finished here.

I will show you the high cliffs where they say a dragon sleeps, and the lakes so clear you can see rainbow-scaled fish dancing in the depths." He said it as though the invitation was already accepted.

"I should get some sleep. Busy day tomorrow." Sylvie shifted, brushing off her skirt as she moved to stand.

Malekai rose instantly, offering his hand without hesitation. He lifted her as if she weighed nothing at all, his touch sending a shiver down her spine despite the warm summer air.

"Goodnight, Miss Sylvie," he said gently, and bowed his head to kiss the back of her hand. His eyes never left hers, even as she turned and stepped into her tent.

By morning, the camp was already alive with movement. The Thorns had cleared the brush and ivy from the sanctuary grounds. Their power turned over the soil, coaxing food-bearing plants to sprout in orderly rows, meant for both the people and the returning wildlife.

The Darra began work on Brenvek's blueprints, dismantling the old Axis structures that had long been swallowed by time. They conjured tools from light and energy, crafted ropes and pulleys, and took down the crumbling walls piece by piece until the land was reduced to rubble. Then the Zephs swept through, wind clearing the debris in great spirals until the land was smooth and clean, ready for rebuilding.

Talons drew water from the sea and filtered it until it ran clear and sweet. They would rely on this until the Thorns uncovered a freshwater spring to build a proper well. Every group had its role. Every hand had a task. They were building a future together.

The days grew shorter, the air crisper, and the leaves turned shades of fire and rust. Autumn crept into camp, unnoticed at first, until the birds began their migration and the animals rushed to store food for the coming snow. What began as a settlement became a community. Strangers became companions. Companions became something more.

Poppy and Brenvek married beneath a golden tree, her simple stone ring carved by one of Malekai's men. She wore it proudly, often waving it in Brenvek's face during arguments over the placement of nursery walls or kitchen doors. They teased and bickered, changing their minds daily, but always with laughter in their voices.

Six months had passed. Soon, Kivani and the twins would return to Glacia, sailing back with Malekai and his crew. And Sylvie would stay behind. She had grown fond of the prince. Their conversations had grown easier, filled with shared smiles and thoughtful silences. The boundary between friendship and something else had begun to blur. And yet every time she felt herself falling, guilt pulled her back.

Slek was still out there, somewhere, lost to time. Trapped behind mirrored glass. He should have been here, beside her, helping to lay these stones, sharing in the future they once imagined. Her grief for him had not faded. If anything, it had become sharper in the absence of news.

There had been no word of Vallorith or Zepher. No sign of the missing priest. No new knowledge on how to free the imprisoned. Orentheon's voyage to Morbessa had only brought more questions, more silence.

Then came winter. Snow drifted down in soft, heavy clumps, covering the half-built roads and unfinished fences in white. But the sanctuary itself was done. Everyone stood back as the final hinges on the grand oak doors were fixed in place. The building rose pale and proud before them: smooth grey walls trimmed with dark wood, elegant arches stretching into the sky like branches. It was part temple, part keep, a miniature castle crowned with a domed roof. And above the doors, where once the golden sun of the Axis had loomed, was a circular stained-glass window.

A tree. Its roots curled into the earth, its branches reached for the heavens, all contained within the symbol of a circle. The message was clear to all who looked upon it: life, death, rebirth. Change and return. Echoes and those who carried them were always welcome here. It was the vision of the goddess, now made real. A home for all who wandered.

"Goddess Danira would be proud," Poppy beamed, shaking her sister's shoulders with excitement.

Everyone had gathered inside. Despite the bite of winter clinging to the air, the sanctuary was filled with warmth and the sweet fragrance of fresh flowers. Vases along every windowsill overflowed with gardenias, a gift from a particular Thorn who adored them. Their delicate white petals softened the grey stone, transforming the space into something sacred.

It felt like walking into another world. A house for the gifted. A pillar of reform. A place for all to belong. The great hall branched out into two wings, one leading to the kitchens and dining area, the other to libraries and classrooms. The central chamber was circular, and at its heart stood an altar bathed in morning light. The statue of Danira, salvaged from the ruins, now rose proudly in the glow that filtered through the stained glass. Hues of green, blue, and orange painted the floor like scattered gemstones. Benches circled the altar, their placement mimicking the ripples of a drop in water. It was more than architecture; it was vision. A shared dream brought into being.

Poppy tugged at Sylvie's hand, grinning. "Come on. I want to show you something." She led her sister to a narrow door hidden behind a carved pillar. A winding staircase waited beyond.

"I do not remember any stairs in Brenvek's sketches," Sylvie said breathlessly as they climbed, her voice laced with suspicion.

Poppy only bounced ahead, smiling widely. "Maybe that is because I had him keep this part a secret."

At the top, she flung open the door, and Sylvie stopped in her tracks. It was a small sanctuary of its own. The walls were the same smooth grey stone, softened by winding vines and blossoms tucked into cracks and corners. Warm wood framed the tall windows, and above it all, a crystal sat in the center of the domed ceiling, scattering soft rainbows across the floor with every turn of sunlight.

A fire crackled in a modest hearth, lending warmth to the crisp, winter air. Shelves lined the walls, packed with old books; worn spines, weathered pages, the scent of earth and ink. A sturdy desk sat at the room's heart, a single candle burning beside a neat stack of notes. And there, mounted on the wall, were four silver mirrors.

Poppy stepped inside and ran her fingers along the books. "Brenvek and I thought you might need a place of your own. To think and rest." She plucked a worn volume from the shelf, its cracked leather cover embossed with the faded symbol of the golden sun. "He found this, too. It has drawings of the mirrors. Maybe it could help?"

Sylvie stared at the book, then at her sister. Emotion swelled in her chest and spilled down her cheeks. She pulled Poppy close, holding her tightly, her shoulders shaking with quiet sobs. "Thank you," she whispered. "Thank you."

By the time the last roof was shingled, spring had come to Verdathos. The sanctuary stood at the heart of a growing village. Neat houses curved around its base, with winding roads leading through forest paths toward a bustling market and a newly built blacksmith's forge. People had begun to arrive. One ship at a time. Young and old. Families and loners. Those with gifts and those with none, all in search of belonging. And at the center of it all stood Sylvie and Poppy. Side by side. Smiling, welcoming each new arrival like an old friend.

Kivani and the twins had sailed back to Glacia with Prince Malekai, who had promised, more than once, to return. Poppy teased Sylvie constantly, humming wedding marches under her breath whenever she caught her sister staring wistfully toward the docks. Before she left, Kivani had pulled Sylvie aside and told her gently, *"Do not wait for love. Live it. You only get one life."* And Sylvie, after years of carrying grief like a second skin, had finally begun to believe those words.

Chapter Sixteen

Snow may fall and stars may gleam. You were born of frost and dream. Raise your glass, for days of truth. Luvaren, dear soul, to you!

The glass-sculpted ballroom burst into applause and cheers as the twins blew out the candles on their birthday cake. Time had flown by, and their lanky limbs and awkward laughter had transformed into graceful movements and growing confidence.

Ismaara, now a reflection of her mother, had delicate, striking features. Her sandy, tightly coiled curls tumbled down her back, and her voice was as soft and lilting as a drifting snowflake. Isrend, tall and stoic, carried their father's stature. His hair matched his sister's in color but was cropped just above his ears. His broad shoulders and stiff posture gave him a soldier-like silhouette.

Although their personalities differed, their mismatched eyes reflected the same light. One of hope and the other a quiet restlessness beneath. They smiled and hugged, faces glowing with happiness. Eighteen was not just a birthday; it was the start of something new.

Kivani wrapped her arms around her children, love radiating from her like warmth on a winter day. "Your father will want to hear all about this when he returns." She cupped Ismaara's face with one hand

and Isrend's with the other, her voice thick with pride. "I am so proud of you both."

Isrend gently pulled away from her grasp, frustration simmering beneath his carefully composed face. Around him stood dozens who had sailed across the sea to witness this day, those who had left behind comfort, warmth, and time. Yet, his own father could not do the same. He turned toward the towering glass doors, catching a glimpse of his reflection in the polished surface. His proud mask slipped, just for a moment, revealing his disappointment. His face showed the weight behind his silence before he hid his emotions once more.

Without a word or glance back, he marched out of the ballroom. A hush fell over the celebration. Guests exchanged awkward glances, whispers spreading like frost in the corners of the room. Isrend's disappearances had become expected; he often slipped away from galas, ceremonies, and any moment meant to celebrate him. Never comfortable beneath the scrutiny of comparisons and expectations.

Then came a sharp, echoing clap throughout the crowded room. King Thaloren stepped into the center, a smile forced on his aging face. The murmurs fell silent instantly.

Thanks to the resident Darras, the ballroom had been brought to life. Silken banners in lavender and gold hung from the roof, while small twinkling stars illuminated the glass dome. The tables were lined with the same fabric, and at their center, small crystalline orbs floated. The room that would have normally been bathed in orange light from the sinking sun by now had been hazed to mimic the night's deep black sky. A deep abyss allowed the floating stars to do their job and cast soft glows throughout the room. The end result felt like an oasis in the frozen lands.

It looked just as Ismaara and Kivani had envisioned. Elegant and regal, a party fit for royalty. Fit for the Freyla who had been brought into the world eighteen years ago. Yet, the king standing at its center was no longer the man from that day.

The man immortalized in tales, a father to an Echo daughter, the man who brought down the Axis, the king whose glass-crafted legs had miraculously turned to flesh. Thaloren had become a faint shadow of his former self. His shoulders drooped, his skin grew pale, and his hands shook. The stories still told of him, but so did the whispers. They started when Vallorith disappeared. They grew louder when hope for Princess Kallemena faded into silence. They became unavoidable when Queen Nyssira left her place beside her husband, consumed by grief.

Eight years had passed, and still she remained in self-imposed exile, confined to her chambers. Her body withered from disuse, and her voice raw from prayers gone unanswered. Every day, she clung to the silver mirror that imprisoned her daughter. Every day, she begged for a glimpse, a whisper, a sign, just as the Zeph had once done. But unlike Sylvie, she was met with nothing.

Disappointment carved itself deeper and deeper into her until she was no longer a queen, but a shadow mourning through endless hours. Thaloren tried to comfort her. He reminded her of their son, their grandchildren, and everything she still had. But none of it reached her. Her grief was too loud, too heavy. And no amount of love or royal blood could free her from its grip.

Thaloren stood in the ballroom now, a fragment of the king he once was. A man worn by time and heartache. "Thank you all for coming," he said, his voice hoarse, age and wear tightening around each word. "We are humbled by the love, gratitude, and support you have shown the people of Glacia and all the Echoes who were freed so many years ago." He turned to Kivani and Ismaara, both smiling warmly from where they stood. "And now, you honor us again by being here on this day. The day, eighteen years ago, when my grandchildren were born. Happy birthday to Isrend and Ismaara."

The crowd erupted into a chant, voices repeating the birthday greeting over and over until laughter filled the air and the cake was cut and served. Guests took their slices with cheerful chatter.

Ismaara moved gracefully among them, offering thanks and kind smiles to each visitor, even as she slowly made her way toward the ballroom doors. Catching her mother's eye, she gave a subtle nod before quietly slipping from the room. Her heels clicked softly as she headed down the long corridor. She was bound for the highest spire in the castle, the glass observatory where the frozen tundra of Glacia stretched out in all directions, endless and glittering.

The climb was dangerous in heels and an elaborate gown, and she cursed her brother's poor choice of hiding spots. Just this once, could he not have gone to the gardens or his chambers? Somewhere she did not break a sweat to reach? With a huff, she pushed open the tall door. The hinges, as always, made no sound, crafted with such precision that even age could not rust them. The door gently tapped against the curved glass wall as she stepped inside.

Isrend sat cross-legged in the middle of the floor, surrounded by open books. Scrolls and tomes spilled from nearby trunks and shelves, all filled with ancient knowledge. Ivy curled along the glass walls and ceiling, softening the chill with a hint of green and gold. The vines gave the room a warmth it should not have possessed, one that tried to disguise the sorrow in the prince's eyes.

Ismaara stomped around the room, her skirts rustling as she came to stand in front of him. Her shoe tapped rhythmically against the thick, woven rug. Isrend did not look up, his eyes scanning lines of old script, lost in whatever world the pages offered. Ismaara considered sinking to the floor herself, just to escape the weight of her dress, but she thought better of it; standing again would be an ordeal, and the fabric would wrinkle beyond repair.

"You are being incredibly rude to our guests, brother," she said at last, arms folded tightly across her bodice.

No response.

Her teeth clenched. "Are you listening? Father is going to lose it when he hears about this."

The book snapped shut with a thud. Isrend stood abruptly, his jaw tight and face flushed. "Father would have to be here in order to hear of it." He crossed the room in three strides, stopping at the window. Below, a ship with white sails had just docked, its slender hull rocking gently in the icy harbor. "And the guests," he added, his voice neutral again, "are not here for me. They came for you, dear sister. The miraculous Echo who can cure their every wound." He turned to her, and for a breath, Ismaara did not respond.

Her expression softened, just a little, and she gave him a look full of performative sweetness. Her tone, when it came, was one she reserved for political lies. "They are here for you as well, dear brother," she said, eyes wide with false innocence. "The whole party has practically stopped in your absence."

Isrend gave a slow nod, no longer the gullible boy who once believed in comforting words. The mask had fallen. He gestured toward the window again. The familiar ship had begun to lower its ramp. Crew members were already unloading crates and trunks. Passengers started to disembark. "Aunt Sylvie has arrived."

The years had not been kind to the twin born without powers. Each passing season reminded Isrend just how different his path would be from his sister's. The world had changed. Where once Echoes were bound by laws and servitude, they now walked freely, sometimes recklessly. Many made their way to Verdathos, settling in or near the sanctuary. But not all. Some demanded crowns. Others carved out their own kingdoms, leaving destruction in their wake. Every time Orentheon led the cavalry to hunt them down, he returned changed, harsher, more rigid, with expectations sharpened like a blade.

"You are the future of this kingdom," he would bark, voice full of unyielding command. "Act your worth!"

Isrend trained in diplomacy and war, a prince was expected to rule with dignity and strength, but Ismaara basked in praise. Their father admired her endlessly, her powers, her compassion, her growing abilities. She was a Freyla born of royal blood. A daughter whose birth, alongside her brother's, marked the start of new ways. But only one of them held the power that people wanted to see. Their birthdays were not about a pair of twins born to the crown; they were about her.

Ismaara raced through the halls, bells tolling overhead like jubilant thunder as she burst from the castle's core and down the frosted steps. The docks below were empty of celebration; all the guests had gathered inside to enjoy the warmth and merriment. The ship's ramp had been lowered. Poppy carefully eased down, holding a squirming baby in her arms, with two children toddling behind. Ismaara let out a joyful shriek, her hands flying to her mouth as her heart leapt.

She had not seen Poppy in years, and now her childhood friend was a mother. She hurried up the ramp without hesitation, eyes filling with emotion. The baby's cheeks were pink and flushed from the cold, a tiny cry slipping from its lips.

"Oh my goodness." Ismaara wrapped her arms around Poppy, memories flooding her like a tidal wave, running through halls, giggling until breathless, while Poppy chased her with mock scoldings. "And who is this?" she asked, leaning close to the bundled infant.

Poppy gently passed the baby into her arms. "This is Victor." Her smile was full of pride and warmth. "And these two," she said, scooping up the boys on each side, "are Julian and Bren." Their tiny feet swung freely, and they offered shy, gap-toothed grins.

"Poppy, I told you not to go down the ramp alone with the children," A voice cut through the air, nervous and brisk. "Ismaara?" Sylvie stopped mid-scold, her eyes lighting up. She dropped her bags without care and rushed forward, weaving past the children to throw her arms around the princess. "Oh, it has been so long! And you have grown so tall!" She pulled back, hands still on Ismaara's shoulders, her face beaming before her gaze darted anxiously toward the harbor. "Where is your mother?"

Ismaara nodded toward the towering castle. "Inside with Grandfather, doing her best to entertain everyone until the dancing starts."

Sylvie appeared older now. Her hair, once a rich gold, had started to fade into wisps of silver, neatly tucked into a bun. Worry still clung to her eyes like ghosts from the past. Her youthful face had softened into lines drawn by time. Poppy, although nearly unchanged, showed the grace of motherhood. Her hair had loosened its curl slightly, gently tugged by the breeze.

"Well," Sylvie said briskly, rubbing her arms, "let us not stand out here too long. I forgot just how cold it is in Glacia." She ushered them all down the ramp and toward the castle as the ship's crew continued unloading their belongings. "And happy eighteenth birthday, Ismaara," she added, glancing back with a smile.

Kivani lit up the moment she saw Sylvie enter the ballroom. She pushed eagerly through the crowd, her delighted squeals almost drowned out by the bright sounds of the orchestra. The music filled the room, lifting everyone's spirits. Some guests twirled across the floor, while others stumbled in mid-dance, sloshing ale from delicate glass mugs. When Kivani reached her friends, her eyes immediately went to the bundled infant in Poppy's arms. For a moment, joy shone from her face in pure, unfiltered happiness.

"You have become a mother?" Kivani's voice was a mix of shock and awe as she took in the sight of the toddlers clinging to Poppy's sides. "Three times over. *Luvaren*, Poppy!" She gathered the baby into her arms, holding him close, the scent of the icy sea still lingering on his skin.

Her gaze shifted to Sylvie. Her dearest friend, aging gracefully, the years fleeting yet gentle. "Malekai is with Oren," she said softly, rocking the infant as he let out a tiny yawn. "They are hunting the rogue Echoes causing trouble in my homeland." She looked down at the sleeping baby, surprised he could rest amid the noise. "He should return in a few days." She winked at Sylvie, whose correspondence with the prince of Aetheria had become something of a well-known secret.

"Friends, Kivani," Sylvie replied quickly, trying and failing to hide the warmth rising in her cheeks. "We are just good friends, like you and me."

Just then, Victor let out a piercing cry, twisting in Kivani's arms, eyes wide with panic as he searched for his mother. Poppy was at her side instantly, cradling her son close and rushing toward the doors in need of a quieter space. Her other children followed like ducklings.

Kivani hugged Sylvie tightly, the swell of reunion catching in her chest. "I have missed you both so much," she whispered, brushing a tear from her cheek. "It has been too hard to leave. With Nyssira's health fading and Oren always gone. Thaloren needed me here." She paused, wiping away another tear. Her voice dropped low. "But that will soon change."

Sylvie gave her a curious look, but before she could ask, the room erupted into applause. Isrend and Ismaara had taken the center of the ballroom. The guests parted respectfully, forming a wide circle around them. It was time for the ceremonial dance. The moment when parents danced with their children.

Kivani stepped forward to take Isrend's hand, adjusting her gown with practiced grace. King Thaloren appeared opposite them, bowing low before Ismaara. The musicians began a soft, elegant tune, their crystalline instruments humming with beauty and magic.

Kivani smiled as Isrend led her into the first steps of the dance. "Why do you always look so glum, my son?" she asked with teasing warmth, her breath touched with wine. "Is the life of a prince truly so miserable?"

Isrend did not laugh. He did not even smile. She asked him this every year. And every year, he answered the same. "The life of a prince is easy," he said. "The life of a son is hard."

Before she could reply, the ballroom doors slammed open with a thunderous bang. The music immediately stopped. Guests turned as one. A man stood framed in the doorway, sun-worn and wind-tossed from days at sea, but proud and smiling, nonetheless.

"Father!" Ismaara cried, her ocean-blue dress trailing like a wave as she rushed to greet him.

Kivani released Isrend's hand and quickly crossed the room, wrapping her arms around her husband and kissing him without hesitation in front of the gathered guests. The hall filled with gasps, cheers, and whispered greetings. The heir to the throne had returned. All eyes were on them. No one noticed the boy still standing at the center of the dance floor. No one noticed the twin who was not embraced. Not greeted. Not celebrated.

Isrend stood motionless, eyes fixed on the sea-stained man who had never looked at him the way he looked at Ismaara. A thousand moments surged through him, nights spent alone with books, maps of the nine continents memorized by candlelight, achievements unrecognized, devotion unrewarded. He was the twin with no gifts, the son who never seemed to get it right. The child too ordinary, too normal, too strange to be loved the way she was. He clenched his fists, and without a word, he turned and walked out of the ballroom. Tonight, the fantasies that had haunted him since childhood were no longer just dreams. They were about to become reality.

Sylvie watched the family embrace, her gaze flicking just in time to see Isrend slip away through the crowd. She moved instinctively, weaving past dancing nobles and servants with trays, her pace quicker than her body liked. "Isrend," she called, breath already catching in her chest.

He halted mid-step, posture straight and rigid, as though carved from ice. "Aunt Sylvie." His voice was calm but not unkind. "It is good to see you." He motioned loosely back toward the ballroom. "You should return to the festivities. You would not want to miss them."

"I am not your aunt." Her correction was gentle, not a rebuke, only truth. She would never take the place of her friend, the twins' true aunt, who had been lost to a mirror long ago. "What about you?" she pressed softly, one hand braced over her ribs, an ache blooming beneath. "Come back with me. I know I am not your family, but I would be honored to have a dance with you."

Her smile was soft and unwavering. The affection in her eyes was real. She remembered holding him moments after he was born, his tiny hands, his mismatched eyes. She had watched him grow up in the shadow of his sister, and her heart had broken a hundred quiet times for him.

Isrend's expression eased. Of everyone in his world, Sylvie had always seen him, not just the title, not the absence of power. She had seen him, and for that, he always admired her. She had never flaunted her Echo gift. She never used it for show. Even after abandoning the Axis, she carried its structure within her and used her gift only when it served others.

Isrend welcomed that. Envied it, even. He often wished he could have lived in the time of the Axis, training under the hand of a figure like Vallorith. A man who understood discipline and order. Who understood power.

"You will always be family to me," Isrend said softly. "Aunt Sylvie." Then his gaze shifted, and the smile on his face brightened with something sly and amused. "And I think that man would prefer the next dance."

Sylvie arched a brow and turned. Her breath froze in her already aching lungs. Malekai stood just down the hall, flowers in hand, his gaze fixed entirely on her.

"The boy is right," Malekai said, nodding once to Isrend with quiet gratitude. "I would be honored if you would share a dance with me, Sylvie."

The sound of her name on his tongue stirred butterflies in her stomach. The childish, ridiculous things she thought she had long outgrown, and yet there they were. "It would be my honor as well," she murmured.

Isrend stepped away, giving them space. He had no desire to overhear their sweet words or shared history. He made his way up the stairs, through winding halls and vaulted doors, until he reached the tallest spire of the castle. His place. His sanctuary. His fortress of solitude. The glass room welcomed him with silence, the world below muffled by thick panes and high walls. Here, no one demanded he smile. No one asked why he could not be more like his sister.

He moved to the bookshelf, a place ignored by others, and slid out his favorite volume. A thick, leather-bound text embossed with a golden sun. He had found it by accident, years ago, during a game of hide-and-seek with Poppy and his sister. He had been exploring the old halls of the sanctuary when he stumbled into a hidden study, Sylvie's study. He had marveled at the silver mirrors lining the walls, each one casting his reflection back at him: a boy with a green eye, a blue eye, and the world behind both.

Among the dust-covered books and parchment, something had called to him. The golden sun gleamed faintly beneath a stack of papers. He had pulled it free and read the title, *The Holy Text of the Axis*. And when he read it, he *believed*. The rules made sense. The structure gave meaning. Echoes were powerful, too powerful to roam unchecked. Without laws, without limits, they would only destroy. He pressed the worn cover against his chest, his smile now full and dangerous.

"Time to call on the mad priest," he whispered.

* * *

He waited until the sun dipped below the mountains, bleeding its final light across the snow-covered horizon. Tonight, the moon would not rise. Its silver glow hidden, swallowed by the world's turning. A moonless night. A night for secrets.

Isrend slipped a dark robe over his shoulders, its hood casting his face in shadow. He opened the tall window of the spire and leaned over the edge, icy wind nipping at his cheeks. Below, faintly lit by the castle lanterns, the frozen footholds he had carved weeks before still clung to the slick stone.

He took a deep breath and carefully lowered himself over the railing. His boot hit the first groove, and slowly he started descending. The book was pressed tightly underneath his tunic; a small knife hung from his belt. The climb was slow and tense, with each gust of wind threatening to knock him off balance. Every move felt risky. He slipped twice and nearly fell once. But at last, he reached the frozen earth below, just as the first snowflakes began to fall like soft white embers from the black sky.

Isrend kept to the shadows as he crept to the stables. He ducked into a stall, his cold fingers trembling as he harnessed his steed. Snow crunched beneath the horse's hooves as he led it past the gates, where the open tundra stretched wide and waiting. He climbed into the saddle, the robe fluttering around his boots.

"Ya!" he called, snapping the reins.

The horse bolted forward, hooves pounding across the white-covered land. Trees blurred past. Frozen geysers steamed quietly in the distance. The wind howled like a warning, but Isrend did not slow.

He was heading to the place he had discovered long ago. A place where the snow refused to fall. Where the ground had burned so hot it turned sand to glass, scorched into spirals and sigils. It was a place the heat of a Cairn had touched.

As they reached the edge of the dead zone, the horse slowed, snorting steam into the air. Isrend dismounted and trudged forward, the snow rising to his waist. His legs ached, soaked to the bone, but he pressed on through the sludge of snow and ice. At last, he stepped into the clearing.

Warmth licked at his boots. Here, the sand was bare, melted smooth, black, and glinting under the faint aurora above. He sat in the center, panting, letting the heat soak into his skin like the breath of a god.

He pulled the book from beneath his tunic and flipped through its yellowed pages, each one more fragile than the last. He stopped at the text he had spent half a year translating, each word once forgotten, now sacred.

Isrend set the book gently down and drew his knife. A hiss escaped through his teeth as he carved the symbol into his palm, an hourglass circled by time's endless loop. Blood welled and spilled into the hot sand, sizzling as it met the ancient glass.

He read the words again, just once, sealing them in his mind like a vow. Then he stood, blood dripping from his hand, and spoke with steady breath: "Valta shek, oruun nai. Velken da'sor ethra kai, brell tu'mar vi talorai."

Nothing. Only the low snort of his horse. The wind brushed against him like a ghost. His jaw clenched. He fell to his knees, trembling, furious. This was meant to work. It *had* to work. He slammed his bloody hands into the sand, crying out once more as the grains buried themselves deep into his palm. He yelled louder now, with every ounce of grief and want and buried shame in his soul: "Valta shek, oruun nai! Velken da'sor ethra kai, brell tu'mar vi talorai!"

The air stilled. Snow froze mid-fall. The ground began to tremble. A brilliant light cut across the clearing like fire drawn in runes, tracing the lines burned into the earth. It burned so bright that Isrend had to shield his eyes. Then, a pulse. A teeth-rattling hum. And finally, silence. He fell backward into the snow, blind and breathless.

The silence was too perfect. The kind of quiet that made the hairs on the back of his neck rise. It took long minutes before his sight began to return, outlines forming from the black. And there, at the center of the clearing, where the heat had once slept, now sat two objects: An hourglass, tall and thin, filled with red sand that stood still, and beside it, a **mirror**. Pure-black, silent and waiting.

Chapter Seventeen

Orentheon awoke to the soft, rhythmic snore of his wife. Kivani lay tangled in the sheets, her hair spread across the pillows like strands of ribbon in water. The blankets twisted around her slender body, holding onto the warmth of sleep. He smiled at the scene, tracing every detail of her with his eyes and storing the moment in his memory like a sacred vow.

He slipped from the bed, his body reluctant to leave the cradle of silken sheets and down-filled comfort. The floor was cool beneath his feet as he moved toward the balcony. Beyond it stretched the kingdom, one day his kingdom. He stood in quiet reflection, remembering when its borders were half their current span. When the weight of rule was still new, and the map had more blank space than claimed land.

Warm arms wrapped around his waist. Kivani pressed her face against his back, breathing him in with a sigh. "I missed your smell," she murmured, her accent husky from sleep. She nuzzled closer, her nose buried in the folds of his shirt.

Oren turned and pulled her into his embrace. Time had barely touched her. If anything, she had grown more radiant, her sleep-tousled hair falling in waves, the faint indentations of the blanket still marking her skin. He tipped her chin up and kissed her with slow reverence. The passion that had been held at bay while he was at sea finally came forward. "And I missed you," he whispered.

He scooped her up, laughter shared between them as he carried her back to the bed. There, they remained entangled in each other until the late morning sun streamed through the curtains. When Kivani finally drifted back to sleep, Oren slipped out quietly, careful not to disturb her.

In the hallway, attendants were busy with their daily tasks. Changing the linens, sweeping dust from corners, and tying back the heavy fabric curtains to let in more light. The castle stirred with motion, yet one sound cut through it all: the muffled cries of his mother.

He paused outside the royal chambers, heart tight, every instinct pulling him toward her. But he did not enter. He could not. Her mind was lost to time now, her cries repeating the same haunting plea.

"Bring her back. Bring my daughter back." She cried.

Nyssira had not recognized him or anyone in months. With a long, heavy sigh, he reeled back his hand that had moved to the door's handle on instinct and pressed on. He made his way to his father's study, where the old king sat hunched over a thick stack of parchment. Thaloren did not look up, his eyes scanning the reports his son had written about the rogue groups of Echoes.

"Five Talons and one Darra," the king said, raising a brow. "Tough work. I see the disbanding was peaceful, though."

Oren nodded once.

Thaloren looked at him closely, truly looked, and the weight of years settled on his face. "I am proud of you, son."

The words landed like a knife. Oren inclined his head in thanks, though the praise accosted him. "Still no sign of Vallorith or his hound," he murmured. His gaze dropped to the floor. "I heard Mother earlier. Is she still?"

Thaloren nodded solemnly. "Worse every day. The healers do not offer much hope."

Oren scrubbed a hand down his face, weariness in every motion. "Has Ismaara tried to help? If not, I can find her now."

"She has tried," Thaloren interrupted gently, raising a hand. "She says your mother's suffering is not something she can heal. It is grief. And even a Freyla's touch cannot mend a heart shattered by loss." His elbows rested on the desk, his candlelit face shadowed and gaunt. "Son," His voice broke. "I think it is time."

Oren froze. He had known that this moment would come, of course. But still, he had hoped to delay the inevitable. Hoped to finish what he started. "No, Father," he said, his voice steady but firm. "Not yet. Just a little longer. I am so close. We keep arriving just weeks too late. I *will* find the mad priest. I *will* free Kallemena."

A knock sounded, sharp and sudden, cutting through the tension like a blade.

"Enter," Thaloren said, though his voice no longer commanded the room as it once had.

The door opened, and in stepped Malekai, Sylvie at his side.

Thaloren stood up, the burden of grief briefly fading. "Oh, my dear," he said with a tired smile. "Sylvie, I am sorry we did not get more time to talk last night." He hugged her close and kissed her cheek. "It is so good to see you." He shook Malekai's hand. "How was your journey?"

Sylvie's smile bloomed like a sunrise. "Long. I came with Poppy and her three boys. It is not easy keeping children entertained on a ship for days on end."

Her gaze flicked to Malekai, who leaned in to whisper something into Orentheon's ear, quiet, intimate words that only the prince could hear.

Thaloren nodded, his thoughts drifting to distant days when his own children were young, clinging to his arms aboard ships bound for council gatherings. He remembered his daughter, her laughter, her cheer, her light. A life meant to unfold in joy and love had been stolen before it even began. He looked at Oren, his decision firm.

"We will hold the coronation tomorrow. Most of the council is already here, having come for the twins' birthday. There is no sense in delaying it any longer." He turned briskly and left the room before his son could object. There was much to prepare before dawn.

Malekai clapped a hand on Oren's back. "Well then, I suppose I will have to start calling you King Orentheon from now on."

Oren stared ahead, too stunned to respond. He sank slowly into one of the chairs across from the desk, chairs that had always seemed too large when he was a boy sitting across from his father. In the corner, Malekai leaned toward Sylvie, their whispers flickering in the room like a trapped fly.

Oren's eyes narrowed. "What are you two whispering about?" His voice was sharper than intended, his patience thin. The weight of the crown pressed against his chest, and they were chatting like this was just another normal morning.

Malekai stepped forward, his hand slipping into Sylvie's. He held it with all the love he could show. "I asked Sylvie to marry me," he said, his tone gentle. "She has accepted. And now that you are to be crowned, I would like to formally ask for your blessing to be named King of Kalyra. I have already spoken to the rest of the council; they are all in agreement." He looked at Oren, his eyes pleading. "Will you give me your blessing?"

Oren felt the air leave his lungs like a blow from an ornery mule.

To name Malekai king was to admit that Ashar was never returning. That Kallemena was gone. All of them, truly gone. Silence lingered. The war inside him raged, grief clashing with reality. Vallorith remained always a step ahead, his power beyond anything Oren had ever faced. He thought of his mother, clinging to the mirror like it still held life. The years she had lost to mourning a daughter while a son and grandchildren stood right before her. Oren stood abruptly, the chair behind him rocking on its legs.

"I see no reason why this should not be done." His voice was tight. "After all, you have proven yourself to be a fair and wise ruler."

He turned to Sylvie. "We have not always seen eye to eye," he admitted. "But Kivani loves you. And I believe you will make a fine queen." He reached for the silver bell on his father's desk, one of many things he would inherit come morning, and summoned a guard.

A man in armor entered, posture straight and polished, a veteran of service.

"Bring me my son, please," Oren instructed.

The guard nodded, disappearing down the hall.

Sylvie gave Malekai's hand a firm squeeze, then stepped over to Oren. He was more than the brother of her friend now; he was the man bearing the burden of a fractured legacy. She could see what the decision cost him. She took his hands in hers, her eyes glistening. "We have already agreed," she said softly. "When Kallemena and the others are freed, Ashar will be named the rightful king of Kalyra. With her at his side."

Malekai laughed aloud, wholeheartedly. "She would not accept my proposal until I agreed to that." He stood straighter, Oren's gaze on him. "I meant what I said all those years ago. I would never keep a king from his throne."

Oren's hope was renewed. Even now, someone else still believed. Someone still held on to the hope that Kallemena and Ashar would one day return. That they would walk their homelands again, live the lives that had been torn from them. He swallowed, his voice nearly a whisper. "Thank you both."

The door creaked open. Isrend entered, posture precise, hands behind his back. Not a hair out of place. He offered quick greetings to Malekai and Sylvie before crossing the room to the shelves that lined the wall, repositories of knowledge from every corner of the world.

"If you would excuse us, we have a lot to discuss." Oren watched his friends depart, their footsteps fading into silence. The study felt suddenly too large for the man about to take his father's throne. He turned to his son, the tall figure with his mother's complexion, his own height, and build. "Your grandfather has announced his abdication of the crown and kingdom. I am to be coronated in the morning," Oren stalled, waiting for a reaction. When none came, he continued. "And you, Isrend, will be named heir."

Isrend did not blink. He did not breathe. He stood still as stone, the words landing like frost on a statue.

Oren approached, his steps muffled by the thick rug. "Do you understand what that means?"

Isrend finally turned, his gaze cold. "It means I will take command of the guards. I will be the one hunting Echoes. Your replacement." His voice dripped with venom. "No, thank you."

He moved past his father, but Oren caught his shoulder in a firm grip. "You must have mistaken me for someone asking your opinion," Oren accused. "This is not a request. You will be my successor." Under Oren's hand, his son's shoulder trembled.

Isrend whirled, his eyes alight with fury. "No, I will not," he spat, yanking his father's hand away. "Give it to Ismaara. She will not disappoint you the way I have. The way I always do." He stormed from the room, leaving silence in his wake.

Oren looked down at his hand, where his son had just touched him. Horror quickly bloomed when he saw blood staining his fingers.

***

As night fell, birthday decorations were swiftly replaced with royal regalia. Silver and deep blue banners now lined the halls, echoing the colors of their kingdom. The castle buzzed with activity. Chef Delli was hard at work preparing additional meals for the extended guests. News of two coronations and a wedding had spread, and a week's worth of events now needed to be coordinated. Staff rushed through the halls, sleeves rolled, voices hushed but urgent.

In the grand ballroom, women twirled in gowns of ivory and sapphire. The men, clad in crisp black and white, held their partners close as the glass orchestra played its delicate harmonies. The floor shimmered with motion and music.

King Thaloren stood at the edge of it all, watching with distant eyes. In his heart, he pictured his wife in his arms again. He would find her in her darkness. He would bring Nyssira back to the light. And when he did, they would dance like this once more. His gaze softened as it landed on Oren and Kivani, moving in tandem. A noble son. A worthy heir.

Nearby, Sylvie danced with Malekai, the two whispering and laughing about their future in Kalyra. Ismaara spun across the floor with Poppy, reminiscing about their childhood days and dreams they once believed impossible. For a moment, everything felt right. No one noticed Isrend was missing.

He paced around the hourglass in his quiet retreat, lit only by the soft glow reflecting up from the ballroom below. The castle lights flickered like a beacon against the dark. Outside, the blue aurora shimmered through the sky, brushing the clouds with ghostly waves. But Isrend saw none of it. His eyes were locked on the hourglass, thoughts racing for an answer. The obsidian mirror rested atop a chest like an object awaiting a purpose. Its surface gleamed. Unmarred and untouched by time. Positively perfect.

"What are you?" he muttered, circling the two objects. The hourglass's black frame matched the mirror. The red sand within remained still, immobile. No matter how he tilted it or how hard he shook it, the sand was fixed.

He had searched every book, every translation, and none referenced a literal hourglass. Only metaphors. Only time. Useless riddles. Frustrated, he slammed the final tome shut and threw it aside. His breath was ragged. He balled his hand into a fist, forgetting the wounds from the night before. His palm stung, the skin inflamed and weeping. He hissed in pain as he peeled away the bandage.

"That is going to get infected."

Isrend spun, startled. The voice had come from just behind his ear, so close he could feel the speaker's breath on his skin. A man stood in the room. Tall and fully cloaked in crimson robes. The golden sun of the Axis emblazoned on his chest. His pale blond hair was slicked back against his scalp, and his piercing green eyes seemed to glow with a hunger just beneath the surface.

"Vallorith?" Isrend breathed. "Is it really you?" He circled the figure, stunned by the detail.

His perfect features, his commanding aura, the way his very presence changed the air he now breathed.

"I did it," Isrend whispered as a smile adorned his face. "I found you."

Vallorith raised a brow as he took in his surroundings. "Aurora. Glass. Unbearably cold." His eyes flicked down to Isrend. "And you... a perfect mix of your mother and father." He smirked faintly. "I was there when they wed, you know. A beautiful affair." He sneered at the prince. "No one knew your mother was a Talon. If I had, she would have been brought to the axis just like Kallemena." He straightened his shoulders, dusting off his robe. "No matter, all will soon be dead, just like you." He lifted a hand, magic gathering at his fingertips, light crackling, radiant and deadly.

"No!" Isrend threw up his arms, shielding his face, but all that came was silence.

He opened one eye cautiously. Vallorith stood still, staring at his own hand in confusion. The glow was gone. He flexed his fingers, the tingle of his powers fading. His eyes shot to Isrend, his anger evident before he searched the room. Eyes darting everywhere in seconds. Then he saw it. The hourglass.

"What did you do?" Vallorith hissed.

He shoved Isrend aside with unnatural strength and stepped toward the relic. The sand inside remained frozen, as if time stood still. The priest reached out, palm grazing the glass, before a sizzling crack slammed through the room. He recoiled with a snarl, cradling his burned hand. The room filled with the sharp, acrid scent of scorched flesh. He turned on Isrend, fury radiating from him like heat.

"What did you do?" he roared, seizing the prince by his tunic and lifting him from the ground.

"Unhand me!" Isrend squirmed, kicking free. He hit the floor with a thud, breathless but grinning.

"No," Vallorith stared at his hands, his blistered fingers growing cold. "No, no, no."

Isrend's grin widened. He understood now. "Stand on one leg."

The priest obeyed.

"Turn around three times."

Again, he obeyed.

"Hop up and down."

He reluctantly obeyed.

Vallorith scowled. "Are you finished?" he snapped. "Where is the book?"

He spotted the worn volume nearby, its pages bent and fraying from Isrend's earlier fury. He thumbed through the text until he found the incantation. His eyes scanned the page, then narrowed.

"You summoned me," he muttered. "With this?" His voice was flat with disdain.

Isrend nodded. "From what I could translate, it was supposed to bring you here, to me. And it did! The words were easy: *Valta shek, oruun nai. Velken da'sor ethra kai, Brell tu'mar vi talorai.* Come forward, what I seek. Use the power where I stand to bring you through to this land."

Vallorith gave a dry laugh and began pacing. "That is what the words say, yes. But what you sought... was not me as I am." He stopped, his gaze falling to the ballroom below. Through the glass dome, he saw the swirling dancers, the glitter of the celebration. His face darkened. "Why did you want to find me?"

Isrend hesitated. "I wanted to help you. I wanted you to be free."

"No," Vallorith snapped. "The truth. Why did you want to find *me?*"

Isrend opened his mouth, but the words caught in his throat. Until now, he had not truly asked himself what the end goal was. Never allowed himself to fully fall into his hatred for them. The want to eradicate a species. He swallowed. "I want you to help me rid the world of the Echoes."

Vallorith studied him for a moment, his expression unreadable. "So, '*bring me what I seek,*' you were not calling for me." He tapped the hourglass. "You were calling for a tool. And now," He rolled his eyes. "I am *your* tool."

A single grain of red sand dropped. Then another. And another. The hourglass had begun.

"By the looks of it," Vallorith said, watching the sand descend, "I will be your servant for another fifty or so years." He turned to Isrend, his green eyes burning like emerald fire. "What are your commands, dear *master?*"

Chapter Eighteen

All of Glacia lay still in the night. The lights had dimmed, and the guests had long since drifted into slumber with dreams of a newly crowned king coming with the sunrise. Guards remained posted at the royal chambers, castle gates, and scattered among the frost-covered gardens. The snow had stopped sometime after midnight, an unspoken mercy from the skies that earned quiet prayers to Nuval, the god of protection.

One soldier stretched, arms rising above his head as a yawn filled his chest with the icy night air. From a distance, he could hear the hush of waves lapping against the harbor walls, boats creaking softly as they bobbed in rhythm. He passed the outer gate, boots crunching lightly in the snow. Any minute now, his shift would end. He pictured his warm bed, the welcome weight of his cat curling against him, her impatient meows until he lay still enough for her to knead his stomach before falling asleep. The thought lulled his eyes heavier before he blinked hard, shaking the dream away, and rounded the next corner.

He stopped. Something was wrong. He turned slowly, eyes narrowing toward the castle's main gates. The lanterns burned low, casting faint halos on the icy stones. The gate was closed, locked tight. But where were the other guards? Retracing his steps in careful silence, he scanned the empty yard. The docks were unguarded. No sentries at the corners. A chill unrelated to the cold climbed up his spine. He pushed lightly against the gate, which was assuredly still barred. His tension eased ever so lightly, for it did not explain the absence of his fellow men and women.

"Hello?" he whispered. "Loro? Glen? Where is everyone?"

A prickling sense of dread crawled into his gut. Was there an emergency? An attack? Was there something he had missed in his dreary state? He turned toward the side passage used only by the guards and approached the wooden door cautiously. Its iron hinges, usually loud and temperamental, remained unnervingly still. He pushed once, but nothing happened. He leaned into it with his shoulder, all the weight he carried pushing to move the stubborn door.

Finally, it groaned open with effort, snow shifting beneath his boots, and something sliding back on the other side. And then his eyes shot open wide as he froze mid-push. Lifeless bodies were strewn across the courtyard like discarded puppets. Blood pooled beneath them, thick and glossy against pale skin. Their eyes stared upward, glassy and unblinking. His comrades. His brothers and sisters.

He staggered back, horror rising in his throat, when a hand clamped hard over his mouth. Muffled cries escaped him before a strange, creeping calm began to cloud his panic. His limbs slackened. It felt wrong but also good. He should be terrified. He was terrified. But a tide of stillness washed over his thoughts. Soothing like a warm blanket in the middle of a winter storm.

From across the yard, just past the fallen, a tall figure emerged. Robed in crimson so dark it appeared black beneath the dim torchlight. His emerald eyes pierced the gloom, studying the guard like a page in a book.

"You should have just kept walking," the man said, his voice smooth and final. He gave a small nod to whoever held the guard in place. "Make it quick. We have work to do."

The pressure in the guard's chest changed. Not pain, just unfamiliar. Foreign. He tried to look down, breath catching in his throat as his eyes saw what was happening. A blade. Its tip protruded through his ribs, gleaming silver, and dripping red droplets to the snow at his feet. His knees buckled as the knife was slowly withdrawn. The sound of it, flesh, steel, and sickening suction, would have turned his stomach, had the numbing calm not still held him in its grasp. He collapsed into the snow. Warmth spread beneath him, soaking into the ground as his vision began to dim.

A shape moved beside him. A creature, catlike in form, but wholly unnatural. Its skin slick as oil, its amber eyes glowing like twin coals. It crouched beside his body and wiped the blade clean using the soldier's cape.

"Fast enough for you?" it asked, voice low and venom-laced.

The green-eyed man nodded, and together they turned and vanished into the darkness.

***

Sylvie awoke with a start, the sound of tolling bells reverberating through the castle walls. She sat up quickly. Her room was still dark, the sun had yet to rise, and the air held that hushed stillness just before morning. Kicking off her covers, she scrambled to the window and pressed her nose to the cold glass. No new ships in the harbor. No sails on the horizon. Just the stillness of snow-covered roofs and quiet streets of the town. She gripped the frozen latch and forced it open, the mechanism groaning in protest. Frigid air spilled into the room as the bells echoed again, across the harbor, through alleyways, off every ice-slick surface.

She watched lamps flicker to life in nearby homes. Doors opened and people stepped out, bleary-eyed, staring toward the source of the disturbance: the towering glass structure at the heart of the city. Sylvie followed their gaze, unease knotting in her stomach.

"Why are the bells tolling?" she murmured.

A sudden *clang* jolted her, and she recoiled from the window, heart hammering against her ribs. She flattened herself against the wall, eyes darting around the room. No movement. No shadows shifting. Then, another thud, this one louder than before. It was not coming from the door, but instead somewhere within the room. Her gaze snapped to her trunk at the foot of the bed. The lid was latched shut, but the whole chest gave a small jump with a muffled *thump*. Breath catching, she crept forward and unlatched it.

Inside, nestled among folded clothes and worn books, lay the four mirrors, silent and still. She stared down at her reflection. Her face looked drawn, shadowed by purple crescents under her eyes. The years weighed heavier now, and yet she felt more like the girl she once was, frightened and uncertain. Still caught between one breath and the next.

"Sylvie."

The voice sent a chill straight through her. She gasped and spun around, a startled cry escaping her lips as she clutched her chest. He was there, just as he had been before. Slek, standing in the shadows of her room, was unchanged. Time had not marked him. His hair was only slightly longer than she remembered, his face still framed by the same quiet intensity that had once made her heart flutter.

She wanted to run to him. To bury her face in his chest, to breathe in the scent of the past and all the years they had lost. But her body held still. Even though he looked like the boy etched in her memory, she was nearing forty now. A lifetime had passed between them.

"What are you doing here?" she asked, voice low. "How did you leave your mirror?"

Slek looked down at his hands, his expression muddled, as if the world still spun too fast around him. "I am not sure," he said. Then his gaze lifted to meet hers, steady and unblinking. "But you are in danger."

***

Oren and Kivani stood on their balcony, gazing out over the village below. Lanterns flickered to life one by one, glowing like fireflies in the early darkness. People moved through the streets, far earlier than they should have been awake. The usual stillness of the hour had been replaced by quiet urgency.

"Something is not right." Kivani's voice was hushed as she gripped her husband's arm.

Oren wrapped his arms around her, drawing her closer. His heart had already begun to race, matching the rhythm of her fear. She was not one to be easily startled. If she felt something was wrong, it almost certainly was.

"I will go check," he murmured, gently easing out of her hold and turning toward the doors.

"No!" Her hand caught his, firm, stronger than necessary. Her eyes were unwavering. "We go together."

He hesitated, weighing the risk, searching her face for any softness that might let him convince her to stay. But he found none, only resolve, shining like steel. He sighed and gave a nod, stepping aside as she moved toward the armor stand. Without a word, she began fastening plates over her nightdress, hands swift and practiced.

"Is that really necessary?" he asked, trying for a lighter tone.

Her eyes met his in her silent answer. The one that told him to dress for war.

His expressions hardened, his light tone gone in the face of the situation. "You are right." He reached for his own armor and sword. "Something is not right."

***

"What do you mean, Vallorith is here?" Sylvie screeched, tugging her dress over her tangled curls, which stubbornly clung to the garment's buttons.

Behind the privacy screen, Slek's footsteps thudded heavy and fast. Trunks opened and slammed. Something shattered against the floor, and something else groaned a nasty-sounding crack. Sylvie peeked around the screen and gasped. Her room was in disarray, her books toppled, her notes scattered, and her undergarments embarrassingly strewn across the floor. Her face flushed with heat.

"What in the chains are you doing?" she sputtered, stumbling from behind the screen. She fastened the last button in the wrong hole and frantically kicked her scattered belongings beneath the bed.

Slek held up a bag. One Malekai had brought her from Kalyra. It was green with purple beads. Inside, the four mirrors clinked softly. "You have to take these. Find a ship and leave now." He shoved the bag into her hands and pushed her toward the door.

"Wait!" She protested. "I do not even have shoes! Or stockings!" Her resistance was useless as Slek seized her wrist and took off running.

They blurred down the hallway in a rush, Sylvie's feet barely brushing the ground. His Zeph power swept around her like a windstorm, whipping her hair into wild spirals as they stopped at the grand staircase. Slek raised a finger to his lips and nudged her behind him. Footsteps echoed; others were running too. A sudden gust of air whooshed through the corridor. Steel hissed from its sheath, and harsh, unfamiliar shouting rang through the cold glass hall.

Oren's blade slashed through the space, its edge narrowly missing Slek's shoulder. A follow-up blast of air sent the prince flying. Kivani caught her husband midair, flinging water from the air and floorboards alike toward the intruder.

"I will drown you where you stand, shol'ven!" Her voice rang with the full force of her islander accent as a crashing wave surged forward.

Sylvie threw herself between them, redirecting the torrent with a twist of her hand. The water curved harmlessly around her and Slek, dissipating into vapor. Kivani gaped, still poised to strike. Oren shook droplets from his armor, eyes narrowing. Sylvie waved her hand again, drying the prince instantly.

"He is not an intruder," she explained, standing awkwardly between her friends and the man she once loved. Their death stares did not help.

"Then who is he?" Oren stepped closer, sword still in hand.

"Slek. He is the one I told you about, from the mirror. The Zeph captured by Vallorith."

Kivani's brows shot up as her gaze slid from Sylvie to the towering man beside her. "I see now why you refused Malekai for so long." Her soft mutter was louder than Sylvie wished.

"Who is Malekai?" Slek looked to Sylvie, his face flooded with questions.

"Not important," she snapped, face flushed. "Vallorith is here. We are all in danger."

Oren's eyes darted between Sylvie and Slek. "He is here? How?"

Slek shook his head, features drawn. "I-I do not know. I saw him. And Zepher." He rubbed his temple, as if trying to claw through the fog in his mind. "He is hunting the mirrors. He knows they are here." He looked at Sylvie. "With her."

Oren's gaze dropped to the bag clutched tightly in Sylvie's arms. "Kallemena."

All four turned toward the darkened hall. The bells still tolled above, low and grim. Oren felt the truth of it settle like a stone in his gut. If Vallorith was truly here, then everything was at risk; his family, the guests, everyone. The coronation and the nobles from across the continents.

"Where are the guards?" he asked quietly, eyes scanning the rows of doors. He hurried to a pair and pushed them open with all his frustration. The bed was empty, sheets undisturbed. He tried three more rooms, all of which were the same. "Where are all the guests?"

"I need to get Poppy and her children to safety," Sylvie said urgently. She turned to Kivani. "And Ismaara and Isrend."

"We will go together," Kivani said, already moving toward the hall.

"No," Slek countered, faster than Oren, who had opened his mouth to say the same.

"Vallorith is here for the mirrors," Slek said firmly. He stepped in front of Sylvie, taking her hands in his. His touch engulfed hers completely. "All of them. And this time, he means to fill every last one."

Sylvie shivered. She stared up at him, her voice cracking. "I have to save my sister."

She rose onto her toes and pressed a kiss to his cheek. For a heartbeat, she was twenty again, a girl running through Axis corridors, hunted by the same mad priest. A girl in love with her classmate. Slek cupped her waist and drew her closer, his lips brushing hers. She was older now, different, but he knew, in the deepest part of his soul, he would always love her. Always wonder about the life they might have shared. He lingered too long, a moment stolen from the past. Then he gently pulled back, brushing hair from her face, memorizing every line he had never gotten to witness form.

"Be careful," he whispered before letting her go.

* * *

Malekai strapped his twin blades to his back and stepped out of his chamber. Five Zephs stood at attention, already gathered at his door.

Their eyes met his, each one ready, loyal protectors trained for moments just like this.

"We find King Thaloren and Queen Nyssira first," Malekai ordered. "Then Orentheon, his wife, and their children. The royal family is our priority. With me."

No hesitation. His guards fell into step, silent but alert. The castle corridors stretched before them, eerily still and quiet but for the low, relentless tolling of the bells. At each corner, only emptiness greeted them; no guards, no servants, no guests.

"My lord," one Zeph murmured, his voice tight with unease. "I saw something there." He raised his arm in a point.

The words had barely left his mouth when a blade flew through the air. It struck with a sickening thud, sinking deep into the Zeph's shoulder, piercing the bone. The man grunted in pain, his body buckling. A shadow darted across the wall, just a glimpse, and then laughter. Cold, sinister, and then gone. Like a predator playing with its meal.

The remaining four Zephs moved instantly, closing in around their prince. The wind howled down the halls, whipping tapestries from the walls and tearing curtains free. Together, the Zephs extended their arms, wind churning between them, forming a barrier of air that spiraled outward and created a living shield.

Malekai caught his wounded guard before he could fall, tying off his wound and hoisting him over his shoulder. Blood seeped through his tunic, hot and fast.

"We need a healer," he barked, his voice nearly drowned beneath the roar of the wind.

The four Zephs clasped their hands together again, and the wind responded instinctively. A shimmering, humming dome of air formed around them, protecting them and beginning to move, gliding them swiftly through the castle, powered by their own elemental strength.

***

Oren and Slek moved cautiously through the darkened castle, steps hushed, senses sharpened. The halls felt wrong. Fires in the sconces were long extinguished. The rooms they passed were abandoned; the beds were cold, the sheets undisturbed, and belongings left behind. Guests had vanished as if they had been swallowed by the night.

Oren cast a glance at the Zeph beside him, the one who had known his sister all those years ago at the Axis. Questions churned in his throat, but the knot of emotion tightened his chest and sealed his lips. Now was not the time. They reached the royal chambers. Oren gently eased the heavy door open.

Inside, the flickering light of a single lantern danced against the walls. His father stood at the balcony, face pale, tense, his hand on the hilt of his sheathed sword. On the bed lay Queen Nyssira, her breath shallow, sunk in sleep under the effects of the healer's tonics.

"Orentheon?" The king turned quickly, startled.

"Father," Oren said, ushering Slek forward, "this is the Zeph from the mirror. Sylvie's friend."

Thaloren's eyes widened as he took in the man, tall, quiet, a mountain in human form. His gaze flicked instinctively to the ornate hand mirror his wife clutched in sleep, never far from her fingers.

"Can you bring Kallemena out?" Thaloren's voice cracked with desperate hope. "Maybe then her mother will believe she is alive."

Slek's stomach twisted at the sight of the frail woman. Queen Nyssira looked like a ghost, her skin pulled tight over her bones, her once-thick hair now thinned, her strength drained by grief.

"Death would be kinder than what is inside the mirrors," Slek said quietly. "To bring her out would only mean restarting the torture at the beginning." His words landed like a blow. Both Thaloren and Oren turned toward the mirror in the queen's hand, their expressions darkening.

"We have to go. Vallorith is here." Without hesitation, Slek crossed the room and gently lifted Nyssira into his arms. She weighed nearly nothing, far too light for a woman of her age. Her fragility struck him more than her age. "Take the mirror," he said, glancing at Oren. "Give it to Sylvie. She must keep it safe. I will get your parents to a ship."

Oren opened his mouth to protest when a gust of air exploded past the door, rattling the frame. All three turned sharply. Malekai and his Zephs appeared outside, wind magic crackling around them. The air dome they had conjured sputtered into a breeze as it slowed. One of the Zephs lay slumped in Malekai's arms, blood soaking the prince's tunic. Oren rushed forward and took the wounded man.

"We need to find my daughter," Oren said. "She will be able to heal him."

Malekai gladly surrendered the weight, rolling his shoulders before drawing his blades with a practiced grace. "What is going on?" he demanded. "Why are the bells tolling? Where are the guests?" His gaze slid to Slek, the recognition instant as he recalled how Sylvie had described her lost love. "You are Slek? Out of the mirror at last?"

Slek stiffened at the question, jaw tight. His eyes flicked briefly to Oren.

"No time for introductions," Oren cut the awkward moment in two.

He bent to tie a new strip of linen around the injured Zeph's arm. The young man's skin was pale, his pulse faint.

"What happened?"

"A shadow hit him," Malekai said. "A blade, maybe. But when I looked, there was nothing there but a laugh in the dark."

Slek stepped forward, his presence suddenly looming. "Zepher," he said grimly. "Vallorith is using him to strike from the dark. He is setting the chaos in motion."

"Zepher?" Malekai echoed, confused.

"A Morin," Oren confirmed, glancing at Slek for assurance.

King Thaloren finished fastening his chest plate, his aged hands moving with the surety of a man who had worn armor most of his life. His sword glinted as he buckled it to his waist.

"No more talk," he said, eyes steely. "We need to move."

***

Poppy jolted awake to the shrill cries of her infant son. His wails echoed unnaturally, bouncing off the low ceilings and wooden walls, rather than the soft, muffled warmth of their chambers. Her eyes fluttered open. The feather mattress was gone, replaced by damp, creaking boards beneath her back. The glow of candlelight and hearth had given way to darkness, the steady groan of wood and water pressing all around her.

She realized she was on a ship. She sat up stiffly, her muscles aching, and reached for the baby. His tiny face was cold, cheeks damp with tears. She cradled him close, breathing warmth into his skin as her pulse thundered in her ears. Julian and Bren lay curled beside her, still asleep. Relief swept through her in a dizzying wave, but it did little to quiet the rising panic. She looked around.

They were in the cargo hold. Crates had been shoved aside, and instead of dry goods, people lay shoulder to shoulder. Every guest, every noble, every servant from the castle was now packed into the ship's belly like cargo for selling. Most were still asleep. A sharp blush crept up her cheeks as her gaze landed on one man who had not bothered with clothing. She turned away, shielding her son's eyes with a corner of his blanket.

"I need to find Sylvie," she whispered, struggling to her feet.

But the moment she moved, a harsh clink stopped her. Cold metal bit into her ankle. She looked down. A silver chain bound her to a loop bolted in the ship's hull. Realization peaked as she reached for

Julian, his ankle too, shackled in place. Then Bren. All of them. Every soul aboard was chained like prisoners. Her stomach turned. They were not just passengers on this ship.

***

Kivani burst into her daughter's room, relief flooding her chest at the sight of Ismaara still asleep in bed. She hurried to her side, shaking her shoulder gently. "Get up," she whispered, urgency thick in her voice. "We have to go."

The bells had stopped. Their silence made the night feel wrong, like the breath had been sucked from the world. Ismaara blinked herself awake and climbed out of bed, following her mother into the hall. They found Sylvie there, her face pale with panic.

"Poppy is gone. So are her boys," Sylvie said, her voice trembling. "Oh, Kivani, what if Vallorith?"

"We will find them," Kivani said, squeezing Sylvie's hand firmly. "But first, we gather the others. We are safer in numbers tonight."

The three moved swiftly through the corridor. Ismaara glanced into her brother's room; his bed was empty. The blankets were untouched. Kivani grabbed her daughter's hand and tugged her down the hall. Their footsteps were light and slow. Their breath held every time a door creaked or a whisper of sound came too close. As they reached the main hall, they stopped short. Kivani's hand flew to cover her daughter's mouth as Sylvie stifled a scream with both hands.

Before them lay the bodies of the palace guards, cold and broken where they had fallen. A wind slipped in from outside, sparse snowflakes drifting across the blood-slicked floor. Sylvie doubled over, bile rising too fast to stop. She vomited into the corner, her whole body shaking. Kivani scanned the fallen, eyes wide and wild, searching for her husband and son. Ismaara slipped from her mother's grasp and dropped to her knees beside the nearest corpse. Her hands hovered over his chest, eyes glowing white as she summoned her gift. Nothing happened. No heartbeat. No spark. She moved to the next, and the next. Each time, failure. Her nightgown soaked in blood, Ismaara began to shake. Kivani pulled her daughter close, cradling her tightly as the girl sobbed onto her shoulder.

"I cannot help them," Ismaara cried. "They are all dead."

Malekai rounded the corner, sprinting to Sylvie's side. He gripped her shoulders, scanning for wounds. Then his eyes landed on the bodies. "What in the gods...?" he breathed.

Behind him came Oren and King Thaloren, with the Zephs close behind. Orentheon embraced his wife and daughter. But one face was missing.

"Where is Isrend?" Oren asked, his voice low.

"His room was empty," Kivani answered.

"Same for Poppy's," Sylvie added, voice cracking as fresh tears slipped free.

The Zephs brought their wounded companion forward. Ismaara wiped her face and stepped toward him instantly, placing her hands over the torn flesh. Her eyes lit once more, and this time, the wound closed. Color returned to the Zeph's face as he opened his eyes, smiling weakly. A flicker of triumph lit Ismaara's tired features. She had saved at least one.

Slek approached, the Queen still sleeping in his arms. His face pained as he took in the two's embrace. Sylvie then noticed how closely Malekai still held her, his hands on her waist, his cheek against her forehead. Guilt prickled her skin as she took a step back, dropping her gaze to her bag in her hand.

"We need to get everyone off this continent," Slek said, weaving air to gently clear the bodies from their path. "To the ships, now."

"No." Orentheon's voice rang through the hall. "I will not leave the guests to the whims of a mad priest. I will find him and end this."

A voice echoed, chilling the blood in every vein. "Oh, are you so sure?"

Everyone froze. Then, with a shimmer of silver light, an ornate box appeared, filigree glinting, its surface carved with arcane scrollwork. Vallorith emerged, calm and composed, just as he had looked the day Kallemena trapped him. He smiled slowly, relishing the look on their faces.

"Well now, my dear Sylvie. Still running?" His eyes flicked to Malekai. "Tell me, between your two suitors, which do you prefer best? The hulking man made of muscle, or the prince that will make you a queen?"

A dark figure stepped from the shadows. The creature's black claws wrapped around Malekai's throat, a gleaming blade pressed to his heart.

"Queen Sylvie? Can you imagine it?" Zepher's voice was cruel.

"You will not harm him if you know what is good for you, Hound!" Sylvie warned, raising her hands instinctively, water beading in the air, ready to strike.

Zepher only smiled as his blade dug deeper into Malekai's chest.

"We all know how this ends if you proceed, Miss Havander." Vallorith tapped his nose. "Now, the mirrors, if you would." He snapped his fingers, the lid of the silver box slowly lifting open.

Oren stepped forward, his blade halfway out of its housing. Malekai gave an involuntary plea as the creature's blade dug deeper and deeper with every step Oren took.

"Take one more step and the prince of Aetheria will be no more." Vallorith smiled as he clasped his hands together. "It has been a while since I had to perform last rites, but I am sure I can think of a few kind words for him." His smile was greedy for bloodshed.

Sylvie bared her teeth as she lowered her hands, her magic fading as she pulled her bag's strap over her head. She cautiously approached the box, ensuring her actions were not mistaken, and carefully lowered the bag inside.

Vallorith grinned. "And now the other one."

When Orentheon did not move, Vallorith waved his hand. Queen Nyssira vanished from Slek's arms. The crowd gasps as Thaloren unsheathed his sword and pointed it towards the priest.

Vallorith clicked his tongue, clearly unbothered by the threat. "One heroic action, and she dies," he warned as he waved his hand again.

The queen's frail body appeared next to the priest, suspended in the air. Vallorith cupped her cheek, trailing his thumb across her wrinkled skin.

"Poor thing. Really let herself go over the years." His eyes lingered on her grief-stricken face.

"Do not touch her!" Thaloren spat, his voice echoing through the castle.

Vallorith smiled. "Oren, give your dear father the mirror. I want to see if he actually has any bite behind that bark of his." He turned to the king. "Go on. Put your daughter's mirror in the box." His hand still rested on Nyssira's throat, his grip tightening with each step Thaloren took.

The queen's pitiful gasps were faint, but they halted the movement all the same. Everyone stood motionless, waiting for the priest to loosen his hold.

The king did as he was told. Thaloren lowered the mirror into the silver chest, his hand trembling as the lid clicked shut. It was the same box from his study, one he never imagined would hold such ruin for his family and kingdom. Guilt choked his breath, knowing that his wife would never forgive him for this. He stepped back to where his son was standing, relieved that Vallorith's hand dropped away.

Oren stepped forward, his sword drawn despite the danger surrounding them.

"Where is my son?" he growled, his voice like steel dragged across stone.

Vallorith's smile only widened. He tilted his head slowly, first to one side, then the other. "How does it feel to be so blind, with working eyes?" He raised a single finger and pointed upward.

On the stairs above, Isrend stood cloaked in crimson. The Axis book was clutched in one hand. His other hand was tucked behind his back.

"Isrend," Kivani whispered, reaching toward him. "Come to us. Hurry before…"

But Isrend shook his head. His demeanor was calm and detached. "Mother. Father." His tone was disturbingly cordial, as if he were welcoming them to tea. "Let me introduce the man who will change the world." He descended the stairs slowly, his eyes sweeping across the bloodstained room and those who stood frozen beneath it.

"We know his name," Malekai spat, Zepher's blade still pressed against his ribs. A trickle of blood stained his white shirt.

"Not Vallorith," Isrend said, straightening with pride. "Me." He pressed a hand to his chest. "His Holiness of the New Axis Order. High Priest Isrend!"

His voice cracked on the title, the final words landing like a petulant child playing dress-up. A boy too young for the immense weight he tried to carry.

Kivani shook her head. Oren stepped toward their son, disbelief etched into every line of his face. *How had it come to this?* How had their boy become what they now saw before them?

Then Sylvie broke the silence. "What did you do with Poppy?" she asked, voice rushed and worried. "Where is everyone?"

Flashes of that night years ago flooded her memory. Her sister missing, and the children gone. Kallemena searching. But now, instead, she was searching, praying it would not end the same way. Hoping her days would not be spent inside a mirror.

Isrend turned toward her, his oldest friend. Someone who had once held his hand on darker days. "They are safe. All sleeping on the ships," he said gently. "No harm came to any of them, Aunt Sylvie, you have my word."

Vallorith rolled his eyes behind him, clearly unimpressed with the boy's misplaced compassion. While they spoke, his magic crept unseen. Darkened tendrils of power slithered across the floor, curling like smoke over the bodies, seeping beneath feet. A portal began to open, inch by inch, beneath them all.

Slek noticed it first. Then Kivani. Then Oren. With a thunderous gust, Slek hurled a blast of wind that sent Vallorith skidding backward.

"NOW!" he bellowed.

Kivani responded instantly. Water surged beneath their feet, and with a snap of her hands, she froze it solid, an icy platform forming just as the floor split below. Malekai twisted hard, breaking Zepher's grip just long enough to strike. His blade slashed down, catching the creature's leg. Zepher howled in pain and leapt back, eyes blazing as he landed in the blood-slick mess. With one hand, he touched two of the nearest corpses.

They convulsed. Twitched. Then rose. Their limbs jerked unnaturally, black eyes soulless as blood leaked from them in slow drips.

Slek wasted no time as he turned and charged. His massive frame slammed into Zepher with the force of a thunderclap, knocking the creature backward. They skidded across the ice, tangled in fury and limbs. At the last second, Slek twisted and flung the beast to the ground, using wind to keep himself upright. Zepher landed hard, slipping on the frozen pools beneath him.

Kivani shoved Ismaara behind her and flung her arms into the air. Snow roared in from the shattered doorway, melting into torrents that she shaped with deadly precision. *CRACK.* One whip of water struck Zepher. *CRACK.* Another followed, leaving jagged gashes in his skin.

Sylvie sprinted for the silver chest, skidding to her knees. She reached inside, fingers grazing the cool edges of a mirror, when the lid slammed shut on her wrist. Vallorith's face was inches from hers, his green eyes gleaming like a predator.

"Eager to see your new home?" he purred, his grin too wide. "I can tell you from experience that inside the mirror is your own personal hell." He raised his hand, his powers glowing throughout his figure.

Sylvie did not hesitate. She twisted her arm, summoning water from the melted snow, and blasted it straight into his face. He staggered backward with a hiss, steam rising as it scalded his skin. The fight was loud and messy. Everyone giving their all, refusing to let the sun rise on their own failure.

Zepher gave new life to each soldier he touched, and before long, all the slain walked again, their bodies slumped and mutilated. Ismaara helped Sylvie push the chest's lid off her crushed wrist, her eyes glowing as she mended the bone within. Oren and Malekai fought off the horde of the undead, while Slek and the other Zephs kept the monster and the priest at bay with a shield of wind. But once again, the boy who had always been overlooked was forgotten for the last time.

He picked up a blade, rage boiling inside him at how everyone could be fighting right now. He had a speech. He had plans. He had seen his vision unfolding perfectly. Every want, every whim, had been answered by his loyal servant, one of the strongest Darra to ever walk the world. Vallorith should have controlled the situation. No one was supposed to interrupt his most significant moment.

Isrend inched forward, his boots slick on the fresh ice conjured by his mother. Around him, the whirlwind of the Zephs focused only on the true threats. The two enemies that mattered. *This* was his moment. *This* was his time to carve his name into history.

He raised the sword above his head, his father square in his sights. "I will act my worth!" he screamed and swung the blade toward Oren's skull.

Before the steel could bite into flesh, Malekai caught the weapon mid-air, the blade slicing deep into his hand; through muscle, through tendon. He cried out as he slammed his foot into Isrend's chest. The boy flew backward, his head cracking against the floor. Malekai crumpled to his knees, his hand nearly severed, only a ragged piece of flesh keeping it connected. Through the haze of agony, his eyes found Sylvie. Her lips parted in a silent scream, her blue eyes wide with horror. Then he felt it. The hot sting of metal cutting through his back.

"Sylvie," His last word, before the world went black.

Zepher's amber eyes locked on Sylvie as his blade was slipped from Malekai's back. His silver scars shimmered in the broken light of the palace. His grin, a cruel taunt for the girl who had always been helpless.

"No!" She tore free from Ismaara's grip and spun her hands through the air. The world itself seemed to shudder. Moisture from every wall, every breath, every tear gathered above them in a swirling vortex.

Water, dense and heavy as death, echoed her pain. Sylvie's eyes blazed bright blue. Her power peaked as she threw her hand forward toward the grinning Morin. The sound was deafening. Bones shattered. Walls exploded. Everything was swept away in a violent stream of divine fury. Zepher and his undead army were consumed by the wave, bodies crushed, skin shredded, and broken.

"Kivani, grab the chest!" Sylvie shouted, spinning to face Vallorith, whose own power coiled in shadows behind him. "Slek, get them out, now!" She turned back, hurling the full weight of her flood toward the priest.

He met her with a force of his own, black and burning, convulsing in one radiant wave after another. The clash sent shards of stone and glass slicing through the air. The ground trembled as the castle around them began to fracture. Everyone obeyed her earlier command. Slek swept up the Queen's body and rushed the king outside. Oren and the remaining Zephs carried Malekai's limp form. Kivani and Ismaara took the chest.

"To the ships!" Oren yelled, eyes locking on his wife. "We will need to make a fast escape."

Kivani gave a solemn nod. She understood what had to be done. They raced across the courtyard, past the lifeless forms of their soldiers, now unrecognizable heaps in the snow. Their blood had been washed clean by Sylvie's fury, leaving only silence and bone behind. At the docks, five ships bobbed gently in the calm waters, already heavy with passengers.

Kivani handed the chest to Ismaara, who trembled in her grip. "Follow your father. I will be there soon."

She watched her daughter go, heart splintering for what she knew was coming.

"How can we help?"

She turned to find the five Zephs, Malekai's guards, standing close together. Their faces were drawn and grief-stricken, eyes dark with the weight of their prince's death.

"One to a ship," Kivani ordered, her voice brisk but hoarse. "We have to move quickly, put wind in those sails."

Just as she turned to the ships, a thunderous crack split the air behind them. They all spun around, just in time to see the castle collapse. The towering glass walls shattered in a cascade of crystal. Snow billowed outward in a cloud of white and ash. The once-grand stronghold was gone.

"Sylvie!" Slek cried out. He shoved the queen into Thaloren's arms and sprinted toward the ruins.

One of the Zephs moved to follow him, but Kivani raised a hand, stopping them. "Leave him," she snapped. "We have got lives to save. Get to the ships. Now!"

They scattered, falling into practiced roles. One Zeph to each ship, cutting ropes, guiding panicked hands. They raised the ramps and checked the cargo holds. Just as Isrend had claimed, the guests lay within, asleep and untouched. The Zephs lifted their hands, fingers weaving through the wind. The air obeyed. White sails billowed, glowing faintly in the pre-dawn dark. So much magic had saturated the night that it felt as if the sun itself had settled on the decks where they stood. A beacon for all to see.

Kivani stood at the shoreline, arms outstretched like a tide mother coaxing the sea. Her hands moved in rhythm, strong and sure, ebb and flow. One by one, she turned each ship, aligning them toward the open waters. Her waves rose higher with each breath, her strength pulsing through them like a heartbeat. With the Zephs' winds guiding the sails and her waters beneath them, the ships raced out to sea. Each one vanished into the horizon, tiny flecks against a fading sky.

All headed toward safety, or what she *hoped* would be a safe haven. Kivani turned back to face her home. Or what was left of it. The castle was now nothing but smoke and snow, settled in a haze. Then, movement. A crack of shattering glass split the stillness. Slek's wind blew the debris aside, clearing a path through the ruins. Sylvie stood beside him, bruised and bloodied but alive. They climbed out together, staggering.

Relief overwhelmed Kivani. She bolted forward, forcing herself not to think about who *was not* climbing out. Her son was still buried beneath tons of broken stone and frost. Their home, where she had borne her children, where she had wed her love, was now a tomb. She shoved the ache away and rushed to Sylvie, arms flinging around her friend.

"I am sorry about Isrend," Sylvie gasped, breathless. Her voice cracked with grief. Her body was battered and on the verge of collapse.

"And I am sorry about Malekai," Kivani whispered.

Both women had lost a piece of their hearts tonight. They stayed like that for a long time, their cries the only sound rising above the wreckage. But the quiet did not last. The ground trembled and a shrill shriek split the air, sharp and unnatural. Glass shifted again, groaning beneath an unseen force. A black sphere rose from the wreckage, its edges pulsing into view. Suspended within it, untouched and unmarred, floated Vallorith and Isrend.

They hovered there, glistening with otherworldly light, then streaked across the sky like lightning, bright, fast, and hot, heading directly toward the fleeing ships.

"We have to get there," Sylvie choked out, lifting a trembling hand to summon her magic. But her power faltered. Her strength was gone.

Slek did not hesitate. He grabbed them both, arms tight around their waists, and ran. His feet pounded through the snow, magic coursing through his lungs. Then he leapt. With a powerful breath and a push of wind, they soared into the air.

***

Oren and Ismaara stood at the ship's railing, watching the shoreline shrink into a blur as Kivani's waves and the Zephs' winds carried them farther from home.

"How will Mother get to us?" Ismaara questioned, her face streaked with soot.

Oren pulled his daughter close. "She is of the water," he said softly, trying to keep the tremor from his voice. "She will be with us soon." But even as he said it, he worried for her still.

He turned his gaze to the deck. Guests had begun to stir and roam, blinking up at the moonlit sky as their chains were unfastened. Poppy was one of the first on deck, her baby in her arms. She went to sit beside the king, who sat with his unconscious wife, eyes locked on the silver box resting near Ismaara.

Everyone flinched when a crack split the sky, sharp and sudden. All heads turned upward just in time to see a black streak arcing toward the ship.

"Everyone, hold on!" Oren shouted a moment too late.

The ship jolted violently. Bodies were flung across the deck. Heat quickly encompassed them, sweat instantly slicking their skin. The wood beneath their feet sizzled and blackened. Smoke curled up from the now burned scorch marks. At the center of the wreckage stood Isrend and Vallorith.

"I will say the company this kingdom keeps is very rude," Vallorith said with a grin, emerald eyes fixed on Oren. "Try to do better if you are ever king." He snapped his fingers. Ismaara vanished from Oren's side and reappeared beside Isrend, a blade pressed to her throat.

Oren's heart seized in horror as the boat rocked again, nearly capsizing. Sylvie, Slek, and Kivani landed hard on the deck beside Oren. Slek collapsed to his knees, his skin paling, his time almost up.

Before anyone could speak, Kivani surged forward. A tidal wave crashed around Vallorith, spiraling upward and freezing solid in an instant, encasing him. Her glowing eyes turned on her son, the water curling just inches from his hand.

"You let ya sista go this instant!" she commanded. Her voice roared like the ocean.

Isrend released his sister. His hands trembled as he stared at his mother's power, so immediate, so undeniable. Ismaara stumbled back to her father, all eyes shifting to the prince.

"Why, Isrend?" Kivani's voice cracked with pain. "Why do this?"

"Why?" he spat, mocking her. He threw the knife down, his hair was matted with blood, and stood out wildly. "*Why?* Because of her!" He jabbed a finger at his sister. "And her!" He pointed to Sylvie. "And you. And *him.* All of you with your precious gifts. Born with power, adored for it. I hate you!"

His whole body shook with rage as veins bulged along his neck. "No one ever looked at me the way they look at *her.* No one ever loved me like you love *her.* My whole life has been lived in her shadow. And no matter how hard I worked, how much I gave, I was never enough. Never as precious as your echo. The perfect Freyla." His words struck true, echoing years of neglect, of aching silence. "No one notices when I am gone. No one comes searching for me. No one *needs* me."

He lifted his chin, hands clenched at his sides. "But that ends now. I will be the new era. I will be the reason the Echoes go extinct. I will be the one people envy. *I will* be the one they seek. I will be ruler over all!"

Ismaara screamed as clawed fingers yanked her from her father's side. Zepher had her, and in his other hand, the silver chest of mirrors. Vallorith appeared beside them, all four gathered at the railing. Kivani glanced at the frozen sphere that had held Vallorith only moments ago. It was still sealed.

"Did you really think *that* would stop me?" Vallorith asked, smirking. His grin twisted cruelly across his face. "As much as I have enjoyed the reunion, we must be going. But first," His eyes moved to where Sylvie sat. "A Talon needs to go into her mirror."

Sylvie gasped, her power depleted, her fears becoming a reality.

"No," Isrend commanded his servant. "Find another Talon. Aunt Sylvie is to be left alone."

She shook her head, forcing her voice to steady. "I am not your aunt!"

At this, Isrend looked hurt, knowing his favorite person was now one of his enemies. "Vallorith, take us to Verdathos."

With a flick of the priest's wrist, they vanished. Oren lunged forward, fingers outstretched, but Ismaara's hand was already gone. Silence fell across the deck. No one moved. No one dared to breathe. Kivani stepped to Oren's side and slipped her hand into his. He wrapped his arms around her, and together they wept for their children. Sylvie turned, locking eyes with Slek. She knew he would not last much longer. She crawled to him, arms wrapping tightly around his fading form.

"I love you," she choked, her voice muffled in his shirt. "I always have. I wanted you to know that before."

His hands trembled as he held her back. "I always knew." His voice cracked. "I am sorry about Malekai."

His last words faded, like dust on the wind. He was gone, vanishing in her arms, returning to his prison once more. Sylvie collapsed, her sobs pouring out, raw and uncontrollable. Grief bled from every inch of her. For Malekai. For Slek. For the pieces of her heart now missing. Forever gone.

A baby's cry broke through the silence. Sylvie looked up, blinking through her tears. Poppy stood before her, Victor in her arms, a green and purple satchel clutched in one hand. Sylvie struggled to her feet and embraced her sister and nephew tightly.

"Bren? Julian?" she gasped, taking in Poppy's face.

"They are safe." Poppy's cheeks were tearstained, her voice tight with emotion. "Here," she said, extending a bag to Sylvie. "I grabbed them. Before that monster took the box."

Sylvie looked down at the satchel. Her dumbfounded expression showed her shock. In her sister's hand was her satchel, the one Slek stuffed the mirrors into. She opened it, and there they were. Four silver mirrors glinting in the moonlight. *Thron. Zeph. Talon. Vira.* The Darra missing.

"How did you know they were in there?" she whispered.

Poppy gave her a flat look, one brow raised. "I remember the box from the king's study." She gave a quick shrug. "I guessed there was something important inside if that monster wanted it. Looks like I guessed right."

Sylvie held the bag to her chest, as if it might vanish again. They may be missing one, but Vallorith was missing four.

∗ ∗ ∗

Isrend shoved open the door to Sylvie's old study, now his own. A smile spread across his face, wider than any he had ever worn. He strode to the window and flung it open. Screams echoed across the sanctuary. The first of many that signaled the death of the Echoes. Vallorith's powers were thorough.

With a careless sweep of his arm, he sent books and papers scattering from the desk. At the center, he placed the hourglass, the red sand trickling slowly downward. Behind him, Zepher entered, ducking slightly beneath the doorframe. His long white braid brushed against his back, pointed ears twitching at the chaos outside. His clawed hand gripped Ismaara's arm, dragging the trembling girl forward.

"Where do you want these, oh master?" he asked dryly, holding up the chest.

When Vallorith had pulled Zepher from the mirror and explained the plan, he had laughed in Vallorith's face. The boy, a prince so emotional and green, was barely a man. How did someone like him manage to bind a strong Darra into servitude? The priest must have been jesting, right? But when Vallorith did not laugh, he knew the priest's words were true.

Zepher scowled. "Leave me in my mirror until he dies," he had said. "Then I will help collect the rest."

But Vallorith only smiled. "We could have the mirrors *and* our revenge. Why wait when we can watch our enemies die now?" His smile was dangerous.

Zepher frowned at the memory, already hating the idea of another person he had to answer to.

"On the desk," Isrend said, nudging the hourglass aside.

Zepher crossed the room, his clawed feet tapping the stone, the scent of rot thick around him. He dropped the silver chest on the desk with a dull thud and turned to go.

"Zepher." Isrend's voice cut through the air, now cold and controlled, no trace of the boy who once sobbed in the halls of his castle. "Disobey me, and I will have Vallorith kill you."

Zepher stopped. He turned slowly, amber eyes narrowed, and in a blink, his blade was at Isrend's throat. But before he could press deeper, he felt the cool sting of a blade at *his* back. Vallorith stood behind him, silent and still, ready to strike. Isrend did not flinch. He only smiled. Every piece on the board belonged to him now. Zepher pulled back, and so did the priest.

"That will be all," Isrend said coolly, waving them off. "Continue the slaughter."

Without another word, they both left, leaving Ismaara alone with her brother. She was trembling where she stood. Her twin before her was unrecognizable. The man was completely different from the one she had teased the day before. Isrend turned to her and snapped his fingers.

"Come. Heal me."

She stepped forward, eyes drawn to the blood matted in his hair where he had struck his head earlier. Could it be a fatal wound? What if she only healed the skin?

"Now, Ismaara. Or I will have Zepher kill you."

She was across the room in an instant, the monster's orange eyes haunting her memory, his sharp claws still etched on her skin. She pressed her palms to the wound, whispering a healing chant. As her magic took effect, the red sand in the hourglass brightened, its glow pulsating. Both their gazes shifted to it, eyes wide at what they saw. The sand had begun to recede. Flowing *upward*. Rewinding time already spent. Isrend shoved her back and snatched the hourglass from the desk.

"Fifty years," he murmured as he looked at his sister. "Could be five thousand thanks to you." He carefully placed the hourglass back on the desk and waved his hand towards the door. "Go to your room. If you try to escape, Vallorith will find you before you can breathe a sigh of relief."

Ismaara nodded and slipped out, silent as a shadow. Alone, finally, Isrend lifted the silver chest and carried it to the wall where Sylvie once displayed the mirrors. Hooks and stands still waited, prepared to house the whole collection. He set the chest down and opened it.

Only one mirror remained. His stomach dropped. He lifted it slowly. His mismatched eyes stared into the glass, meeting a reflection that was not his own.

"Kallemena," he hissed.

The woman who had started it all. The ghost that haunted his father's every step. With a roar, he hurled the mirror back into the chest and slammed the lid shut.

"You will *drown* before you ever watch me rule. You took my life away from me. My father spent years looking for you. *Always* you. Never me!" He kicked the chest, his foot screaming in pain.

He stormed out of the study and into the sanctuary. The smoke of burning halls curled in the breeze. Screams had faded to echoes, and bodies littered the cobbled ground. Annoyed that they were in his way, he stepped over them without pause, eyes fixed on the docks.

Ahead, the sea churned. A storm gathered on the horizon. Waves crashed violently against the stone steps. He stood there for a moment, looking out to the ocean, the power his mother wielded. He would never admit he was envious. Jealous that he had been born too soon. An hour before the day of turning. He gripped the silver chest in his hands, its weight nothing compared to the loneliness he had carried for years. With a mighty heave, he flung the chest into the ocean. The silver glint vanished beneath the dark surface of the water.

Part III:
The Forsaken Land

Chapter Nineteen

Everyone stared at Ismaara as her tale finally came to an end. The sun had begun to rise, casting pale light through the cracks above, yet the cave held its breath in silence. Even Rhubarb the donkey seemed spellbound by the story, swaying gently in his pen, ears still.

"What happened to your family?" Edna inched closer, her voice soft. "Your mother and father?" Her eyes were wide. "What about Sylvie and Poppy?"

Ismaara shook her head slowly. "I am not really sure. I heard my grandparents passed not long after I was taken." She looked toward the dragon resting in her nest, watching her with unwavering eyes. "As for my parents, I only know they died of old age, hidden away from the Axis my brother created."

She turned back to Edna, a faint smile breaking across her face. "But Sylvie and Poppy lived to be very old. The children grew, had families of their own, which is why you are here now." She beamed at the old woman, her expression far too bright for the heaviness lingering in the cave.

"So, you just lived with them?" Nemeah's voice cut through the silence, cold and sharp. "Vallorith. Zepher. You stayed in the sanctuary while they slaughtered Echoes and did nothing?"

Ismaara's smile vanished as her eyes locked onto Nemeah's. "What was I supposed to do?" Her lip started to quiver as her eyes watered. Her voice took on a childlike pitch. "I am a Freyla. I cannot summon water or command wind. I cannot create, like you, a Darra." Her gaze swept across the small gathering, her voice cracking. "All your gifts are useful in a fight." She covered her face with her hands as her shoulders slumped, and her voice turned to a whisper. "I just heal people."

The tears came fast. Her body trembled as she made a show of wiping them away, sobs echoing in the now dimly lit cavern.

Keanoff rose and crossed to her, wrapping an arm around her shoulders. "You did what you could." His voice was easy, meant to comfort, but Nemeah heard the accusation within.

Ismaara clung to him, burying her face in his chest as her cries deepened, muffled by the fabric of his tunic. Nemeah stood frozen, her insides knotting. She had heard this kind of cry before, when she had once tricked Henry into thinking Nemeah had hurt her cellmate. The sound was too familiar. She watched as Keanoff gently led Ismaara to her bed of moss, helping her beneath the blankets.

Nemeah curled her fingers into fists, her pulse thrumming in her ears. The urge to lash out simmered beneath her skin, nearly beyond control. She turned and strode from the cave, her boots crunching against gravel and dirt.

Outside, the morning light was cresting the mountains. The air felt warmer than it had in days; summer was stirring, rising like the sun. A new season on the horizon. A reminder that their time was running short.

"That was unfair."

Nemeah turned sharply, her heel grinding into the earth. Keanoff stood a few paces behind her, his eyes like daggers as he stared at her. His tunic still bore the damp mark from Ismaara's tears, fluttering in the breeze. She said nothing, just stared at him and his ever-judging eyes. His gaze pulled toward the distant tower of Highspire's castle, silhouetted against the sky.

She felt her emotions growing. "What was unfair?" Her voice was flat, her jaw clenched. She knew exactly what he meant, but needed to hear him say it aloud.

Keanoff exhaled, the breath slow and weary. "You know there was nothing she could have done. Like she said, Freyla are healers. She is not like you." He paused a little too long. The weight behind those words landed harder than he likely intended.

Nemeah felt her chest tighten, her blood turning to frost. *She is not like you.* The words rang in her head, echoing deeper than she wanted to admit. She turned away from him just as the tears threatened to spill down her face. She did not want him to see that his words could hurt her so easily. Not when he thought her a monster, an evident danger. She now needed to hear the words that he held back. The ones he thought of every time he looked at her. "And what am I like?" she asked quietly, ready to confront the answer. The silence stretched. "Tell me."

She spun around, but no one was there. She stood alone in the golden light, the world quiet save for the rustling grass and distant birdsong. Her braid slipped from her shoulder as she yanked at it, walking down the trail that led to the cliffside. Her thoughts tangled, unraveling fast. *She is not like you.*

"No one is like me," she whispered through the ache in her throat as her boots slipped on the loose dirt and rocks. "Why? Why do I have to be different?"

She thought of the Axis house burning. The swirling wall of water that had loomed over the city. The faint memory of her finger pressed to Keanoff's forehead. Of sitting astride a black-scaled dragon, soaring toward the mountains. She rubbed her temples. The memories stabbed through her skull like tiny needles of light. Why was this happening? Why could she not control it anymore?

The questions, the confusion, the guilt, the trust that had unraveled. It was all bubbling to the surface, begging to be released. She stepped to the cliff's edge, her body a furnace of emotions and fractured thoughts. The memories, hers and those that did not belong, collided in her chest.

A shriek tore from her throat, sharp and wild, echoing across the mountains like a wounded animal. In that instant, fire burst from her, a brilliant, blistering eruption. The air hissed and steamed. Flames danced around her, spiraling, cocooning her in heat and light.

Her fire roared to life, fed by months of buried anguish. Her family, afraid of her. The Axis, hunting her. Kallemena, trapped and silent in her mirror. Her friends whispered when they thought she could not hear, avoiding her gaze.

Everything in her life was unraveling. None of it was like the future she had once imagined as a girl. She dropped to her knees, her flames flickering out. Her limbs trembled from exhaustion. She pressed her hands into the dirt, now warm from her outburst. Smoke clung to her skin. The sparse grasses around her smoldered, edges curling and blackened. She drew in a deep breath, then another, grounding herself.

"Wow."

The voice startled her. Nemeah turned, slow and wary, to find Yuli standing nearby, batting at the sleeves of her jacket. The fabric was scorched and still smoking, the smell of singed cotton curling through the air.

"Really caught you at a bad time." Yuli offered a crooked smile, half-friendly, half-cautious. "Was going to see if you wanted some chow. Edna's out cold, but I can scramble up a tasty egg or two."

Nemeah glanced toward the cave entrance, feeling tension at the thought of going back so soon. The feeling of eyes watching her as if she were a spectacle was humiliating. Hearing the whispers haunting her in the darkness was torment. It all twisted something in her gut.

"No," she murmured. "You go ahead."

Yuli raised an eyebrow, unconvinced. "You just put out a lot of energy; you will need to put some back in." Before Nemeah could protest again, a massive grumble escaped her stomach. Yuli's smirk deepened. For the first time, Nemeah noticed her teeth, specifically her incisors, sharper than any human's. With an easy grin, Yuli stepped forward and grabbed her by the arm. "Come on. Everyone is already asleep. We will practically have the place to ourselves."

She helped Nemeah to her feet, brushing the soot and ash from her skirt. The two of them made their way back into the cave. The air was filled with the soft rhythm of snores, deep and peaceful, utterly unaware. Nemeah moved cautiously, eyes scanning the figures sprawled in their beds. Edna. Then Keanoff. Then Ismaara. All asleep. All undisturbed.

Yuli pointed toward her husband, who had claimed the biggest moss bed and somehow managed to sprawl across it entirely, arms and legs dangling off the edges.

"Honestly," she whispered, "I do not know how I get any sleep with that man." She tiptoed to where the chickens had left their morning offering and plucked five eggs from the dirt floor. With a cautious hand, she snatched one of Edna's cooking pans from the hooks on the cave wall. "Go grab some peppers while I warm the pan."

Nemeah obeyed without a word, her movements quiet as she padded across the stone floor toward the tidy rows of vegetables. She selected a few red and yellow peppers, their skins smooth and cool beneath her fingers. The sweet scent filled the cave as she carried them back.

Yuli diced them in a blur of motion, tossing the colorful pieces into the pan. The sizzle rang out, sharp and satisfying. The aroma that followed, of hot eggs and sweet peppers, made their stomachs even more impatient for the treasure that awaited them. Yuli scooped equal helpings into bowls, and together they ate in silence, the sounds of the others sleeping around them. Noa shifted in her nest, the soft scrape of her scales adding to the dreamy atmosphere of the cave.

Yuli watched as Nemeah's gaze wandered over the dragon. "So you can speak her language now?" she whispered, mouth still half-full.

Nemeah considered the clicks and whistles. Before, the words had been clear, whole sentences. Now they were just sounds swirling in her head. "I am not sure," she said, setting her bowl aside. "It is like I only understand it when my powers allow me to." She looked over at Yuli, eyes shadowed with uncertainty. "I could not even tell her hello right now." She set her bowl aside, half a meal left uneaten.

"I picked up a little from what Keanoff was translating when Ismaara was speaking," Yuli told her, glancing back at the dragon again. "But most of it was just nonsense. Whistles and clicks. Nowhere near fluent yet." A pause. "Did you really turn him into one?" She nodded toward the sleeping Vira. "Scales and all?"

Nemeah's face flushed with shame, the memory igniting guilt in her chest. "I did," she admitted softly. She tugged her braid over her shoulder, twisting the stray hairs around her fingers. "I did not know I could do that. And when it happened, it was like I was watching myself from outside. Like, I was not even the one doing it."

She looked toward Keanoff, who lay still, his arm draped across his eyes. "He told me afterward that it goes against Vira ways." She turned back to Yuli. "Why? If you do not mind me asking."

Yuli finished the last of her breakfast and chewed thoughtfully. "Vira get their gifts from Dathmor, the god of all animals. I do not know if our tribes share the same traditions," she nodded at Keanoff, "but in mine, it is forbidden because it is unfair to nature. In the stories, it is said that Dathmor once became a dragon during the gods' war, the one that ended with us Echoes being created." Her voice grew softer. "They say he grew a hundred times his normal size, fire pouring from his jaws, scorching the land. He caused so much pain so quickly that the goddess Brynna could not heal people fast enough. Too many lives were lost, all because of selfish gods."

Nemeah shifted closer, curiosity piqued. "But it was a war, was it not? That is part of the cost?"

Yuli shook her head. "He did not attack the gods. He attacked humans. He knew Brynna would crumble if they suffered. He knew she would bend. And she did. She gave up her place. Bowed to her brother."

Nemeah looked over at Ismaara, her thoughts heavy. A brother and sister, at odds, even back then. "What was the point of the gods' war?"

"What every war is about."

Both women turned at the voice. Agnes sat up in bed, her black hair tousled from sleep.

"And what is that?" Nemeah asked.

"Love," Agnes said plainly. She pushed back her covers and crossed to the fire, settling beside Yuli with a groggy sigh. "I am starting to believe the Axis lied about more than just the Echoes," she said. "But the gods' war, that story has never changed. Every version I ever found said the same thing." She nodded toward Nemeah's unfinished bowl of eggs, and when it was passed to her, she dug in happily. "I was dreaming of these," she said with her mouth full, swaying from side to side as if the food itself was a lullaby.

Nemeah and Yuli watched her, amused and warmed by her new-found ease. Agnes had been so timid when she had first arrived, and now, she glowed with quiet joy.

"I never learned about the gods' war," Nemeah said quietly. "That is not something they taught in schoolhouses on Tirnmoor."

Agnes scraped the last of the eggs into her mouth and placed the bowl beside her with a satisfied sigh. "I know it like the back of my hand," she said, lifting her hand in proof. "It all started when the Freyla was born," she continued.

"Brynna, youngest of the gods, was known across the world for her beauty. She healed the small, the sick, and the wounded. I mean, what was not to love?" Agnes chuckled softly. "Mortals adored her. Every-one wanted to be her chosen one, to stand at her side, to live in her light." She drew a half-moon in the dirt with her finger.

"So many men turned their hearts to her that they stopped wor-shipping Caerwen, the moon goddess. And Caerwen did not like be-ing second to anyone." Agnes's tone grew darker. "She went to Arvayn, the god of death, the one who adored her, and asked him to kill every man who had pledged his love to Brynna." She looked at Nemeah. "And he did. Young and old. No mercy."

Nemeah felt the weight of the tale pressing in on her like a stone. The thought of so many dying because someone deemed it so. It reminded her of Isrend and Vallorith.

"And Brynna?" she whispered.

"She went to her brother, Dathmor," Agnes said, "and begged him to stop the god of death."

"But wait," Nemeah said, eyebrows knit, "I thought you said it was Dathmor who killed the people. Why would he help his sister if he turned around and betrayed her?"

Yuli nodded, just as confused. "Why become a dragon if not to fight another god?"

Agnes lifted a finger, clearly ready to explain. "Love," she said again, letting the word settle. "When Dathmor went to face Arvayn, he found something else instead; they both loved the moon goddess. Both wanted her approval, both wanted to rule by her side. If two gods came together, they would be more powerful than the rest, combining their gifts. And to Dathmor, that sounded like a pretty good deal. So, he decided he would not just kill the men, he would kill the women too. To show Caerwen exactly what he could do. How powerful he could be. A contest for her affection."

She paused dramatically, the firelight flickering across her face. "He turned into a beast the mortals could not even comprehend. A dragon the size of the world, burning continent after continent. All of it, a show for Caerwen's heart. But after he turned into the horrible beast, the urge to rule over all became too great. He then turned on the other gods, forcing them to kneel before him to save their people."

Yuli yawned and rubbed her eyes. "How was he stopped?"

Agnes turned to Nemeah, voice softer now. "The queen."

The word fell like a promise in the silent room, both women leaning closer.

"Lirian, the god of the sun, saw the destruction. His worshippers dying in a war that was not theirs. So he went to the queen and begged for her help." She leaned back, warming her hands by the fire. "The books were vague. Hazy and full of symbolism and fragments, but from what I could gather, the queen told him no. She said it was their mess to fix. But she gave them something. A single seed. One that, when grown and touched by an Echo, would suppress their powers."

"Silvervane," Nemeah whispered, and Agnes gave a slow nod.

"So Lirian gathered Danira and Nuval, Thorn and Glade. Resourceful gods who answered the call. They were the ones who took down Dathmor. Bound him in cuffs made with the plant woven through them."

Nemeah sat frozen, entranced in the tale.

"Then Turan and Lysar joined the fight. Their people had been caught in the destruction long enough, even after they had admitted defeat. And that is where the stories splinter, everyone fighting, the heavens shaking, and then... it happened." Agnes's eyes gleamed, her voice rich with reverence. "The Echo." She wiggled her fingers through the air.

Yuli raised an eyebrow. Agnes had their full attention now, like a bard holding an audience in the firelight.

"What is the Echo?" Nemeah asked, fully drawn in.

"It is what happened when all the gods' powers collided at once. A shockwave that cracked through the universe. The day the Eclipse Veil began." She traced waves in the dirt around the moon she had drawn earlier. "All those powers, all that magic, scattered like a tide pulling away from the shore. But tides come back and eventually, those waves find land again." Her finger tapped the center of the moon. "That is what happens when Echoes are born. A wave finds its way home, sinks deep into a newborn's soul."

Yuli raised her hand as if she were a student in a class. "But why just babies? Why not everyone?"

Agnes tapped the center of her chest. "It is about timing. When we are born, our lungs are new, and our bodies are still forming. We are open. More absorbent, but only for a few seconds. All that magic in the air seeps in. It settles deep. Then it lies dormant until one day it comes out." She turned to them, eyes bright. "When did your powers start?"

Now it was Agnes who leaned in, hungry for a story. Yuli looked at Nemeah, hesitating. But finally, she relented. "I was seven," she said quietly. "Playing with my friends when the fever hit me like fire. I thought I was dying. My bones felt broken, my skin felt as if a thousand knives were slicing into me. Then, there was fur. All over my arms. Claws sprouting from my fingers. It lasted only a second, human one moment, wolf the next." She looked down at her hands, brushing a thumb over the tribal markings etched into her skin. "After that shift, I knew my life would never be normal again. I knew the Axis would come for me eventually."

Agnes nodded slowly, an apology unspoken in her eyes.

"Seven years old?" Nemeah asked quickly, glancing between them. "When do Darra usually show signs? Because honestly, I did not know until a few months ago."

Agnes frowned, thinking. "Most start showing around ten or eleven. All of them show by puberty. Every Darra does."

"You only just discovered your powers a few months ago?" Yuli asked, eyes wide. "But they are so strong, it feels like you have lived with them your whole life."

Agnes leaned in. "What was the first thing you manifested?"

Nemeah felt the heat of their attention. She raised her hand, and Alban appeared beside her in a ripple of silver light. His armor shimmered with the flickering firelight, casting fractured shadows across the cave walls.

Agnes's eyes never left Alban. "And when did the fire start? The other powers?"

"A few weeks ago," Nemeah replied. "Just before I was caught by the Axis. It began with a dream. There was this girl, trapped inside the Axis house, and then the fire started. It spread everywhere." She flexed her fingers unconsciously. "That is when I burned my hands. I caught the cave on fire while I slept."

"And who was the girl you dreamed of? Did you ever find out?" Agnes followed Nemeah's solemn gaze to Ismaara, huddled beneath a pile of blankets. "So the girl was her," she said softly. "You can see visions. You have fire. Water. You can speak the Vira language. You can manifest like a Darra," She reached out, gently taking Nemeah's hand. "Can you control the wind? Or grow things? Plants, vines, anything?" Her questions spilled out in a rush, her voice rising with excitement.

Nemeah pulled her hand back, unsure how to answer. "No, I do not think so." She rubbed her palms together. "But I have never really tried. Have your books ever mentioned someone like me?" she asked, searching Agnes's face. "Someone who had more than one Echo gift?"

Agnes went quiet, her thoughts turning inward. "There was one," she said at last. "I always thought it referred to the god. The Queen. It never said what she could do, just that she was unlike the others. But," Her eyes lit up. "If we could get back into the Axis house, there are books there, countless journals. I bet I could find something. Something to explain this."

Yuli gave a soft laugh and clapped her hands. "Oh, I am *so* in. When do we leave?"

Nemeah's eyebrows shot up. "We *cannot* go back there. We barely made it out last time."

Agnes was already on her feet, pacing. "The fire damaged the building. I doubt they have repaired anything yet." She looked down at her tattered robe and smirked. "I could get in, no problem."

"No," Nemeah said firmly. "That is way too dangerous." She turned to Yuli for backup, but the girl only smiled, already on board.

"If we got more robes," Yuli offered, "we could pretend we were sent to help. Repairs, cleanup, just a few loyal workers doing our duty."

"Absolutely not!" Nemeah snapped, stomping her foot. She instantly regretted it. She sounded exactly like her mother.

Yuli placed a hand on her arm, a soothing gesture, though not entirely calming. "We have to go back," she said, her tone low. "We all need answers, and right now it is looking like that is the only place to get them."

Chapter Twenty

The moon hung high in the sky by the time everyone began to stir. Edna muttered about her sleep schedule being ruined for weeks, while Henry joked that it made him feel like he should be out on nightly patrol for the Axis.

The three women had not yet shared their plans with the others, nor did they really want to. Yuli knew her husband would forbid it outright, and Nemeah expected the motherly look from Edna and the quiet concern from Keanoff. Only Agnes moved freely, unbothered by others' opinions.

Scrubbing at her soot-stained robe, Agnes frowned at the frayed collar where she had tugged it too many times. The hem was beginning to unravel as well.

"I need new clothes," she announced to no one in particular, her voice echoing off the cave walls. When no one responded, she cleared her throat and tried again, louder. "I need a new dress."

This time, everyone turned, even Ismaara, who had been in a quiet conversation with Keanoff.

Nemeah stood, recognizing her cue they had discussed that morning. "I have a few dresses you could look through. They are not much, but they should work."

Yuli chimed in next, holding up her scorched jacket. "Got something for me in there?"

Henry raised a brow. "What happened to your jacket?"

"She threw a hissy fit and burned it," Yuli said, nodding toward Nemeah.

"You what?" Keanoff gawked as he stood, Ismaara close behind. "You burned her? What were you thinking?"

Agnes shot Yuli a worried glance. This had not been part of their morning plan.

"It was an accident," Nemeah said quickly. "I thought I was alone, and I was just so angry." Her voice trailed off, her hands lifting in a helpless gesture.

Keanoff's face showed his anger, a face Nemeah did not like directed at her. "You cannot let your emotions take over like that," Keanoff snapped. "What if you had hurt Yuli?"

"But she is fine. It was just her jacket, and we can—"

"Just her jacket?" His voice rose. "And what about tomorrow? You going to roast her hair off next? Maybe a leg or two? You are one outburst away from losing control again."

Nemeah's eyes darkened, sparks flickering from her fingertips. Her voice dropped, growing deeper, resonating with something ancient and wild. "I told you I would find a way to control this."

Black smoke bled from her hands, swirling around the room until it consumed everything. One by one, the others faded from sight. Only she and Keanoff remained, standing in the heart of a growing void. The air thinned. The warmth from the day vanished.

"You need to trust me," she said, her voice echoing in the dark.

Keanoff's brows drew tight, his mouth a firm line. "How am I supposed to trust you," he said grimly, "when you do not even realize what you are doing right now?"

He swung his hand through the smoke, but it only thickened, coiling tighter. Light disappeared in folds around them. Nemeah's eyes darted around. She had not even realized it had gotten this far. Her powers were moving without her will. Panic crept in. She drew in a long breath, then another, forcing herself to concentrate. The rage clawed inside her, begging to be released. But she held it in, a silent struggle inside her.

Slowly, the smoke receded. The air warmed, and the pressure around them lifted. Keanoff scoffed and turned his back to her. Ismaara rushed to his side. Nemeah stood frozen, the urge to explode still burning in her chest. She clenched her fists so tightly her nails pressed into her palms. She wanted to lash out, for just a second, to let the power run wild and free. But if she did, she would become exactly what Keanoff feared. A danger to everyone around her. She spun on her heel, throwing up her hands in frustration, and stormed out of the cave. Agnes and Yuli followed without a word.

Henry walked over to Keanoff, his grip firm as he clasped the Vira's arm. "Was that necessary?" he asked, voice filled with disapproval like a father warning a son.

Keanoff tried to jerk away, but Henry's grip was iron. "She has to see that she is not in control of whatever the hell is inside her," Keanoff snapped, trying again to pull free, but failing.

"And you think provoking her was the best idea?" Henry yanked Keanoff a step closer, his voice low but firm. "Next time you pull a stunt like that, make sure it is only *your* life you are risking." He released Keanoff and stormed from the cave after his wife.

Keanoff rubbed his arm, quietly impressed by the strength a "normal" human could wield.

"I think you did the right thing," Ismaara said softly, appearing beside him. Her hand landed gently on his arm, easing the ache. "I saw what she did back at the Axis house. It was terrifying." A shudder passed through her as she wrapped her arms around herself.

Keanoff let go of his frustration and instead rubbed her back, trying to comfort her. "Have you ever known an Echo who could do the things she does?" He scanned the mouth of the cave for any sign of Nemeah returning and was not sure if he felt relief or regret.

Ismaara shook her head slowly. "No. I have never seen someone with multiple Echo abilities before. She is the first of her kind."

He turned fully to face her. "Her kind?"

Ismaara watched Keanoff's features relax, his previous concern now toddling into something that looked like fascination. Something that made her insides ignite with jealousy. She curled her fingers and spun on her heel, leaving Keanoff with his questions.

***

Outside, Agnes had caught up with Nemeah, a cheerful smile on her face. "Well," she said brightly, "I think now is the perfect time to leave. No one would even notice us gone."

Yuli came running up the hill, her scorched jacket still balled in her hand. "Are you alright? He could have been a little less dramatic about the whole thing."

"Yuli." Henry's voice made her wince. She squeezed her eyes shut and turned, offering him a too-bright smile. "She just needs a moment," she said quickly, trying to steer him back toward the cave, but moving Henry was like trying to push a stone wall.

He looked between the two women, concern furrowing his brow. "Are you sure you should be out here? With her like this?"

Nemeah felt her body tense. She wanted to scream. To tell him to leave with his judgment and doubt, but deep down, she knew he was right. If she could not control her anger, then how could anyone feel safe around her?

"I am sorry I worried you, Henry," she said, voice soft but steady. "I will try to do better next time." She turned to Yuli. "And I am sorry I burned your jacket."

Yuli smiled, her usual mischief returning. "Henry, we are going into the woods for a bit. See if we can find some more—"

"Moss," Agnes interrupted, voice pitched higher than usual. "My bed is still pretty lumpy." She gave a nervous laugh.

"Moss?" Henry echoed, skeptical. "Why not just ask Edna to grow more?"

"Oh, she has already done so much," Agnes said, scratching her head until her short hair stuck out in odd directions. "I just, well, I want to try doing this on my own."

Yuli coughed.

"With my new friends," Agnes added, recovering quickly. "Just us ladies."

Henry raised a brow. He had worked with Agnes for twelve years, and she was always precise, meticulous to a fault. This sudden spontaneity did not sit right. His gut told him something was off.

"I could come with you," he offered. "Just to keep an eye out. Security." He looked up at the moon. "I do not like the thought of you being out there by yourselves."

Yuli leaned up and kissed his cheek. "No offense, honey, but we are scarier than you." She nodded at Nemeah with a wink. "We will be fine. We will come back with moss. Loads of non-lumpy moss."

Before Henry could argue, Nemeah waved her hand. Alban materialized beside a portal that shimmered open in the air beside them. Dark woods lay on the other side, bathed in moonlight that filtered through the branches above. Alban went first, checking the perimeter. Then the women stepped through quickly, and the portal snapped shut behind them.

Henry sighed, rubbing the back of his neck as he made his way back to the cave. The scent of cooking herbs and roasted root vegetables hung thick in the air. The dragon blinked at him with large blue eyes and let out a soft clicking noise. Keanoff stepped up beside him and gave a low whistle in reply. Then he let out a long breath and shook his head.

"What is the matter?" Ismaara questioned, her voice innocent as she traced circles on Keanoff's arm with her finger.

"Nemeah is being reckless again," Keanoff muttered, breaking out of Ismaara's hold and setting off into a run.

Henry followed close behind. "What did it say?" He yelled as he met Keanoff just outside, his eyes scanning the horizon.

Behind them, a low growl rumbled through the cave. Henry flinched as the dragon padded up silently, its massive body nearly weightless on the stone. Another series of clicks and whistles shattered the tranquil backdrop.

"*She*," Keanoff corrected Henry aloud. "What did *she* say?"

Henry gave an apologetic look at the dragon, his reflection showing in her glacial eye. "What did she say?"

"She said they are sneaking into the Axis house. Agnes is searching for a book or something. They are looking for answers."

"Answers about what?" Henry watched as Keanoff climbed onto Noa's back.

"About what is happening to Nemeah." He replied, giving Noa a slight kick with his heel.

The dragon lurched forward, her massive wings giving a few test flaps. Henry ran out in front of her, his arms open wide.

"I am coming with you!" He shouted, his guts making him seriously consider what he was saying. "My wife, my responsibility. Besides, I know how to navigate the Axis house."

Keanoff leaned over and offered him a hand. Henry's weight nearly pulled Keanoff off Noa's back, as he strained to hoist the massive figure up.

"Hold on." Keanoff offered as Noa took to the sky.

***

In the woods, Nemeah focused her energy. She visualized the veil of invisibility coating her skin, imagined it sinking into every pore, winding over her like a second layer. Her hand vanished, then her arm, until she was completely see-through. She took a breath, feeling the magic cling to her like mist.

"Me next!" Yuli clapped, giddy as her fingers turned translucent. She watched her limbs fade until even her shadow was gone. "This is amazing!"

"It may feel that way now," Agnes said cautiously, "but we do not know how long it will last. If there is still silvervane in the lower halls, your disguise will be limited. We need to reach the storerooms quickly." She was talking to just Alban, now that both women were invisible. "And that is if any robes survived the fire," she added, her voice dropping. "What if this does not work? What if I get you both caught again?"

Yuli nudged her shoulder, making Agnes jump. "We will be fine. You said the storeroom's right down the stairs. We will be changed before anyone knows we are there."

Agnes took a deep breath and nodded. "Third door on the left. If I am delayed, keep going. I will catch up when I can."

She turned to go, then paused, staring at the space where she hoped Nemeah stood.

"The Darra who designed the Axis house built it like a maze," she warned. "There is a pattern to follow. You can turn left three times and still be heading the right way, but any more, and you are lost. Take a right before the third left? Lost again. And if you go past the fourth right, you will need three lefts again."

Nemeah groaned. "What?"

"Just follow me," Agnes said with a weary sigh, and all four moved out of the trees.

The streets of the city were a ruin. Blackened stone, collapsed roofs, and water-logged alleys. What Nemeah had not scorched in her rage, she had swept away with her tide. The devastation was complete. Homes reduced to ash, shops crumbled beyond recognition. Families slept among the rubble. Merchants sat silent in the streets, their livelihoods shattered.

Agnes kept her head low and her steps brisk, silently praying no one would stop her. But when they reached the city square, all of them froze. The Axis house was gone. A heap of splintered beams and scorched marble marked its place. The grand stairway was buried beneath a tangle of charred wood and broken stone. Agnes staggered forward and shoved at a thick beam. Her boots skidded on the soot-slick stone. She grunted, hands blackening as she tried again, to no avail. She straightened slowly, defeat etched in every line of her face.

"How are we supposed to get inside now?"

Yuli poked at the ground, nudging loose stones with her boot. "Maybe," she whispered, "If I shift into something small, like a mouse or a beetle?"

"Shh!" Nemeah hissed. Two armored men were walking toward them. She waved her hand, and Alban quickly vanished into thin air.

The men wore the gold-plated Axis armor, but it was battered, dulled with ash, and scorched in streaks. Their gazes fixed on Agnes, eyes trailing down her smoke-stained robe.

"You were the cook," one said, his expression lighting up with recognition. He pointed to the ruined stairs. "We thought you were trapped."

Agnes shook her head quickly. "No. I fled to the woods and got turned around. I was relieved to see the city again, or what is left of it." Her voice was careful. "Has anyone gone inside since?"

The second soldier shook his head. "The beam is too heavy. We have no idea what is beneath it." He pointed down the street. "Survivors are holed up at the Barbs Tavern. Father Leon is there. He will be glad to know you are alive."

Nemeah and Yuli held their breath at the name, Father Leon. The man who had nearly poisoned them with their last meal. They watched helplessly as the two soldiers led Agnes away, her eyes darting back toward them. Uncertainty clouded her face, unsure of where their invisible forms stood, whether they would still be there when she returned.

Only once the street was clear, Agnes and the guards disappearing around the corner, did Nemeah move. With a wave of her hand, the fallen beam groaned, sliding aside with slow resistance. Beneath it, to their surprise, the stairs remained intact, descending into a black void.

"Third door on the left," Yuli whispered. "We change first, then we go look for that book."

Nemeah's nerves prickled. She had been dragged through these halls before. Agnes had not exaggerated; they *were* a labyrinth. Nemeah tried to recall the pattern she had been told: three lefts, then a right, but already it felt like it was slipping from her mind. Before she could voice her doubts, she heard footsteps ahead. Yuli was already barreling down the stairs.

They descended quickly. Only when at the bottom did the thick darkness swallow them whole. Even invisibility did not matter now. They could not see a thing, not even the space between them. Nemeah opened her mouth, but the bitter metallic tang of silvervane coated her tongue, her powers already thinning.

"We will have to feel our way through," she whispered, reaching out until her fingers found the cold wall. She pressed her palm against the stone and started forward.

"Just give us a lantern or *something*," Yuli muttered, her voice close behind.

"We do not know if anyone is still down here. The last thing we need is to draw attention to ourselves."

They shuffled forward, blind and quiet, each footstep a calculated risk. The dark played tricks on them, shapes morphing, shadows stretching, and Nemeah had to count every doorway just to stay sane. One. Two. Three. She found a handle, sleek and cool, and turned it slowly, afraid the creak would give them away. The door opened into an even darker room, but at least it was empty.

They slipped inside and closed it behind them. A dim orb of light bloomed from Nemeah's hand, small and muted, just enough to see by. They searched the space, Albans' dim form fading from the effects of the silvervane. Nemeah waved him away, her head starting to ache as she helped Yuli search.

"Here we go." Yuli moved straight to a pile of robes, brushing dust from pristine white cloth. Somehow, the room had been spared the fire's hunger.

They dressed quickly, adjusting to the stiff fabric and pulling the sun-stitched patches into place.

"I did *not* miss these," Nemeah muttered, stuffing her dress beneath the pile of robes. A headache throbbed behind her eyes, dull at first, then pounding. Her magic was draining fast. "Find something we can use for light. Anything."

They turned over benches, shoved aside piles of cloth, and rummaged through forgotten crates. Cobwebs clung to their sleeves. The dust tickled their noses, and sneezes were stifled. At last, Yuli held up an old stub of a candle.

"It will have to do." Nemeah cupped it in her palms. She rubbed her fingers together until a small flame sparked to life, just as the last of her power fizzled out.

The candle flickered, but held. They returned to the hall, now dressed as if they belonged there.

"Three lefts, then a right," Yuli reminded, taking the lead.

If the halls had been confusing before, they were far worse now. Every corridor looked the same. Every turn was a guess. Even with the candle, shadows reached up like claws. The silence was thick, pressing against their ears. At each door they passed, they checked. Most revealed more closets, rows of robes, and shelves of abandoned armor. Bunks were stacked in tight lines, and stalls for bathing smelled of stagnant and moldy air. One room had more candles; they each stuffed several into their pockets, just in case.

Then they opened another door. It creaked open to reveal a long corridor of cells, just like the ones they had been locked in. They checked each one, their breath held, and were thankful to discover that each one was empty.

Time passed in unknown spurts; had it been only minutes or several hours? Down here, they could not quite tell. The world above felt like it had stopped turning. Door after door, they moved silently until they came to what looked like a study. Papers and scrolls littered the floor, ink wells cracked and dried in sticky pools. Shelves lined the walls, filled with books whose golden titles shimmered in the candlelight.

"There are *hundreds*," Yuli groaned. "How are we supposed to know which one?"

Nemeah scanned the spines. Each title blurred into the next. *Axis Laws, Continents Alphabetized, Historical Leaders by Region.* Her temple throbbed. The silvervane was in her bloodstream now, numbing her thoughts and dulling her senses. She rolled her neck, a satisfying pop echoing through the quiet. Then, as her eyes flicked back to the shelves, one book stood out.

The ink-stained burgundy leather stood out from the rows of neat books. *The Gods' War.* Could it really be that easy? She pulled it from the shelf, its cover worn, the spine cracked from age. She turned it over in her hands, unsure what she was hoping to find. Her head suddenly pulsed with pain as she fell to the floor, a vision flashing before her eyes. She clutched her head and let out a scream. Yuli was by her side, her hand over Nemeah's mouth, stifling her cries.

A vision of a woman played through her head, sending a searing pain racing down Nemeah's body. The woman was running down a dark hall, her white robe fluttering behind her. Everything seemed to move with accelerated speed, and Nemeah had to concentrate on the vision to see it clearly. She watched as the woman ran up a spiral staircase, taking the steps as quickly as her feet would allow. She bursts through a door, the warm wood leading to a study lit only by a single candle. The woman spun in the middle, her brown hair clinging to her sweat-littered face, obstructing Nemeah's view of who she was. Then, as if spotting it together, Nemeah and the woman stared at four mirrors on the wall, all of which circled around one made of black glass.

The woman hurried to the wall, staring at her reflection in each one until a voice boomed from somewhere below. *"Stop her now!"* The woman hastily grabbed a mirror from where it hung on the wall and hurled it to the stone floor with all her might. A blinding light erupted from the shards that now flew everywhere, and the sound of shattering glass echoed slowly around them. Nemeah now stood behind the woman, watching the open door of the study, curious to see who was coming. Then Nemeah saw him, a man who looked identical to Ismaara, with one green eye and one blue. "No!" He yelled as the woman between them shattered into a million pieces, mimicking the mirror she had successfully destroyed. The woman turned around, now staring at Nemeah, her broken face giving way to a smile before fading.

"Wait!" Nemeah's body jerked, her eyes now looking up to Yuli, who was focused on the door, her hand still clamped over Nemeah's mouth.

She craned her neck, her eyes seeing a dim glow under the door growing brighter and brighter. Footsteps shuffled from the hall, the sound scraping against the two women's eardrums. Yuli looked at Nemeah, worry in her eyes. Both were now helpless to whoever would find them in this room.

"What do we do?" Yuli whispered as she helped Nemeah up.

"Maybe they will pass up this room, go to the next?" Nemeah searched the floor, finding the book, cautious to pluck it from where it lay.

Yuli scooped it up, her finger pressed to her lips as the shuffling feet stopped outside the door. They stopped breathing, their eyes wide as their hair stood on end. The glow under the door flickered, orange and warm, as a shadow appeared to be reaching for the knob. The door handle turned, and both girls felt their hearts skip.

Chapter Twenty-one

Nemeah quickly blew out the candle as the door creaked open. Both women crouched behind the desk, holding their breath and praying to any god listening not to be found. Shuffling footsteps entered the room, uneven and quick. The flickering light cast long shadows across the wall, twisting the shapes of the chair and scattered items on the desk into monstrous forms. They watched the glow shift from one wall to the next, inching closer as the girls squeezed each other's hands tighter, knowing they were just moments from being caught. Then, a voice spoke.

"Yuli? Nemeah?"

Both girls exhaled in relief as Yuli peeked up from behind the desk. Never before had she been so happy to see a furious husband staring back at her, with his furrowed brows and downturned mouth. Yuli hurried out from her hiding spot and threw her arms around Henry, who instinctively pulled her close.

"What in the chains do you think you are doing?" Keanoff snapped, quickly shutting the door behind him. "Sneaking in here like a couple of idiots."

"Watch it," Henry warned, tightening his hold on Yuli. "They must have had a reason." He looked down at his wife, her face buried in his chest. "Right?"

Yuli nodded and pulled a thick purple book from beneath her robe. "We needed this. Agnes thinks it will help us understand what is happening to Nemeah." She nodded toward her friend. "And if we can figure it out, we might actually be able to help her control it." She met Keanoff's glare with one of her own, the kind that said *you are supposed to protect your friends, not abandon them.*

Keanoff looked away, pretending to focus on the door. "We need to leave before someone notices we are not part of their precious order." He cast a sharp glance back at the others. "Where is Agnes?"

"A few of the guards recognized her," Nemeah said, rubbing her temples. The strange pulsing in her vision still had not faded. "They took her to a tavern where some Axis survivors are staying."

"How did you even know we were here?" Yuli asked, her voice softer now as she looked up at her husband.

His expression held a familiar mix of relief and worry. "The dragon ratted you out," he said with a crooked smile.

Yuli grinned back as she leaned up to kiss him, her fingers gently threading through his thick brown hair.

Nemeah turned away, heat rushing to her face. Her eyes flitted to Keanoff, then quickly back to the bookshelf, hoping the shadows might swallow her embarrassment. This was not helping their mission progress.

"Come on, love birds, we need to move." Keanoff slowly eased the door open, checking the corridor beyond. It was still as empty and dark as it had been before. "Henry, take the lead."

They slipped back into the passage, the dim candle barely lighting the way. It felt like wandering through a catacomb, each turn a mirror of the last. Nemeah's balance wavered, her thoughts clouding more with every step. The silvervane in the air dulled her senses, pressing like fog against her skull. She caught a glimpse of Keanoff shaking his head as if trying to clear his own mind. Even Yuli was starting to sway, blinking hard as her pace slowed.

Only Henry moved with certainty through the shadowed tunnels. He led them forward, his familiarity with the labyrinth their only hope of escape. Then, finally, after what seemed like hours, a sliver of light appeared. The morning sunlight, bright and golden, poured down the stairwell ahead. A collective sigh broke the tension, followed by soft laughter. Nemeah could smell the fresh air flowing down through the opening, her blood tinged with excitement at the thought of escape. One by one, they climbed the stairs, tired but relieved. Henry reached the top first and froze.

Above ground, more than twenty soldiers stood waiting. Their armor showed the full force of destruction Nemeah had caused the last time she was here. Their capes were ripped or discarded entirely. Their once polished plating was now dull and charred. Not one man wore a full suit, but all wore the same smug expression. Two men held Agnes between them. Her eyes were wide, her face streaked with dirt and tears. A bruise lined her jaw, where someone had hit her.

"Oh, Henry," said a familiar voice.

Father Leon stepped forward from the center of the group. His priestly robes were blackened with soot, the hems soiled. He looked disheveled but disturbingly calm. "I feared you had perished in the fire," he said, almost gently. He placed a hand on Henry's arm and gave it a patronizing pat. "It will be good to have you back by my side." Then, leaning in close, he lowered his voice. "This lot?" His gaze swept over the men standing at attention in their battered plating. "They are a bit daft."

Henry looked into the faces of his former comrades, men he had stood beside for years, hunting down Echoes and celebrating their demise. Shame twisted in his chest for all the blind loyalty he had given the Axis. For every life taken in its name, his heart ached for his young and naive past self. He finally looked at his friend, Agnes. Her wide, terrified eyes were locked on the stairwell behind him as Nemeah, Yuli, and Keanoff emerged one by one, hands raised. More

Axis soldiers followed behind, their blades drawn and pointed, corralling the group like prey.

"Hello again, Yuli," Father Leon said smoothly. "Always a pleasure to see your beautiful face, even if it belongs to an Echo." His gaze shifted to Keanoff, his grin widening, but when his eyes landed on Nemeah, the smile vanished. "And *you*," he said, practically spitting the words. He snapped his fingers. "Kill her. Take the other two."

Yuli thrashed against the guards grip. "Leave us alone!"

Henry stood frozen, feeling helpless; there were too many to fight on his own. Keanoff was not so cautious. He landed two hard punches before a guard kicked him in the gut, doubling him over. The hilt of a sword cracked down on the back of his head, and he dropped to the ground, unconscious.

The world spun around Nemeah; Yuli biting at her captors, Agnes weeping, Keanoff helpless on the ground, Father Leon grinning, and Henry backing away. She felt something inside her shift then, mending the blood that was tainted by the silvervane. Its magic going from one cell to the next, cleansing her from the inside out.

It stirred deep within her, rising from the base of her spine like a wave building in the depths. Pressure surged through her limbs as a soldier's blade lunged straight for her chest. She felt the power stir, clawing its way through her body, as if every cell in her had become its own tiny echo, pushing back with a startling defiance.

In an instant, her vision cleared. The pounding in her skull was gone, leaving her mind sharper than before. Her hand snapped up, and just before the blade pierced her white robe, she *released it*. A burst of energy exploded from her like a hurricane, tearing through the air with raw force. Bodies flew backwards, their feet unable to keep them grounded. The buildings that had somehow survived fire and flood were finally reduced to rubble. Dust and soot billowed into the air, blinding everyone, turning the world into a storm of grey ash.

Soldiers groaned and shifted in the debris as they regained consciousness. Father Leon gasped in pain, his leg bent at an unnatural angle, his arm hanging uselessly at his side. Yuli rolled onto her back, stunned to see Henry already next to her. He helped her to her feet, caressing her face, examining her for wounds. The tender moment was interrupted by a scream that pierced the haze. They turned, squinting through the fog. Visibility was almost zero, with barely enough light to see a few feet in any direction. Then a voice cut through the haze.

"You." A lone soldier stepped forward, his sword dragging along the stones of the street. His voice trembled with rage. "I *knew* you were an Echo lover." He raised his blade to strike, but something coiled around his ankles before he could.

A black vine, slick and sinewy, snaked up his legs and *jerked*. The soldier fell, his sword clanging and echoing between his pleas for help. Panick fueled him as he clawed at the road. The vine dragged him backward as his fingers scraped between cobblestones, desperate to hold on. But it was of no use; with a final shriek, he vanished into the fog. Henry pulled Yuli into his arms, holding her close as they stared into the swirling grey.

Agnes awoke with a start. A hand was still clamped around her arm. She jolted, turning her head to find her captor slumped beside her, blood trickling from his ears and nose. Dead. Carefully, she slipped from his grasp and stood on trembling legs. All around her, screams rang out, some distant, others alarmingly close. The air was thick with dust and soot, burning her lungs with every breath. She pressed a sleeve to her mouth, stifling a cough. She did not dare reveal her position.

"Agnes?"

She froze. Her gaze darted through the smoke until she spotted Keanoff sprawled across the ground. Two bodies lay atop him, Axis soldiers, motionless. She rushed to his side, struggling to push one corpse over. It was heavier than she expected, and she cursed herself for her weak limbs. With one final shove, she managed to roll the body off, and Keanoff squirmed free from under the second, his hands brushing frantically over his clothes as though he could wipe away the lingering touch of death.

"Where is Nemeah?" he asked, voice low, eyes scanning the haze.

"I think that is her," Agnes whimpered, hands covering her ears as another scream tore through the fog.

Keanoff gripped her arm and pressed forward. They stumbled over debris and slumped bodies, unknown if they were dead or just unconscious. Neither wanted to check to know for sure. Keanoff tried to hold his breath, only breathing when he thought the air was cleaner than the area before. The smoke was suffocating, blanketing the city square. They stuck to the outskirts, eventually finding Yuli and Henry standing still, backs tense, their eyes wide with fear.

"We have to get out of here," Keanoff whispered. He gently nudged Agnes toward them. "Noa is waiting, but I need to signal her." He closed his eyes, ready to shift into his hawk form, but nothing happened. He grunted in frustration.

"You have too much silvervane in your system," Yuli said quietly, her voice chastising. "You will not be able to change for a while."

Keanoff stared down at his hands. His head throbbed while panic bloomed in his chest. Never had he felt this helpless. He had never experienced the numb obedience of a body that refused to listen. Shifting forms had always been a part of him, *his* gift, his identity. Now it was silent. *Is this what it is like for Nemeah,* he wondered. *When her magic breaks through her control?*

Another distant cry cut through the air. Then another and another, all echoing, clashing together like a wave of anguish, and then silence. The kind that settles before a storm. They waited, still as statues, ears straining for any sign of movement. But instead of footsteps or swords, a breeze brushed past them. Slow and steady, it cleared the soot and dust, sweeping the ash from the air. The grey lifted, and there she stood.

Nemeah was alone beside what remained of the Axis house, black smoke drifting off her skin, her eyes dark as pitch. Her chest heaved, each breath shallow and strained. Magic curled around her like a living shadow. She stared at them, watching as her senses took in each one, waiting for their reactions.

They stared back, watching her with unblinking eyes as her magic coiled at her feet, prodding for something to manipulate or hold onto. What they could not see was the battle raging inside her, every heartbeat a war cry as she fought for control. She raised a trembling hand, pointing to the beam that now sealed off the stairwell.

"They are still alive," she panted, her voice ragged and hollow. "I put them all in the hole." Her eyes swept over them. All looked terrified as if they were her next victims. She wanted to scream at them for it. To let the fury rise and consume everything. To make them see that it was only by her that they were now safe. The monster they stared at was their protector. But instead, she clenched her fists, her body shaking as she forced the magic back.

"Obey me," she willed it. *"Obey!"*

She opened her eyes, feeling the world around her calm. Her friends approached slowly, watching her with wary eyes, as if they were looking for danger.

"You alright?" Yuli's voice was soft and careful.

Nemeah looked down at her hands. The smoke had vanished. Her breath was steadier. The rage was gone.

"Yes," she rasped. "I think so."

A thumping echoed from beneath the beam, soldiers hammering against the sealed entrance, their cries muffled but persistent.

"We should get going," Keanoff said. He cupped his hands around his mouth and let out a long, continuous whistle.

In the distance, Noa appeared. Her massive wings blended almost seamlessly with the sky, feathers shimmering as the sun struck the glossy surface of her scales. She was radiant, a creature pulled from myth, both beautiful and terrifying. She landed as softly as a swan, her enormous frame barely disturbing the cracked earth beneath her. With a low whistle and sharp click, she called out to Keanoff.

He answered in kind, a series of matching sounds. "She can only take two or three at a time. Same as before," he said, turning to Henry and Yuli. "You two go with Agnes. We will wait."

Yuli reached into her robes and pulled out the book. "I hope this was worth it," she said, pressing it into Nemeah's hands. She hugged her tightly, then stepped toward Noa and climbed aboard.

Noa stretched her wings wide, then charged across the square. With one final leap, she caught the wind and vanished into the sky.

Keanoff shaded his eyes, watching until the dragon disappeared. "We should head for the woods," he said, glancing toward the distant tree line. "It will be safer to wait there."

But Nemeah stood still, her gaze locked on the broken stairwell and the beam she had placed over it. "Do you think they will make it out?" she asked quietly, her voice no longer ragged, but weary and small.

Keanoff stepped beside her, resting a hand on the beam. "Did you leave them with weapons?"

She nodded without meeting his eyes.

"Then if they are smart, they will chip their way through." He turned and started toward the woods. "Come on."

They walked in silence. The town around them looked hollow and haunted. Shops abandoned, homes burned or broken. Cleared out of any life that was here before. Nemeah bent to collect a few dresses scattered in the street, most of which were ruined by fire or water, while some had miraculously been spared. She carried them in her arms, the fabric draped over her like fallen petals.

Her thoughts drifted to the vision. The woman smashing the mirror. Her body splintering in sync with the glass. To the voice that whispered in her head after her magic subsided. Who *was* that voice? She was so deep in thought that she did not realize Keanoff had stopped walking. When she looked up, he was staring at her, one brow raised.

"You did not hear a word I said." He let out a frustrated breath and kept walking, scooping up some clothing from the roadside. "I asked what in the stars possessed you to walk right back into the same place that imprisoned you." His voice was mean, his usual carefree composure starting to fray.

Nemeah shrugged, arms already tired from the weight she carried. "Because I need answers. And if anywhere held them, it was the Axis house. I thought maybe... I do not know. Maybe I could understand what I am."

Keanoff shook his head as a small chuckle left his throat. "What you are is an impulsive Darra who keeps dragging herself and her friends into dangerous situations." His words were blunt.

Nemeah stopped walking, nerves tightening. "Do you *really* think it is that simple?" She rushed past him and dropped the pile of clothes at his feet. "I am *not* just a Darra," she snapped, her voice rising. "You have seen what I can do. I am different!"

Keanoff rolled his eyes, though the tension in his shoulders betrayed him. "Do *you* believe that?" he asked.

"You do," she shot back. "You said it yourself."

He stopped and dropped his own bundle to the ground. "I do not know what I believe," he said. "You seemed normal enough before." He paused. The rest of the sentence hung in the air between them, unsaid but understood.

"Before everything changed? Before Jacob died. Before the monster who killed him tried to kill *us*. Before his army of corpses rose from the ground." She stepped toward Keanoff, wishing, just for once, that she did not have to tilt her head to meet his gaze. She wished she did not feel so *small*. Wished she did not feel an attraction to a man who looked at her as if she were the Morin she spoke of.

"I can feel it," she said, her voice cracking. "That I am different. And I do not *want* to be. I want to go back to my family. I want to stop running. I do not want the Axis hunting me down. I do not want the visions, or the shadows, or the nightmares. I do not want these powers." She pressed the heels of her palms into her eyes, trying to erase the image, *the woman shattering like glass, smiling as she splintered.* "I just want to be *normal.*"

Keanoff froze. The guilt struck fast, rising like a tide, crashing through the careless armor he wore like a second skin. He remembered the way they had fought in the cave. The coldness of his tone. The things he had said were selfish and unfair. Where had that even come from? But then he remembered her *eyes.* That unnatural black, endless, and void-like. The way her magic tore through the Axis soldiers like they were nothing, like their lives were flames ready to be snuffed out.

He did not know what he was supposed to feel. Gratitude? Fear? Both? He raised his hand slowly, meaning to touch her shoulder, to pull her in, to say *something* kind. But she stepped back, just out of reach, as the sky darkened. A great shadow passed over them as Noa descended from the clouds, her enormous wings beating the air. She landed in silence, feathers raised, body alert. A whistle and a click sounded a bit uneasy.

"More are coming." Keanoff quickly moved, collecting the garments they had salvaged and handing them to Nemeah once she climbed onto Noa's back. He mounted after her, careful not to sit too close. The silence between them was louder than any words.

With a strong push from her hind legs, Noa charged forward, caught the wind, and lifted off. They rose into the sky, bound for the cave that had begun to feel less like shelter and more like a cage. When they returned, a hush fell over the group.

Henry stood beside Yuli, his expression hard but worn, like he had already had a long, quiet argument with her. Ismaara rushed to Keanoff's side, fingers threading around his arm like she always did, a signal of their ever-growing relationship. Agnes lit up at the sight of Nemeah, eyes going wide when she spotted the soot-streaked dresses in her arms.

Edna did not speak, just nodded from behind the small fire where she stirred a pot. Relief softened her face, though she kept her hands busy. Nemeah made her way to her bed, Agnes following in her wake, excited chatter about the new clothes.

"I have not worn anything besides these robes since I was a small girl. I do not even know what is in fashion these days." She gave a nervous laugh as she held up the corset. "Oh dear."

Nemeah had to smile at this, her innocence that of a child. Her eyes lingered on the woman's bruised jaw, the mark now black and purple. Agnes lowered the garment, feeling her face with her fingers.

"Is it bad?" She traced the bruise. "I will get Ismaara to heal it as soon as she is done," She trailed off as her eyes caught on the Freyla snuggled in Keanoff's arms. She shot her eyes back to Nemeah. "I may just keep it, let it heal on its own. Does it make me look tough?"

Nemeah hated that she allowed her eyes to roam across the cave. She hated the feeling in her chest as she watched the two of them embrace, the whispers they shared. She shook her head as she flexed her hand.

"Agnes?" She looked up at the woman, who was now holding up a dull green dress, the long sleeves only slightly burned. "Could I try something?"

Agnes lowered the dress, nodding, though her eyes said no.

"Tell me to stop if it hurts, alright?"

Agnes gave another nod as Nemeah scooted close enough to cup Agnes' face in her hands. She closed her eyes, remembering the feeling she had felt in the square. The feeling of her body ridding itself of the silvervane. She let that feeling flow from her, feeling the magic creep along Agnes' skin and sink into her flesh. She felt the blood vessels healing, the blood returning where it should have stayed. The swollen tissue calming and shrinking. A gasp brought Nemeah out of her trance; her eyes shot open to see Agnes smiling at her, her face healed.

"Did you just?" Yuli was standing next to them, her voice low.

Agnes felt her face; the sore tissue like new. "Yes, she did."

Chapter Twenty-two

Nemeah tossed and turned that night, the vision refusing to release her. Again and again, it replayed: the woman in the white robe, her brown hair streaming behind as she raced through dark corridors. Damp footprints smeared the stone steps as she climbed, bursting through a wooden door into a silent chamber. Her eyes searched frantically, her hands clutching the mirror. Then, a crash like thunder erupted from the dark night. Glass scattered across the floor like a thousand falling stars. And before vanishing, the woman turned and smiled directly at Nemeah.

"No!" Nemeah bolted upright, skin slick with sweat, her heart hammering against her ribs.

The cave around her was still, black as a void, shadows clinging like velvet curtains. For several long minutes, she sat frozen, breath rasping until it steadied, pulse easing back from panic. She wiped her forehead, the damp chill of drying sweat clinging to her skin. The images looped in fragments: broken glass, that uncanny smile, the sudden absence.

Did she die? Nemeah wondered.

A faint sound tugged her back. She turned toward the cave mouth, where Alban stood, bathed in the dim glow of the crescent moon. His posture was rigid, his eyes locked on the tree line below, one hand already curling around the hilt of his sword.

Nemeah scrambled to him, bare feet slapping against stone. "What is it?" Her eyes strained through the haze, focusing on the forest far beneath.

A distant wail floated up the mountainside, high and thin. It made her spine shiver as if something cold had slid down her back.

"What is that?" Yuli's groggy voice drifted from behind, followed by Henry and Keanoff. They stumbled out half-asleep, eyes squinted, hair sticking every which way.

"It sounds human." Keanoff rubbed his face, trying to shake off the fog of sleep. "But who would be out here at night?"

The cries grew louder and closer. The group fell silent. Not even breaths stirred as they strained to listen. Then, another shriek, right below them, shrill and panicked.

"It sounds like a child," Yuli whispered, one hand pressed protectively to her stomach. Henry slipped an arm around her shoulders, steadying her.

Alban drew his blade. Moments later, a figure stumbled from the trees. A small body in a shredded dress. Mud smeared her face and hair, and blood streaked her scraped knees.

"Chains," Yuli gasped. "It is a child." She started forward, but Henry caught her arm.

"Wait. It could be a trap," he warned, his voice low but weighted.

He was not wrong. They were perched on a remote mountain; no one should have reached them here, much less a child alone.

"Help me!" the voice broke, ragged with sobs. The child lurched from the undergrowth, long black hair tangled, bare feet stumbling. "Please! Someone, please!"

Something twisted inside Nemeah. Horror, disbelief, and recognition. Her body moved before she thought, pushing past Alban and Keanoff. Her lips formed a name she had not spoken in months.

"Orla?" She flew down the rocky slope, feet slipping on loose shale. Stones cut into her soles, but she barely felt them. She skidded to her knees beside the girl, pushing damp hair from her face.

"Orla, is it really you?"

The child's tears streaked her mud-smeared cheeks, but her eyes were unmistakable. Her little sister's gaze met hers, wide with fear, her small body trembling violently.

"Orla, what happened? Where are Ma and Pa? How did you get here?" Nemeah pulled her close, desperate to shield her.

The small girl's sobs wracked her frame until she could hardly breathe. Snot ran down into her mouth as she coughed and choked, clinging to her sister.

"Get Edna!" Nemeah barked up the mountain. "Warm some water, food, anything!"

She hoisted Orla onto her back and began the climb. Sharp slate bit into her feet and palms as she clawed her way up, the added weight pulling at her shoulders. Alban reached down and hauled her the last stretch. Yuli rushed forward to take Orla's weight from the now-exhausted Nemeah.

Together, they ushered the girl inside, where the fire was already crackling, and Edna had a kettle set over the flames. Within minutes, a steaming cup was pressed into Orla's trembling hands. The Thorn's herbs worked their quiet magic, slowing her breathing, softening the edge of her terror.

"Orla, can you tell me what happened? How did you come to be here?" Nemeah's voice was soft, coaxing, but her sister only shook her head. She swallowed and tried again. "Do you know where Ma and Pa are? Why they are not with you?"

Another shake and still no answer. Nemeah forced her lungs to fill, pushing down the sharp edge of frustration. By now, the whole cave was awake. Everyone was watching the small, dirt-smudged girl who had somehow crossed oceans and continents to collapse into their firelit refuge.

Ismaara stepped forward, her practiced smile glowing as she knelt and lifted one of Orla's scraped feet into her hands. "I bet these cuts do not feel too nice, do they?"

Nemeah's chest tightened, jealousy flaring as her sister nodded. Orla's lips even curved faintly as the Freyla's touch mended her wounds. That look of awe, like she had never seen real magic before, stabbed at Nemeah.

"Would you like to tell us how you ended up in the woods?" Ismaara's voice was a silk thread that made Nemeah want to scream.

"What makes you think she will answer *you* when she would not even answer her own sister?" The words snapped out like acid on her tongue.

Ismaara's eyes narrowed, but she did not rise to the bait. She turned back to Orla, taking the girl's trembling hand. "Orla, how did you get here? Where are your parents?"

Orla's gaze flicked between the Freyla and her sister, and then the circle of strangers staring from the shadows. Her voice, when it came, was barely audible. "A bad man came to the door."

Nemeah's whole body jerked, brows furrowed, lips parting. "What bad man?"

But her words were swallowed as Ismaara pressed gently, "What bad man, Orla? Can you tell me about him?" Her fingers sifted through the child's tangled hair.

"He banged on the door. He woke me up. When I came downstairs, Pa was already there, telling him to leave. He tried to shut the door, but the man pushed his way inside." Tears welled again, spilling down her cheeks. "He had powers like Nemeah. He could make things appear."

The air around Nemeah crackled. She hissed a name through her teeth: "Vallorith." Her insides blazed with hate. She lurched forward. "Did he send you here, Orla? *Did he send you here?*"

Her voice rang off the cavern walls, louder, sharper, until Orla shrank against Ismaara's chest, clutching the princess as if she had always belonged there. The sight made Nemeah's stomach twist. She could not stay, could not breathe. She tore her golden compass from her bag. She would not stand idle. She would not let Vallorith touch her family again. She would kill him.

"Nemeah!" Keanoff caught her arm, his grip iron-tight. "Where are you going?"

"To do what needs to be done." She wrenched against him, wild-eyed. "Let me go."

"No." His voice was granite. He caught her other arm, forcing her to face him. "You are rushing into a trap. We need a plan."

"I *have* one!" Nemeah roared, rage boiling over. "I am going to kill him and then everything will be solved!"

The power inside her surged, screaming for release. She let it go. Wind exploded outward in a violent gust, hurling Keanoff across the chamber. He struck the ground with a heavy thud.

"Keanoff!" Yuli rushed to his side. "Nemeah, you cannot do this alone!" she shouted above the roar of the storm. "Let us help you!"

But Nemeah was beyond reason. Her hair whipped around her face, strands stinging her cheeks as she tore open a portal, the air shimmering with raw energy. Her gaze flicked across them all: Alban's taut expression, Yuli kneeling by Keanoff, Orla curled in Ismaara's arms. And then her decision hardened. With a flick of her hand, she summoned Alban to her side. Before anyone could move, she stepped into the portal and vanished. Silence rushed back in her wake.

"We have to stop her," Yuli said, hauling Keanoff to his feet. "Where did she go?"

Keanoff's chest rose and fell with ragged breaths. Dust clung to his clothes, but his eyes never left the space where Nemeah had disappeared. "Tirnmoor," he said grimly. Then he turned, shoulders heavy with defeat.

***

Nemeah stood with Alban on the hill behind the barn. From their perch, she could see the yard below, firelight flickering across armored bodies. A dozen Axis soldiers lounged around the flames, laughing, muttering, trading stories as though this land belonged to them. Inside the house, shadows moved. She recognized her parents' forms and felt slight relief to know they were somehow safe.

Above, the crescent moon drifted across the sky, casting its cold silver glow. Nemeah tipped her head toward it, a plan coiling in her mind. As she raised her hands, black veins spidered across her pale skin as she summoned powers she should not have been able to wield.

The clear heavens clouded. Moon and stars smothered beneath a fog that thickened until even the horizon vanished. Distant thunder growled, and the smell of rain was fresh in the air. The soldiers' chatter faltered, dropping to uneasy whispers. She heard their question pass from one mouth to the next: was this normal weather for Tirnmoor?

Nemeah sank to her knees and pressed her palms into the wet grass. Her power slid outward, creeping through each blade and stone, slithering like a serpent toward the enemy camp. She *felt* it stretching, covering the fields, surrounding them. She smiled as her shadows fell all into place. The soldiers were sluggish with fatigue, their talk drifting lazily between women and the spoils of war. Nemeah eased her magic closer. So close she could smell the salt of their sweat, and then she struck.

The fog thickened and split open with snarling maws. Wolves, vast and black as shadow, tore free, jaws of jagged teeth snapping shut on flesh. Screams ripped through the camp as one by one the men fell, their fear pouring into her like a drink she had been craving for years. She felt it all. The crunch of bone, the ripping of tendons, the exact moment life fled from their eyes.

The massacre ended in heartbeats. Not one soldier stood. Rising, Nemeah strode down the hill. A storm churned above, lightning flashing through the haze. The house loomed ahead, its door flung open. Three more soldiers stumbled out, swords half-raised and faces tight with panic.

"What is happening?" one barked.

"How should I know?" the other snapped.

They were afraid, and Nemeah relished it. She lifted her arm to the sky, then slashed it down like an executioner's blade. Light blazed while thunder shattered the air. When the smoke cleared, their scorched bodies sprawled across the grass.

She stood in the wreckage, her eyes dark voids, magic curling around her like a pack of hounds. "Find them," she ordered. Alban rushed into the house.

Nemeah prowled the firelit yard, wolves at her heels. Something itched in her thoughts. She crouched, examining the fallen soldiers more closely. Their wounds were right, but not *real.* Her wolves pressed against her side, nuzzling for comfort. Absent-mindedly, she stroked their damp fur, her gaze snagging on the thing she had missed before. Her stomach dropped.

"No blood."

A pulse cracked through the air, and her wolves dissolved into mist, the bodies evaporating into nothing. The yard was suddenly clean, untouched, as if the massacre had never been. Nemeah spun and saw a man standing in the moonlight, in robes the color of fresh-spilled blood. His blonde hair gleamed, slicked close to his scalp. Emerald eyes glittered with cruel delight.

"So," he said, voice like a constant ache in her ears, "you are the one who found my mirrors?"

Nemeah froze. The crimson robe. The golden hair. *Him.*

"Where are my parents?" The words ripped out of her throat, her magic stirring wildly, barely leashed.

"Your parents?" He tasted the words, his smile widening. "Why care for them now? Were they not the ones who cast you out? Who made you feel unwanted?" His voice dripped with mock sympathy as he stepped closer. "But forgive me, introductions first?"

Her veins burned. "I know who you are." Her voice was a growl. "Vallorith."

The name on her lips thrilled him. He lit up like a child who had been handed their favorite toy. "Ahhh, and what may I call you?" His gaze swept over her; black eyes, veins pulsing, magic swirling like smoke. He flicked his attention to Alban, silver armor gleaming as he stood ready. "And your companion. Though never mind. I will be dealing with you alone."

He flicked his hand. Another pulse rippled through the air, but Alban did not vanish. Vallorith's brow furrowed for the briefest moment. Only a second, but Nemeah caught it.

"Where are my parents?" she shouted, voice cracking like a whip. She stepped forward, power searing at her fingertips. "Tell me *now.*"

Vallorith only smiled, his posture shifting into a calculated stance. "A name first," he murmured, settling into a stance of his own.

Nemeah clenched her fists, patience shattering like glass in the wind. She hurled her hand forward, releasing a storm of jagged ice.

The shards whistled through the air, all aimed for the priest. Vallorith raised his arm, and the frozen blades burst apart before reaching him.

Her teeth ground together. She thrust both hands forward. Darkness swallowed the world, a void of frost and shadow closing around them. The air went black, the cold so deep it cut. She drew her palms together, willing the void to crush inward, to squeeze the life out of him. But then it fractured. Her spell frayed like strings being sliced, fragments falling to the earth as Vallorith kept walking, closer and closer.

"You know who I am," he said, his voice steady and smug, "and yet you think you can best me?" He flicked a finger. Nemeah's limbs turned heavy. She looked down in shock. Chains, black and iron-hard, coiled around her waist and shoulders, biting into her skin.

"Her name is Nemeah."

The voice came from behind. She twisted against her bonds, and a tall, hooded figure stepped into the moonlight. Clawed feet scraped the dirt. Amber eyes gleamed from beneath the hood.

"Zepher," she hissed.

"Oh yes," Vallorith said lightly. "I almost forgot you two had already met."

Her gaze locked with those burning eyes. Memory surged, Jacob's body crumpled at Zepher's feet, Edna screaming as the Morin held a blade to her throat. The shambling corpses he had raised, their soulless stares still haunted her. Pain twisted with fury until it burned hot enough to consume her. She pulled at the chains, a ragged groan breaking from her lips.

Vallorith chuckled. "How precious. She thinks she can—"

The crack of snapping metal cut him off. The chains fell, and this time Nemeah was the one smiling. Her arms swept forward. A gale slammed into priest and monster alike, flattening them against the ground. She did not think, nor did she plan. Her magic roared out of her, untamed. Flames erupted around them, wind stoking the blaze until it raged tenfold.

Zepher tore off his burning cloak and vaulted through the fire, daggers flashing. He lunged for Nemeah, desperate to carve her open, only to be met by a crashing broadsword.

"You again," Zepher snarled, eyes narrowing as Alban forced him back. He remembered the manifestation in the antique shop, the fight in the woods. Steel rang on steel, sparks bursting into the night. The duel raged, Alban and Zepher locked in a deadly rhythm.

Vallorith's confidence faltered. His smile twitched. "It was you," he spat, his voice sharp with realization. "You were the one at the Axis house in Highspire. The one Zepher fought in the forest." A shrill laugh tore from him. "The cursed Echo of Tirnmoor."

He raised both hands, conjuring a shimmering barrier around himself. Nemeah twisted her fingers, and the howling wind died. Moisture bled from the humid air, creeping into the sheltering bubble, seeping past the cracks. The water swelled around Vallorith's ankles, then rose to his knees. She felt savage joy watching him flinch and *squirm.*

Snarling, he dropped the shield and called his army. Soldiers materialized, ranks upon ranks hemming her in. Nemeah struck again. Her fire roared higher as her fog smothered the world in grey. All starlight and moon beams vanished until only the priest's burning prison still glowed. Sweat poured from his skin as blisters bubbled along his arms. He spun, shielding his face, mind racing for escape.

A wolf's howl cut through the haze. The sound of teeth on metal brought about screams and the dread of death. Nemeah was nowhere to be seen. Vallorith turned in frantic circles, the fire painting him in shifting gold and red. A sickness coiled in his gut. It was new. Unwelcome. The word broke from his lips like a curse. "Fear."

Vines writhed from the ground, coiling around his legs and arms. Ice crept into his lungs. Through the flames, a figure advanced, Nemeah, her skin blackening, peeling, only to regrow and heal with each step.

"You have them all," his voice trembled with fascination. "All nine Echo abilities." Fascination overtook fear as his eyes followed her approach. "Tell me, what does it feel like?"

Her stride faltered. "What?"

The smile returned to his lips. "What does it feel like to have all that power and still lose?" Behind him, a portal unfurled, its edges burning with light.

Nemeah's eyes widened. Her parents huddled together in a cell, pale and trembling. She bolted toward the portal, hand outstretched, but it dissolved before she reached them. She spun on the priest, fury swallowing her panic. Her eyes darkened into pits of shadow.

"Where are they!" The fire flared brighter, bands of blue and orange crackling around her.

"No," Vallorith said simply, menace back in his voice.

Her vines coiled tighter. "No?"

"You are going to let me walk away. In return, I will not kill your parents right now." His gaze cut into her, certain she had no other choice.

She paced back and forth before him, her anger bursting as her flames rose and fell like the waves of the ocean. What was she to do? She had forgotten about her parents for mere seconds, the priest's death all-consuming. Could she kill him and still get her parents? Could he harm them if he were dead?

Question after question swirled in her mind until her arms dropped. The flames guttered out, and the fog thinned into nothing. The vines withered at his feet, and for a moment, silence stretched between them. She could not risk her parents' lives.

"Kallemena would be proud of you," he said, brushing ash from his robe. The charred fabric left soot stains on his hands. "She taught you well. But now," His lips curled into a smile. "Now it is time for her to return to me."

Steel clashed in the distance. Alban and Zepher were still locked in battle. The knight's blade slashed low, catching the Morin's leg. Zepher staggered, muffling his groan, then lunged again and again. Each strike failed to break through Alban's guard.

"Make your knight disappear," Vallorith said, his tone flat as stone.

"You make him." Her words were a challenge, knowing he could not.

He raised a brow. "Do you think your parents would prefer hanging? Impalement? I hear poison can be unforgettable." He clapped his hands together. "Or shall we do it your way? Drown them? Burn them? Both, perhaps. Roast them first, then let them choke for water. Yes." He nodded slowly. "That suits me."

Her stomach lurched, and Alban vanished in an instant. Zepher dropped to the ground, gasping, his sweat-drenched chest heaving. His body shook with fatigue.

"See?" Vallorith sneered. "Not so difficult." He snapped his fingers. Zepher staggered upright, swaying, but still dragged himself to his master's side. "Now, time for a deal."

"A deal?" Nemeah mocked, though her voice faltered. She already knew why she would have to listen.

Victory gleamed in the priest's eyes. "I had planned to trade your parents for the other mirrors. But no, there is something far more valuable." He tapped his chin, circling her like a vulture. "You." He brushed a hand through her hair, snickering when she flinched away. "You carry all the abilities." He glanced at Zepher, who was still struggling for breath. "You for your parents. Do we have a bargain?"

Her chest hollowed. This was not the plan. This was not how the night was supposed to end. Panic clawed up her throat, bile searing her tongue. Her thoughts spiraled: shame, rage, helplessness, when fingers yanked her hair back and cold steel pressed against her neck.

"Zepher," Vallorith spoke the name as if it were filth. "What are you doing?"

The Morin steadied his breathing. His words came out as if he had been rehearsing them for some time. "I will not be trapped in a mirror any longer. You will free me and the others before she surrenders to you."

Vallorith was stunned motionless as he watched his faithful servant. His mind whirred, piecing the betrayal together. "I told you. When Isrend is dead, I will release you."

"I want out now, Vallorith. Not later." Zepher's knife pressed harder, a bead of blood sliding down the blade. "I yearn to be free. Release us, or she dies here."

The priest's eyes flicked between them, his scowl deepening. "I will not forget this." He turned his piercing gaze on Nemeah. "Do you accept?"

Her thoughts spun. Zepher was not bargaining only for himself; he wanted all the echoes freed. Why? What did that mean? But then she pictured her parents. Her choice was already made.

"You free the echoes and my parents," she said hoarsely, "in exchange for me."

Vallorith nodded slowly.

"I want your word," Nemeah said, her voice shaking as Zepher's blade pressed tighter, "that you will not touch my family or friends. Ever again."

He nodded once more.

"Then I will take this deal."

The knife lifted from her throat. Zepher's grip fell away, leaving only the sting of his betrayal. Vallorith's eyes slid to his servant, cold and cutting, before he turned back to her. A flick of his wrist and something clamped around Nemeah's arm. A metal cuff, heavy and pitted with age, bit into her skin. Its surface was scratched and dull, its weight unnatural.

"What is this?" She yanked at it, panic rising. "Get it off me."

"Insurance," Vallorith hissed. With another wave of his hand, the world fell.

The farm dissolved into smoke and shadow. Damp rot clogged her throat, and a fine ash drifted in the air, stinging her eyes and making her lungs burn with every breath.

"Where are we?"

"Morbessa," Vallorith said, plucking strange flowers from the earth. Their petals shimmered red and blue like shards of glass, cutting his skin until beads of blood swelled. He did not flinch. "This is where the last mirror lies."

"No. The last mirror is on Verdathos. Sylvie hid them."

"Sylvie hid them," he mocked in a shrill voice, twisting his lips. "Sylvie Havander, thorn in my side, little meddler, and no good thief. She did not hide the final mirror on Verdathos. For five hundred years, I searched." His roar cracked the silence, rattling the very air. "It is here. On Morbessa." He held the bleeding flowers out to her. "Proof. Born from a Thorn, guided by those cursed twins who linger inside the mirror. Created for one purpose."

"To look pretty?" Nemeah muttered defiantly.

Vallorith's face purpled, rage quivering at the edges of control. "To keep me away. Anyone beholden to a mirror cannot set foot here." He hurled the flowers to the ground, their glow snuffed out. With another wave, the smoke peeled back, and Tirnmoor's jagged cliffs surrounded them again.

"Find the mirror," he said, voice low and dangerous. "Bring me the ones you already possess. Then," he cut a sharp glance at Zepher, "I will free your parents and the echoes, in exchange for you." He extended his hand.

"I am not shaking your hand." She crossed her arms, though her cuff burned against her skin.

He pinched his brow, exasperated. "Child. I am a man of honor."

"You are a monster."

An amused smile lit his face. "Every monster knows its own reflection."

A mirror shimmered into being before her, and Nemeah felt a blow she did not expect as she stared at her own reflection. Her blackened veins crawled beneath her skin, and her irises were twin pools of ink. Slowly, the darkness receded, but not enough. Not yet. She raised her hand, power thrumming in her veins, yet nothing happened. She tried again. Nothing. Again. Still nothing.

"What did you do?" Panic cracked her voice as she clawed at the cuff, skin tearing beneath her nails.

"I told you," Vallorith said, almost tender. "Insurance." He offered his hand again. And this time, trembling, she took it.

The ground split beneath her, and she fell. Her body fell, and she slammed onto the stone; her shoulder erupted in pain. Vallorith's voice thundered above her.

"Bring me the mirrors before the next full moon, or your parents die."

The portal snapped shut, and only the crescent moon remained. She staggered to her feet, the night air thin and cold as she looked around for clues to where she had landed. Ahead, a faint glow flickered, and she recognized the cave she now called home. It was unsettling knowing that Vallorith knew where they were, and even more disturbing that her time was almost up.

Chapter Twenty-three

Agnes examined the cuff on Nemeah's wrist. Ancient script was etched into the metal, its mysterious message long lost to the people of this time. The band itself was made from metal, unlike any they had seen before. It was not heavy on Nemeah's arm, yet it was strong enough to withstand their prying. It was weathered and tarnished, its brownish-gold coloring marred by bits of bluish-green corrosion, revealing its age. The cuff, firm and unyielding, offered no chance of slipping free from its new owner's hand.

Keanoff paced near the fire; his silence seemed worse than any outburst they expected of him. Yuli sat nearby, rapidly thumbing through the pages of the old book they had recovered from the Axis house, her fingers constantly working until they stilled on a particular passage.

She turned the book so Nemeah and Agnes could see the worn pages with faded drawings on them. "This." She tapped the page with her finger, urgency in her voice. "It sounds as if it is the same cuff Agnes told us about, in the story of the god war. Listen."

Flipping the book back around, she began to read aloud. "Danira wove the weapon from her garden, using what the mother had gifted her. Each vine, every root, thousands of petals, all weaving through the air. She took the rock from the river, the molten liquid from the inner earth, and waited for the offering. Nuval gave his golden cuffs from his armor, the clothes that had protected him from so much harm, and together they created a weapon fit for a god. An item so powerful, it would end the tyranny of the god of beasts."

She flipped back a few pages. "How did Vallorith get one of Dathmor's cuffs?"

"Maybe the god gave him one?" Nemeah flinched as Agnes prodded at her skin. "Does the book say if Dathmor ever removed them?"

Yuli searched again, flipping through more pages, until she finally shook her head. Nemeah exhaled slowly. Without her powers, all she had left was her rage. She glanced toward her sister, now curled up with Edna on her bed, both asleep. Edna had cleaned the girl up after Nemeah left, her face and hair washed, her knotted mats carefully combed out. Ismaara had healed the shallow cuts on her arms and feet, and Agnes had fashioned a new dress for her from an old nightgown Nemeah had found in town.

"Thank you," Nemeah whispered, voice thick. "For looking after her." But the gratitude sat heavily, laced with guilt.

Guilt for abandoning her sister in her moment of terror. Guilt for lashing out at her friends. Guilt for hiding what had happened in Tirnmoor. She watched Keanoff pace, his braid swaying with each step. He had not yelled, but his silence screamed enough. She knew he was furious that she had not let him come with her. But if he had, if any of them had followed, they might all be dead. Vallorith would have surely killed them, and if not him, then her own powers would have. The realization eased its way through her, her stomach growing queasy.

"I have to go to Morbessa." She blurted the words like she had to say them before she allowed her body to react to the nausea she was now feeling. "Vallorith said that is where the last mirror is."

Keanoff froze mid-step. She did not need to look up to feel the weight of his stare. A thick silence settled over the cave. Everyone seemed to be processing what that meant.

"What if it is another trap?" Agnes asked gently, slipping a strip of cloth beneath the cuff on Nemeah's wrist. "This should keep it from chafing."

Nemeah gave her a grateful nod.

Keanoff sat down by the fire. His gaze was stern, fixed on the dying embers. "Let me get this straight." He spoke slowly; each word was like an accusation. "He ambushed you with the Morin, shackled you with a power-draining cuff, and then told you where to find the last mirror." He turned his stare to her, eyes scanning for any crack in her story. "Feels like there are chunks missing from this meal."

From the other side of Yuli's bed, Henry stirred. "Meal?" he mumbled, sitting up.

Yuli rubbed his back gently, coaxing him back down with a soft laugh. She shut the book and handed it to Nemeah, its worn purple cover almost black in the firelight. "Keanoff is not wrong. It does sound like parts are missing." She raised her hands quickly at Nemeah's glare. "I am not accusing you, just saying maybe *Vallorith is* setting you up again." She sat back on her bed, sliding under the covers beside Henry. "I will sleep on it. Maybe the morning will bring better answers."

Agnes stood and stretched, stifling a yawn. "Same. Goodnight, everyone." She padded to her bed in the far corner, wrapping herself in a thick blanket and disappearing beneath it.

Nemeah watched her sister breathe, inhale and then exhale, her eyelids fluttering with the signs of restless dreams. Nightmares, no doubt. Nemeah felt her chest tighten. The ache in her heart was nearly unbearable. None of this had been meant for Orla. Not the mad priest or the fear, and definitely not the darkness creeping into every corner of their lives.

She buried her face in her hands, dragging her palms down slowly before letting out a long, defeated sigh. When she looked up, she was startled to find Keanoff still watching her. His expression was intense.

"What are you not telling us?" he asked softly.

Her heart stuttered. How could she make him believe a lie that was, in part, the truth? The thought made her flinch. She did not *want* to lie to him. She did not want to lie to any of them. Her eyes drifted to where Ismaara lay sleeping, curls splayed like a halo around her. A darker thought surfaced, ugly and intrusive: Would Keanoff even care if she left? Now that he had Ismaara? Someone prettier and less dangerous.

She waved him over, cautious not to speak too loudly. Her face flushed as Keanoff sat beside her, his presence a welcome warmth against her cold side.

"I made a deal with him," she murmured, so low he had to lean in to catch it.

"You *what?* Nemeah, what were you thinking?" he hissed, louder than she wanted.

In a flash, her hand was over his mouth. Her dark blue eyes locked on his, silently begging him to listen first, judge later. He nodded, and she lowered her hand, the cursed cuff dragging across her skin with a dull scrape.

"I do not have another option." She thought of her words, knowing they were not the whole truth, but also that they were not entirely a lie. "The last mirror for my family. Without it, he will kill them." She looked back at him, "That was the deal."

She felt Keanoff tense beside her. Her breath caught like a stone in her throat. She hated to lie, hated the feeling of tainting their friendship with falsehoods, but she could not bear to see the relief on his face if she told him the truth. She did not want to know he would be glad to see her gone.

"Why would you agree to that?" His voice was strained. "Nemeah, that is, chains, that is a *terrible* deal." The scent of pine clung to his clothes, earthy and clean.

It pulled her back to the moment they first met, when she had shared her food with the strange, silent hare who had turned out to be far more than it seemed. That moment felt like another lifetime.

Before running and fighting. Before the blood. The image of Ismaara hugging him tightly struck her like a dagger. She swallowed the pain, forcing the tears back.

"I do not have a choice," she said, voice thick. "My parents' only hope is that I find the missing mirror and bring it to him before the full moon." She paused. "And then."

She looked at him, wanting to tell him everything. She wanted him to tell her not to sacrifice herself, to beg her to stay with him, and to promise that they would find another way.

"And then he will have everything he needs to become a god." Keanoff cursed under his breath, his hand reaching out and grabbing hers.

She froze; his touch in that moment was what she had wished for. A sign that he still cared; that their friendship still meant something to him as well.

"Nemeah," he whispered, "I know they are your parents, but we cannot give the mirrors to him. There has to be another way."

Before she could say anything, Orla started to whimper in her sleep. Her body thrashed in the bed, still locked in her nightmare. Arms flailed, legs kicked violently, and her head whipped from side to side as she groaned out in terror. Edna tried to hold her steady, keeping her from rolling off the edge of the bed and onto the hard cave floor.

Nemeah rushed to her, hands on her sister's shoulders. "Orla! It is me! Wake up, please!"

It took long, agonizing seconds of gentle coaxing before Orla's movements subsided. Her eyes, red and streaming, locked on Nemeah. Her voice was hoarse as she shrank away, curling back into Edna's arms.

"Not you," she cried, yanking the blanket over her head. "Go away!"

Nemeah's chest pulsed with dread as she covered her mouth, forcing the sobs back down. The fear was not just a result of the night terror. It was here. Orla was afraid of *her*. She looked at Edna, the shared understanding passing between them silently.

"Come now," Edna said gently, her voice calm and warm. "Let us soothe you with some tea." She led the child to the wall of herbs and vines, softly instructing her on which leaves to pick.

Nemeah stumbled to her feet and bolted from the cave. She could hear footsteps behind her, someone giving chase, but she did not look back. She could not bring herself to let him see her tears. She reached the fork in the trail. The left would take her to the cliff, and the right to Jacob's grave. Neither was a place she wanted to go.

Desperately, she waved her hand through the air, calling for a portal. Nothing. She let out a frustrated groan and waved again. Still nothing. Another grunt tore from her throat as she lashed out, kicking at the dirt and throwing whatever was in her vicinity. She dropped to her knees, grabbing rocks, flinging them as far as her arms would allow. Again and again, until her limbs trembled and her chest heaved with sobs. Her fury drained into exhaustion, and she collapsed into herself, curling her knees to her chest. She heard footsteps crunching behind her. Measured and slow. Cautious to approach.

"Nemeah?" Keanoff said softly. He crouched beside her, his voice careful. "She was just startled by a dream. It will be better in the morning."

Nemeah turned to glare at him, her grief swirling like a storm inside her. "Everyone is scared of me," she spat. "You all look at me the same way." Her gaze drifted to the distant mountains, her tears glinting in the rising light. "He was right."

Keanoff's hand rested lightly on her arm. She flinched but did not pull away. "Who?" he asked.

"Vallorith." Her voice cracked as she met Keanoff's eyes. "I called him a monster. He told me we know our own reflections." She wiped her face, suddenly furious with herself, and stood. Her legs were weak, but she forced herself up the trail. "He was right."

"Nemeah, no." Keanoff caught up quickly, wrapping his arms around her shoulders, pulling her into his chest. His voice was low, his face pressed into her hair. "You are not like him. You are *not* a monster." He slid his hand slowly through her hair, again and again, each pass a quiet attempt to soothe her. To say everything his words could not. His fingers threaded gently from crown to nape, trailing warmth in their wake. He gently lifted her chin until she met his eyes. "You might be different. Reckless, even. But you are *not a* monster."

Something broke inside her, and tears rushed back, hot and fast. She sniffled, embarrassed by how small she felt, how *young*, but she did not pull away. This was the Keanoff she remembered. The man who told her dumb jokes by the fire. The one who ate like an animal, his hands covered in food, with his cheeks stuffed full. The one who made her feel like she belonged. His hands slipped down her arms, and his fingers brushed the edge of the metal cuff. She drew back, her heart racing and her mind spinning.

"Why are you being kind to me now?" she asked quietly.

His face shifted. The warmth drained, replaced by confusion. "What?" he asked, as though the question had slapped him.

"You talk to me like I am a child," she said, voice rising. "Impatient. Inexperienced. Dangerous. You walk away from me. You do not even *look* at me half the time. And now, suddenly, you are telling me I am not a monster?" She held up her arm, the metal catching the pale gold of dawn. "Is it because of this? Because I no longer have powers? Because I am weak?"

"No!" Keanoff snapped, too quickly. He paused and took a breath. "Look, I will admit, it is intimidating. Watching someone break every rule I have ever known. But I," He trailed off, eyes searching hers. And then, finally, he saw her. Not the power. Not the danger. Just her.

The farm girl who had once shared her food with a hare in the woods. The Darra who had saved him more than once. The woman who had somehow, without either of them realizing it, found her way deeper into his life.

"You what?" Her voice struck like a whip, sharp with hurt. Anger now fueled her words. "You know what?" She threw her hands up. "I do not care." She turned on her heel to leave.

Keanoff lunged forward, stepping into her path and blocking her escape. "I was wrong. I do not know why I acted that way." He reached for her hand, but she yanked it back. "Nemeah, I am sorry. I guess I let my own emotions take over, and I did not stop to think about yours." He ran both hands down his face, frustration tightening his voice. "You saved my life, and I repaid you by acting like a fool." He stared at her, the hurt on her face breaking something inside him.

This time, she stared back, really looking at him. His warrior's braid had come undone, loose strands catching in the wind. His beard was scruffy, and his clothes were torn and dirt-smudged, in need of a stitch and a soak. She noticed something she had not before: one ear was shorter than the other, the tip missing.

"What happened to your ear?"

Keanoff brushed a finger over the healed edge. "A guard got lucky. Back when you ran into the Axis house."

"You should let Ismaara heal it." She said the Freyla's name like it were a curse.

He shrugged. "Figured you might like it."

She gave a confused smirk. "Why me?"

"Keanoff?" Ismaara's voice echoed sharply down the trail from the cave. "Keanoff? Keanoff!"

Neither moved nor dared to speak. They stood in the stillness, unwilling for the moment to end. Ismaara's voice rang louder, each call more insistent than the last.

"You should go." Nemeah gestured toward the cave. "It would not be good for her to find you here with me." She turned away and headed down the path, not daring to look back.

Keanoff remained still, eyes fixed on her until she vanished from view. A confession left his lips. "I want to be here with you."

***

Nemeah stayed on the path all day until the sun began its slow descent behind the mountain peaks. Hunger gnawed at her, but she ignored it, unwilling to return to the cave too soon. Orla needed time to form her own connections and build trust with the others. It was better for her to have someone inside she could rely on, even if that someone was not Nemeah.

The scent of something savory drifted on the wind, Edna's cooking pot, no doubt. The older woman had moved the fire outside, taking advantage of the cloudy summer day. Her voice rang out across the clearing, sharp and commanding.

"Keanoff, you are in charge of the animal pens. Henry, give Rhubarb a bath. Yuli and Agnes wash the clothes. Orla, dear, you help with dinner."

Nemeah hesitated, half-tempted to turn around and wait until all the chores were done. But, she thought better of that idea. The last thing she needed to be labeled as, on top of already being dangerous and hot-headed, was selfish and rude. So, she made her way slowly up the trail, her nerves easing slightly when Edna offered her a warm smile over the bubbling pot.

"Nemeah, I am glad you are back," Edna said. "You can help Ismaara move the bedrolls and sweep out the cave." She spotted Orla squinting between two leafy vegetables. "Go help your sister. I need a fat cabbage for my stew."

Inside the cave, Henry groaned dramatically. "Stew again?"

"Yes, Mister Grumpy. It will be stew, and you will love every bite," Edna snapped back, without missing a beat.

Nemeah bit her tongue to keep from chuckling as she stepped into the garden. Narrow footpaths wound between neat rows of vegetables and vines heavy with fruit. She knelt beside her sister.

"These are cabbages," she said, pointing to the thick, waxy leaves tinged with blue-green. "And these," she added, plucking a ruby-colored berry from a soft, brambly bush, "are raspberries."

She popped the fruit into her mouth, her eyes fluttering shut as the tangy sweetness danced across her tongue.

"Try one," she whispered, picking a few more and holding them out.

Orla took one cautiously, chewed slowly, then smiled. Wide and bright. She reached for more, juice staining her lips and teeth red. Nemeah smiled back, a tightness easing in her chest.

"There," she murmured, "See? Not so scary." She nodded toward a tree tucked in the corner of the cave, its broad leaves shading small clusters of plump fruit. "Those are figs. My favorite."

She bent and tugged a cabbage free from its stalk as Orla skipped away, plucking a few figs from the branches. The little girl bit into one and gave a delighted squeal.

"Do not let Edna catch you," Nemeah warned, half-laughing. "She will fuss just like Ma does."

Orla giggled and ran off, clutching the cabbage like a prize. It was not how things used to be between them, not yet. But maybe, in time, it could be again. Nemeah stood, brushing her hands clean, and caught sight of Ismaara and Keanoff across the cave. The beds remained unrolled. Ismaara leaned close to him, her fingers brushing his arm, her mismatched eyes locked on his. She whispered something, her lips a breath away from his ear. Nemeah's stomach twisted.

"Need help?"

She jumped and turned. Yuli stood beside her, already rolling up one of the moss beds.

"Thanks." Nemeah pulled her gaze away and bent to help.

They rolled up one of the bedrolls and stood it on end, leaning it against the cave's wall. Each time they moved one of the beds, Nemeah could feel Ismaara's eyes on her, watching from where she stood with Keanoff while he did his chores.

"She makes you feel weird, too?" Yuli whispered as they rolled up a fourth bed.

Nemeah nodded and kept her voice low. "I am not sure why, but I just do not trust her."

Yuli nodded. "Probably the way she talks." She pitched her voice high. "I just could not do all this hard work, I am a princess."

They both laughed as Nemeah helped Yuli push the bed to the side before starting on another. "It is just," She took a breath. "It is the way Orla was with her, I guess. She was so comfortable with a stranger instead of her own sister." They heaved the heavy roll onto the stack with the others. "I guess I am just jealous."

Yuli stretched her back, twisting around until she could see Ismaara. She turned back and touched her toes. "I would not be too jealous. Everything about her makes me uncomfortable. Should not be long before Orla feels it too."

"I hope so." Nemeah pulled her gaze from Keanoff just as Ismaara placed a kiss on his cheek.

They worked side by side, chatting lightly as they cleared the space and swept. Laughter and dust filled the air. More than once, Nemeah caught herself snapping her fingers or flicking her wrist, forgetting her magic would not answer. Each time, she glanced down at the cuff on her arm, her frustration growing with every failed impulse.

When the cave was finally spotless and dinner was ready, they gathered outside under a sky strewn with stars. They spoke of the days before the mirrors, before prophecies and curses. Of homes left behind and memories that felt like dreams. Henry was on his third helping of stew when the inevitable question surfaced.

"So, how are we getting to Morbessa?"

A sharp hiss came from flames under the stew pot as Henry fumbled his bowl, stew sloshing out as he scrambled to catch it.

Edna cleared her throat, her eyes steady. "More importantly, how are we getting there without Nemeah's portals?"

Silence settled like a blanket. All eyes turned to the old woman, as if she had grown a second head.

"It is a fair question," she said, sipping her stew. "And one that needs an answer."

Orla stirred her own bowl silently, gaze fixed downward.

Nemeah set her food aside and straightened. "I thought I could ask Noa. Flying would be faster than going by foot or sea." She looked around at the faces gathered around the fire. Their silence spoke volumes. "And I will also be going alone."

The group erupted in arguments of disapproval, everyone except Ismaara, who remained notably silent.

"No, we go with you," Yuli said firmly. "You have no powers right now. How do you expect to find the mirror alone? What if you run into trouble?" She nudged Henry, spilling some more of the stew from his newly filled bowl. "Tell her."

Henry froze, his eyes wide while his spoon still hung in his mouth. He quickly swallowed and nodded. "You will need protection." He cleared his throat and tried again. "Can you wield a sword?"

Nemeah shook her head. "I never needed to learn."

"She fired Pa's muzzle loader once," Orla chimed in brightly. "I do not think she hit the target, though." Her voice dimmed as she shrank back into her seat.

"Muzzle loaders are fine for animals," Henry said with a shrug, "but not so great against a group of people who actually want to kill you." He shoved another bite into his mouth just as Yuli's elbow jabbed him hard in the ribs. "Ow!" he wheezed through his mouthful, eyes darting to his wife.

Yuli nodded toward Orla, who was again staring down at her bowl, slowly stirring the contents with her spoon.

"I just meant they are better for hunting than defense," Henry muttered, stuffing more food into his mouth to avoid further commentary.

Yuli rolled her eyes. "Point is, someone should go with you."

"I will go," Edna announced, setting her bowl aside. "I can keep her safe."

"No," Nemeah said quickly, shaking her head. "You need to stay here. The animals, the gardens, this is your home now. I would not ask you to leave it. Besides," She glanced at Orla and lowered her voice. "I was hoping you could look after my sister while I am away."

Edna's gaze shifted from the child to Nemeah. After a pause, she gave a quiet, resolute nod. Her expression said more than words: she was willing to stay and protect what mattered most.

"I will be fine," Nemeah continued, reaching into her pocket. She pulled out a small, shimmering object and held it up for them to see. "I have Kallemena's compass. It will take me straight to the mirror and back. A week, maybe two, at most."

"Well," Ismaara said with a soft smile, daintily lifting a bird-sized bite of stew to her lips. "It sounds like you have thought of everything. Happy travels."

Agnes was the first to look away from the bluntness of the princess. "I can go," she offered. "I know a little about Morbessa, the customs, the language." She rattled off a few smooth syllables in a foreign tongue. "I could translate."

"That might actually help." Nemeah's shoulders dropped with a breath of relief. "But only if you are sure."

"Of course," Agnes said with a grin. "It is a once-in-a-lifetime chance. Hardly anyone travels to Morbessa, and knowledge of the place is, well, limited to say the least." She sprang to her feet. "I need to pack!" And with that, she darted into the cave.

"I can go."

All heads turned toward Keanoff. The offer caught everyone off guard. Ismaara's hand immediately curled around his wrist. Her voice was low and intimate as she leaned in to whisper something into his ear. Keanoff's smile faltered. His brow furrowed slightly, confusion clouding his expression. Ismaara turned to the group, her tone light but her eyes locked on Nemeah.

"Keanoff really should stay," she said sweetly. "To help Henry guard the remaining mirrors. Especially now that Vallorith knows where we are."

Her meaning was clear; this was not a suggestion. She stood and extended her hand to Keanoff. Nemeah watched as he took it. It felt like her heart was on a chopping block, diced into pieces too small to gather again.

"Ismaara is right, I should stay," Keanoff said, voice deflated. "Just in case." His shoulders slumped as he followed Ismaara into the cave, leaving Nemeah with silence and the weight of his choice.

Chapter Twenty-four

Agnes circled Noa with the intensity of a storm cloud, muttering under her breath. Her satchel swung from one hand to the other as she paused at intervals, lifted it, frowned, then repeated the process on the opposite side. Round and round she went, gathering a crowd of onlookers.

Edna watched from a short distance, lips twitching with amusement. The old woman stifled a laugh as she observed Agnes pacing around the dragon like a circling shark. Noa, clearly unsettled, followed the woman with wide, wary eyes. Her long neck bent left, then right, tracking Agnes's every move with mounting confusion. Never before had such a towering creature looked so nervous. Eventually, Noa gave a sharp series of clicks and huffs toward Keanoff. He laughed, translating her concern aloud.

"Agnes, what are you doing? You are making Noa very uncomfortable."

Agnes stopped mid-step, her satchel bumping against her hip as she turned. She bowed deeply to Noa with her hands pressed together.

"Apologies. I did not mean to alarm her." She straightened with a slight annoyance in her voice. "I am just not sure where to put my bag."

The others paused, glancing toward Noa with the same question. The flight to Morbessa would take days, and they would need to bring supplies with them. But how exactly would they carry them?

"I think I can help with that," Edna said, approaching cautiously. She extended her hand, letting Noa sniff it with a hesitant snort. "I can weave a saddle, if she will let me." Her weathered eyes flicked to Keanoff for translation.

He nodded and turned to Noa with a string of clicks and whistles.

"What is a saddle?" Noa asked, her tone tinged with confusion and suspicion.

"You know, like what horses wear." Keanoff dropped to all fours, puffing out his cheeks to mimic a horse's snout. "It goes on their backs; humans sit on them."

Noa was silent for a moment, processing. "Will I still be able to fly?" she clicked back, the concern in her tone unmistakable.

"Fly, swim, glide, whatever you can do now, you should still be able to do with the saddle," Keanoff assured her. "If it is uncomfortable, Edna can adjust it."

More silence. Then: "We can try? And if I do not like it, she removes it?"

Keanoff gave a firm nod. "Exactly."

After a long pause, Noa let out a low rumble of agreement. Keanoff gave Edna a thumbs-up, and she wasted no time. Sinking to the cave floor, Edna placed both hands against the stone and whispered an ancient phrase. The earth answered her call. Vines and roots pushed through cracks in the rock, winding toward Noa. The plants crept up her body with surprising gentleness, threading between feathers and scales. Twisting and weaving, they formed a sturdy frame.

A wide oval seat took shape across Noa's back, large enough for both women to sit or even lie down. The straps were made from supple, living vines that expanded and contracted with Noa's breathing. Edna watched intently as the saddle settled into place.

Noa shifted. She turned in a slow circle, then carefully lay down and rolled onto her back, wings tucked close. She stood again, shook herself, then clicked toward Keanoff.

"She says it will work," he relayed, already accepting Agnes's bag and securing it to the saddle's left side. He glanced at Noa for her reaction. "She says the weight's fine. Does not bother her." He gave Edna a small nod. "Good work, Gran."

Edna's face lit up with pride as she stepped back, watching Nemeah hoist her own bag toward the saddle. The young woman struggled, her arm trembling from the weight, until it lifted easily. Keanoff was holding it for her, a faint smile curling his lips.

"Thanks," she murmured, fumbling quickly to secure the straps.

"What have you got in here?" Keanoff asked as he lowered the bag. "Bricks?"

"Clothes. Books. The compass. Some food. A blanket," Nemeah listed off, ticking each item on her fingers.

Agnes stepped forward with another bag, handing it to Keanoff. "Here, do this one next."

He took it, eyeing the two packs. "Why do you need two?" he asked, weighing the second one. "And why is this one heavier?" Curious, he flipped open the flap, then blinked. "Gold?"

Agnes straightened, nonchalant. "It is not *just* gold."

Nemeah leaned over and peeked inside. Her brows shot up. "Planning on making a hefty purchase?"

Agnes swept her hair out of her face with a huff, irritation sharpening her tone. "Morbessa is a continent in poverty. They do not trade with any of the other continents, which means most people there probably have next to nothing." She paused, calming herself. "It will be faster to bribe for information than to just ask."

Nemeah blinked, caught off guard. She had been so focused on finding the mirror and the journey ahead that she never once thought about the people they might meet along the way. She had not considered what desperate measures might be needed in a place so closed off.

A chill ran down her spine. Her eyes drifted through the cave, searching for Orla.

The child was crouched near the chickens, chattering and clucking as if she were one of the flock. She giggled, gently petting a golden hen that allowed her close. The bird's stiff feathers ruffled under her small hand. Edna stepped beside Nemeah, giving her a comforting pat on the back.

"She will be fine," she said softly. "I will watch her like she is my own." Her weathered hand rested on Nemeah's shoulder. "Just like I did with you."

Then she pressed a kiss to Nemeah's cheek and moved toward Orla. Raising her hands, Edna twisted her fingers through the air, and before their eyes, grass unfurled beneath the chickens, lush and seeded, dotted with small fruits. Orla let out a delighted laugh as the hens rushed to peck at their sudden feast.

"We need to go," Agnes called out from the saddle, already astride Noa with little elegance but a great deal of urgency.

Noa rocked in place, her talons scraping the stone. Her wings twitched. Nervous energy rippled through her body. Yuli hurried forward, her face tight with emotion, as if she was about to say goodbye forever. She pressed a small blade into Nemeah's hand and pulled her into a fierce embrace.

"Just in case," she whispered. Her grip tightened. "You run into trouble, you use this."

Nemeah held her close for a beat longer. When Yuli stepped back, she turned to Agnes. "I really think I should be the one going."

Henry appeared behind his wife, his face knotted with concern. His arms hovered near Yuli's shoulders, unsure whether to pull her back or support her plea.

"Noa can only carry two," Nemeah said gently, giving Yuli's hand a squeeze. "And we have got our bags, too. Besides," She looked at Henry. "He is starting to look ill."

Everyone turned to see that Henry's face had paled considerably.

"She is staying here," Nemeah said with a small laugh, watching the relief wash over him like a tide. His color was returning slightly.

"You two be safe," Henry said, voice gravelly with worry. "I have heard that Morbessa is no place to let your guard down. Watch your back."

Nemeah and Agnes nodded solemnly; his warning landed like a stone. Yuli hugged Nemeah one last time. "Keep an eye on her," Nemeah whispered into Yuli's ear before stepping back. The moment stretched. Then Nemeah turned and approached Noa, ready to climb up, only to feel a pair of strong hands lift her easily by the waist. She gasped, startled, and met Keanoff's amused smile as he set her on the saddle. Her cheeks flushed. Out of the corner of her eye, she caught Ismaara watching, expression sharp like daggers.

"What is the signal for fly?" Nemeah asked, clearing her throat. The warmth of his hands lingered in her thoughts.

Keanoff responded with two crisp clicks of his tongue. She nodded, mimicking the sound.

"And for land?" she asked.

He wet his lips, then whistled low and steady, the tone rising quickly to a sharp pitch.

Nemeah tried several times to mimic the sound, failing with each attempt. Behind her, Agnes nailed it perfectly on her first try.

"I can handle that part," she offered with a grin, her tone friendly and teasing.

From their perch on Noa's back, both girls glanced down at the group below. Their nerves churned in unison, and neither could stop their minds from conjuring every reason this was a terrible idea.

"Hang on tight," Keanoff warned, clicking and whistling to Noa.

The dragon stirred beneath them, her powerful steps shifting their balance with each sway. Nemeah adjusted quickly, recognizing the familiar rhythm; it was not unlike riding a horse. Agnes, however, clung tightly around her waist, clearly less steady.

As they emerged from the cave, the sky opened up above them. Puffy white clouds drifted lazily overhead, and the air smelled warm, laced with the faint sweetness of sun-warmed stone and summer wind.

"Ready?" Keanoff gave Noa a gentle tap on her flank and backed away.

Nemeah let out the signal to fly, and before she could even finish the call, Noa surged forward. Her wings flared wide as she sprinted along the cliff face, picking up speed. Faster and faster she moved until she launched into the air with a powerful kick of her legs.

Yuli and Keanoff watched in awe as the dragon climbed higher with every beat of her wings, the girls now just specks against the sky, shrinking into the vastness.

Yuli elbowed Keanoff lightly, a knowing smile tugging at her lips. "Go on, you know you want to."

He turned to her. The sun glinted in her brown eyes, catching golden flecks that sparkled like flame. Behind them, the sound of foot-steps echoed softly, light and dainty. Ismaara was approaching, her pace slow and purposeful. Keanoff's eyes flicked to the sky, the dragon now a distant silhouette above the cliffs.

"Keanoff." Ismaara's voice was sweet, almost too careful as she called his name.

His gaze shifted between Yuli and the sky, his body already decid-ing before his mind caught up. Without another word, he turned and bolted down the path. Dirt kicked up behind his boots as the cliff edge drew near, the sheer drop looming just ahead. He did not hesitate. He leapt.

The wind tore past him, thrilling and dangerous. The ground rushed up to meet him far too quickly. Then, he closed his eyes. His body began to shift. Feathers burst from his skin. His bones hollowed, limbs shortening. His nose elongated into a sharp beak. Within sec-onds, he was a hawk, sleek, swift, and agile. Wings spread wide as he caught the wind beneath him and soared, cutting through the air in pursuit of the dragon above.

Behind him, Ismaara reached the cliff's edge, her face flushed with exertion and rage. She stomped her foot and clenched her hands, tension rippling through her muscles as she screamed after him.

"Keanoff!"

***

The Night Before

Keanoff looked out from the cave, watching his friends gathered around the fire. Laughter danced on the night air. Yuli and Henry were spinning in an uneven, joyful balter, while Nemeah and Orla clapped along to the beat of a childhood folk song. Everyone looked so alive and free. He wanted to be out there with them. To dance. To share stories. To laugh with everyone. He looked at Nemeah, watched her smile, and heard her laugh.

He loved her happy, the way her whole face lit up, how her eyes sparkled like all her worries had drifted away on the tide. He stood, feet already carrying him toward the warmth of the fire, when a gentle hand caught his arm. Ismaara's fingers were soft against his rough skin, silk on stone. She tugged him back down onto the mossy bed, her hand trailing along his back in slow, deliberate circles.

"Where were you going?" she asked, her voice as sweet as a ripened plum.

Keanoff hesitated. His thoughts, once clear, now churned and clouded, softening beneath her touch. "I am not sure." He turned toward her, locking eyes with those strange, mesmerizing irises of hers.

"Good," she whispered, resting her head on his shoulder.

He felt an overwhelming need to press a kiss to her curls and did. The scent of honey and sage flooded his senses. She shifted, placing a bowl of fruit in his hands, then reclined on the bed, her sandy curls fanning around her like a halo on the moss.

"Feed me?" she asked, lips already parted in invitation.

Keanoff plucked a strawberry from the bowl and gently placed it between her lips. Juice stained her mouth a deep red, and he watched her tongue sweep across her bottom lip. More laughter rang from outside. He turned toward the fire just in time to see Agnes and Nemeah dancing now, their clumsy steps igniting another wave of giggles from the group. Everyone joined in, stumbling, singing, circling the flame like it was the heart of their world.

A dull ache stirred inside Keanoff. He wanted to be out there. He wanted to be laughing and stumbling. He wanted to feel alive. He wanted to be with them. With her. He set the bowl aside and shifted to stand, but Ismaara's hand found his arm again. The ache inside him vanished, his longing drowned beneath that feather-light touch. His thoughts dulled, his purpose faded. Only Ismaara remained.

She propped herself on one elbow, twirling a curl between her fingers. "You were feeding me, Keanoff. Remember?" Her voice slipped into his ear like a secret. "You would not want me to starve, would you?"

He shook his head, already reaching for another berry. One by one, he fed her until the bowl lay empty and her appetite was gone.

"I am going to sleep," she murmured, patting the spot beside her. "Will you keep me warm?"

He opened his mouth to respond, but her hand found his arm once more. A wave of warmth and calm rolled through him. His limbs grew heavy as his mind ceased all thoughts. His stomach growled, but the thought of leaving her side flickered and died. She curled into him, slipping her hand into his, and he drifted to sleep before he could whisper goodnight.

Hours came and went, and everyone fell into a deep slumber except for the dragon. Noa's clicks were soft and deliberate, spaced just enough to gently stir her target without rousing the woman beside him. Keanoff's eyes cracked open. A weight pressed into his shoulder, and strands of hair brushed his cheek. Ismaara was still tucked against him, breathing slow and even. A strange tightness coiled in his chest.

Memories hovered in his brain like fog, fragments of the fruit and everyone's laughter. He remembered the firelight he had walked away from, the look on their faces as he told them he would be staying here. He looked down at Ismaara, the feeling that she was everything good and true crept through him like a warm tide. He glanced around the cave. The others were still sleeping, except for the dragon.

Noa watched him from her nest, eyes glowing faintly. She let out a soft click and a low-pitched whistle. "Just listen," she instructed in her own language, her gaze flicking between Keanoff and the sleeping girl at his side. "Do not answer. Just listen."

Keanoff nodded faintly, his muscles tense.

"She is doing something to you. When she touches you." Noa's nostrils flared slightly. "I can smell her magic. It clings to you. Strongest when she is near."

Keanoff stilled. A flash of clarity split through his haze. He started to click a response, but Ismaara stirred beside him, rolling onto her back with a sigh. Careful not to wake her, Keanoff slowly sat up and crept away, silent on bare feet, until he reached Noa's side.

"How can she do that?" he whistled softly, casting wary glances back. "Can Freyla do that? Control the mind?"

Noa gave a curt nod. "It is part of their gift. To ease pain during healing. To trick the mind into forgetting the injury." Her next whistle was lower, more deliberate. "But this one seems especially interested in *you*."

They both glanced toward Ismaara, relieved to see her still asleep. Keanoff turned back to Noa, panic fluttering in his chest.

"How many times has she done it to me?" he clicked. "Is there a way to block her?"

Noa only shook her head. Her knowledge came from observation, not instruction. "The short-haired human might know." She tilted her head toward Agnes, who was snoring, mouth wide open. "I like her stories."

Just then, at Noa's final click, Yuli shot upright from her bedding, her eyes narrowing as she spotted them. She tilted her head, wordlessly asking, *What are you two doing?*

Keanoff gave a helpless shrug, which only prompted Yuli to crawl out of bed. She shoved Henry's leg off her and rolled out awkwardly, still half-asleep. Straightening her rumpled shirt, she made her way over to Noa's nest.

"What is with the midnight gossip?" she asked, arching an eyebrow at Keanoff before shifting her gaze to Noa. Her next clicks and whistles came out slow and clunky. "Has you yell him about the chicken's powder?"

Keanoff winced at her attempt at dragonspeak. Noa responded, more slowly than Yuli had asked, to ensure her words were understood. Then she gave an exaggerated yawn.

"You tell him," she said, curling herself into a ball that looked impossibly small for her massive frame. "I need my sleep for tomorrow."

Yuli grabbed Keanoff by the tunic and tugged him away. "Come on." She did not let go until they were well out of earshot of the others. "How much did she tell you?" she asked.

Keanoff blinked at her. "No, no, *you* first. Since when do you speak dragon?"

Yuli gave him a blank look, as if he had asked whether water was wet. She pointed to herself, with messy hair and drool still drying at the corner of her mouth. "Vira, remember? It is not hard when you actually pay attention." Then she exhaled. "Now, what did she say?"

Keanoff ran a hand through his hair, the weight of everything pressing in. "She said Ismaara's been putting some kind of spell on me. Every time she touches me." A shudder ran down his spine. "Ugh, gods, it feels like I have got bugs crawling under my skin." He dropped to the ground and started rolling in the dirt, as if it might scrub the sensation away.

Yuli narrowed her eyes, struggling not to laugh. "What *are* you doing?"

"I am trying to get it off!" he grumbled from the ground.

"Okay, drama king, stop. We need to *talk*."

Keanoff sat up, brushing dirt from his sleeves and pants. "Did Noa tell you first, or did you tell her?"

"We both noticed it around the same time," Yuli replied, arms crossed. "You are different when she is near, like the light goes out in you. And, look, I know you got feelings for my girl Nemeah." She smiled with her eyes when he looked uncomfortable. "So you can imagine my shock when you and *Miss Priss* got all cozy overnight."

Keanoff's face twisted in horror. "Why me?" Then, trying to pivot, he straightened and flashed a crooked grin. "I mean, not *surprised* really. I *am* incredibly handsome. You would have to be blind *not* to want to bewitch me."

Yuli rolled her eyes and smacked his forehead, three sharp taps.

"Alright, alright," he groaned, rubbing his face. "Does Nemeah know?"

Yuli shook her head. "Noa and I only just figured it out."

"Do you think I *can* block her?" His voice dropped. "Noa said Agnes might know something. But they are leaving in the morning. I cannot live like this, being someone else every time she lays a hand on me." He shot her a grin. "I mean, I cannot help it if a woman wants to put her hands on me." His smile faded when he saw Yuli's serious face. "Right, yes, not a joking matter."

Yuli took a long breath, then placed both hands on his shoulders. "Go with them," she said softly. "Make sure they stay safe. Agnes has no magic. Nemeah, she is defenseless now."

Keanoff frowned. "What about you? Henry? Edna and Orla?"

Yuli lifted her chin. "We will be fine. Henry and I can handle anything that comes our way." Her voice hardened with resolve. "But they will need *you*. Nemeah will need you."

Chapter Twenty-five

They flew northeast, the golden compass point pulling them onward over the wild expanse of Kalyra. Nemeah held it tight, guiding Noa with the smallest nudges whenever the needle shifted. Two days of flight had carried them through whipping storms and open, cloudless skies. Sunburn had begun to stain their skin, and their tailbones ached as if carved from splintered glass.

Leaning over Noa's side, Agnes peered down at the endless sweep of ocean, the sun shining silver across its rippling surface. Far below, scattered islets rose like jewels, waves breaking in white foam against their painted shores. She nudged Nemeah's shoulder and pointed.

A sharp pat to Noa's flank, followed by Agnes's whistle, sent the dragon into a steep dive. Nemeah's stomach lurched into her throat as the wind roared past. Agnes laughed in delight, arms cinching tighter around Nemeah's waist. In less than half a minute, the dizzying height gave way to a sudden, sandy landing on a narrow beach.

They climbed down, awestruck by the patch of paradise that would be their shelter for the night. A fringe of lush palms ringed the shoreline like sentinels, blocking the view of whatever lay beyond. To Nemeah, the vertical trunks looked too much like the bars of a cell in the Axis house. She drew in a slow breath and tried to shake the memory away.

Strange birdcalls echoed from somewhere within the canopy. The undergrowth shivered. Nemeah froze, eyes searching for movement. Again, the brush stirred, and this time she caught sight of a small animal darting between the bushes.

Noa's head swiveled toward the sound, her posture sinking low. Like a hunting cat, she advanced, tail swaying in slow arcs, claws pressing into warm sand with each step. Then she sprang, only to slam into the dense palm trunks. A spray of fronds dropped from above as she found herself tangled, the saddle caught fast.

The women rushed to her side, coaxing her to stillness while working to free the straps. It took smashed fingers, muttered curses, and several minutes of tugging before Noa was loose again. She shook herself vigorously, the bags at her sides bouncing. Nemeah's own had come unbuckled, spilling its contents across the sand.

"Noa, no," Nemeah chided, hurrying forward.

With an impatient snort, the dragon allowed them to unfasten the bags. She cast a lingering glare toward the jungle before heading for the shallows, clearly preferring prey that did not hide behind trees.

Nemeah began gathering her scattered belongings, brushing off the sand. The purple-bound book lay open to the tale of Dathmor and his monstrous form. She shook it gently, grains spilling in slow trickles. Agnes joined her, arms full of loose items.

"I wonder what we can find to eat here," Agnes mused, scanning the curve of the beach in both directions. "It is a shoreline, so there should be something unless you would rather try in there." She tipped her chin toward the palm forest.

Nemeah met her gaze, both silently agreeing the trees could wait.

"Let us stick to the shore. Just in case."

Agnes nodded, and they split up, each taking a side of the tiny island in search of food that might spare their dwindling supplies. Nemeah spotted quick crabs darting into their sandy burrows, far too fast for her to snatch. Even if she caught one, she had no fire to cook it. She cast another glance at the jungle and decided against risking its labyrinth. Her stomach growled, so she settled for an apple and a stale scrap of bread from her pack.

Back at their landing spot, she sat cross-legged on the hot sand, paging through the book. She read of the gods, their jealousies, and their hunger for worship.

"Is that what Vallorith wants? Followers?" she murmured, biting into the apple, its crunch loud against the hush of waves.

Agnes trudged into view, dripping wet, her skirts heavy with sand and something bundled inside. She headed to the rocks and beat the hem of her dress against them. She waddled over to Nemeah triumphantly, the culprit to her disheveled look still wrapped in her dress.

"What happened to you?" Nemeah asked around a mouthful of apple.

Agnes dropped beside her, unrolling the bundle to reveal the catch. "I," she panted. "Caught a fish."

"I see that," Nemeah replied, eyeing the slick body, the briny scent rising between them. "So, what do we do with it?"

Agnes glanced from the fish to Nemeah and gave a casual shrug. "I figured we could cut it up and cook it. Save our rations." She wiped her hands down the front of her dress. "Hand me your knife."

Nemeah passed it over, watching as Agnes's long years of kitchen work in the Axis house came to life. With swift, practiced motions, she slit the belly and eased out the entrails, careful not to pierce the stomach. Then she sliced behind the gills, running the blade along the spine until the fish opened like a folded blanket.

Nemeah, still chewing her last bite of apple, wandered to the shoreline and tossed the core into the sea, then returned to find two thick, glistening fillets laid out in the sun.

"Now we cook it?" she asked, suddenly feeling like a child. "How exactly are you making fire?"

Agnes opened her mouth, then shut it again. "I had not thought that far." Her gaze drifted to the water. "We could wait for Noa, and then she could, you know." She mimicked fire coming from her mouth.

"She cannot," Nemeah interrupted. "She lost her fire when Ashar's mirror cracked, and the fire I gave her was apparently only temporary, faltering as my outbursts come and go."

Agnes's shoulders sank. She studied the fillets, then picked one up, rinsing the sand from its pink flesh. After a quick inspection, she sank her teeth into it.

"What are you doing?" Nemeah shot to her feet, half-ready to slap the fish away.

"It should be fine as long as there are no worms. And I do not see any." Agnes chewed thoughtfully. "It is salty." She swallowed and took another bite.

Nemeah eyed her own portion lying in the sand. The idea of eating it raw made her stomach twist, but she thought of Agnes, catching it, cleaning it, and decided to try. She rinsed hers in the shallows, then took a tentative bite. The slick texture nearly made her gag, but she forced herself to chew, swallowing with effort. Agnes's grin flashed in the corner of her vision, and Nemeah managed a few more slimy bites before tossing the remains into the waves, her taste buds relieved to be done. She turned just in time to see Agnes hopping on one foot, tugging off her boot, then the other.

"What are you doing now?" Nemeah laughed as Agnes peeled off her dress and danced in her undergarments.

"I smell like fish. I am getting clean." Agnes waded into the water and let out a contented sigh as she sank beneath the waves. "Come on, it feels amazing!"

Nemeah scanned the empty beach, still half-wary of unseen eyes. Then she unbuttoned her skirt and untied her blouse, folding them neatly in a sunlit pile. Clutching her chemise, she stepped into the shallows, savoring the shock of cold on overheated skin until gooseflesh rippled up her arms. Soon she was floating beside Agnes in the crystalline water.

"Nice, right?" Agnes splashed her, droplets hitting her square in the face.

"Better than that fish."

They both laughed, knowing the meal had been far from ideal. Together they explored the cove, drifting into rocky tide pools and even a half-flooded cave. Nemeah pocketed a few shells for Orla, knowing she had never seen the ocean before.

When the cold left their fingers and lips tinged blue, they staggered back to shore, collapsing into the sun's embrace. Warmth soaked into their skin as they drifted in and out of light sleep.

"How long before we get there, you think?" Agnes asked, tugging her dress over her head and ruffling her hair dry. "To Morbessa?"

"I am not sure." Nemeah laced her boots and glanced at her pack, where the golden compass glimmered in the light. "Hopefully not too much longer. I do not think my backside can take another day in that saddle."

They both laughed, knowing it was the truth.

"Would it have killed Edna to put some moss on it?" Agnes grumbled, rubbing the small of her back and working her hand slowly down toward her tailbone. "I am sure we will both have bruises."

Nemeah was halfway through lacing her boot when a thunderous crash split the air, followed by the heavy beat of wings. Both women froze, eyes going wide. From the waves emerged the largest fish they had ever seen, its body nearly half the size of Noa herself. The creature's glassy eyes were as big as their heads, its mangled fins reduced to tatters, leaving it helpless in the surf.

Noa shook salt water from her scales, dousing the women in a fine spray. She paced in a slow circle around her catch, watchful, as if making sure it was truly dead. Then, with a sudden lunge, she sank her jaws into its side. Pearlescent scales cracked and shattered between her teeth.

"And I thought my fish was big," Agnes whispered.

They stood transfixed. Noa's beauty was matched only by the fear she inspired, sharp teeth tearing through dense flesh, while dragon scales and fish scales alike shimmered in the fading light. She ate without pause until the sky deepened into a blueish black. Only then did she leave the carcass, curling into herself for a long, needed rest.

Agnes gathered fresh palm fronds to make two small beds beside the dragon, soaking in her warmth against the chill. Nemeah tossed her single blanket over both of them, and in the comfort of shared heat, they whispered stories.

Nemeah spoke first about her family farm, the day her powers accidentally killed their cow, the dead merchant she had stumbled upon, and her first meeting with Zepher. To Agnes, every tale sounded like an adventure.

Her own story felt far plainer. Her ailing mother had given her to the Axis at the age of two, and she had grown up steeped in their teachings. She told of meeting Henry, and of the way his tone shifted whenever he mentioned the Vira prisoner. "I knew he liked her," Agnes admitted softly. "I just did not know they were married."

"You knew and did not turn him in?" Nemeah yawned.

Agnes shrugged. "I suppose I did not want to. I have seen so many Echoes pass through the Axis house, most of them kind, even friendly. I guess I started to care for them in my own way." She rolled onto her side to face Nemeah. "I am glad you escaped, and I am glad you will stop His Holiness and that mad priest."

"Me too," Nemeah murmured, and sleep took them both.

That night, dreams plagued Nemeah. A black, airless world closed around her, lit only by a hundred pairs of slit-pupiled eyes. Unintelligible whispers slid across her mind like cold fingers. She saw a woman running through shadowed halls, a mirror breaking, and the woman shattering with it, her mouth twisting into an unnatural smile.

"Good work," a voice whispered from nowhere, both strange and disturbingly familiar.

Then came silence. A silence so complete it rang in her ears. Nemeah stood, though her feet rested on nothing solid, in a place high above the world. Far below, the land spread like a painted map. A dragon appeared in the distance, its scales the color of ash, its body streaked with black markings. It exhaled a torrent of fire, and the world beneath withered and melted under the heat.

Nemeah tried to scream for it to stop, but her voice was gone. Her limbs were locked, weighted by the cuff clamped tight around her wrist. The dragon's gaze fell to her. Its maw twisted in a sickening grin.

"We must stop him."

A new voice was beside her now. Nemeah turned to see a striking woman with waves of deep red hair spilling down her back. Dark green eyes held a desperate plea as they fixed on the destruction below.

"Please, Mother."

Nemeah bolted upright, breath tearing in ragged gasps as her eyes adjusted to the deep blue darkness. The steady hush of waves rolled in a slow, hypnotic rhythm, and above her, the stars burned clear and unblinking. A hand landed gently on her shoulder, nearly causing her to leap out of her skin.

In one swift motion, she was on her feet, Yuli's knife drawn, the blade glinting faintly in the starlight. Her mind told her to doubt her eyes, but her heart knew before she could breathe the name.

"Keanoff?" Her voice was breathy, trembling at the edges.

"You were having another nightmare," he murmured, hands raised in surrender, a half-smile softening the worry in his eyes. "I just wanted to make sure you were alright."

The knife slipped from her grip and landed blade-first in the sand, the hilt standing upright. Nemeah closed the distance between them, collapsing into his arms. He pulled her close, rubbing slow circles between her shoulder blades. The tang of sea salt clung to him, sharp and stale, and for a moment she simply breathed it in.

She drew back, still stunned. "What are you doing here?" she whispered, glancing toward Noa and Agnes to make sure they slept undisturbed. "You should be with the others."

"Yuli told me to come," he replied just as quietly. "Although keeping up with Noa was a challenge."

Even in the dim light, she could see the toll the journey had taken. Lines deeper than his years etched into his face, shadows like bruises beneath his eyes. A cold breeze swept over the island, and she shivered before she could stop herself. Keanoff wrapped his arms around her again, warmth swaddling her like a winter coat. She rested her head against his chest, listening to the steady beat of his heart.

"Nemeah?" His voice softened, almost breaking on her name.

She lifted her gaze to meet his. The stars stretched behind him, outlining his features. She wanted to stay here forever, in his arms, with that gaze locked on hers. But there was something inside her, pressing like a weight, something that should never have been there.

"Nemeah, I," He stopped as warm splatters hit his boots.

Nemeah's body heaved, and she doubled over, emptying her stomach into the sand. Sweat drenched her skin, her chest tight as another wave of sickness tore through her.

"I am so sorry," she mumbled between breaths, cheeks burning with humiliation. "I think I got your boots." The words had barely left her before her stomach rebelled again.

Keanoff stood frozen, caught between the urge to strip off his boots and the urge not to leave her alone in such a state. The stench of bile and half-digested fish curled unpleasantly in his nostrils. Still, he crouched and rubbed her back in long, steady strokes, hoping to anchor her through the misery.

"I think that is everything." Nemeah straightened, wiping her mouth with the back of her hand. "I am so sorry. I will clean your boots." She crouched, fingers fumbling at the laces. "I will do it now." Her shaking hands knotted the ties worse than before.

"How about," Keanoff said gently, "you get some sleep, and I will handle these."

She did not resist as he steered her back toward the blanket beside Agnes. Her eyes drifted closed almost instantly.

Only when she was breathing evenly again did Keanoff take a long breath of his own. He walked the foul-smelling boots into the surf, working the knots loose before yanking them free. The cold water bit at his feet as he scrubbed them clean, setting them on a sun-bleached rock to dry.

Circling to Noa's other side, he found the dragon's great glacial eyes open, glinting as if she found amusement in his plight. He gave her a shove on the shoulder before curling against her side, the rise and fall of her ribcage lulling him toward sleep.

Morning came bright and brisk. Nemeah's color had returned, and Agnes could not resist a few teasing remarks about the night's events. They packed their belongings, fastening them to Noa's saddle, and winced as they settled onto the root-woven seat. Keanoff checked the bags, gave Noa a firm pat, and shifted back into his hawk form. Together they took to the skies, the compass needle pointing them onward.

Five days later, the smudged line of Morbessa rose from the horizon. Dark clouds swirled over its shoreline, thick and heavy, as if they were flying toward the mouth of doom. Noa began her descent, wings stretching wide to catch the air for an easy landing on the dark shoreline, when a piercing wail ripped from her throat. She jerked violently midair, twisting and rolling as if something invisible was tearing through her.

"What is happening?" Agnes shouted over the dragon's roar.

In an instant, Nemeah remembered Vallorith's warning: *Those bound to a mirror cannot set foot on Morbessa.*

"We have to jump!" she yelled back, fumbling with the straps on the bags and shoving them over the side. They tumbled toward the churning backwater below. "Keanoff!" She pointed sharply.

The hawk dove from the sky, vanishing beneath the surface in a blur of feathers. Seconds later, a sleek seal broke the waves, the bag straps clenched between its teeth as it swam hard toward the shore.

Nemeah grabbed Agnes's hand and signaled for Noa to pull away. Without hesitation, both women pushed off the dragon's back, plummeting into the icy water. The cold was nothing like the gentle tides of their island; it bit deep, stealing their breath in a single, sharp grip. They broke the surface, gasping, air clawing its way into their frozen lungs.

"Come on," Agnes wheezed. "We need to reach shore!" She barked the order as her strokes sliced through the water with effortless precision.

Nemeah glanced up. Noa hovered above, wings faltering, torn between the instinct to stay and the agony racking her body.

"Go!" Nemeah shouted, slapping the water with one hand. "Go, get away from here!"

The dragon's eyes lingered for a heartbeat longer before she wheeled around, vanishing into the low clouds. Nemeah pushed herself after Agnes, waves shoving her toward a shore of smooth, rounded stones. Each pebble was light to the touch, pocked with tiny holes. Keanoff was already there, hauling her the last few feet onto dry ground, the sodden bags piled beside Agnes.

"What happened?" Keanoff asked, wringing out his hair, his voice a mix of frustration and worry.

"The flora here keeps anything tied to a mirror away," Nemeah coughed water from her lungs, shivering as she wrapped her arms around herself. "Noa is made from Kallemena and Ashar; she cannot touch this land."

Keanoff knelt beside the bags, pulling out a blanket. It was sodden and heavy, his apologetic look saying more than words could. Agnes suddenly let out a sharp cry. She tore her own bag open, pulling out a stack of books. Pages hung limp, their ink bleeding into unreadable blots. Her shoulders sagged.

"Well, this is a fine mess." She tossed the ruined books aside, grief quickly hardening into anger.

"At least the gold made it." Keanoff offered a faint smile. "Maybe you can replace them here." He straightened, looking out over the jagged landscape ahead. "I guess," he said quietly, "this means we made it."

Chapter Twenty-six

The land around them was as dark as midnight. The air felt too heavy to hold in their lungs, and sight was a constant struggle with their burning eyes. Overhead, a ceiling of dense clouds smothered the sky, swallowing any hope of sunlight. Nemeah and Agnes kept shoulder to shoulder, their steps slow and deliberate in the suffocating black.

They followed Keanoff's eyes, who had taken a form so small that Nemeah had trouble believing such a creature existed. Even the field mice on her family's farm had more heft. He could fit easily into her palm, a round head with impossibly large, liquid eyes that dwarfed his tiny, fur-covered body. Tawny hair clung to him in a soft halo, and his long, sticky fingers clutched her hand as his head darted in sharp, twitching motions, scanning a world only he seemed able to see.

The roar of the surf had faded long ago, replaced by the hiss of unseen steam vents and the ghostly glimmer of alien flora. Every flower matched Vallorith's warning, serrated petals in blistering shades of blue and red, stalks armed with cruel thorns. Even from a distance, they seemed to slice at her skin. An itch crawled over her arms, and each breath scraped her lungs raw as they pressed deeper inland.

Step by step, Nemeah's body rebelled. A lightness filled her skull, and her tongue tinged with the taste of copper. Beside her, Agnes coughed into her sleeve, leaving rust-red specks behind. On her shoulder, Keanoff's tarsier form swayed, his heavy eyelids blinking slower and slower.

"Look for shelter." Nemeah's cough punctuated the words. "We need to get out of this," she motioned at the air, thick and poisonous, "before it kills us."

She fumbled for her compass, focusing hard on the thought of refuge. The needle spun wildly, paused, then whirled again. Her heart pounded in time with its restless turn, panic chewing away at her patience.

"Come on!" she barked, ready to hurl it into the dirt, when suddenly the needle froze. "This way, hurry."

Her hand clamped around Agnes's, and she made sure Keanoff was secure before plunging forward. They ran with all their might, the air shredded their throats, every gasp bringing blood to their lips. Their eyes burned, streaming bloody tears, and red blotches blossomed over their skin. Keanoff returned to his human form, pressing a sleeve over his mouth and nose as he took the bags from them, urging them onward.

Agnes's stride faltered, her steps sluggish and uneven. Nemeah all but dragged her, fury simmering in her chest. The cuff on her wrist throbbed like a shackle. If she had her powers, she could shield them, blast the toxins away with a single gust. Vallorith's smirk came unbidden to her mind, had he known? When he told her where the last mirror was? When he locked her magic away? Was this indeed one last trap?

"There," Keanoff rasped, pointing toward a shadow just a shade darker than the suffocating air.

A cottage, or something shaped like one, emerged from the fog. Its roof and walls gleamed wet, coated in a viscous, tar-like slime that oozed in slow rivulets. Even the door was lacquered in the stuff, and if there were windows, they were sealed under the same suffocating layer.

Agnes stumbled to the entrance, pressing her hand against the sticky surface. She tried to knock, to pound her fist, but the clinging muck swallowed every sound and coated her arms with each desperate blow. Shoulders sagging, she stepped back just as Keanoff pushed past her, gripped the handle, and shoved hard.

The door gave way with a reluctant groan, and the three of them spilled into the dark interior, leaving the heavy air outside. They all coughed as Keanoff slammed the door shut, their ragged hacks echoing in the cramped space. Nemeah cracked her eyes open, only to meet a darkness just as thick as the air outside. Her hands swept along the rough surfaces around her while Keanoff and Agnes fought to catch their breath.

Fingers met a wall. She stretched her arms out and was surprised when she felt another. She shuffled sideways along the perimeter, six steps, then another wall.

"This place is tiny," she said, her voice too loud in the confined space. "Feels more like a shed than a house." The words scraped from her burning lungs.

"It would be nice if we had a light," Keanoff rasped, his cough a harsh bark that made the women's hacking sound mild in comparison.

"What now?" Agnes asked between shallow, wheezing breaths. "We do not know where we are, and we cannot see an inch in front of our noses." She groped her way through the black until her shoulder thudded against the wall. "No wonder so little is known about this place."

"Because it kills anyone who comes here?" Keanoff's morbid reply dropped like a stone, pulling whatever hope they had left down with it.

They stayed there for what seemed like hours, trading ideas on how to escape, none of them viable. With no light, no map, and no way to shut out the deadly fog, their survival seemed limited. Eventually, Agnes dozed off, her breathing shallow but steady despite the hell they had just gone through.

Nemeah leaned against a wall, legs stretched in front of her. She tilted her head back, tapping it lightly against the wood as if a plan might shake loose. All that came instead was anger. She hated being powerless. Hated having no control. The realization stung; she had spent weeks wishing to be normal, to be rid of what made her different. And here she was, fully human, wishing for anything but. The bitter irony twisted in her chest as she pulled her knees up, curling into herself.

"I am going to have the weirdest boogers for a week," Keanoff muttered as he blew his stuffy nose. "So, how do we get out of this?" His tone was oddly calm, almost casual, after what they had just endured.

"I honestly have no idea," she murmured, her mind still circling what she could do if only her powers were hers again. Her fingertips traced the rough cuff, its edges catching on her skin. "If I could just get this thing off!" She yanked hard, her wrist twisting painfully until she let out a groan.

"That is not coming off until Vallorith gets what he wants," Keanoff said, feeling his way toward her until his hand found the crown of her head. He settled beside her, his shoulder brushing hers. "You ever wonder why it was us? Why were we the ones to hunt down these mirrors?" he made an expansive gesture she could feel more than see. "Why are we the ones trying to save the world?" We have barely lived in it. The mirrors should have found more experienced leadership."

Nemeah could picture him scowling, even here in the dark. They lapsed into silence again, broken only by Agnes's gentle snores, proof they were still alive, still trapped in a shed with no light and no plan.

"I wondered, once," she said at last. "When I was alone. Before you found me in that snowstorm. Back when I thought you were just a plump hare that might make a decent supper."

Keanoff let out a rich laugh, and Nemeah jabbed him in the ribs. "Quiet or you will wake Agnes," she whispered.

He smothered the rest of his laugh and rubbed his side. "I would not have been worth eating. I was skin and bones before you started sharing your food with me. I thought you were just a runaway farm girl. Figured you would eventually turn back and head home."

Nemeah thought of that time, her mind seeing the forest clearing in the pitch-black room. "Would you have been sad?" Her voice was soft, uncertain. "If I had left?"

The silence stretched uncomfortably. Keanoff's warmth seeped into her chilled skin, steady and grounding.

"I think," He paused, choosing his words carefully. "I think I would have been happy either way. If you had gone, it would mean you found your way back to your family." His thoughts drifted to his father, still trapped in one of Vallorith's mirrors, the Morin monster lurking in memory. "But I was glad you stayed." A faint grin colored his tone. "And definitely grateful for all the food you shared."

His words settled over her, unsatisfied. She felt an ache in her chest as the cave and its inhabitants flashed through her mind. The image of Keanoff with Ismaara implanted itself front and center. She cleared her throat, hoping he did not sense the hurt in her voice. "Well, Ismaara barely eats, so I am sure you will have plenty from now on." Her fingers traced the cuff again, feeling Keanoff stiffen beside her.

"It is not," he began, but she cut him off.

"We need sleep if we want to make it out of here." She eased away from him and lowered herself to the hard floor. "Goodnight."

Keanoff sat in silence, a dozen unspoken thoughts lodged in his throat. His gaze swept the blackness, searching for even the faintest glimmer of light, but found nothing.

"Goodnight," he said at last.

They shifted in the dark, each finding a barely tolerable spot to rest. Neither spoke again before sleep claimed them.

The dream returned, racing through Nemeah's mind as though time itself were fast-forwarding. The mirror. The woman. The shattering glass. The grin.

"We must stop him." The woman with the red hair pleaded, her hands lifted toward Nemeah as if in offering, a silent prayer resting in her palms. "Take anything from me, anything, as long as we stop him."

From somewhere beyond, a mighty roar rose, followed by the thunderous beat of colossal wings.

"Tell us how we can stop him." A man's voice now spoke, firm, yet edged with desperation.

Nemeah turned. A young man stood there, far younger than she would have imagined a god could be. His face was square, his jaw unshaven, the beginnings of a beard little more than shadow. Blond hair brushed his shoulders, and his eyes, burning with fierce determination, met hers with unflinching intensity.

"If you do not help us, everything you see will be gone forever." His words were a plea, though his face remained composed.

Nemeah's gaze dropped to her own hand. Her fingers were outstretched, and resting in her palm was a single white seed. The voice that came next was not her own; it was the one that had whispered in her mind for weeks, uninvited yet familiar.

"Take it, and it will be done. But know this, its power can be turned on any who bear gifts."

She watched as the two gods accepted the seed and vanished from sight, swallowed by the shifting dream.

A sound dragged Nemeah from her slumber, the long, pained groan of rusted hinges moving after ages of stillness. She lifted her head, muscles stiff and tendons tight from sleeping in such an awkward position. Her joints protested as she stretched, muttering to herself about the price of falling asleep like that.

Then, a light. Orange and warm filled the room. It seared her eyes until tears welled up. She threw up a hand to shield her face, ears catching the faintest of whispers.

"I told you, Korven. I told you I heard something up here last night."

A meaty slap echoed, followed by a yelp.

"What was that for?"

"That is for sneaking through the tunnels alone." The second voice sighed, heavy with guilt. "Father is going to be so mad we came up here."

The voices sounded young and nervous. The groan came again, and the light vanished.

"No, wait!" Nemeah scrambled forward, palms brushing over dirt until her fingers met something foreign: a cold and solid edge. She traced a circle embedded in the floor, then found the hinge. A laugh burst from her throat, startling Keanoff awake. He thrashed in the dark, and the chaos of his flailing made her laugh harder while Agnes yawned somewhere nearby.

"There is a hatch here, in the floor," Nemeah said breathlessly, her need for light clawing at her. "Keanoff, help me." His rough hands found hers and followed the metal rim to the hinge.

"How did we miss this?" he murmured, still feeling around the edges.

"We did not exactly look on the floor," Nemeah admitted with a shrug no one could see. "I woke up because I heard it open. There was a light, and I heard people talking. One of them was named Korven."

Agnes cautiously shuffled toward the center of the room, fingertips brushing against the hatch in the darkness. "That actually makes sense," she said, her voice nearly trembling with excitement. "If the world above is too dangerous, then the people here must live underground." Her tone climbed toward a giddy squeal. "Keanoff, open it! We need to introduce ourselves." She drew in a deep breath, then let it out in a dramatic groan.

"Agnes, what is the matter?" Nemeah tried to find her in the dark, reaching for comfort, but her searching hand found only another wall.

"I have no idea how I look right now," Agnes said gravely. "We must look awful after yesterday. First impressions matter, Nemeah. What if they take one look at us and decide to shut us out because we look like we have been crawling through the wild for days?"

"We *have* been crawling through the wild for days," Keanoff pointed out.

A sharp smack echoed in the darkness.

"Chains," he yelped. "Agnes, what was that for?"

"That was me," Nemeah's voice chimed from the shadows. "And you did not have to point out how terrible we look."

"I am just being honest." He waited a beat, an unseen smile spreading over his lips. "I should be honest more often if it means you will hit me like that some more."

Heat rushed to Nemeah's face so fiercely she was certain it could light the room. Agnes broke first, laughter spilling out of her in an uncontrollable fit. The image of their ridiculous circumstances, trapped in a dark room, huddled over a trapdoor, fretting over their appearances, and Nemeah smacking Keanoff in the dark, was simply too much. Soon her giggles filled the space, echoing off the walls.

"Got it!" Keanoff's triumphant voice cut through the laughter as he pulled on the handle. The hatch creaked, giving way slowly.

They leaned over the opening, surprised to find a narrow tunnel below, a ladder descending into its depths. A single torch glowed faintly, throwing flickering light up toward them. Nemeah glanced at Agnes, who looked from her to Keanoff.

In the torchlight, they all wore the same shell-shocked expression, like they had walked into the god of death's domain and somehow walked back out. Smears of dried blood streaked their faces from the day before, and stains marred their clothes with the poisonous ash that still clung to the air outside.

Agnes immediately dug into her bag, producing a brush and dragging it through her salt-tangled hair. "Turn around," she ordered.

Nemeah and Keanoff obeyed without protest, too weary to argue. Agnes worked through Nemeah's hair with brisk, decisive strokes, a few strands pulling painfully free. When she finished, she pivoted to Keanoff. One firm tug on his braid sent him shuffling forward, his hands snapping up to guard his hair.

"No. It is fine the way it is," he said, holding out a palm as though that alone might stop her.

Agnes narrowed her eyes at him, every inch the scolding matron. "Fine. But at least wipe your face."

Once they were marginally cleaner, they descended the ladder, taking the torch with them. Keanoff led the way, the tunnel stretching endlessly ahead. Their footsteps echoed against dirt-packed walls, and their stomachs growled in the oppressive quiet. The passage seemed freshly carved, its earthen sides crumbling to the touch yet mending themselves instantly, no risk of collapse.

"This must be a Thorns magic," Nemeah whispered, running her fingertips along the self-healing dirt. "Maybe they are the ones who grew the flowers. Maybe they know where the mirror is."

"Let us not get ahead of ourselves," Keanoff cautioned as they reached another wooden door, similar to the hatch above, its massive hinges gleaming dully in the torchlight.

They exchanged a glance, none of them sure what waited beyond.

"First impressions," Agnes murmured as Keanoff eased the door open.

The sight stole their breath. A vast cavern sprawled before them, lit by hundreds of lanterns, casting a golden glow over the stone. Temples and homes flanked a wide central road; people bustled along it, their shadows stretching across the walls. Around the city's edges, farmland thrived in lush, ordered rows, fed by a waterfall that emptied into canals veining the entire settlement.

Only when Nemeah looked down did she realize how high they stood. She stepped back from the ledge, heart lurching at the dizzying drop to the tiled rooftops below. Roofs that crowned what appeared to be an immense temple complex, its walls hung with colorful banners.

Agnes's quiet nudge snapped her back. "The welcome party," she whispered.

Three figures climbed the long stairs toward them, their appearance striking and strange: catlike ears and noses, hair in shades of silver and snow, and skin patterned in intricate patches of black and white like living mosaics. Their brightly colored togas blazed against their muted skin, each hue rich under the lantern light.

The eldest stepped forward and spoke, his language a quick, fluid rhythm of sounds more than words. Agnes slipped past Keanoff, bowing low. Straightening, she replied in the same unusual tongue, her words slower, careful, as if placing each sound precisely. Back and forth they went, the man's speech rapid, Agnes's responses deliberate, until a sudden burst of laughter from the men broke the tension. Agnes bowed again.

She turned to her companions, her expression a mix of excitement and unease. "They are taking us to the king."

Then together, they began their descent into the unknown.

Chapter Twenty-seven

The three walked in single file through the winding streets, shadowing the elders who had wordlessly taken the lead. Every step drew more eyes. People paused mid-task, hands stilling over wares, tools, or baskets, their gazes following the pale-skinned strangers with dark hair. The ones who so clearly did not belong.

Agnes led the way, her eyes darting like a child's in a sweet shop, drinking in every sight, scent, and sound her senses would allow. She studied the curve of rooftops, the bright fabrics hung to dry, the rhythmic clang of a distant hammer. Every detail was tucked away for the notes she would feverishly write later. To her, this underground world was not just a city; it was a discovery of a lifetime.

Nemeah walked behind her, head lowered, arms folded tight across her middle as if to shield herself from the stares. She wanted to move faster. She wanted walls. She wanted *anything* to break the force of the onlookers' eyes. Her gut twisted with unease, whispering that whatever awaited them in the temple-palace ahead would not be kind. She stole a glance around. The faces watching them all carried the same weight: outsiders, unwelcome invaders. The look was all too familiar, dredging up memories of her family's faces the night they saw her powers.

Keanoff brought up the rear, flashing an easy smile at everyone he passed, radiating a charm that said, *I am harmless.* He nodded to the men and aimed his most disarming grin at the women, earning a few coy giggles behind their sheer veils. Children whispered to each other, pointing, and then breaking into laughter as the strangers walked by.

The streets undulated with the land, flat and bustling in the market plains, then sloping upward over arched bridges that spanned rivers fed by the ever-present waterfall. The city's quiet was such that the distant roar of that cascade was a constant hum, even here in the heart of this strange civilization.

At last, they reached the base of the temple. Up close, it shared the sculpted elegance of the town, yet something about it felt more *made by hands* than by magic. Thick walls of dried mud still bore the imprint of the palms that had shaped them, immortalized in hardened clay. A vibrant mosaic of tiles paved the walkway and stairs, each depicting fragments of the world above. They climbed the steps in measured pace, following the elders, until a shout split the murmuring crowd.

"Crutulo! Mika haa buu talla na!"

A young man shoved forward, his face markings forming the illusion of a battle helmet. His eyes burned with fury as he raised his hand, a stone resting in his palm. Without hesitation, he hurled it straight at Nemeah.

"Crutulo!"

She saw the rock flying toward her, heart lurching, but Keanoff's arm shot up, catching it mid-flight. He let it drop to the tiled step with a sharp *clack.*

"Not the warmest of greetings," he murmured dryly.

The elders rushed between the strangers and the crowd, hands raised, voices in a low, calming rhythm. But the tension hung heavy, the people's glares unsoftened. Then another voice rang out, a woman's, also shouting the unknown word.

She hurled a stone. Another followed. Then another. Soon, the air was thick with the thud and crack of rocks striking the stairs, the sound echoing in every ear. The elders shielded themselves and urged the outsiders forward, up toward the sanctuary of the temple doors.

They ran now, feet skimming over the mosaic tiles as the mob's chant grew louder, pounding in rhythm with each stone thrown. "Crutulo! Crutulo! Crutulo!" The last of the elders crossed the threshold, and the two massive stone doors swung shut, muting the voices to a low, ominous hum.

Breathless, Nemeah turned to Agnes. "What does that word mean? *Crutulo?*" Her voice shook. That man's eyes were burned into her memory, eyes that had looked at her as though she were a curse given flesh.

"I do not know." Agnes's brow furrowed. "It is not a word I was taught." She glanced at one of the elders, a deep cut marring his forehead where a stone had struck. "Oh no." In an instant, she was at his side, pulling a rag from her pack and pressing it gently to the wound.

Nemeah watched as Agnes, still tending the injury, spoke in the locals' quick, clipped tongue. The three elders exchanged hushed glances, then gave an answer so quiet it seemed meant for no one beyond them.

Agnes nodded slowly, then turned to her companions, her face drawn tight. "If I understood them correctly, it is part of a prophecy. One passed down by the god of death himself. *Crutulo* means," She hesitated. "The Mother."

Keanoff frowned. "You studied their language and never learned the word for mother? That is some *magnificent* Axis education."

Agnes's glare could have cut glass. "It does not mean mother as in someone who raises children," she said sharply. Her voice rose. "It means *Mother* as in *Creator*. It means Morwyn."

The moment the name left her lips, the elders inhaled sharply, then dropped to their knees. In unison, they began to chant urgently as if the word itself had cracked the air open.

"Who is Morwyn?" Keanoff's eyes stayed on the robed men, their foreheads pressed to the tiled floor, the one with the cut leaving a smear of blood on the tiles as he repeatedly bowed.

Before Agnes could answer, Nemeah spoke. Her voice was distant, almost hollow.

"The queen."

At this, the three elders spoke, all pointing to the far side of the hall. Nemeah turned around, and there in front of her was a tiled picture. One that depicted a dark-haired woman with blue, almost black eyes. It looked like Nemeah.

***

They were quickly whisked away without explanation, separated at the first doorway they were brought to. Agnes and Nemeah were pushed into one room, and Keanoff into another.

The women were stripped of their clothing, attendants carrying away every last scrap of the contaminated garments. Warm water was poured over them, followed by a gritty yellow mud scrubbed from head to toe until their skin tingled. One attendant tried to remove the cuff on Nemeah's arm, tugging and twisting until her mutters dissolved into frustrated curses.

When the washing was done, they were rinsed, dried, and dressed. Agnes was wrapped in yellow silks embroidered with tiny green leaves that trailed like vines across the fabric. Nemeah's gown was deep midnight blue, a silver shooting star streaking across its folds. Matching scarves were wrapped and twisted around their hair, draping neatly down their backs.

In the other chamber, Keanoff's ordeal was far less cooperative. He refused to surrender his clothes and nearly came to blows when he saw the shears. It took eight men to force him down, five to pin his limbs, and three more to hack and shape his overgrown beard and brush his hair into a severe knot atop his head. His toga was patterned in layered greens, like grass after rainfall.

When he finally emerged, adjusting the strange folds of the garment, he froze mid-step. His gaze locked on Nemeah.

"What are you staring at?" she hissed, fingers nervously fiddling with her cuff.

He cleared his throat. "Nothing. Just did not recognize you without dirt on your face." A smirk tugged at his mouth.

"Same to you," Agnes shot back, earning a quick laugh from him.

The room they were brought to was understated in its elegance, with low tables carved from dark wood and enormous pillows in jewel tones scattered across the floor. A kettle of steaming tea sat at the center, the scent of warm spice curling into the air. They eyed it in silence, hunger gnawing at their bellies.

"What if it is poison?" Nemeah murmured.

"Or silvervane?" Keanoff countered.

Agnes and Nemeah exchanged a look. Neither of them would be bothered to have the herbs' effects in their system if it meant something warm inside their aching bellies. They reached for the cups simultaneously. Agnes drained hers in one long swallow, closing her eyes as she sighed.

"Oh, that is heavenly." She poured herself more, unashamed.

Nemeah sipped more cautiously, recognizing the notes almost instantly. "Heather, honey, and something else." She tipped back the cup, reassured. "Not silvervane."

At that, Keanoff downed his share and helped himself to seconds and thirds until the kettle was empty. The tea only deepened their awareness of how empty their stomachs were; three days without a proper meal had left them weak.

The door behind them swung open. A pair of hands clapped sharply, and they all jumped. A plump woman in a sapphire blue toga trimmed in gold stepped inside, her movements brimming with authority. She spoke her language quickly, her words lilting like music.

"This is the king's daughter, Oleeta," Agnes translated. "She will escort us to the banquets they have prepared."

"Banquets?" Keanoff's head snapped up. "As in food?"

Oleeta smiled, clearly pleased by his reaction. "Come," she said in accented common. "Let us properly welcome you to the kingdom of Mortava."

The princess led them through winding halls of rich earthen tones. Dark brown walls streaked with ochres and rust-red clay rose high above, the ceilings draped with dangling roots that twisted like grasping fingers.

"It was my brothers who found you," Oleeta began, her voice as light as a hostess sharing a charming anecdote. "My father was angry at first. But when the townspeople said you looked like the Mother, we had to see you at once. We were just going to throw you into the pits." She laughed, a quick, warm sound that did not reach her eyes. "Luckily, that did not happen."

Nemeah lengthened her stride to walk beside the princess. "How do you all know what the mother looked like?"

Oleeta did not answer directly. She glided on, her tone airy. "Our traditions have not changed since we came to live underground two hundred years ago. We are still ruled by a monarchy." She touched her tiara, a delicate crown molded from the same earthen material as the walls. "But my father will tell you more at the feast. I would not dare steal his stories." Her gaze flicked over each of them. "It is so nice to finally have visitors."

Nemeah's fingers worried at the cuff on her wrist, agitation starting to leak through her calm façade. "Oleeta," she pressed, "the tiled picture in the main hall."

"Father will answer all." Oleeta's smile was sugar-sweet as she swept open a towering set of doors, revealing a cavernous hall filled with long tables sagging under the weight of food.

The hum of conversation died instantly. Every head turned toward them. A man stood on a dais, a stone throne looming behind him, a crude crown of hardened mud perched on his brow. His cheeks were full, his grin wide, and his arms spread in welcome as he spoke in the lilting language of this strange world.

The crowd broke into applause as Oleeta led the three forward, the way a handler might parade livestock at market. Eyes followed them from every direction, whispers threading through the air. The whole scene felt less like hospitality and more like a snare being sprung.

Nemeah's gaze flicked across a sea of faces, skins of black and white cut through with bright sashes, jewel-toned togas catching the torchlight. The sheer press of color and movement made her dizzy. Without thinking, she caught Agnes's hand in one of hers and Keanoff's in the other, drawing them close as they trailed Oleeta toward the dais.

"Father." Oleeta bowed low before gesturing toward them. "These are the ones who found their way below ground to our marvelous kingdom."

The king clapped his hands together, the sound booming off the stone. "Finally, the Mother has arrived!"

He descended the steps with surprising speed for his size, eyes fixed on Nemeah. His white hair was braided tight to his scalp, his sunny yellow toga hanging in loose folds, and his crown looking as though a child had shaped it in the mud after a rainstorm.

"Your hair and your eyes." His slit-pupiled gaze drank her in from head to toe, his delight unmistakable. "Welcome to Mortava." He circled her like a man inspecting a rare treasure before turning abruptly to Keanoff. "A Vira," he said with interest. "We have heard of such people with markings." His thick fingers gripped Keanoff's arm, tracing the tribal tattoos. "Our Vira also had them long ago."

Keanoff's eyes narrowed. "You have Vira here?"

The king stared blankly before moving on to Agnes. "Not since we were banished." His voice trailed off as his attention returned to Nemeah. "Not since the Mothers' poison forced us underground."

"Then, who grew the flowers?" Nemeah asked, matching his movements so he never stood behind her. "The red and blue ones on the surface?"

"Questions for another time." The king smiled a toothy grin, his pupils tightening unnervingly. "I know what it is you seek."

With a sudden pivot, he climbed the dais again, his bulk surprisingly quick. From a small table beside the throne, he lifted an object. Nemeah's breath caught. The final mirror. The one that held the Thorn twins. The room erupted in clapping, as though the king had performed some great act.

"Thank you," Nemeah said, her voice steady but her pulse racing. "With this, we can stop the mad priest and free the prisoners trapped inside. This can all be over soon." She stepped toward the dais, and the atmosphere shifted like a sudden change in weather. From above, the roots hanging from the vaulted ceiling whipped down like striking snakes, coiling around her arms and legs. Keanoff lunged to pull her free, but more roots shot down, tangling him in place. Agnes stood frozen, her face pale, shock locking her limbs.

The king set the mirror down with exaggerated care before lowering himself onto his throne. "You uppers," he said with a slow shake of his head. "Always grasping for what you want without thinking of what we need." His tone carried a hint of laughter. "You may have the mirror when the Mother releases us from our confinement."

"Confinement?" Keanoff strained against the bindings.

"Yes." The king's voice swelled. "The punishment of our god. We have served our time. We wish to see the sun again, to sail the seas, to walk the lands beyond. This is our new beginning." He thrust a hand toward Nemeah. "The Mother is finally here! Crutulo es tulu Morwyn fret frey hanna Morbessa!"

The crowd roared, cups lifted high. They drank deep, stomped their feet, and slammed utensils against their plates in a deafening chorus.

"Sima rue bik walla!" the king bellowed above the din.

The roots loosened, only for guards to seize Nemeah and Keanoff. They were marched from the hall, the intoxicating scent of roasted meat and ale tormenting their empty stomachs. Down a barren corridor they went, into a small, rootless chamber. The heavy stone door slammed shut behind them, locking tight.

Keanoff's eyes swept the walls, seeking any weakness. Finding none, he cursed under his breath. "No way out," he muttered. "Not unless someone opens that door."

"What was he talking about?" Nemeah turned to Agnes, whose face was still pale, the color yet to return. "The queen punished their god? Arvayn? How? Why?"

Agnes shook her head, "I have no idea. I have never read anything about this."

Nemeah groaned in frustration. "None of this is helping us," she muttered, "and why do they think I am the queen?"

"Probably because you look just like her." Keanoff spat, still examining the door. "Dark hair, dark eyes." He turned to Nemeah. "Even the same nose and mouth."

The scrape of stone interrupted their talk. The heavy door swung inward, and the guards entered first, rough hands clamping around their arms to keep them still. One by one, women filed in behind them, balancing trays and baskets. Soft pillows and thick blankets were set against the wall. Platters of roasted meats, steaming bread, and glazed roots filled the air with a heady, mouthwatering scent. Jugs of water and dark ale clinked against each other. Baskets spilled over with ripe fruit, their skins shining in the dim light. No words were spoken. As quickly as the procession came, it was gone, the stone door grinding shut and locking once more.

"At least they are feeding us," Keanoff said, dropping to his knees by the nearest tray. He wasted no time tearing into the food.

The questions that had been crowding Nemeah's mind scattered like startled birds. She dropped down beside him, hunger drowning out every other concern. Even Agnes, still somewhat dazed, reached for the platters, eating as though she had not seen food in weeks. They did not stop until every dish was scraped clean and every crumb gone.

Chapter Twenty-eight

They spent the night in uneasy silence, each one lost in restless half-dreams. Their borrowed garments clung strangely to their skin, the muffled echoes of the temple unsettled their ears, and the foreign tongue of the guards outside was a constant reminder: this was not their world. Everything was unfamiliar, yet Nemeah could not shake the hollow familiarity of being a prisoner once more.

She shifted again on the heap of oversized pillows, but sleep never came. The dreams had no room to intrude; her mind was already crowded with tension. Hours slipped by until exhaustion seized her every fiber, and still she could not sleep. She gave up trying and slouched against the cold wall. She fixed her eyes on the strip of shadow beneath the locked door, watching it pulse with the flicker of torchlight beyond.

Agnes stirred. She rubbed her red-rimmed eyes and sat up with a groan. "No sleep for you either?"

Nemeah shook her head, both of them turning instinctively toward Keanoff, who snored so loudly the pillows seemed to vibrate.

"I wish I could do that." Agnes stretched, straightening the folds of her toga. Her voice carried a hint of guilt now, softer than usual. "I am sorry I went all strange yesterday. I was so fascinated by this place, and when you and Keanoff and those awful roots. I just panicked." She lowered her head.

"There was nothing you could have done," Nemeah said gently, trying to soothe her shame, though her own unease gnawed deeper.

From the hall came the scrape of boots, a tide of footsteps that swelled closer. The shadows under the door thickened. A metallic click echoed, and the stone slab swung inward. The same guards as before seized the women's arms without a word and had to lift Keanoff's dead weight from his still slumbering state. Once everyone was on their feet, they were marched through Mortava's dim corridors.

The banquet hall looked twice as vast without its crowd. The tables had been cleared, the air heavy with the faint ghosts of last night's feast. At the dais, the king lounged on his throne, the mirror in his hand. He waved it lazily back and forth as though it were nothing more than a fan. Nemeah's stomach twisted. That mirror was no ornament; it was a prison. Two Echo lives still clung inside, yet the king dangled it recklessly, as if it could be replaced.

Beside him sat Oleeta, radiant in a deep blood-red fabric, and two slender boys who looked much younger than their sister sat quietly, watching the prisoners being brought in. To the king's other side rested a woman draped in pink, her swollen belly leaving no doubt that she would soon bring another heir into this strange, shadowed world.

The king leaned forward, his eyes bright with theatrical delight as he addressed the one his people called Mother. "It seems that you, our strange upper world visitors, know nothing of our history and what we have endured. Clueless about the curse put upon our god and the land he had shaped for his followers. Today you will hear your story and refresh your ancient memory." He gestured to his sons. "My boys will show you. They are our finest storytellers."

At his signal, the two boys rose. Thin, graceful, and sure of themselves, they descended the dais steps. The torches dimmed until only a single pale light fell across the elder's mosaic skin, black and white as if chiseled from stone. His amber eyes locked onto Nemeah's, unblinking.

"Ladies and gentlemen," his voice rang clear, carrying far beyond his slight frame. "Tonight, you will witness the tale of our land, the curse that binds our people, and the one who will set us free." He bowed low, and in an instant, every flame in the room winked out.

For a breath, there was only silence and darkness. Then, light blossomed again. This time, five figures stood at the center of the hall, clothed in shimmering costumes, their presence so sudden it stole the breath from the audience.

"Long ago," The eldest son's booming voice filled the chamber like a god himself as he narrated. "The gods struck a bargain with the Mother."

A woman stepped forward, her hair streaming black ink that dripped to the floor, staining her toga into a living shadow. Another figure followed, red sashes hanging from her hair, her green robe woven with vines and sparkling emeralds.

"Mother, we must stop Dathmor," she cried, bowing low before stepping back, the vines at her waist trembling as if alive. "His beast form will destroy us all!" Her voice carried the theatrics through the room.

Another figure stepped forward; it was the youngest son. He wore armor of rough stone, a blazing sun carved into the breastplate. Wisps of golden straw crowned his hair, catching the torchlight until it seemed to burn.

"Mother," he cried, voice ringing with youthful desperation. "Tell us what we can do. Help us stop this madness."

"I have seen this," Nemeah whispered, the words slipping from her before she could stop them. Her stomach tightened, for she knew what was to come.

The woman in black raised her hand, revealing a white stone that gleamed against her ink-streaked skin. "Take this, my children, and use it upon the dragon. Save the world from his tyranny." She pressed it into the brother's palm. "Go now, save our world!"

Nemeah's nose wrinkled. That was not right. The vision she remembered was different.

The actors lifted the stone in triumph, and the hall went dark. Only shuffling feet and hushed voices stirred in the blackness. When light returned, a massive beast loomed at center stage. Its body was a framework of roots bound with grey sashes, jewels glittering where eyes should be. Two silhouettes moved inside the frame, and the giant wings beat the air in staggering rhythm.

The woman with the red sashes and the brother reappeared, holding the white stone aloft. Their voices rose together, echoing against the chamber walls: "If you must consume, then consume this seed from the Mother!"

They hurled the stone into the dragon's gaping maw. The people within the frame jolted it violently, making it lurch as if in battle. Sashes tore loose, the wings crashed to the floor, and at last the dragon's jeweled head sagged lifeless.

Nemeah tugged at her cuff, words burning her tongue but refusing to form. Again, darkness fell.

A lone spotlight burst to life. A figure stepped into view, his face hidden behind a mask of bleached bone, antler-like branches rising above his head. Draped in flowing black, he stalked to the fallen beast and laid a hand upon its ribs. When he spoke, his voice rasped with grief and rage.

"I will heal my brother," he vowed. "And together, we will rule the world."

He spun around the carcass in a fluid dance, each step deliberate as a performer. From the folds of his robe, he drew long sashes dyed the color of fresh blood. With a flourish, he cast them over the dragon's body. "Rise, Dathmor! Rise from death!"

The torches blazed higher, revealing the dragon's body lurching upward. Its wings unfurled, rattling against the hall. From inside, a hidden actor bellowed a guttural roar. Darkness consumed the hall again. More murmurs interrupted the silence as shuffling gave away that the stage was changing again. When the light returned, the woman in black stood at the center once more, the masked figure bowing at her feet.

"You have gone against my wishes," she shrieked, her voice splitting the silence. "You have gone against your kin. For this, I curse you and your land, a poison to plague you forever, until I return."

The masked man cried out, collapsing in anguish. "Oh, Mother, please! Punish me, but not my people!" His last word stretched into a wail.

The woman turned her face aside, nose tilted high, voice cold as stone. "You harmed others. So shall your punishment be equal."

He grabbed at her robes with trembling hands, groveling at her feet. "When will you return? When will our torment end?"

Her gaze snapped forward, straight at Nemeah. The hall dimmed again, shadows choking out the corners. When she spoke, her voice carried the weight of prophecy.

"When man grows too large and his goodwill too small, I will rise from my island with power to enthrall. Should I require aid, a bargain will be made. One prison for another, the debt shall be paid."

Once more, the room plunged into blackness. When light returned, everything had been swept away. The actors, the dripping ink, the dragon's bulk, all gone. The hall was pristine, the actors back in their seats as if nothing had happened.

The king rose, his belly straining against his purple toga. Spittle flew from his lips as he spread his arms wide. "So now you see? You understand? You will lift our curse, Mother. A prison for a prison." He brandished the mirror like a trophy, its surface gleaming under the light.

Nemeah stood, her eyes locked on his slit-pupiled stare. Her hand lifted, trembling not with fear, but fury. "Your tale leaves out truths."

The king froze.

"It was not only the seed that felled Dathmor. Danira and Lirian forged a cuff using the ones given by Nuval. Together, they bound it to the beast's arm, draining its power." She raised her wrist, the metal catching the light. "This cuff is the very same as the one the gods used. I could not wield magic even if I wished to." She took a step forward, her frustration edging her on. "And Dathmor did not die. So, there would have been no reason for your god to revive him. There is another reason your land is cursed, and maybe rightfully so."

The king's grin faltered. His eyes dropped to the cuff at her arm, and for the first time, his mask of confidence cracked. The king's face flushed red as he swung toward his sons. "Korven. Does she speak the truth?"

The princes answered in their native tongue, voices sharp and fast, each word like a blade. Their gazes darted between the mirror and the uppers, their arguments rising until the air itself seemed to thicken with tension.

Nemeah's earlier confidence began to fray. Her stomach coiled, and she realized once again that her anger had made things worse.

Keanoff leaned to Agnes, whispering, his voice tight with worry. "What are they saying?"

Agnes tried to keep steady, but her hands trembled in her lap. "They say that Nemeah is lying. Calling her names, I dare not repeat." She took in a quick breath, her eyes widening. "They want to send her up there to clear the curse."

"That would kill her!" Keanoff bellowed, ripping against the guards' hold. "She is telling you the truth!" Three men pinned him, but he thrashed like a storm. "She will die if you do that!"

The king's eyes burned with hate as he turned on them. "If she dies, then she is not the true Mother. She is an imposter." He lifted the mirror high, spit flying as he shouted, "This only goes to Morwyn!" With a snap of his fingers, the order was given.

A guard seized Nemeah's arm, his grip iron around her flesh. Oleeta gave a shrill, delighted giggle, bouncing in her chair like a child at a feast.

"Father." The youngest son rose, voice trembling. "If what they claim is true, then sending her up will kill her. We are the ones who named her Mother. She never once claimed it for herself."

"Silence, Mavren!" The king's roar shook the chamber. A hush fell so heavy it rang in Nemeah's ears. His face twisted with rage as he glared down at her. "Take her topside. If she dies, then we will know."

"No!" Keanoff's roar tore through the silence. With a violent surge, he hurled one guard over his shoulder. He dodged another strike, body shifting in a blur. In seconds, a tiger stood in his place, pelt striped with his tribal markings, fangs bared, and claws gouging the stone. The guards stumbled back as another roar rattled their bones. Saliva dripped from his jaws as he stalked toward the throne.

"We can all talk calmly," Mavren began, only to yelp as his brother cuffed him on the head.

"How many times must I remind you?" Korven snapped. "You have no authority."

"Korven is right, darling," the queen drawled from her seat, entirely unfazed. She licked honey from her fingers, eyes never leaving the sweet treats she had been consuming the entire time. She lay in her throne, as if the fate of the room only bored her.

The tiger prowled closer, inch by inch, every muscle coiled to spring until a scream split the air. All eyes snapped to Oleeta. She had Agnes in her grasp, her thick arm wrapped around Agnes' neck. Her lips curved into a smile that chilled Nemeah's blood.

"Change back, kitty cat," she sang sweetly, "or I will snap her neck."

Keanoff froze, his green eyes blazing.

Nemeah's heart thundered. Her gaze shifted between the predator and her friend, the world narrowing to the fear that took over Agnes' features. "Turn back, Keanoff," she ordered firmly. "Turn back."

For a long, terrible moment, he did not move. Then, with a shudder, the tiger was gone. Keanoff stood human again, his eyes locked on Nemeah's, the fight still burning in them.

"Take her to the surface," Oleeta said, her smile sinister at the thought of what might happen to Nemeah once exposed to the toxic atmosphere.

The guards dragged Nemeah from the hall, the sound of the door slamming behind her like a final verdict.

***

Nemeah was pulled up a flight of stairs, shoved through winding tunnels, and forced up a narrow ladder until she and two guards stopped in front of a wooden door that looked eerily similar to the hatch in the small house. Her body trembled, nerves sparking through her like fire. Her mind raced, conjuring every possible outcome, and all of them ended the same way, with her death.

The door creaked open, revealing the dark, poisonous world beyond. One guard flinched and took a hesitant step back, while the other gave Nemeah a hard shove through the threshold. She stumbled forward, unable to keep her footing, and crashed to the barren dirt. Dust exploded around her, filling her lungs until she choked and hacked against the air itself. Her fingers clawed at the ground, desperate for something to defend herself with, until they closed around something solid. She lifted it close, then instantly recoiled. The object slipped from her grip as horror jolted her upright.

It was a bone. Her gaze darted outward, and her stomach lurched. Thousands of bones littered the wasteland, a carpet of the dead stretching in every direction. Panic took hold, and she bolted for the door that was already shut. She pounded against the wood with raw fists, praying and begging that one of the guards might take pity and drag her back inside. Deep down, she knew that hope was nothing but a cruel lie.

Slowly, she turned, facing what her future held. In hours, perhaps less, she would join the collection beneath her feet. The forsaken and rejected. Those denied refuge in the underkingdom of Mortava. The ones who died alone. Tears spilled freely, and every gust of wind pressed the stinging dust into her wet cheeks.

"If I can find another house," Her hope was now desperate.

She pushed through the haze, lungs already burning as if fire had taken root inside them. She pushed her sashes over her nose and mouth as she broke into a run, aiming for a shadow on the horizon. Any hint of structure, anything that might mean safety, was what she aimed for. Without her compass, she was blind, stumbling toward nothing, yet clinging to the desperate illusion of direction.

Minutes stretched into hours. The poisonous air exacted its toll. Her skin erupted in angry blotches, swelling until it felt as though it might split. Blood streaked from her eyes and nose, painting her face in red stains that dulled her senses further. Her stride faltered as her feet met the razor-sharp petals of the flowers here, each step agonizing as she waded through the thicket of them. Her very breaths rasped like a saw inching its way through her chest. She staggered, collapsed to her knees, and clawed forward through the dust, leaving streaks behind her in the dirt.

Her body gave out before her will. Nemeah crumpled to the ground, spasms wracking her frame as her lungs begged for air. Her vision narrowed to black, and sound collapsed into a high-pitched ring as she made her last, desperate plea.

"Morwyn, help me."

Part IV:
The Frayed Fates

Chapter Twenty-nine

The light tapping of rain stirred Nemeah awake. The damp scent of earth drifting through an open window reminded her of home. She tried to force her eyes open, only to find them crusted shut. Pain surged through her body, dragging the memory of what she had endured back into her mind. Each breath scraped like glass in her lungs, a cough ripping its way up her raw throat.

She curled in on herself, regretting the sudden motion as her heart hammered against her ribs. Waves of agony rolled through her battered frame until she cried out, her voice a broken moan. Was this death? Was this the eternity she had been waiting for? An endless prison of pain?

The window shut with a soft thud, startling her. She blinked against the blur, desperate to see, but the world was still a smear of shadow and light.

"Who is there?" she tried to rasp, but her tongue was swollen, her throat too raw for more than a whisper.

Footsteps circled, steady and deliberate. Then came a low hum that was melodic and almost soothing. She lay still, her body refusing any effort, listening as a jar was opened, a cork popped, and liquid bubbled in some unseen pot. A sweet fragrance of cinnamon and honey soon filled the room and forced her stomach to release a painful growl deep within her.

Her mouth watered, but all she tasted was blood. The memory of Morbessa came rushing back. The poisonous sand and how it burned her lungs. The way her body had given up, falling to the sand. Tears threatened, but she had no strength to shed them. She could not move. She could barely even speak.

A cool hand slid beneath her neck. Gentle motions to keep the pain at bay. Careful not to aggravate her already irritated and feverish skin. Her head lifted, and the rim of a cup brushed her lips. Warm liquid touched her tongue. She hesitated, then gulped greedily. Milk spiced with cinnamon and sweetened with raw honey spilled down her throat, sugary and rich, crashing into her hollow stomach. She knew she should pace herself, but hunger and thirst devoured her restraint.

The cup pulled away, and panic flared. "More. Give me more," she begged, coughing between the words. Her voice sounded small and hoarse. Childish, even, but she could not stop herself. "Please."

The cup returned, but this time her caretaker's voice guided her. "Slowly. Or it will come back up. That will only bring more pain."

The voice was calm and firm, and Nemeah obeyed. She forced herself into measured sips, each one precious. When the last drop slid into her mouth, she almost wept. She wanted more. She wanted bread, cheese, anything solid, but her body was not ready.

Her head was lowered gently back to the pillow, and her mysterious caretaker's footsteps retreated.

"Please," she croaked after them, her chest hitching. "Who are you?" She tried again to force her eyes open. The firelight flickered faintly on the far side of the room, but the rest was shrouded in darkness and blurred shapes. "Where am I?" Her words slurred, tangled by exhaustion as sleep clawed at her again.

Panic surged. She could not surrender, not here. Not in an unfamiliar place, not with a stranger close by. She fought it, but her body betrayed her, pulling her back under. She dreamed of Keanoff and Agnes. Pacing a stone room, whispering too low for her ears to catch. Keanoff pounded on a locked door while Agnes continued to cry. Nemeah tried to shout, to tell them she was alive, but her voice was swallowed, her mouth feeling heavy and stuffed with cotton.

When she woke again, the air had turned colder. The rain drummed harder against the roof; the fire crackled closer now. She peeled her eyes open at last and found the room cloaked in perfect black.

Another wave of worry surged as she forced her arms upward. Her muscles screamed in protest, skin burning as if stripped raw. The effort made her eyes water, her pulse thudding in her ears. She brought trembling hands to her face and found soft fabric wrapped across her eyes, tied tightly at the side of her head.

Panic jolted through her. She clawed at the knot, tugging desperately, until another hand caught hers. She gasped, a small yelp slipping free before the hand gently guided hers back to her side.

"Your eyes are badly damaged," the stranger said. Their voice was both familiar and strange, carrying a weight that unsettled her. "The cloth is soaked with herbs to heal them. Leave it be unless you would rather be blind."

Nemeah's breath shuddered out of her, and she slowly shook her head. The hand retreated, and shuffled feet sounded in the silence once more. She listened to the stranger moving about the room: jars opening, corks popping, liquid simmering. Metal scraped against ceramic, and water sloshed as dishes were cleaned. When they returned, they lifted her gently, helping her drink warm milk and propping her up on more pillows. Their movements had a rhythm to them, steady and practiced. Soothing in a way that pulled her back toward sleep again and again.

By the fourth day, her voice returned in fragments, though it rasped like stone dragged across wood. Her throat no longer burned with every word, but her chest still seized if she pushed too far. She lay listening to the stranger's routine, questions pressing at her lips until one finally slipped free.

"Am I dead?" Her voice sounded strange even to her, hoarse and low.

The stirring stopped. The hiss of boiling rose louder in the silence. She caught the scent of food before the stranger answered. "No."

The word was a stone dropped into water, short, hard, rippling without comfort.

Nemeah tried to shift upright, her body still weak despite the days of rest. "Is this still Morbessa?"

The clang of a spoon against a pot cut through the air. A heavy lid was set in place, followed by the sharp, quick rhythm of chopping. The answer came only when the blade paused. "No."

Nemeah rolled her head slowly across the pillow, her neck stiff and aching. Not dead. Not Morbessa. Neither truth gave her peace.

"Then where am I?"

The footsteps drew closer. The voice was mere inches from her ear. "My home."

The sudden nearness made her flinch. Pain flared in her body, stealing any strength she might have used to lash out. She clenched her jaw instead.

"We need to get you out of bed so I can change the sheets," the voice said calmly. "Ready?"

Nemeah opened her mouth to object, but a firm grip closed around her arm. With surprising ease, the stranger pulled her upright. She winced as the sashes against her skin scraped raw flesh. She let out a groan as she was hauled to her feet. Her legs trembled beneath her, glass-brittle bones threatening to splinter. Her breaths came in labored puffs, every step a battle as the stranger guided her across the cold stone floor. At last, she was lowered into a chair. She clutched the arms, fighting the dizzy spin of her head and the sweat-induced nausea roiling in her gut.

"Do not move," the stranger warned before hurrying away.

She listened: the flap of fabric, pillows beaten and fluffed, the sound of liquid ladled into a container. A moment later, the bowl was nudged toward her. "In front of you is a bowl," the voice instructed. "To your right, a spoon. It is hot, so eat it slowly."

Nemeah raised her hand, brushing the underside of a table. Fingers slid along smooth wood until she found the clay bowl. Her other hand reached right, fumbling until it closed around the spoon. She dipped it into the broth, trembling as she lifted it to her lips.

The first taste made her want to cry, evoking memories of cold winter days and her family sharing jokes around the fire. Salt, herbs, the softness of vegetables cooked down into warmth. Tiny bits of potato, carrot, onion, and beans, all reduced to a savory mash. She ate cautiously, savoring each spoonful, the joy of fullness almost overwhelming after so much emptiness.

While she ate, the stranger tended to the room: stoking the fire until the heat thawed her skin, pouring water into a bath, the kettle steam whistling shrilly and constantly. She barely noticed, intent on the food, until the bowl scraped empty beneath her spoon.

Then the stranger's voice returned, low and unflinching. "Strip down."

Nemeah froze. "Strip down?" Her voice rasped, her head turning slowly as though the air itself weighed her down. She did not know where to direct her words. "In front of you?"

The stranger pulled open a drawer, the wooden slides groaning in protest. Fabrics rustled as they were lifted and tossed aside, the sound oddly loud in the tense room. Nemeah's stomach tightened with unease.

"We are both women," the stranger said plainly. "You have nothing I have not already seen." A drawer shut with a solid thud, followed by footsteps drawing near. "You are covered in blood and poison sand. Your skin is torn in a thousand places. If you do not bathe, infection will finish what the desert began."

A hand, firm but not unkind, settled on Nemeah's arm. She hesitated, weighing the strength left in her body against the futility of resistance. The memory of her earlier staggering steps came back to her. How even crossing from bed to chair had nearly undone her. She knew she had no choice.

She pressed her palms against the table, forcing herself upright on trembling arms. The stranger guided her carefully, and together they crossed to the waiting tub. The air against her bare skin was cruelly cold as the stranger began loosening the sashes that clung to her. Each strip of cloth was peeled away with a tug that stung, sticky with dried blood, sand, and sweat. Her flesh itched under the slow, deliberate movements, but she kept her head high, clinging to the thought of the warm water that awaited her.

When at last the final layer was gone, Nemeah could feel her body shuddering, more from weakness than shame. The stranger eased her down into the tub, and the water embraced her. Heat unfurled through her like a sigh. Her arms floated limply, her hair drifting about her shoulders, heavy and wet. She could feel grit and filth loosening from her skin, clouding the water in a faint swirl.

A soft cloth traced over her arms, back, and neck. The sharp tang of soap cut through the sour stench of sweat and blood. Nemeah's body sagged against the water, half-submerged, half-dreaming, as if she were being remade piece by piece.

Time blurred. When the water cooled and her hair was rinsed, the stranger gently lifted her out. A fresh dress was slipped over her aching frame, a towel pressed around her damp hair. Every motion was unhurried, reverent in its simplicity. By the time she was returned to the bed, sheets newly turned down, blankets folded over her, Nemeah's limbs had no strength left for protest.

The stranger tucked the covers snugly around her, and Nemeah let out a great yawn that filled her lungs with the room's warm air. Sleep pressed heavily against her.

"Who are you?" she asked, the words dissolving into drowsiness.

The figure moved away, footsteps soft against stone. A chair creaked near the fire. The flames crackled hungrily, their light painting the edges of the room. The stranger filled a bowl, lifted it to her lips, and sat in silence.

For a long moment, she did not answer. Names rose in her mind like ghosts. Titles, epithets, false faces worn across decades. She stared into the fire, into the memory of all she had been called. She sipped her broth, then chose the simplest truth.

"Morwyn."

Chapter Thirty

The days blurred into one another. Darkness felt endless when no sunbeams pierced the eyes, no silver moonlight marked the hours. Nemeah and the goddess settled into an unyielding rhythm: eat, sleep, bathe, change the bedding, change the dress. Always with the blindfold. Always in shadow.

Over time, she grew attuned to Morwyn's murmurs, the steady pattern of her steps, the way she moved through the small house. Like clockwork, the woman rose at the same hour each morning and retired at the same hour each night. But Nemeah noticed something else. Each afternoon, when she surrendered to her habitual nap, the woman slipped away. That knowledge thrilled her. Her body grew stronger every day; her lungs were less fragile, and her muscles were slowly returning. All she needed now was patience.

After the midday meal, a hearty stew of carrots, beets, and onions, its sweetness and salt lingering on her tongue, the stranger carried away her bowl and checked her bandages. Nemeah yawned, full and content, the warmth of food urging her toward drowsiness. She lay her head on the pillow and stilled her body, refusing to scratch at her healing cuts.

She listened instead. Six steps from hearth to bed. Twelve from bed to sink. Five more to the door. Her heart quickened when hinges groaned and a breath of outside air slipped inside. Rain scented the breeze, pulling at her chest with a pang of homesickness. The door closed, and the silence remained. No footsteps, and no clatter of dishes. She was finally alone.

Nemeah counted her breaths, then moved. Carefully, she reached for the blindfold's knot. Her fingers trembled as she unwound the cloth, layer after layer, her arms aching from the effort. When the last strip fell away, she kept her eyes closed. Even through her lids, the light stabbed, shocking her after days confined to darkness.

Tentatively, she opened one eye, then the other. Tears blurred her sight. She wiped them away, blinking until the dim shapes of the room sharpened into form. She drank it in greedily. The hearth of smooth river stones with its heavy wooden mantel. The table carved from knotty timber. A stone sink fitted with a pump, its spout dark with water stains. The ceiling of thick, neatly thatched straw. Vases of wildflowers lined every sill, their bright faces oddly familiar.

With effort, she pushed herself upright. Her legs trembled, but she held. Muscles ached yet obeyed. She took a few slow steps, savoring the simple miracle of being able to move on her own. At the window, she froze. Beyond the glass stretched a sunlit sky, where a storm gathered faintly at the horizon. Rolling fields of green swayed in the breeze, scattered with tiny purple flowers. Birds drifted lazily overhead. Cows dozed beneath the shadow of trees. Her breath felt like a betrayal in her lungs, and her heart ached with a familiar pull inside her.

"No, it cannot be." She stumbled to the door, gripped the heavy handle in her stiff hand, and pulled. The wood resisted, but she summoned every scrap of strength until it groaned open, spilling the world into view. And there it was. The songs of the birds, the bend of the grass, the scent of the earth. All familiar, all remembered. She had run across these very fields as a child. This was Tirnmoor. This was her home.

She stepped outside, trembling with the effort, but unwilling to stop. The air wrapped her in its cool embrace. She staggered forward, determined to see more, to believe her own eyes. She did not make it past the grazing cows before a woman appeared, walking back toward the house. Nemeah froze, questions overtaking her. Would she be punished for what she had done? Would the goddess be angry that she had dared remove the blindfold and seen where she lived?

The woman's figure drew closer, her pace steady, the gait of one who had carried years upon her shoulders. Her footfalls were sure, deliberate, as if the earth itself made way for her. Nemeah's blurred eyes strained to bring her into focus.

Silver hair streaked with strands of black framed a face older than she had expected. Lines traced the corners of her eyes and mouth, though there was strength in them, not frailty. Her skin was pale, smooth as a daisy petal, and her eyes bright, unyielding, shone like a sky stripped of clouds. Suddenly, she understood why the people of Mortava had mistaken her for the figure they believed haunted their land.

"Morwyn?" Her voice cracked, but it was stronger than it had been in days, her throat no longer raw with ruin.

The woman shuffled past her, arms laden with two baskets brimming with herbs and fresh vegetables. Without pausing, she gave a single nod, her chin flicking toward the cottage. "A storm is coming, and you are in no condition to weather the elements." Her tone was calm, almost dismissive. "Come on." She kept walking, offering no arm of support.

Nemeah lingered, torn between wonder and disbelief. The fields stretched before her, lands she knew as intimately as her own heartbeat: the orchard where she had climbed trees as a child, the barn her family had mended every summer, the woods she had once feared after dusk. Thunder grumbled far off, rolling across the sky, and her strength began to drain. Her muscles shook, and her limbs faltered as she turned back to the cottage. Its frame was set snug against the dark backdrop of the woods, the white-washed stone almost blinding against the trunks of the trees.

"Come on!" Morwyn's voice cut through the air as the rain's first drops spattered the ground. She vanished inside the door yawning open behind her.

Nemeah staggered up the path. By the time she crossed the threshold, the storm had broken in earnest, rain pounding against the thatch, wind rattling the shutters, the hearth-fire answering with a low hiss and crackle. She sank onto the bed and watched.

Now, every sound had an image. She saw the quick, efficient rhythm as Morwyn chopped and peeled the vegetables, dropping them into a pot suspended over the flames. After they ate, she saw her scrape the bowls, wash the dishes, and dry her hands on her apron. The same motions Nemeah had heard for days, but now married to the sight of them. And through it all, Morwyn said nothing. Silence filled the room, broken only by the storm. It might have stayed that way had Nemeah's curiosity not pressed so hard against her chest that the words spilled out.

"We are on Tirnmoor." Her voice wavered as she watched Morwyn skim the milk before ladling it into a kettle.

The older woman crushed heather with a pestle, added it to the milk, and slid the kettle close to the flames. Dusting her hands against her apron, she lowered herself to a chair.

Nemeah's heart thudded. "And you are the goddess Morwyn."

A sigh escaped the woman's lips, heavy with years of silence. "Is that a statement, or a question?"

The sharpness startled Nemeah. "I am not sure." She thought, then admitted, "A question."

"Then you must ask it as one."

Nemeah blinked, unsettled by the gravity in her tone. "Are we on Tirnmoor?"

"Yes."

"And are you truly a goddess?" She sat up straighter, her breath quickening.

"Yes."

Joy lit Nemeah's face. "This is unbelievable. You are a god! You could help me, and in turn, help us. You could stop Vallorith, stop his plan to become one of you." She covered her mouth with her hand, the thought bringing new energy to her weakened state. "You could save me from the mirror. I will not have to give up my life."

Morwyn's hand curled into a fist on the table. At each word Nemeah spoke, her body withdrew, recoiling as though the sound itself stung. Then, with sudden force, she struck the table with her palm. The sharp crack silenced the room. Nemeah bit back her words, startled.

The kettle by the fire steamed, releasing the soft note and the fragrance of heather. Both women were glad for the interruption and allowed the silence to be their companion for a short while. Morwyn rose, retrieved the bubbling kettle with a ragged hand, and poured two cups. She handed one to Nemeah without a glance, then returned to her seat. She blew gently over the rising steam, eyes fixed towards the shifting firelight.

Nemeah studied her closely, taking in the way she sat, the way her gaze drifted yet never quite landed, and the unfocused light in her eyes. The realization struck her like a stone.

"You are blind." Her voice cracked with shock.

Morwyn sighed, the steam from her cup curling briefly before vanishing into the air. "Is that a statement, or a question?"

Heat rose to Nemeah's cheeks. Was it rude to ask? "A question."

"Yes. I am blind." Morwyn took a sip of her milk and set the cup down with practiced ease.

Nemeah's astonishment only grew as she watched the woman stand and move through the cottage with a precision that surpassed anyone with sight. Each step was deliberate, each gesture meaningful. She opened a cupboard, retrieved a jar of honey, and returned to the table without flaw. After spooning a generous dollop into her milk, she extended the jar toward Nemeah. She took the jar, the outside sticky from the many droplets that had fallen from the spoon. She swirled the wooden scoop through the thick golden liquid and carefully dropped it into her own cup.

She handed the jar back to the goddess, still amazed by her fluid movements. When both women had settled again, Nemeah dared to ask the question that had been burning inside her. "Can you help me and my friends stop Vallorith?"

Morwyn shook her head. "No. I cannot."

The words stung, and Nemeah's heart sank. "But with your gifts, you could. You could free the echoes trapped in the mirrors, stop him from using me as a siphon. You could prevent him from ascending."

Silence met her words. Morwyn only stared toward the window, her blank eyes unreadable, her lips pressed shut. The old woman before her was acting more like a stubborn child than an ageless goddess. Frustration bubbled in Nemeah's chest, surprising her with its force.

She wanted to pace, to lash out, but her body remained too frail. Instead, she gripped the blanket and glared at the goddess.

"Why not then? You are a god, with more power than anyone alive. I have read the stories about you, about all the things you can do."

"Could." Morwyn's correction was hushed. "What I *could* do."

She rose, carried her empty cup to the sink, and then stoked the fire until the flames leapt high. Without another word, she crossed to a stairway Nemeah had not noticed before and disappeared. The silence that followed was heavier than stone, leaving Nemeah with more questions than answers.

***

The next morning, a harsh clatter startled her awake. Morwyn was dragging the table across the floor, its legs scraping loudly against the boards. She positioned it beside Nemeah's bed and began arranging items on its surface: a jug of water, bowls of fruit and bread, a pot of soup still steaming. Lastly, she placed a plain brown book on top of the stack.

"What is all this?" Nemeah asked, reaching for the book. Its cover bore no title, only worn leather stretched tight across the binding.

"The past," Morwyn answered, fastening her cloak. "It will show you the answers you seek." She paused at the door, her hand resting on the handle. Her expression looked troubled, though her voice was soft and calm. "Just know it is not what you have come to learn." With that, she left.

Nemeah sat in silence, staring at the book. Outside the window, she watched Morwyn's form grow smaller against the horizon until it vanished. Alone now, she opened the book. The first page was blank. So was the next, and the next. She flipped through every sheet; the smell of old parchment filled the air, but there was not a single drop of ink on any page.

"Well, this is useless?" She dropped the book into her lap.

She plucked an orange from the bowl and peeled back its sun-golden rind, its juice spraying the corner of the page. A low hum filled the cottage as the blank book in Nemeah's lap shifted and jumped. She stiffened under its movements and watched as the pages filled with markings she did not recognize. Nemeah carefully picked up the book, and she felt her consciousness get sucked in.

***

When Nemeah came to, she was standing in a land that was unknown to her senses. The world that stretched around her was ravaged and storm-swept. Lightning split the sky without pause, thunder roaring so loud it shook her bones inside her. The soil was barren, trees stood like blackened husks, and famine clung to every breath of air. Wrapping her arms around herself, she felt like a child who had strayed too far from home.

Then a bolt of blinding light cleaved the heavens. Heat and sound tore through the land as Nemeah shielded her eyes. When the commotion settled, the storm was gone. In its place stood five figures. They looked down at their hands, flexing their limbs and testing their muscles, marveling at the weight of their new forms. Slowly, their eyes turned to Nemeah.

"Where is this place?" asked a woman with hair as red as fire. Nemeah recognized her instantly, the goddess Danira.

"This world will be named Ardoria." The word slipped from Nemeah's lips, but it was not her voice that spoke. It was Morwyn's. "This is our new home. The place where your gifts will flourish and bring forth a new age."

A bearded man stepped forward, his voice low and rough, thick with an accent Nemeah had never heard before. "And what of the others? When will they be drawn from their slumbers?"

"When the world is ready and their punishment has ended, I will bring them here," Morwyn's voice declared through Nemeah's mouth. "Now go. Do what you were born to do."

The five turned, and as they did, the barren land transformed. The moon rose, followed by the sun, as they took turns across the sky. Grass spread like fire across the soil, flowers blossomed, and trees unfurled new leaves. Rivers carved through stone, filling vast oceans. Shadows birthed life, first fragile, then growing stronger and more elegant. The creatures grew until flocks of birds littered the sky and animals roamed freely.

Nemeah stood among it all. She watched as the world she called home was born, creation unfolding before her very eyes. Her body moved of its own accord through the newborn land, her hair still against her back, until another crash split the now mountainous horizon. From the impact rose a man. His features mirrored those she had seen first, though his beard was cropped short and his dark hair was tied back in a knot.

"Turan," Nemeah said, her arms lifting to his face as if she had known him all her life. The god returned her embrace warmly. "How are the others?"

"They grow restless," Turan replied, his gaze sweeping over the trees and flowers already pushing skyward. "Aching to be freed." His hand clasped hers, his grip strong and sure. "You have chosen well, mother." He inhaled deeply, then exhaled a gust of wind so vast that it wrapped around the entire world. The breeze carried through valleys and over peaks, and Nemeah's hair lifted, swirling in the current. "That is better," he said with a smile, releasing her hand.

As he walked away, Nemeah felt a strange certainty settle in her chest. These were her children. Not in flesh and blood, but in the way she had nurtured and provided for them, guiding their gifts as they learned to wield them. She counted their abilities in her mind: Darra, Cairn, Zeph, Talon, Thorn, and Vira. All born, all thriving. That left only the Freyla, Morin, and Glade.

Time leapt forward, days blurring into weeks, which blurred into centuries before another crash shook the rocky surface of the planet they now called theirs. Two figures emerged: one scarred and weathered, the other radiant with young beauty.

"The world is ready for you now," Nemeah, yet not Nemeah, said. Her eyes narrowed on the scarred man. "Behave, Arvayn, or you will find yourself in an eon's slumber again." She looked to the Freyla, the girl's face revealing her youth. She was not aged like the others; her skin was too smooth and unmarked. "Brynna."

The young goddess looked to Nemeah, her eyes screaming of mischievous glee. "Yes, mother?"

Nemeah inhaled slowly, her words needing to be a warning but not threatening. "Behave this time."

The goddess beamed at the mother before turning to Arvayn, her smile sending a chill through Nemeah as she closed her eyes in delight and her power spread. In a heartbeat, the wilderness transformed into bustling settlements. Mortals filled the land, raising statues to the gods they worshipped. The world was alive, thriving, and perfect for a time.

When the wars came, Nemeah felt her heart break, the past repeating like all the other times. Nemeah had no idea how many times this had happened, but from deep within her, she could feel that there had been more than a hundred different worlds. More than a hundred tries to give her children the world she so desperately wanted for them.

Blood was spilled, cities burned, and the peace was shattered. From her home, Nemeah watched her children tear at one another. This was not the love-scorned goddess that the mortals' books made everyone believe. This was petty sister jealousy and brother rivalry.

It hurt Nemeah's heart to see her children fall into the same routines they had in every other world. This world was supposed to be different. She clenched her fist. This world would be different. Closing her eyes, she envisioned a savior for the fragile mortals. A protector against her children's constant bickering. She waved her hands, and her magic flowed from her, her will coming into form.

Before her, a man took shape. His body drew substance from stone, soil, and sky. In his grasp, a spear and shield formed. Cuffs clasped his forearms, and a helmet crowned his head. He looked to Nemeah, breathing deep, as if tasting life for the first time.

"You are Nuval, god of protection," she declared. "Guardian of mortals. Teach them to defend themselves and each other." She looked to the heavens where her children resided. "And keep your siblings in line."

The man bowed, and when he rose, he was already a god. His name was on the lips of mortals from the moment of his birth. Nemeah watched with awe, reminded of her own protector, Alban.

Time spun onward, cycles of peace and war, until Morwyn herself was plagued by visions. Nightmares clung to her: a dragon, fire, and the knowledge that she would be forced to slay one of her own children.

Grief hollowed her as she carried this vision for years, never speaking of it to anyone. She distanced herself from her children, becoming a recluse in her small cottage near the woods. Time continued as she sought a way to keep the vision at bay, but even her powers were not enough to stop fate. The vision would come to pass, and there was nothing she could do about it.

Dathmor became a dragon. Silver fiery flames split the earth as he raged, and hate devoured the world. Nemeah watched as the gods came to her for help, and all she could offer was a single white seed. Her children placed the cuffs on their brother's scaled arms, and his body changed from beast back to man. Nemeah felt the burn of his fury as he looked for the mother, questioning why she would help in his downfall. He pleaded and begged as his brothers and sisters chained him, the sting of silvervane coated metal never leaving his arms and legs. Nemeah felt his madness consume him and watched as his form withered into bones and shadow. At his bedside, she, Morwyn, laid a hand to his brow and forced him into eternal sleep. But the visions did not end there.

As her hand pressed to Dathmor's skin, flashes of another fate struck her. She stood over all her children, the world a blackened wasteland. Her body was being torn apart by her powers. The land and sky shook around her as her hair caught on fire and her skin slid from her bones. Nemeah watched in horror as she realized the meaning of this vision. Morwyn would destroy the world. Everything she had created would come to an end at her hand, and she would be the last to fall.

***

Nemeah jolted awake. The book slipped from her weakened grasp and struck the floor. Her breath came ragged, her throat raw as if she had been screaming. She could still smell the fire, still feel her hair burning, skin blistering. Her heart pounded against her ribs as she realized she had only been asleep.

Her mouth was dry, her body aching with a hunger that clawed at her insides. She dragged the jug of water to her lips and drank acquisitively, gulp after gulp, until it was empty. Then she tore into the bread, cramming mouthfuls between frantic breaths. She bit into fruit, juice running down her chin, and pulled the pot of stew to her chest. She drank straight from the rim, without regard for spoons or bowls.

When at last her hunger was sated, she collapsed against the mattress. She felt ancient, as though centuries had passed while she slept, though the sun told her it had only been half a day.

"So, you saw." Morwyn hung her cloak by the door and crossed the room with unhurried steps. She bent to retrieve the fallen book, flipping absently through its blank pages before setting it on the table.

"What was that?" Nemeah rasped. Her throat still burned from the visions, her chest heavy as though she carried the weight of centuries.

Morwyn's blind eyes turned toward her, finding her without effort. She let out a long breath and shook her head. "That," she said softly, "was the history of the gods. How we came here. What we did." Her hand pressed the cover of the blank book closed with a dull thud. "Now is the part where you ask your questions. And I answer." She nodded once, as though granting permission.

Nemeah's lips parted, then closed again. She thought of the endless years she had just lived in a single afternoon. The births, the wars, the burning. It felt too immense, too unreal to even put into words. And yet she forced the question out. "You brought the gods here?"

Morwyn inclined her head.

"From where?" Nemeah whispered, gripping her cup as if to steady herself.

Morwyn tilted her head back, eyes turned to the rafters as though searching for leaks in the thatching. "I do not know how many times our history has repeated, nor do I know where we originated," Her gaze dropped to her own hands, pale fingers curling and flexing. "But each time, we fail."

"Fail?" The word left Nemeah brittle, her voice already braced for an answer she knew.

"Each time we start, we start with a singular goal in mind. Make a world, thrive there, and have everlasting peace." Morwyn said. Her voice was flat, unadorned, like someone reciting a duty they had long since grown tired of. "This has gone on for longer than your mind could even fathom. The gods, their duties, each with a purpose. One for rain. One for leaves. One for beasts and flight and flame." She gestured toward the window, toward the world beyond. "All of it to make the world beautiful. A heaven anyone could reach."

"I saw it," Nemeah whispered. "I saw it all. The crash, the world changing, the fires, the wars."

Morwyn's lips curled faintly. She nodded once. "Of course you did. Because it comes with the territory."

Nemeah blinked, confusion snapping her upright. "With what?"

"You are an Alune," Morwyn spoke calmly. "A seer. One who sees visions. Who walks the past, glimpses the future, and bends the present." She rose from the table and crossed to the hearth, tossing two logs into the fire. Embers hissed and flared as the fire grew larger, flooding the chilled room with warmth. "The one who brings life to worlds and also snuffs it out. The bringer of death, no matter where you go or how hard you try."

Nemeah shook her head, her mind swimming as if she had just spun in circles for hours. "None of this makes sense."

Morwyn chuckled dryly. "It was never meant to. But it seems the fates enjoy mocking me." She turned back. Her pale eyes blackened like ink spilling through glass, and the air shifted, twisting heavy in the room.

"How is this for some clarity?" Her voice deepened, edged with something ancient and terrible. "You think it will be this Vallorith who ascends? That his flame will pierce the heavens?" She shook her head slowly. "No, child." She stepped closer, the shadows bending with her. "It will be you who brings the destruction of this world."

Chapter Thirty-one

Nemeah stood in the yard, rain soaking through her thin dress and dragging her hair down in heavy strands. The chill clung to her skin, making her shiver and her teeth chatter, yet she refused to retreat inside. She could not bear to hear more of what the goddess had to say. She did not want to imagine the things the woman would confront her with. She could not be responsible for destroying the world. She would not.

Morwyn had said it would be her fate. Did she believe in fate? Yes, she believed everything happened for a reason, and those reasons were of the gods' design. Did she believe in what Morwyn had told her? She clutched her hand to her chest, and the ache under her ribs told her her answer. She knew it was yes.

She tipped her face toward the sky and let the storm punish her. The cold drops stung as they slipped past her lashes, running down her cheeks until she could no longer tell where rain ended and her own tears began. Her sobs rose, raw and uneven, the more the visions twisted through her head. The images blurred together, truth tangled with confusion, and though she knew she needed answers, in that moment, she only wanted solitude.

When her body finally gave out, she dragged herself back inside. Warmth wrapped around her instantly: a crackling fire in the hearth, the scent of herbs simmering in a pot, and a steaming bath waiting by the flames. Morwyn sat at the hearth, stirring her stew, her blind eyes distant. Nemeah slipped into the tub, the hot water leeching the ache from her bones until, all too soon, it was as cold as the rain. She watched Morwyn move with sure hands, never once calling on her gifts.

"Why do you not use them?" Nemeah asked, wringing her wet hair over the tub before wrapping herself in a towel. "Your gifts."

Morwyn did not pause in her work, her voice thoughtful, almost absent. "Because I do not have them anymore."

Nemeah sank into one of the chairs at the table, trembling more now from exhaustion than cold. "Why not?"

Morwyn lifted the pot from the fire and set it carefully on the table. The stew's aroma filled the room, rich with the scent of a meal that was sure to thaw their insides. She ladled it into bowls and finally sat across from Nemeah. "I am the twelfth Alune to rise since the dawn of time," she said evenly. She stirred her stew once, then looked up. "Do you have children?"

Nemeah blinked. "No. I am not wed."

Morwyn's lips curved with a sly smile. "And you think I am?"

Heat rushed to Nemeah's face. She ducked her head, busying herself with her bowl. Chunks of tender goat and vegetables swam in the broth, and when she took a hurried bite, the scalding heat made her fan her mouth as steam rushed from her nose. "I have a younger sister." She mouthed through the simmering pain of the hot food on her tongue.

"Then you should still understand," Morwyn continued, her voice low but firm, "what it is to love as a mother does. To want to protect the weaker. To never see them harmed."

Nemeah's throat tightened. She thought of Orla that night in the cave, bloodied and terrified. She remembered the wild surge of anger and fear that had ripped through her when she saw her sister used as a pawn in Vallorith's plan.

Morwyn's spoon stilled. "I have watched my children grow. Shaped them. Taught them. Given them everything. And when I saw that it would be me who destroyed them, me who undid all we had built," Her voice cracked, and she pushed her bowl aside with sudden force. She drew a shuddering breath. "I thought if I stripped my powers away, I could prevent that future. That perhaps fate would release me."

Nemeah lowered her gaze to her own hands, the cuff still locked tight around her wrist. "But I was born with your gifts."

Morwyn inclined her head, her expression unreadable. "Yes. My children's fate has only been delayed, not erased. You will ascend, Nemeah. You will become the goddess, just as I did. You will build worlds and watch them fall, ending the cycle of gods and man."

The words landed like blows. Nemeah shook her head, stumbling to her feet and pacing, her tired legs barely carrying her. "No. That is not how it will be." Her voice trembled, rising with each word. "The prophecy says an Echo of Tirnmoor will rise and stop Vallorith. That his reign will end, and the world will be whole again." She slammed her palms on the table, making the bowls and spoons rattle.

"You are an Echo of Tirnmoor," she said, waving her hand at the window as if the blind woman could see her gesture. "That is why you live here, no?" Nemeah pressed, her breath ragged. "You can stop him. The world does not have to burn. My family, my friends, your children, they do not have to die!"

Morwyn laughed as her hand shot out, gripping Nemeah's wrist with unsettling precision. Her fingers tightened until Nemeah winced. The goddess's blind eyes darkened, and when she spoke, the words spilled as though dragged out by some unseen force.

"You think the mortals' prophecy holds any weight in deciding our future? How the gods will live and end?" She laughed again, a low, booming sound that seemed to shake the rafters. Laughter she had not uttered in centuries. "No, child. *You* will be the one to ascend. You will rise to the heavens and become the destroyer of worlds. You will bring death to all who dwell on this rock, and afterward the universe will be as it should, void of beings like us. This will come to pass, and there is no undoing it. The cycle will finally be broken."

When her last words fell, Morwyn released Nemeah's wrist and collapsed back into her chair, her breath uneven. Sweat dotted her brow, a sheen of strain across her aged face.

Nemeah staggered backward, tears hot in her eyes. She shook her head, choking on her denial. "No! No, I do not accept this. I do not want this." Her voice sharpened with desperate hope. "Tell me how you got rid of your gifts. I will do the same. The world will be safe if I do this, yes?"

Morwyn shook her head. "That does not stop fate, child." Her voice was harsh, and her brows furrowed as she tracked Nemeah with her pale eyes.

Nemeah wanted to scream. To stamp her feet like a child denied a toy. Instead, her voice tore out, wild with desperation. "Maybe if we at least try!" She whirled toward Morwyn. "How did you get rid of your powers?"

"It will not stop anything," Morwyn murmured.

"Then we delay it until we find another way. And we can keep delaying. The world will not end because of me." Nemeah slammed her fist onto the table again, desperate for the right answer. "There has to be a way to stop this!"

Morwyn sagged, looking suddenly older, as though each denial tore away at whatever time she had left. "You can pull a single thread from a tapestry," she said softly. "It will unravel. More and more strings will be revealed with each tug. But in the end, no matter how you pull, the picture is always ruined."

"And what picture is that?" Nemeah spat defiantly.

Morwyn's answer was cold and final. "The picture of our world."

Silence fell heavy between them. Their meals sat untouched, broth congealing, the hearth's warmth doing nothing to ease the cold pressing down. Eventually, Morwyn rose without a word and retired upstairs, leaving Nemeah alone with the faint crackle of the fire.

Nemeah ran through the visions in her mind as her fingers absently traced over the cuff at her wrist, her thumb mapping the grooves. She found no rest, only the gnawing truth of her helplessness. *Powerless.* The word burned in her mind. She looked again at the cuff, and her heart lurched. "Morwyn." She shot to her feet. "Morwyn!"

Her voice carried up the stairs. A groan answered her, then the slow creak of floorboards as the goddess descended. Her hair was loose now, spilling in silver waves around her face instead of its neat braid. She drifted to the hearth first, coaxing the flames until they roared back to life, bathing the room in heat.

"What could not wait until morning?" she muttered, moving with weary grace. She filled the kettle as if nothing were amiss, and before Nemeah realized it, she held a steaming cup of tea in her hand.

Nemeah thrust her arm out. "Vallorith put this cuff on me. The same as the one from the stories, the one Dathmor wore. If I just keep it on, then I will never have my powers again, and I cannot destroy the world."

Morwyn's brow arched. She waited as Nemeah shuffled closer, placing her wrist beneath the goddess's touch. Morwyn's fingers brushed the cold metal, tracing its lines. Then, to Nemeah's shock, she chuckled.

"Child, this is no god's cuff."

Nemeah blinked. "But it drains my powers as such, and it looks exactly like Dathmor's."

"Like it, yes." Morwyn lifted her cup, sipping with deliberate calm. Her pale eyes never wavered. "But it is not. This trinket was crafted to play with your mind, not your essence. It tethered your thoughts, made you believe you were powerless." Her fingers clamped the cuff and, with startling ease, pried it loose.

Cold air rushed against Nemeah's bare wrist. The weight vanished, and in an instant her arm felt light again. She stared at the cuff, which lay twisted on the table, bent like soft tin.

Then it came. The surge. Her power flooded back, rushing into every vein and sinew, burning with fury and release. Wrath and rage filled her until laughter broke from her lips, wild and unrestrained. For the first time in weeks, it was not despair that consumed her; it was joy.

"Better?" Morwyn asked.

"Yes." Nemeah was still smiling faintly, rubbing at her freed wrist. "But how did you take it off, if you do not have your powers?"

Morwyn tapped the side of her head with one finger. "You never forget how to wield it, and with you here, it is like I never lost them."

Nemeah lowered herself into the chair again, thoughts sparking behind her eyes. "What does my being here have to do with your powers?"

Morwyn sipped her tea, patient as though she had been waiting centuries for this moment. She sighed heavily as she explained. "Powers like ours cannot be destroyed." She moved her hand through the air, a soft, glowing orb appearing in her palm. "It is passed from one god to another." She snuffed out the light, and Nemeah watched as small strands of the magic raced back to where she sat.

"Me? It passed it to me?" She looked at the goddess, hope flaring in her chest. "Are we related? Am I like some kind of ancient descendant?"

Morwyn could hear the excitement in her tone, and the shake of her head told Nemeah that the truth was not a fairytale. "When an Alune dies, our powers choose the next rightful heir. This does not come by blood ties, but rather echo abilities." The old woman shifted in her seat. "It will choose a strong echo, someone who has all strands within them."

Nemeah looked down at her hands, "How did I get your gifts if you are still alive?"

"We can also choose to pass our gifts." Morwyn clasped her hands together, and when she pulled them apart, ten strands of magic stretched between her palms. "You have to understand, I wanted to stop the destruction of my children. The loss of life and world." She touched the table, and the strands wound around the wooden surface until they found Nemeah.

Nemeah stood and backed away from the woman, her hands still in front of her, shaking with the only emotion she could fathom: betrayal. "You chose me?" She looked from her hand to Morwyn. "Literally chose?"

The goddess sat straighter, her hair framing her face and highlighting her ancient age. "Yes. And when I sought a replacement, you were the closest with all ten lines of magic."

Nemeah scoffed. "The closest? Because someone could not be bothered to travel?"

She ran her fingers through her tangled hair, pressing her fingertips into her scalp as racing visions filled her mind. Her destruction in the woods where Jacob died, the fire in their cave, the flattened town. Why did she have to be the one Morwyn picked?

"Was I even born an echo?" The room was silent except for the crackle of fire, and Nemeah already knew her answer.

Morwyn's voice was soft. "You would have been like the others in your family, had I not interfered."

Nemeah felt her legs give way as she fell to the floor, resentment screeching through her gritted teeth. "I could have been normal. I could have had a family like others. Instead," She turned her head to Morwyn. "Instead, I am feared and hated by them. And for what?" She yelled. "For me to kill them in the end? Why would you do this? How? How could you do this to me?"

Morwyn's fury was equal as she yelled back, her black eyes staring at Nemeah. "Because I needed my children to live. I needed to know they would be safe from the one person who is supposed to love and protect them forever!" She furrowed her brows. "You were never even supposed to make it this far. You were supposed to die when the Axis came, and yet somehow you survived." Morwyn picked at the wooden table surface, her lips moving as she spoke to herself.

"And do not act like you have not relished the power I have given you. I felt the joy that rushed through you when you first wielded your magic. The mighty roar you felt in your heart as you did things no echo has ever done. You loved it!"

The cottage rattled around them, the floor heaving and sinking as Morwyn stood and stomped towards Nemeah. "I will not pity you when it gives my children longer to live. Without me shedding my gifts to you, you and your family would have already perished in my flames! So do not think for a second you are a victim here. You are just the replacement who brings destruction in the end! The end where no one survives."

The room settled, and the two women remained silent, all their anger gone. Nemeah felt her insides freeze as Morwyn's words hit home. Without her actions, the world would have already been lost. She thought of her friends and family. She thought of Orla and Keanoff. She would never have met them without the extra time. She looked up to the goddess, her eyes back to their usual pale blue.

Nemeah pushed herself off the floor and walked to her bed. She fell onto it in defeat, feeling smaller than she ever had before. Who was she to question a god? Who was she in a world that had just been delayed in being destroyed? She looked at her wrist, the weighted cuff gone. Her eyes drifted to the table where the crumpled metal still lay.

"Passing my powers only delays fate." She sat up, eyes still fixed on the cuff.

Morwyn rubbed at her temples. "Is that a question or a statement?"

"A question." She looked to Morwyn, sadness seeped deep within her bones.

"Yes." The goddess answered, solemnly.

Nemeah nodded. "Then I know what I must do."

Morwyn nodded, already knowing what she was about to say. "You must go into the mirror, and never come out."

***

The next morning, Nemeah dressed with deliberate care. She braided her hair, smoothed her gown, and tried to quiet the pounding in her chest. One question lingered like a shadow, one she dreaded to voice but could no longer keep inside.

"Morwyn?"

The goddess moved about her home as if it were any ordinary day, her steps measured, her hands steady as she arranged things in their place.

"When I do go back?" Her words were hesitant.

Morwyn stepped up beside her, opening the door. Beyond the frame, Nemeah could see the dark land of Morbessa. The smell of rot filled the small cabin, and the sand was already grating against Nemeah's skin.

"It will be as if you never left. Your body will be once again on the brink of death." She held Nemeah's hands in hers, giving them a squeeze. "When you leave here, your Alune powers will be unlocked, so to speak. You will see rushes of visions, and you must learn to control them or else you will go mad."

Nemeah felt her pulse quicken. "I was afraid of that." She tore her eyes from the poison that awaited her and looked at the goddess. "Will I ever see you again?"

Morwyn lowered her head before standing tall. "No. This is the last anyone will ever see me."

Nemeah sucked in a breath, feeling the tearing in her lungs already. "You mean, you are?"

Morwyn nodded. "I am going back to where I belong." She looked up to the ceiling, her blind eyes searching. "I am returning to the stars."

Those words hit Nemeah harder than she expected. She should hate this goddess, hate that she was now burdened with so much responsibility. However, the truth was that she felt as though she was losing a part of herself. "What if I have questions? What if I need you?"

Morwyn tapped her forehead. "I am in here. All you need to do is ask, and your powers will show you if there is an answer."

"What does that even mean?" Nemeah turned as Morwyn's hands guided her closer to the door.

"It means trust in yourself." And without another word, the goddess pushed Nemeah through the door and back into reality.

The pain struck her at once, sharp as a hammer blow against her ribs. She coughed, and the copper taste of blood filled her mouth. Her vision blurred. Shadows shifted in the haze, and panic clawed its way up her throat. Her arms stretched blindly before her, her knees buckling as the agony dragged her down to the poisoned sand.

She thought of what Morwyn had told her: *ask, and your powers will show you.* Nemeah gritted her teeth as a vision raced through her mind, flames surrounding her, and the land cleared.

"Fire? I do this with fire?" She coughed again, feeling her strength waning as she debated.

Tears of blood fell, staining hot trails across her cheeks. She pressed her hands into the gritty earth, feeling each grain bite against her skin. She summoned her magic, focusing on the raging fury she felt inside her.

First, it rippled through the ground, then surged outward into the air. Flames burst from her fingertips, ravenous and alive. They leapt to the glowing plants, seized the drifting poison, and devoured both in a storm of fire. Her thoughts turned to her family, her friends, the strangers in marketplaces, the birds in their nests, every fragile soul bound to this world she called home. For them, she burned brighter.

The fire swelled, red and orange tongues licking higher, until they blazed white-hot. She poured her anger, her sorrow, her love into the inferno, and the flames shifted, piercing blue, searing and unrelenting. The heat scorched her skin raw. The sand beneath her liquefied, pooling into molten glass. She clung to the last threads of power, forcing them outward, forcing herself empty. And then, one final surge. A mighty burst ripped across the land, flames racing like a tidal wave over the continent, scouring every last plant, every trace of poison, until none remained.

The blast deafened her. The world rang faintly in her ears as she collapsed onto the cooling glass. Above, ash fell in gentle flakes, drifting like snow, cloaking the land in a grey haze. She lifted one trembling hand, catching a single flake in her palm before the world went dark.

Chapter Thirty-two

Agnes watched Keanoff strike the stone door for what must have been the hundredth time. His ram's horns cracked against the marble surface, but the door remained flawless and unmarked. She could not stop herself from wincing at each blow, the sound of bone meeting stone echoing in their cramped prison.

"Keanoff," she pleaded softly, her voice almost swallowed by the thud of his next charge. "You need to stop. Just rest."

He ignored her, driving himself at the door five more times before his body finally gave in. His form shifted back to human, his shoulders heaving as he hammered at the stone with his fists. The fleshy slaps echoed dully in the room, his frustration raw and animal. A primal sound tore from his throat before he crumpled to the floor, head buried in his hands.

Agnes slid down beside him. She could hear the shudder in his breath, the ragged edges of grief and fury. Comforting people had never been her gift; she had always been better with food than feelings, but she wished she had the right words now. Her hand hovered inches from his arm before she withdrew it, settling instead for leaning her head back against the cold wall and waiting.

Two days. That was how long it had been since they had taken Nemeah. Two days of silence and gnawing dread. Both of them knew the truth, that without her powers, Nemeah would not last long on the surface of Morbessa.

Keanoff jolted upright suddenly and threw himself at the door again. His shoulder hit hard, and he staggered back with a groan, rubbing at the raw pink skin before bracing for another hit.

"Keanoff, stop!" Agnes tried to intercept him, but he barreled past her, slamming into the stone again. The sound of it reverberated in her chest. She sighed, her protests drowned by his stubbornness. For two days, he had been relentless, his anger so thick she could taste it, and the awkwardness between them only made the silence worse.

She gave up and dropped onto a pillow, her stomach growling weakly. Her gaze flicked to the trays left from their first night. Empty and licked clean. Not even a crumb remained. Another slam rattled the door, followed by a sharp grunt of pain.

Keanoff slid down again, cradling his shoulder, the skin now blazing red. "There has to be a way out," he muttered, half to himself.

Agnes lifted her brows. "We could try knocking?"

He turned his head toward her, eyes burning. "Knocking?" His voice was dry, cracked like desert earth.

She shrugged, a small, nervous smile twitching at her lips. "I mean, maybe someone will answer."

He gestured at the towering slabs. "Be my guest."

Agnes got to her feet, shuffled over, and raised her knuckles. She gave the stone a timid rap. The sound was pitifully soft, barely carrying in the heavy air. Keanoff let out a strangled laugh at the absurdity.

"If anyone opens that door, I will," His words cut short as a click resounded through the chamber.

Agnes leapt back as the massive stone door groaned open, the grinding of rocks against each other loud in the suffocating silence. A man stood in the opening. He wore black trousers and a long tunic tied at the waist, his face half-hidden behind a sash. His white hair looked as though it had been dusted with coal.

Keanoff was instantly in front of Agnes, body angled low, every line of him a coiled threat. "Where is Nemeah?" he hissed, voice dangerous enough to cut.

The man shifted to keep Keanoff in view, hands raised cautiously. Then he pulled the sash down to reveal a much younger face than either of them expected.

Agnes peered around Keanoff, eyes widening. "You are the king's son," she blurted, tapping Keanoff's arm. "Martin? Marlin? No, that is not right."

"Mavren," the boy whispered, glancing down the hall as though he feared being overheard. "I am letting you out, but only on the condition you take me with you."

Keanoff scoffed, the sound sharp and cold. "And why would we do that?"

Mavren crossed his arms, trying to mirror the Vira's stance. "Because I am saving you. If it were not for me, you would be rotting in here until you starve to death." His voice cracked, betraying the high, unsteady notes of youth.

"We are not dragging some ten-year-old around," Keanoff growled, pushing past him into the hall.

"Fourteen!" Mavren's face flushed, his indignation almost comical. "I have passed my exams and training. That makes me as much a man as you."

Keanoff turned on the boy, towering over him by more than a head. His voice was low and biting. "Maybe down here, but not in the world above." He flicked a hand toward Agnes. "Come on. We need to find Nemeah."

He started down the corridor at a run, Agnes keeping pace beside him. Their footfalls echoed sharply, and a third rhythm quickly joined theirs.

At the hallway's end, Keanoff slowed, exchanging a glance with Agnes. She opened her mouth, but he silenced her with a raised hand.

"No. We do not need him." He jabbed a finger down one tunnel. "That way leads to the throne room." He turned, pointing in the opposite direction. "And that way is the stairs to the city."

When he looked back, Mavren was grinning with the kind of smugness that belonged on an arrogant courtier, not a boy. "But you do not know which tunnel they took your friend," the prince said. His tone dripped with triumph. "And unless you want to spend the next year crawling through passage after passage, you are taking me."

Keanoff's jaw tightened. He clenched his fists but could not deny the truth in the boy's words.

Agnes leaned close, whispering, "We could let him guide us, then ditch him once we are free."

"I heard that." Mavren stomped his foot, the motion childish and out of place in his stealthy garb.

Keanoff dragged a hand down his face. The whole ordeal was spiraling into absurdity. "Alright. Show us the way."

"And then you let me come with you?" Mavren's grin spread, boyish and infectious despite itself.

"Fine," Keanoff snapped. "Yes. You can come."

Mavren tugged the sash back across his mouth, his words muffled but laced with excitement. "Then keep up."

He darted down the hall, moving with a speed that was far beyond human. Keanoff cursed under his breath and pulled Agnes along after him. They darted through chambers lined with relics of the city's history, statues, faded tapestries, and painted ceilings. Agnes lingered on them even as she ran, her eyes drinking in every carving and mural. A whole civilization's story was etched into these halls, and she longed to stop and study it.

They burst into the throne room, the dais at the far end looming empty of its rulers.

Keanoff's voice echoed across the cavernous chamber. "Where is everyone?" He skidded to a halt when Agnes yanked free of his grip. "What are you doing?" he barked.

Keanoff and Mavren watched as she ascended the steps toward the throne. She reached behind it, plucking something from the table. When she turned, her face was lit with a wide, almost radiant smile.

"The last mirror," she said breathlessly, holding it aloft like a prize. "We have it." She nearly skipped down the stairs, her joy unnervingly bright.

"Great," Keanoff muttered, groaning as he turned back to Mavren. "Continue."

The prince did not need to be told twice. He led them through twisting corridors, pulling them into shadows when guards passed and signaling when the way was clear. At last, they slipped out through the temple's main doors just as a patrol rounded the corner behind them.

Keanoff stopped dead. The underground city stretched out before them, once alive with bustle and sound. Now it was silent. Streets lay empty. Windows were dark, and an unsettling stillness clung to the cavern.

"Where is everyone?" he demanded again, voice harsh in the echoing quiet.

"They went to the surface," Mavren called back, already running down the stairs and reaching the street below.

Agnes and Keanoff followed as they made their way down the streets, their footfalls the only sound aside from the towering waterfall at the edge of the city's limits. Keanoff noticed that the street was not only empty, but it was as if the people had just abandoned it. Carts with wares still sat staged for selling. Food lay on pits, and the smell of charred meats filled the air. Tables with dishes still sat as if someone would return to their meal.

The scene they ran through was unnatural. The atmosphere feeling haunting and solemn. Mavren led them onward, towards the water falling from the cliff's edge. They ran through fields of wheat and corn, the stalks blocking their view, but their ears could tell they were getting closer to the roaring water. They reached the base out of breath; Agnes was red-faced, and her hair was damp with sweat.

Keanoff braced his hands on his knees as he took in lungfuls of the damp air. "How much farther?" He looked up in disbelief as he saw Mavren scaling a ladder that rose straight up alongside the waterfall. "You have got to be joking."

Agnes looked up with wide eyes. "He is going to get us killed."

Maven looked down, smiling at his companions. "Come on! It is perfectly safe." His laugh echoed down to them.

Keanoff rolled his neck and pulled the sash free from his chest, revealing his markings for everyone to see. He gestured for Agnes to go first, praying she had the strength to make it up all the way.

"What about the poison that covers the land?" Agnes asked, scrambling after Mavren up the ladder. "Would it not kill them?"

Mavren paused partway up, glancing down as Keanoff caught the bottom rungs. "Morwyn has cleansed the land," he said with almost reverent certainty. "My people can finally live in the upper world as you do."

Keanoff and Agnes exchanged a look. Neither dared voice the thought, but the same question burned in both their minds. If the land was cleansed, was Nemeah alive?

They climbed faster, chasing the boy higher and higher up the cliff-side. Spray from the waterfall drenched their thin sashes, the sound a deafening roar all around them. Agnes's arms trembled, and her legs shook with every rung until she dragged herself on top of a platform. She collapsed to her knees, gasping prayers between each ragged breath.

"Thank the gods that is over." She examined the mirror, noting it was still in one piece.

Mavren only laughed. He strode forward and pulled open a wooden hatch, revealing yet another ladder stretching into a shaft of shadow. "Halfway," he announced cheerfully. "Come on."

Agnes groaned aloud, only to feel Keanoff's heavy hand on her shoulder. "On my back," he ordered. "It will be faster."

She hesitated, then allowed herself to be hauled up, clinging tightly. Her arms locked around his neck, sometimes choking him as he climbed, but he did not complain. Not once.

Keanoff's muscles burned, his chest screaming for air, but he forced himself rung by rung upward. The climb felt endless, stretching on for far too long. When they finally pushed through another hatch, he nearly collapsed, lowering Agnes gently to her feet.

They stumbled into a cramped room much like the shed they had found when first arriving in Morbessa. Its air was thick and oppressive. Black tar oozed sluggishly from the ceiling, dripping into stagnant pools that shimmered with an oily sheen.

Mavren eased the outer door open, and all three froze. The world beyond was grey. Fields that had once bloomed the red and blue flowers was now nothing but charred earth. The flowers had been incinerated, their repelling properties no longer potent. The poison that had long choked the sky was gone, swept clean, and the sun's rays spilled across the land for the first time in centuries.

The light revealed a vastness none of them had ever truly seen. Mountains loomed in the near distance, their stone as ashen as the ground. Burnt trunks jutted up like blackened teeth, bark still smoldering, smoke curling from the ruins of a dead forest.

Somewhere far off, faint music drifted on the wind. Cheers and laughter. Clear signs of celebration were evident. The people of Mortava were above ground at last, stepping into a new life. Keanoff strode out of the shed, boots sinking into ash. Each step sent up small plumes that swirled around him.

His eyes scanned the horizon, frantic. "Where is she?" He spun toward Mavren, anger rising sharp and hot.

The boy lifted a hand, pointing to the mountains. "They would have led her to the center of our land. She should be there."

Keanoff did not hesitate. He broke into a sprint, his movements wild with desperation. Ash shifted treacherously beneath him, hiding dips that sent him stumbling, but he did not stop. He called Nemeah's name again and again, voice hoarse, eyes pleading to see her.

He reached the rocky hills and braced a hand on the hot stone, chest heaving. His gaze darted wildly until it landed on a door. Wooden and rimmed with iron, like the sheds. It was set into the rock as if it had been formed there by long-ago magic. Hope flared painfully in his chest. He needed to find her, but where was she?

Cupping his hands around his mouth, he shouted her name, voice breaking as it echoed back at him. When silence answered, he changed form, fur rippling over flesh. A bear's nose pressed to the ground, inhaling deeply, blowing ash aside with heavy breaths. His fur-lined face twitched as he worked, remembering Noa's words: she smelled of fire and starlight. He clung to it, clung as if that memory alone could keep her tethered to him.

His nose struck something buried. He pawed furiously until tarnished metal glinted in the soot, twisted and mangled, but he knew it, nonetheless. The cuff from Nemeah's arm. His heartbeat thundered as he inhaled its scent, a desperate and wild sensation. Then he pressed his nose back to the ground, continuing his eager search.

Agnes ran up, out of breath and on the edge of passing out as she stooped, lifting the broken cuff. Her expression was unnerving, a mix of pride and strange delight. She turned it over in her hands, marveling.

"She got it off." Her voice carried a note of awe.

Keanoff ignored her, driving forward through the ash as Mavren trailed close, excitement crackling in the boy's steps to see a Vira in action. The bear pushed onward until, at last, a form emerged half-buried in grey. Keanoff shifted back to himself in a blink, heart lurching. He fell to his knees, brushing ash from Nemeah's face with trembling hands. He studied her swollen features. Dried blood streaked around her nose, mouth, and eyes.

Agnes dropped beside him, helping to clear the soot. Her hands were steady, but her face was filled with sorrow. They stared down, waiting for breath, for movement, for anything.

"Is she...?" Mavren whispered, the child in him showing through his princely mask.

Agnes bowed her head. "I am afraid so."

"No!" Keanoff's roar split the stillness, raw and jagged. Both companions flinched. He gathered Nemeah into his arms, clutching her tight against him. He rocked her, his body shuddering as tears pressed against his eyes. "No. No." The word fell again and again, broken and desperate, a plea against the silence.

Agnes touched his shoulder, but he shook her hand off violently. His grief was his own, and no one could share it.

Mavren circled them slowly, his amber eyes fixed on the lifeless form in Keanoff's arms. This was the girl who had cleared the poison, freed his people from darkness. The one they would always remember. He dropped to his knees in the ash, pressing his forehead to the ground.

Keanoff's voice grumbled as he watched, his cheeks streaked with dust and tears. "What are you doing?"

The boy raised his head; ashes clung to his hair and brow. "I am showing respect to the Mother. To Morwyn."

"Do not call her that!" Keanoff roared. His voice was fierce with denial. "Her name is Nemeah!"

Mavren's gaze softened. "Nemeah," he whispered reverently.

He crawled closer and took her limp hand in his own, bowing his forehead against it. For a moment, he stilled. Then his eyes flew open. His body went rigid, and his head snapped up toward her face, then her chest. He pressed trembling fingers to her throat.

Keanoff lunged forward, ready to shove him away, when Mavren gasped.

"She is alive!"

Chapter Thirty-three

Keanoff bent close, pressing his ear to Nemeah's lips, desperate to catch even a whisper of truth in Mavren's words. For a moment, there was nothing, and then, faint as the brush of a moth's wing, he heard it. A breath. A trembling, fragile inhale.

His strength nearly failed him. Tears spilled unchecked down his face as he pushed the hair back from her pale skin. He kissed her cold forehead, clinging to the only thing that mattered: she was alive.

He turned on Mavren, all composure shattered. "Do you have healers here? Freylas? Anyone?"

The boy shifted uncomfortably, shoulders hitching in a shrug. "Not since the banishing."

In the open sunlight, his youth was clearer. His voice was steady, but his wide eyes betrayed fear. His amber gaze, his pointed ears, and the patchwork constellations scattered across his dark skin made him look at once otherworldly and heartbreakingly young.

"We need to get her back to the cave," Agnes said softly. "She needs Ismaara."

Her words twisted like a blade in Keanoff's chest. He scanned the ruined horizon, searching for something, anything. "The flowers are gone. Maybe we could ride Noa back?"

Agnes shaded her eyes and looked skyward. "And how are we supposed to call her?"

Keanoff answered with a sharp, piercing whistle. He tried again, and again, each note thinner than the last, his hope unraveling with every silence. The land itself had driven the dragon away.

"Who is Noa?" Mavren whispered.

"Our dragon," Agnes replied in hushed tones.

"Your dragon?" Mavren blurted, his voice cracking into an excited shout. He flinched when Keanoff's head snapped toward him. "Sorry."

Keanoff rose, lifting Nemeah carefully into his arms. Ash drifted from her hair and clothing, swirling back down around them like dying snow.

"What about a boat?" Agnes asked as she stood, offering her hand to Mavren.

He hesitated before taking it. "We have not built boats in over two hundred years."

"Perfect." Keanoff groaned, adjusting Nemeah's limp weight. "We will have to find another way."

Agnes wrapped the mirror in a strip of sash and tied it at her waist. "Someone from the city must have the means. A carpenter. Someone." She started walking toward the sound of distant celebration, her voice clipped, her steps too quick, too eager.

Keanoff glanced at her, uneasy at the strange brightness in her tone, then turned to Mavren. "Think your family will welcome you after helping us?"

Mavren tugged his sash over his mouth again, his answer muffled. "Guess we will have to see."

The three of them set out side by side, trudging toward the noise of people seeing sunlight for the first time in centuries. The journey was harsher than they had expected. The sun's weight pressed down, and the blackened earth grew blisteringly hot beneath their boots. With no food, no water, and Nemeah's fragile body in Keanoff's arms, their strength dwindled.

The celebration never seemed closer, though the sounds of laughter and music carried on the air like a taunt. They were forced to stop three times, exhaustion hollowing their faces, before the sun began to sink.

"How is this possible?" Keanoff whispered hoarsely. He lowered Nemeah with trembling arms, his muscles raw from carrying her for hours. "We should have reached them by now."

Mavren pulled down his sash, his skin slick with sweat. "I do not know. It feels like they are right there. We should have been among them already."

Agnes dropped onto the sand, her skin flushed red. "The land is empty. Sound can travel farther when there is nothing to catch it." She wiped her brow with a shaking hand, her lips cracked and dry.

Mavren lay back in the ash-warmed sand, his arms sprawled wide, his chest heaving. His wide eyes fixed on the sky as the moon climbed into view, glowing silver with the sun's last touch. Stars scattered after it, pricking the heavens with light.

"I have never seen them before," he whispered. "Stars. Or the moon. I read about them, but I never thought," His voice faltered, reverence softening his boyish features.

Keanoff sat close to Nemeah, holding her hand as though it anchored him. He followed Mavren's gaze skyward. "She loves the stars," he murmured. The words ached in his chest.

The night deepened, the heat of the sand easing into a strange comfort beneath them. One by one, exhaustion claimed them. Mavren drifted off beneath the stars he had just discovered, Agnes curled against herself in silence, and Keanoff, his hand still clasped around Nemeah's, kept watch until his body surrendered to sleep.

***

Nemeah saw the woman, brown hair plastered to her damp face, white robe trailing behind her as she ran. She bounded up the stairs, flung open the door, and scanned the chamber with frantic eyes until she found what she sought. Without hesitation, she seized the mirror and hurled it against the stone floor. Glass exploded in a hundred glittering shards, scattering like fallen stars. A blinding light burst from the woman's body, then she was gone.

Nemeah remained, standing amid the broken fragments. Her mind was ready, bracing for the vision to end, but this time it did not. She looked around the room, knowing somehow that this was Sylvie Havandar's old study, now Isrend's. She looked to the wall of mirrors and then to the floor. "The Freyla. The one who had loved Vallorith. Demetra, that is who broke their mirror, that is who died."

Voices echoed in the corridor. She turned, tense, as the door opened. A man stepped inside. His mismatched eyes were wild with anger, his brows carved deep as he took in the wreckage. Isrend. His chest rose and fell too fast, composure straining on the edge of collapse. Behind him, Vallorith entered, his expression hard, fury flickering beneath his calm.

"What does this mean?" Isrend snapped, whirling toward the priest. His voice cracked like a whip, though his hands remained clasped behind his back, trembling with the effort to stay in control.

Vallorith's gaze lingered on the scattered shards. His lips pressed thin, then curved with a measured calm. With a slow wave of his hand, the glass began to stir. Fragments slid across the stone, scraping as they gathered at the room's center. One by one, they fused, light hissing at the seams, until the mirror stood whole again.

"This means," Vallorith said, his tone smooth, almost satisfied, "we need a new Freyla." He turned to his master, a thin smile stretching across his face. "Where is your sister?"

***

Nemeah choked on a ragged gasp, her lungs burning, her mind drowning in the remnants of the visions she had just endured. Keanoff jolted upright beside her, his hand gripping hers, movements frantic as he tried to help. He hauled her forward, patting her back as wet, heavy clots of blood spilled from her throat. She gagged and heaved, her body wracked with pain until it trembled in his arms.

When she finally sagged back, Keanoff caught her, cradling her against him. Her eyelids fluttered, pupils blown so wide they nearly swallowed their color. He brushed damp hair from her fevered face and pressed his hand against her cheek. Her skin burned beneath his touch.

"Nemeah?" His voice cracked as he whispered her name. "I am here."

Her lips parted, trembling, a single word rasping out between wheezes. "Ismaara."

Keanoff felt his chest hollow out, his breath vanish. He was powerless, utterly helpless to ease the agony tearing through her body.

"Ismaara," he repeated, clinging to the word like a command, like a direction through the storm. His voice rose, sharp as a blade. "Agnes!" He barked her name with the force of a man giving judgment. "Mavren, wake up!"

The two startled awake, eyes wide as they saw Nemeah convulsing in his arms. Keanoff seized Mavren's arm and dragged him forward, thrusting the boy toward her side. Agnes scrambled closer, reaching out, but flinched when her palm met Nemeah's forehead. It was so hot she nearly burned.

"What do we do?" she demanded, looking at Keanoff with alarm. "Keanoff?"

He shook his head, dread settling into resolve. The choice was the only solution, knowing it went against his tribes rules, knowing banishment was what faced him should they ever find out. "We are taking her home."

The words had barely left his mouth before he roared, the sound painful as it shook the air. His body contorted, bones snapping and twisting. Flesh split, stretching into something vast and monstrous.

Mavren stumbled back, horrified as Keanoff collapsed onto the ash. His limbs lengthened unnaturally, and his skin blackened as scales rippled across his body. Wings tore free from his back, shadows spilling out as the great beast took shape. Agnes shielded Nemeah and pulled Mavren close, her jaw set even as the boy gawked in terror.

With a thunderous bellow, the dragon rose, midnight black, fire dripping from its fangs like acid, wings thrashing clouds of ash into the air. His green eyes, unmistakable even in this form, locked on them. Keanoff clicked and whistled, the primal sound of a language no human throat could form. He lowered himself to the ground, waiting.

Agnes gripped Nemeah's shoulders, steadying her limp form. "Mavren, help me."

The boy's voice cracked in protest. "He, he just, Keanoff—"

"Turned into a dragon." Agnes' voice cut sharply. "Now grab her legs."

Together they lifted Nemeah, her body slack between them, and climbed onto the dragon's back. Mavren moved as if in a daze, his hands trembling as he clung to the ridged spines. Keanoff's piercing eyes followed him, and the boy shivered under the weight of that gaze.

Agnes adjusted Nemeah's body carefully across the dragon's back, then looked to Mavren. "Are you sure you are ready to leave your home?"

His lips pressed thin, face flickering with fear, uncertainty, longing, and finally resolve. He gave a single nod.

"Then hold tight," Agnes said.

She dug her heels into Keanoff's scaled sides, giving the signal. With a low rumble, the dragon surged forward, claws gouging at the sand. His pace built into a thunderous gallop before his wings unfurled, catching the night air. In one powerful leap, he launched upward, carrying them higher and higher above the scarred land.

Below, the barren world fell away. In the distance, lanterns flickered, tiny stars against the dark horizon, the sound of celebration still drifting faintly through the night. Keanoff's wings beat with relentless rhythm, every motion pulling them farther from Morbessa. Soon, the broken continent disappeared behind them.

Agnes clutched Nemeah tightly as they flew, the girl's trembling never once subsiding. Her fever burned hotter with every hour, breath breaking into ragged gasps as she whispered the same name again and again.

Keanoff flew without rest. For three days, his wings carried them over island after island, shadows streaking across the sea below. By the fifth day, when Agnes finally recognized the jagged peaks of Highspire rising against the horizon, her relief was comforting enough to sting her eyes. She tapped Mavren's shoulder and pointed ahead as he dared lift his head.

"We are almost there!" she shouted, but the wind tore her words away.

Ahead, a shimmer of light danced against the stone cliffs. Noa waited, her scales scattering prisms of color across the rocks like a beacon. She clicked a greeting, her voice echoing into the cave mouth. Moments later, Yuli appeared, her gaze locking on Keanoff as he descended.

The black dragon stumbled on landing, his massive body crashing to the ground, and passengers were tossed roughly from his back. Yuli darted forward, hands braced against his scales, while Edna and Orla hurried from the cave.

"What happened?" Edna demanded, her sharp eyes flicking from the exhausted dragon to Agnes, who staggered upright, one hand pressed to the back of her spinning head.

"Nemeah," Agnes pointed at a rock, swaying as she tried to steady herself. "Nemeah needs help. She needs Ismaara."

Edna's gaze swept the ground and landed on Mavren, slumped protectively over Nemeah's limp body. She twisted her hands, vines bursting from the stone to wrap around his limbs. He cried out, struggling as the bindings yanked him away, his mask slipping free to reveal his face.

Yuli knelt by Keanoff, whose sides heaved with exhaustion, his body refusing to shift back. He clicked weakly, the sounds rough and broken, but Yuli understood enough.

"Release the boy," she ordered, stroking Keanoff's snout. "He says Mavren helped them escape. We will take it from here." Her words seemed to soothe the massive beast as she rushed to Nemeah's side. The girl's skin was searing to the touch. Yuli pulled back with a hiss before shouting into the cave. "Ismaara!"

A shadow moved, and Henry emerged, eyes widening at the sight before him. "Gods above."

"Help her!" Yuli snapped, waving frantically. She did not need words; Henry understood. He scooped Nemeah into his arms and carried her inside.

Edna loosened her grip on the spell, lowering Mavren gently to the ground. His amber eyes darted across the strangers surrounding him, hesitant, wary, yet full of desperate hope. Edna spared him no more than a glance before turning back to Keanoff, who had collapsed into deep, dreamless sleep.

Inside the cave, Henry laid Nemeah on her bed. Yuli worked quickly, soaking cloths and pressing them to her fevered skin. Beside her, Ismaara finally appeared, her gaze focused, her glow already kindling as she knelt at Nemeah's side.

"Can you help her?" Agnes stumbled into the room, still swaying, one hand clutching her head.

Ismaara's lips pressed into a hard line. She did not answer, only lowered her hands. Light bloomed from her palms as she poured her gift into Nemeah's body. She stitched torn lungs, replenished blood, and mended frayed veins. Pain ebbed, wounds closed, yet something remained. Something deeper, unreachable, hidden far below the flesh.

Ismaara pressed her hand to Nemeah's chest and pushed harder, forcing her gift deeper than she had ever dared. For one fleeting moment, she touched it. Something vast, terrible, and ancient thrumming beneath the girl's heart.

She recoiled with a cry, jerking her hands away as though burned. Her eyes widened, mouth parted, breath trembling as she stared at Nemeah's still form.

Yuli wrung out another rag and laid it across Nemeah's brow, frowning at the unrelenting heat. "You did not heal her? Ismaara, what the hell?"

Ismaara's voice broke as she defended herself, "I did. I tried." She glanced down at her glowing hands, then back to Nemeah. "But I cannot heal what she is."

A silence swept through the cave. All eyes shifted from the Freyla to the girl lying unconscious on the bed, a single question heavy in the air.

"What is she?" Orla asked softly, her child's voice fragile as glass.

Ismaara's glow dimmed. "I do not know."

Marven stepped forward cautiously, feeling nervous among the strange faces. "I know what she is." His voice shook, but he straightened regardless as all eyes turned to him. "She is the Mother. She is a god."

Chapter Thirty-four

K eanoff stood before the mirrors, their cold surfaces reflecting a fractured image of himself. Five were found, though he knew soon they would be in Vallorith's possession. He forced his thoughts elsewhere, hunting with Yuli, sharpening blades with Henry, flying with Noa. Anything to keep from spiraling deeper into the hollow pit gnawing at his chest.

Nemeah's torment weighed heavier than any weapon he had ever carried. She drifted between fevered mutterings, her words tangled nonsense to every ear. Ismaara never left her side, tending to her day after day, but even her healing gifts seemed powerless to help. Each time, her voice trembled with the same refrain.

"There is nothing more I can mend. It feels like before, but this time, it is like something is growing inside her. Something I do not understand."

Keanoff's gaze returned to the mirrors. His beard was ragged, his hair drawn back into its usual warrior's braid, but his eyes betrayed the fatigue that sleep could not mend. He traced the jagged crack across the Cairn's glass, then let his sight climb the curling silverwork of the Thorn's frame before resting on the Darra's.

"We need your help," he whispered, the words a prayer he knew went unheard.

It had become a ritual, kneeling before the mirrors, begging for one of the old Echoes to rise and answer. Each day began with hope, only to be cut down by the insistent silence. A faint voice broke the stillness. Nemeah.

Keanoff turned sharply, leaving the mirrors to kneel at her side. Her skin burned beneath his palm, though not as fiercely as before. He refreshed the rag at her brow, wringing it out with careful hands before laying it gently back against her temple.

Her eyes fluttered, mouth parting to release a low, gravel-edged sound. "Ismaara."

Keanoff squeezed her hand. "She was here this morning. She is doing all she can to heal you." He bowed his head, murmuring a prayer through clenched teeth.

Then, a sudden pressure. Nemeah's fingers tightened around his, her gaze cutting into him with startling clarity. Her lips trembled, but her words were firm. "She is the replaced Freyla. She should not be trusted."

Keanoff shook his head as he leaned closer, certain he had misheard. "Replaced what?"

Pain shuddered through her body, twisting her features. Her teeth clenched, words torn out between spasms. "The mirror was broken. The Freyla died. Vallorith put her in the mirror. He knows where she is, where we are."

Shock rooted him where he knelt. His gaze darted across the cave. There stood Ismaara, beside Orla, her fingers gently braiding the girl's hair, as her voice drifted around the cave. The song she sang was old, in the tongue of her motherland.

He turned back to Nemeah. "Are you certain?"

Her eyes rolled back, then snapped open again, now black as night. Her voice was no longer fevered but ringing, as though drawn from a place far beyond her frail body.

"I have seen it. I see it all. Someone whispers to Vallorith. They told him we were here. They have been watching since the Axis house.

Every secret has been carried to him." Her strength fled in an instant. She collapsed against the pillow, her breathing soft, steady, as though nothing had happened at all.

Keanoff stared, mind churning, questions striking like arrows without a target. He tucked her hand carefully at her side, then rose, his steps heavy as he left the cave. A dull ache built behind his eyes.

Outside, sunlight spilled across the clearing. Edna scattered grain for the hens with steady hands. Orla hummed along to Ismaara's tunes, her smile growing as the older girl encouraged her. Agnes sat nearby, scribbling notes about what she had discovered and seen in Morbessa. Yuli spotted him first. She rose at once, waving Henry back when he started forward. Her hands gripped Keanoff's shoulders, steadying him.

"You alright?" she asked softly.

He glanced from her to Ismaara, who looked up from her braiding with innocent eyes. His voice faltered. "She woke up for a second." His brow furrowed, a storm behind his gaze. "She said," He shook his head. "I do not even know how to repeat it."

"The mother." Mavren's voice pulled everyone's attention as he dropped into a low bow.

Yuli froze, her mouth agape and her eyes going wide. Nemeah stood silhouetted in the entrance, her skin marred by splotches, dark veins threading beneath the surface. Her hair whipped in a wind that had not been there a heartbeat before. Her eyes, black and depthless, locked on them. The clear sky darkened. Clouds surged from nowhere, rolling over the peaks, and thunder cracked through the mountains.

"Get inside the cave." Nemeah's voice boomed, unnatural, echoing from stone to stone. "He is coming."

With a sweep of her hand, jagged rock rose from the earth, sealing the cave's mouth and trapping her friends safely behind the barrier. Another gesture summoned a dome of shadow, blotting out the sky, cloaking all who remained behind it. Rain poured from clouds that had only just been born.

Agnes scrambled to gather her papers before darting inside. Edna pulled Orla and Mavren with her. Yuli and Henry snatched their swords, while Keanoff lunged for the mirrors. His whistle and clicks carried across the cavern, sharp and urgent.

Noa answered with a roar, the dragon's scales bristling with fury, her claws digging deep into the stone. "Let them come. I will tear them apart. I will protect my morakai!" Her growl rumbled through the cave walls, vibrating in every chest.

"Noa." Keanoff's clicks cut through her rising bloodlust. "If Vallorith breaks through, you take the mirrors and keep them safe." He shoved all five into a bag, burying it deep within her golden nest. His hand lingered for a breath before he turned back. "If we fall, you carry them out of here."

The dragon lowered her massive head, eyes narrowing. Her vow was wordless but ironclad. She bared her teeth at the storm beyond. "He comes," she hissed, nostrils flaring. "I smell them, metal bodies and one steeped in death."

"Zepher." Keanoff's pulse spiked. He rushed to Nemeah, who still stood at the threshold. But her form wavered, shifting. A thousand different faces flickering across her own skin. His voice softened, aching with uncertainty. "Nemeah? You need to go rest. We can take care of this."

Her shoulders sagged. Breath rasped from her chest, each inhale shallow. When her eyes cleared for a moment, he saw the cost of her gift etched into her. Her skin was pale, her frame trembling, every ounce of strength spent.

"I will do what I must to keep everyone safe." Her words barely carried above the rain, but her gaze held his. She studied him, memorizing the shade of his forest-green eyes, knowing she would never see them again.

Lightning split the sky. The crack of thunder shook the mountain. Keanoff flinched, and in that instant, he lost her. When his gaze returned, Nemeah's features had warped again. She lifted her hand, and an unseen force hurled him backward into the cave. The mirrors tore themselves free of Noa's nest, drifting weightlessly into Nemeah's outstretched palm.

"No!" Keanoff surged forward, sprinting, arm extended. His hand reached for the bag only to slam against something solid. Pain burst across his cheek as his face struck the invisible barrier. Blood slid hot from his nose. Nemeah approached, holding the bag tight against her chest. Her expression was calm and resolute.

"You will be safe inside," she said, pressing her hand to the unseen wall. "This was the deal. This is how I save you all."

Keanoff hammered his fists against the barrier. The sound rang out like blows on stone, each strike useless. "No!" His roar echoed through the cave, swallowed by the storm.

They all watched in silence as Nemeah summoned Alban and strode to the serrated rocks that divided her from Vallorith. The rhythmic clang of metal boots swelled, growing louder until, with a grinding roar, the rocks before her collapsed into rubble.

Through the dust marched Vallorith and his gleaming host. Golden soldiers funneled into the clearing, their polished armor blinding in the dim light. A smile carved its way across the priest's face as his men fanned out, forming a circle around Nemeah and her guard. Swords flashed from their scabbards, helmets hiding any trace of humanity beneath the gold.

Another figure entered the ring. His crown gleamed, etched with a blazing sun along its band. His blue and green eyes cut like blades as he circled Nemeah, appraising her with a predator's calm.

"So this is the one they call the *Harbinger of Doom*?" His words were precise, clipped, his spine rigid as a staff. He let out a humorless chuckle. "The Echo from Tirnmoor. You lot and your endless craving to be," he rolled his hands with disdain, "*special.*"

Nemeah's blackened eyes tracked him, her lips curling into the faintest smile. "Isrend, leader of the Axis. Twin to Ismaara. Son of Orentheon and Kivani. Heir to the Glacian throne." She bowed with mocking grace, then rose, her grin widening. "You speak as if we are not special, yet it is you who drains your sister's power to preserve your youth. You who send us to do your bidding." Her gaze flicked to Vallorith. "We are special. You are merely a jealous man."

Color rose in Isrend's cheeks. His fists curled tight. "How dare you address me so?" He snapped his fingers, voice sharp. "Enough. Do what you came for, so we may be done."

But Nemeah did not move. Her eyes shifted to Vallorith. "You have not told him."

Isrend's brow furrowed. "Told me what?"

Vallorith's smirk faltered. "Yes, well," His hand waved dismissively, as though brushing away dust. "It was not relevant until now." His grin slithered back into place as he called into the cave. "Ismaara. Come here, my dear."

All eyes turned to the Freyla huddled in the corner. Ismaara shook her head, refusing to move. With a flick of Nemeah's hand, she was dragged across the stone floor, her feet scraping helplessly until she passed through the barrier and stood beside Vallorith.

"How did you manage to keep her outside her mirror indefinitely?" Nemeah's voice cracked like a whip. The question made every heart in the cave jolt.

Vallorith waved it away, casual and smug. "Because I made it so."

Isrend's eyes snapped wide. "You said it was a weakness because the mirror had been reused. You lied to me?" Rage laced his voice. He snapped his fingers again. "Zepher! Kill him!"

The hound appeared in a blur of steel and shadow, blade gleaming as he stalked toward Vallorith. But when he reached the priest, he pivoted, turning his sword instead toward Ismaara. The edge hovered at her ribs, hungry for blood.

"No!" Isrend's voice cracked with disbelief. "You are supposed to obey me!" He jabbed a finger at Vallorith, desperation fraying his composure. "You are bound to me!"

Vallorith dipped his head, smile widening. "I am. But *he* is not."

The words unraveled Isrend's composure. His face contorted, rule slipping like sand between his fingers. He spun on his soldiers, bellowing. "Kill him! Kill them both!"

Not one moved. The army stood still, statues of gold. Their silence was its own verdict.

"Now," Vallorith said, returning his attention to Nemeah, "back to business." His hand stretched outward.

Nemeah hurled the bag, and the priest caught it with ease, his fingers prying free one of the mirrors. He tilted it in the dim light, his grin nostalgic.

"Oh, I remember this one. A feisty little thing." He flicked his hand, and a brilliant flare lit the clearing, then vanished as if nothing had happened.

The mirror remained whole. Confusion rippled through the cave until a low groan shifted their attention inward. On the stone floor lay a girl, small, her curly brown hair spilling across her face. A white Axis robe clung to her frame. Gasps echoed. The impossible had been made flesh.

"Wynna?" Keanoff recognized the girl who had once saved them in the forest. The one who had become a great silver bear. He rushed to her side, lifting her carefully into a sitting position.

She pressed her palms to her forehead, eyes shut tight as though the cavern itself swayed around her. Freedom felt strange: air prickling against her skin, sound scraping her ears, the vastness pressing in after years of stillness. She longed for the silence of the mirror, even as breath filled her lungs again.

"What," Her lips shaped the word awkwardly, her voice foreign to her own ears. "Happened?"

Nemeah's voice broke the hush. "Now the others."

All eyes turned as Vallorith drew another mirror from the bag. Light burst forth, blinding and white, and beside Wynna, a man appeared. His hair was long and golden, falling down his back. The Order's robe strained against his broad frame as though he had outgrown it.

"Slek?" Edna whispered, her frail hands flying to her mouth before she hurried to him.

Like Wynna, he staggered at every sound, flinching at the faint breeze stirred by her approach, his body raw to sensation. Another mirror shattered its glow, and Kallemena lay sprawled across the stone, her black hair spilling like ink. Then came two more, twins with fiery red hair that blazed against the muted cave.

Vallorith's lip curved as he plucked the last mirror from the bag. "This one may not return as he was." He turned it so Nemeah could see the fracture running through the glass. "A pity. He carried such promise."

Light flared, searing brighter than the rest. When it dimmed, a man lay gasping for air, armor clinging to his frame, a crown upon his brow. His breath rattled like someone surfacing from centuries beneath water. The cave stilled, every gaze locked upon him. The long-dead king of the land itself, alive once more.

"My morakai." Noa's voice clicked as she crept forward, lowering her muzzle to nuzzle both her master's cheeks.

At Vallorith's snap, a golden-armored servant stepped forth, bearing the same chest Nemeah had found on the beach. The same one she had found the first mirror in, the one that started this all. The priest lifted a mirror from within, and once again light poured forth, but this time, no new figure appeared.

"You are free, my dear," Vallorith said with a low bow toward Ismaara.

He repeated the motion, nodding to Zepher. "And you as well."

Zepher's smile stretched across his face, too sharp for sincerity. Two more flashes followed, and then the cavern lay crowded with bodies, every mirror empty at last. Beside Ashar, another man stirred, massive as Slek, robed in the garb of the Axis. Another figure appeared next to him: this one looked to be the oldest so far, his furs and leather setting him apart from the others.

"Father!" Keanoff's voice cracked as he lunged to the second man's side. The resemblance was undeniable. He caught him in his arms, steadying his staggering form.

The man's gaze sharpened. "Keanoff?"

Their embrace tightened, rough and desperate. Keanoff's throat ached with the cry he swallowed. He had thought this moment lost forever. Pulling back, he drank in his father's face, then cast his eyes across the cavern floor at the host of strangers rising from stone and light. Something twisted low in his gut.

"Why is he letting them out?" His voice carried a note of concern in this happy time. He glanced at Edna, at Yuli, the same emotions mirrored in their eyes.

Keanoff whirled toward the barrier, his fists slamming against it. "Nemeah!" His shout rang with grief and fury. He drove his shoulder into the wall, pounding with fists and heels. "What was the deal?" His voice broke. He struck again and again, a storm of rage. "What was the deal you made?"

Chapter Thirty-five

The storm outside the protective dome raged louder, and sheets of rain hammered the earth in a deafening roar. All eyes stayed locked on Nemeah and Vallorith, each holding their ground, the air between them thick with unspoken menace.

"Now my parents." Nemeah's voice carried the weight of worry.

Vallorith's smile thinned into a hard line, his patience nearly spent as he closed in on everything he desired. With a flick of his hand, a portal shimmered to life inside the cave. From its glow stepped Maeve and Eoghan, thinner, frailer than Nemeah remembered.

"Ma! Pa!" Orla wrenched free of Edna's grip and bolted to her parents, throwing her arms around them.

The family clung together, Maeve weeping as she kissed every inch of her daughter, while Eoghan stood stiff, eyes darting warily over the crowd of strange faces. He nodded to a few of them, uncertain of where he was or who these people might be.

Maeve's cries echoed off the stone walls, even as Orla tried again and again to assure her everything was all right. Keanoff's fists still pounded against the barrier, his frustration a steady drumbeat under the low murmurs spreading among the newcomers.

Kallemena stirred, rolling onto her side as fragments of memory from the mirror spun through her head. She lifted a trembling hand

and studied her fingers, the smooth skin that stretched across them, as if to confirm the reality of her own existence. Was this real? Was she truly free?

A groan sounded nearby, one she knew instantly. She shot upright too quickly, the world pitching around her, but she forced herself to search for him. Ashar. He lay only a few feet away, his armor gleaming dully in the firelight, his hair just as she remembered. Crawling toward him, her heart thundering, she brushed her hand against his cheek and whispered, "Ashar?" His eyes flickered open, their hazel irises adjusting to the dim glow. "Ashar, it is me, Mena."

For a moment, hope lit his face. Then it shattered. "No." His voice cracked as he seized her hand and wrenched it away. "You are not here. You are never here." He scrambled back, clutching his head between his palms, shaking violently. "None of this is real. You are not real."

Kallemena froze, her fear becoming real as tears blurred her vision. She watched in horror as her betrothed recoiled from her touch. She edged closer, careful not to frighten him further.

"Ashar, please. It is me. We are free at last." She gestured desperately at the cave, the crowd, the storm beyond. "This, all of this, is real." She gathered one of his trembling hands and cradled it gently in both of hers.

Ashar stared down at their entwined fingers, confusion warring with fear in his eyes.

Kallemena turned, searching for someone who might be able to help. Her gaze found the twins. "Fraya," she urged, her voice calm though her pulse raced, "is there any plant that could ease his mind?"

The red-haired woman sat up slowly, her twin brother steadying her. "You will have to wait until my head stops spinning," she muttered, rubbing her temple. Her gaze swept the cave. "Where in Ardoria are we anyway?" Her accent was strange and lilting, unlike anything any of them had heard before. The sound drew every head toward her.

Her brother spoke next, his tone lighter but no less arresting. "It looks like a damp cave." He sniffed the air, then frowned. "Smells like one too." His gaze swept the chamber until it landed on the garden tucked against the wall, thriving with herbs and vegetables. Slowly, his eyes found Edna, still crouched beside Slek. "You." He pointed at her. "You are like us, then. A Thorn?"

Edna nodded, her silver hair bouncing with the motion. "Yes, and there may already be herbs in that garden to clear the fog from everyone's mind." She patted Slek's hand before rising and heading toward the greenery with Finn.

Wynna let out a wry chuckle. "Looks like the gang is all here."

Her eyes swept the cave. First to the unknown man in the Axis robe, then to the older man in fur and leather. She glanced at the family clinging to one another, then at the couple holding hands. At last, her gaze settled on the short-haired figure clutching books.

"And some new faces." She pushed herself up on unsteady legs, relieved to find they still worked after so long entombed in glass. "I am Wynna, a Vira."

Yuli smiled. "I am Yuli, and this is my husband, Henry. I am also a Vira, as is Keanoff." She nodded toward the man still hammering at the invisible barrier.

Wynna's expression softened as memory stirred. "Ah, yes. I know him."

"I am Slek." The hulking man had risen, his head nearly brushing the stalactites above. He pointed to the twins. "Finn and Fraya, Thorns." His thick finger jabbed toward his own chest. "I am a Zeph."

Keanoff's father stepped forward, his long braid streaked with grey but still bearing traces of the dark brown of his youth. The braid matched his son's, a warrior's mark. "I am Yaigen, Talon. Keanoff's father."

Orla piped up then, her voice bright despite the heavy air. "I am Orla, and these are my parents." She outstretched her small hand and pointed to Nemeah, who was outside the barrier. "And that is my sister."

Every eye turned toward the young woman outside, standing opposite Vallorith. They were speaking in hushed tones, too low to hear.

The unknown man in the Axis robes shifted, pushing himself upright. His hair and beard matched in color, his face startlingly young, no more than twenty-five.

"Embric," he said, rubbing his temple. "Glade."

"I am Kallemena, and this is Ashar." The princess's words were soft, her eyes never leaving the man she loved.

A sharp clap outside snapped every head back to the dome's edge. Vallorith stood beside Nemeah, his smile cutting like a blade while she kept her face downcast, refusing to meet her friends' eyes.

"Now that I have upheld my bargain," Vallorith said, his voice smooth, "there remains one final matter." From the chest, he drew the last mirror. Obsidian glass framed not in silver but in plain black, unadorned and ominous.

Kallemena barked a bitter laugh and stepped in front of Ashar, shielding him from the priest's gaze. "And what makes you think I would release you?" She folded her arms across her chest. "I will never let you out."

Vallorith's smile did not falter. His gaze slid over the gathered crowd, hunting. When his eyes fixed on his target, he gave a subtle nod.

A scream tore through the cave. Orla's cries were muffled by a hand over her mouth. Maeve shrieked, and Eoghan shouted, but it was too late. Orla was already pinned, a dagger pressed to her throat. Every face turned, horror etched into their features.

"Agnes?" Henry's voice was scarcely more than a whisper, aching with disbelief. "What are you doing?"

Agnes dragged the girl closer to the barrier, her expression twisting into grotesque delight. The knife wavered dangerously close to Orla's skin as she hauled her along.

"Because she is not who you think she is." Embric's brow furrowed as recognition dawned. His voice hardened. "Hello, Demetra."

The woman let out a jagged laugh, her eyes wild with mania. "Hello, old friend."

Nemeah's head snapped up, fury flaring through her body as her magic surged, anger taking over. A tendril of fire lashed across the ground, coiling around Demetra's ankle and searing her flesh. Demetra shrieked but refused to release Orla. Instead, she dragged the blade down the girl's arm. Blood welled instantly, soaking her sleeve as Orla screamed from the pain into the smothering hand.

"Do that again," Demetra spat, "and I will carve a line from her chin to her naval, letting her insides decorate this pathetic cave."

Nemeah's magic slithered back, retreating at once. Her eyes burned with recognition. "You. The Echo who shattered her own mirror, the one I thought dead."

Demetra's grin flickered, then steadied. "Not dead. Free."

"All it took was breaking the mirror?" Ismaara questioned from where Zepher still restrained her.

"Yes." Demetra's laugh rang hollow. "So simple. Smash the glass, win your freedom." Her head tilted, and her eyes roamed over the faces that stared at her. The once quirky Agnes was now a lethal loon.

Vallorith gave a careless shrug. "A design flaw." He held up his own mirror, its obsidian surface catching the dim light. "But not one I am willing to test."

Kallemena's hands trembled as she lowered her gaze, shame rising like bile. Could it have been so simple all along? She looked at the others, then at Orla. The child bled steadily, her slight frame trembling, her fear spilling into the silence between whimpers.

"Do it, Kallemena." Nemeah's command cracked through the air like thunder. "Free him."

The princess's throat tightened. She turned back to Vallorith, then to the mirror he held. Closing her eyes, she reached into the bonds she had woven in desperation, the failsafe she had clung to for survival.

One by one, she unraveled them. A blinding light burst, flooding the cave. Vallorith dropped to his knees, laughter ripping from his chest as his limbs shook. His ragged gasps rasped like broken glass in his throat.

He stood with the mirror in his hand, then hurled it against the stones. The shatter rang like a bell, shards scattering across the cave floor. Some struck Nemeah's invisible barrier and hissed against it. Vallorith turned his gaze on Isrend, savoring the fear twisting the young man's face.

The priest stretched out a hand, magic lashing forth to drag the prince by the collar of his robe. "Unhand me!" Isrend thrashed like a netted fish. "I said unhand me!"

Vallorith's smile darkened. The moment of realization struck that he no longer had to obey this boy. He glanced at Demetra and gave the faintest nod before returning his attention to the Axis leader. "It seems this is where you and I part ways, *master*."

He opened a portal, shadows curling like smoke, and Demetra slipped through, dropping Orla to the ground. When she reached his side, she handed him the bloodied knife, her eyes alight with wild delight. Vallorith accepted it without pause and drove the blade into Isrend's gut.

Ismaara screamed, struggling against Zepher's grip, desperate to reach her brother.

"Settle down," the hound growled, wrenching her arm behind her back and pressing cold steel to her throat.

"This was not the deal." Nemeah's voice cracked, her body convulsing as magic surged within her.

Vallorith let Isrend's body crumple to the ground and ignored the girl's cry. With a snap of his fingers, a guard dragged the silver chest before him. He hovered his hands over the nine mirrors inside and muttered in a language older than the stone around them.

The box erupted with a blinding glow that was seen through the eyelids. The sound of metal grinding and glass shrieking filled the cavern, building to a piercing ring, and then silence. Vallorith reached inside and withdrew a silver mirror. Unlike the ornate nine, this one was plain, small, practically unremarkable.

He weighed it in his palm, flicked a finger across the glass, and grinned. "This one will not break."

He cast it to the ground. Instead of shattering, the mirror bounced and skittered across the rock. With a wave of his hand, it lifted, floating obediently back to him.

"Now it is time to finish our bargain." He held out his hand, waiting for Nemeah to take it.

Nemeah shook her head, fury tightening her face as magic coiled around her like chains. "You promised my friends and family would be unharmed." She pointed to Orla, who had returned to her parents, still weeping, her sleeve stained crimson. "Does that look unharmed?"

Vallorith shrugged. "A scratch. The scar will build character."

Nemeah curled her fists and felt her power compressing within her. She thought of the lies the priest had told. The honor he claimed but did not possess. The betrayal of Agnes, someone she thought of as a friend. They were pawns the whole time, and she was done with it.

Keanoff's eyes locked on Nemeah, noticing the subtle shift in her appearance. Her hair shimmered with streaks of silver, her face flickering like a shifting mirage. Panic struck him. He seized his father and hurled them both to the ground. "Get down!" he roared, just as a burst of power tore through the air.

Nemeah's rage exploded. Every sorrow, every humiliation, every ounce of pain she had buried erupted outward. The force blasted everyone off their feet. The protective rock formations crumbled, the barrier shattered, and the storm outside rushed in, rain flooding the cavern.

Vallorith staggered upright, ears ringing, and stared at her. Her form shifted, one and many at once, fractured and godlike. Awe and dread knifed through him.

"The Mother," he whispered. "She has Morwyn within her."

Nemeah's eyes burned dark, her mind suddenly alive with memories not her own, with powers she did not understand. A jagged smile split her face as she raised her hand. "And now this ends."

Black smoke poured from her palm, lashing across the distance toward Vallorith. The strike was fast, forcing him back before he could counter. He grunted, flinging his own magic against hers, the clash of their powers splitting the air. The cavern roared like thunder. A low hum pressed into every bone, vibrating the air with unnatural force.

Ismaara, thrown hard against the stone, sat up with blood running down her brow. Her arm throbbed, but she was free of Zepher's hold. She scrambled to Isrend's side and pressed her trembling hands to his wound. His breath steadied, flesh stitching beneath her touch as her power flared to life.

Isrend choked out a sob, his throat raw, eyes burning as he looked up at his savior. "Why?" His voice was hoarse and dazed. "Why save me?"

Ismaara pulled him carefully to his feet. He winced, clutching his tender belly. "Because Mother and Father would have wanted it." Without waiting for his reply, she turned and hurried deeper into the cave, searching for the wounded. She found Orla unconscious in her parents' arms, their grief-stricken eyes fixed not on their youngest but on their eldest daughter. Ismaara dropped to her knees, placing a hand gently on Orla's arm.

"No!" Maeve screamed, slapping the Freylas' hand away. "Do not touch my daughter, you witch!"

Ismaara flinched at the rejection, her frown deepening as she noticed the blood still seeping through the child's sleeve. "The cut is deep. If I do not heal her, it could turn foul, and she could lose her arm." Her plea was desperate, baffled at the mother's hesitation.

Eoghan caught Maeve's hand, forcing her gaze toward him. "Let the girl heal her, Maeve." His voice was firm, though his own eyes carried doubt. He turned to Ismaara and gave a single nod, silencing his wife's protests.

Ismaara drew a steadying breath and pressed her hand to Orla's wound. The blood stilled, the skin knit back together. Relief loosened her shoulders as she realized she had grown fonder of the small girl than she had thought. She looked at Eoghan then, noting the familiar limp he carried. "I could heal that, too," she offered softly. "If you wish."

Eoghan hesitated only a moment, then nodded. She laid her glowing hand against his thigh. Warmth spread deep into his bones, knitting muscle and tendon, setting to rights what had been broken for years. When the light faded, she pulled her hand back with a small smile.

"All better." Then, with barely a pause, she rushed off to find the next soul in need.

Kallemena coughed, dust clogging her throat. She pushed herself upright and realized an enormous wing shielded both her and Ashar. Her breath caught as she gazed up at her dragon, the one she had shaped so long ago, the one protecting her still. Somehow, it had survived.

"Thank you," she whispered.

Noa inclined her head, understanding as only a creature bound to its master could.

Ismaara hurried up, panting, her eyes scanning the pair beneath the dragon's shelter. "Are you hurt?" Another rumble thundered through the cavern, shaking stone from the ceiling.

Kallemena studied the girl's face. Something in her features tugged at a memory. "You look familiar."

"Kivani was my mother," Ismaara answered, her hands sweeping over Kallemena to check for injuries. "And my father was Orentheon. I am your niece." She glanced toward her brother, who had just stumbled inside, pale and shaken. "And that is Isrend. Your nephew."

Her glowing hands hovered over Ashar next, pausing at his head. She felt the tangle within his mind. Memories blurred with falsehoods, centuries of fractured thought twisted his reality. Closing her eyes, she reached deeper, peeling illusion from truth, threading his mind back together.

Kallemena's gaze darted between the boy and girl, her heart lurching. In Isrend's features, she saw her brother, his ears, his eyes, his nose. The sight brought tears that cut through the grime on her cheeks. She turned back to Ismaara, watching her work with practiced ease.

"We need to leave," Kallemena urged, voice tight as she braced for another round of tremors. "The cave will not hold."

When Ismaara finished, she met her aunt's eyes, hope shining through the dust and fear. "I will tell everyone to move to the back of the cave; it is sturdier there. Can you make portals?"

Kallemena nodded as she watched her niece stand and make her way through the rubble. She turned back to Ashar, her breath faltering when clarity sparked in his eyes.

"Mena?" His voice was like spring's first warmth, soft and full of wonder.

Her throat closed. "Ashar?" She threw herself into his arms, clinging as if the world would rip him away again. His embrace was solid, alive, and she wept into his shoulder.

Another boom rocked the cavern. Rocks tumbled from above. Chickens scattered, clucking in panic, while the donkey brayed in terror.

"Easy, easy now," Edna murmured, gathering her flock. She tugged gently on the rope at the donkey's neck, coaxing it back further into the cave. At the same time, she called to the newest member of their small troop. "Mavren, fetch my kettle and pot!"

Yuli and Henry steadied Wynna and Slek, while Yaigen hauled Embric to his feet. Eoghan rose, testing a leg he had not trusted in fourteen years. Amazement crossed his face when no pain greeted his weight. He took Maeve's hand, pulled her up, and lifted Orla into his arms.

"To the back of the cave," he commanded. "Follow them!"

Another blast shook the ground, fire roaring and spitting as rain hissed against it. Keanoff grit his teeth while Ismaara pressed her glowing hands to a gash in his shoulder where a falling spike had caught him.

"I am sorry for my actions before," she admitted, cheeks flushing pink even as she worked. "I was jealous. I have never had anyone look at me the way you looked at her." She gave his arm a quick, awkward pat before darting off to tend the next wounded.

Keanoff barely registered her words. His heart thundered as he looked out from the cave and saw Nemeah seize a blade barehanded, twist it, and fling it back at the priest. Power radiated from her, too much, too dangerous. This was not the Nemeah he knew, yet he clung to the belief she was still in there, somewhere. He staggered upright and lunged for the cave's mouth only to be stopped by a broad arm, silver armor gleaming even in the dim.

"Alban?" Keanoff wheezed, breath ragged from the impact. "Let me pass, she needs me."

"No."

Keanoff froze. The word had come from the guard's mouth. "You can talk?"

"I can now," Alban said flatly, gripping Keanoff's arm with iron strength. "And my orders are to get everyone to safety." He shoved him deeper into the cave.

"We cannot just leave her." Keanoff twisted free, ducked under the guard's arm, and sprinted toward Nemeah, ignoring the protest from his friends.

Behind him, Kallemena hauled Ashar to his feet. Both turned their gaze upward to Noa, who loomed above them.

"I can help her," the dragon rumbled, blue eyes burning bright.

"And we will help as well," Kallemena replied, gripping Ashar's hand tighter.

But Ashar shook his head, his flames already sparking to life in his palms. "No. You must make the portal and get the others to safety. I will go to her." He looked up at Noa, determination steady in his voice. "Ready?"

Noa's answering roar rattled the stone walls. Together, man and dragon surged out into the storm.

Chapter Thirty-six

The battle raged deep into the night. Every strike from the enemy was answered with five more from the misfit trio. Nemeah moved like a shadow, her powers guiding her blade as she felled armored guards with silent precision. Ashar returned Noa's fire to her breath, the two of them unleashing a storm of flame and fury that harried both priest and hound. Blow after blow, they fought, their bodies aching, their magic running thin, both sides knowing this clash could not last forever.

Inside the cave, Kallemena gathered the others and bent her will toward forming a portal that would take them away from the chaos. She pictured the snowy plains, the glittering frost, the spires of her icy castle, her home. A place of safety. A circle of shimmering light wavered into being, but its edges pulsed weakly, warping under the weight of the magic flooding the battlefield. She let out a hiss of frustration, forcing herself to focus again.

Along the walls crept an unseen ally. Keanoff slipped past the guards, hugging the shadows, ducking behind broken stone. With a sudden shift, his body shrank into the small, lithe form of a hare, and he darted past fallen enemies. He had to reach her. He had to help his friend.

Nemeah dispatched the last of the guards and turned her gaze on the mad priest. "Surrender!" she cried above the storm's howl. Her voice rang like the roar of a hurricane. "You are drained and outmatched. Yield, and I will spare your life."

Vallorith clutched his burned arm, the singed fabric clinging to blistered flesh. He spat a curse, his eyes darting between Nemeah, Ashar, and the dragon circling overhead. He needed a plan. He needed them divided.

"I will never surrender my destiny," he screeched, tasting the raw magic that clung to the storm. The air prickled across his skin, every hair standing on end, every breath thick with power. "An unfair numbering, would you not say?" he panted, chest heaving. "Just you and me, little shadow rat. Just you and me."

Nemeah's eyes narrowed. She glanced toward Ashar and Noa, giving them a single nod. Reluctantly, they stepped back. The world shifted. The storm vanished. Darkness swallowed the mountaintop whole, and silence pressed down. Nemeah steadied herself, muscles taut, senses straining.

A jagged bolt of lightning struck at her feet. She staggered back, heart racing, but rose again in an instant, ready.

"You think this is best for the world?" Vallorith's voice boomed from everywhere at once, close and far, impossible to pin down.

Nemeah turned in circles, her shadow-black eyes useless in the void. "I have seen what happens if you succeed," she shot back. "I will not let it happen."

Another strike split the darkness, forcing her to leap aside.

"I would liberate us all!" Vallorith's voice thundered. "I would tear down the walls between god and man, and we would all become what we were destined to be."

A third bolt split the void, but this time Nemeah anticipated its strike. She caught the lightning in her hand, the wild current bucking and thrashing like a beast. With a cry, she crushed it, the sparks dissolving in her palm. Then she hurled the energy skyward, an explosion of light and power. The void cracked, and light ripped through the illusion, shattering Vallorith's conjuring. The storm and mountain returned in a flash.

"You will wake the god," she shouted, her hands blazing with power, "and his fury will tear this world apart!" Her magic flared, striking Vallorith square in the shoulder. He bellowed, collapsing to one knee, his voice ragged with pain.

"And when your powers spiral beyond your control?" he gasped. "What happens when you destroy the ones you claim to love?"

Nemeah's jaw tightened. "I would never harm them. I am not the monster you are." Her next strike lit the air, yet Vallorith rose to meet it, his magic slamming against hers.

They clashed, sparks scattering, their powers locking in a furious storm of light and shadow. Ashar and Noa stood ready at the edges, their muscles coiled. Zepher paced, blades drawn, hunger burning in his eyes as he fixed on the king of Kalyra.

Inside, Kallemena's portal flickered, splitting into five then ten unstable rings as the strain grew. The magic in the air was too much, and she could not control her gifts.

Nemeah's breath came heavy as Vallorith's face twisted through agony and triumph, his lips peeling into a terrible sneer. Then their magic connected, a blast of light and sound, unearthly and immense, fused and radiated outward. The world shattered beneath its force. Everyone and everything was hurled backward; the force itself broke bones and ruptured veins.

Nemeah lay sprawled on the stone, her head pounding, her vision swimming in grey fog. Rain seeped through cracks in the cavern roof, thinning the mud on her face and tangling her hair into wet strands. Slowly, she pushed herself upright. The world spun as she clutched her temple, searching desperately for any sign of life.

A footstep echoed behind her. She turned and saw a hand reach out of the haze. Instinct moved her before thought, and she grasped it with trembling fingers, hauling herself to her unstable feet. The grip steadied her, firm and unyielding, as the world around her slowed and came into view. When her sight cleared, she froze.

Vallorith. His face was streaked with dust and soot, solemn as if cloaked in grief. She recoiled, jerking her hand away, but he caught her arms and held fast.

"Nemeah." His voice was disarmingly gentle, as if coaxing her to his will. "Nemeah, look."

Against her will, she followed his nod. Her stomach dropped. The battlefield was empty of allies, Ashar, Noa, and even Zepher, all gone. Only two figures remained. Demetra and Keanoff.

The crazed woman held his rabbit form by the ears, his small legs kicking and twisting in her grip. She wrapped her other hand around his neck, laughing as Keanoff's teeth sank deep into her hand.

"Stop!" Her heart lurched. She waved her hand, calling for her magic, but it was useless; she was drained completely. A hand grabbed her shoulder. She did not flinch this time; she did not have the strength.

"This can all be avoided," Vallorith murmured. His words slithered like a snake down her spine. "If you honor our deal."

The sound of his voice made her insides twist, as if his evilness seeped into her blood. She lifted her head, her eyes burning. "Our deal was broken when you hurt my sister."

"Technically, Demetra did that. Not I." He straightened, examining the burns down his arm. His tone was maddeningly calm. "Your powers will devour you, you know. And in the end, everyone you love will die."

From behind him, he drew the silver mirror and held it out like an offering. His voice dropped to a near whisper. "I do not wish to do as you fear. I do not wish to release the god from his slumber. I only want what I rightfully deserve." He crouched low, bringing his narrow green eyes level with hers.

Nemeah's gaze searched his features, the sharp nose, the bloodied mouth, the eerie steadiness in his stare. Tentatively, she reached forward. Her fingertips brushed his hand, and a vision struck. She saw Vallorith ascend, cloaked in divine light. She heard him swear the gods' oath never to harm mortals. Then she saw him enthroned among the others, the world below hushed, peaceful, untouched by war. Untouched by her.

The vision shattered. She snatched back her hand, sobs wracking her chest as she turned to Keanoff once more. She begged for him to understand, to believe that this was necessary.

"Do not come for me." She whispered. "Forget about me."

The hurt in his animal eyes broke something within her, tears coming faster than before.

She turned to Vallorith, her voice trembling but resolute. "I am ready."

He lifted the mirror, chanting in a hushed, foreign tongue. A brilliant light bloomed around Nemeah, engulfing her, and then Nemeah was gone. Vallorith cradled the mirror against his chest, a smile unfurling across his face. He snickered as he glanced at Keanoff, nodding to Demetra to release him.

She dropped his form, kicking rocks at him as he scurried away into the ruined cave. Her laugh echoed through the air, the shrill pitch forever ingrained in his memory.

From the shadows, Zepher limped into view, his jaw clenched. "Is it finally done then?"

Vallorith stared at his reflection in the mirror, raw power slowly filling its reflected world. "It is." A portal ripped open behind him, swirling with pale light. "Come along. We have much to prepare."

But Zepher shook his head. "I am free now." He took a step back, his voice flat, heavy with finality. "I am done being your servant. Done with all of this. I wish to see my land. Have solitude as my own being."

Demetra sauntered up beside the priest, her gown torn and charred at the edges, her hair plastered from the rain. "We do not need him, my love." Sliding close, she wrapped herself around Vallorith, standing on tiptoe to kiss his cheek. "Let us go." Together, they stepped through the portal and vanished.

Zepher lingered. His gaze swept the ruined cavern, the scattered bodies of the fallen. He sheathed his blades, shoulders heavy, and turned toward the north. Without another word, he began his long journey home.

***

Kallemena coughed, her chest aching as she forced herself upright. Dust plumed around her, spilling from torn sacks of rice that had broken beneath her fall. She blinked through the haze, noticing the tilt of the floor, the groan of timbers, the sharp tang of salt in the air. A ship.

She scrambled to her feet, swaying as the vessel rocked beneath her. Her legs fought for balance, knees trembling against the unpredictable rhythm of the waves. Another cough sounded nearby. Kallemena spun toward it, heart leaping when a tumble of curly hair rose from behind a stack of crates.

"Wynna?" Relief softened her voice. She stumbled toward the girl, joy breaking through her confusion at the sight of a familiar face.

The small woman sat up slowly, brushing splinters from her arms, and revealed another figure beneath her.

"Embric?" Kallemena's surprise deepened. She pulled Wynna to her feet, and together they hauled the hulking Glade upright.

He rubbed at his head, towering over them, shoulders brushing the low beams until he nearly cracked his skull against the ceiling. For all his size, his voice came quiet as wind through leaves. "Where are we?"

"I think a ship," Kallemena answered, still steadying herself. "But I cannot say where it sails."

Wynna was already darting about, peering under bags and behind barrels. Her voice rang with urgency. "Slek? Finn? Fraya?" She popped up, frowning at the empty corners, then turned helpless eyes on Kallemena.

"I fear the blast scattered us," Kallemena admitted, frustration in her tone. "It twisted my portals and I could not hold them steady."

She pushed open the deck door, sunlight spilling into the shadowed hold. Above, the crew froze in their work. Rough men with weathered faces and calloused hands stopped mid-motion, their eyes fixed on the striking stranger who had emerged from the darkness below.

Kallemena lifted her chin. "Excuse me. Where are we?"

A man stepped forward, his beard grey, his smile a ruin of missing teeth. "Sylvara," he said, the V softened into a B by his accent.

Kallemena ducked back below deck, breathless. "We are in Sylvara."

Wynna's eyes went wide, a smile spreading across her face like sunrise. "I am home?"

***

Alban pushed himself upright, his dented plating groaning with the effort. He unbuckled the chest piece and slid it free, testing his ribs before setting it aside. A handful of shallow cuts marred his hands, but otherwise he was whole. Piece by piece, he stripped away the rest of his armor. First his helmet, and then his arm guards, each clattering into a small pile at his side.

Satisfied, he rose carefully, flexing his leg. A sharp pull bit into his knee. "That is new." He muttered, his voice strange to his own ears.

His gaze fell to the shield lying nearby, propped against a rock. Beneath it was a brown rabbit, one ear shorter than the other, shivering in the night's damp air. Alban nudged it gently until the creature relented, its form stretching, limbs lengthening, features sharpening. Keanoff emerged, blinking as he stood, now human once more.

The Vira swept his eyes over the barren slope. "Where is everyone?"

"I think the blast tore open the Darra's portals," Alban said, scanning the horizon. "I would wager most are not even in Kalyra anymore."

Keanoff's hand dragged through his tangled hair, his sharp gaze settling back on the guard. "How are you here, if Nemeah is?" He could not force himself to finish the thought, remembering watching her form vanish into the mirror.

Alban gathered the remaining armor, threading the straps through his belt before hefting the suit onto his shoulder. "She made me human. Like you."

Keanoff barked a laugh, the sound bright and almost desperate. "She made you human?" His laughter echoed across the hills, wild and unrestrained, until his eyes caught the scabbed cuts across Alban's hands. His smile faltered. "Wait, really? How is that possible?"

"She is the goddess Morwyn reborn," Alban said evenly. "She can create anything." He gestured at himself. "So she made me human. Well, a Glade, I think she called it."

Keanoff stared at him, disbelief plain, before hurrying to match his stride as Alban started down the mountain path. "How do you know this?" He caught Alban's shoulder. "And where are you going?"

"I just know." He looked down at his new solid body, pain still throbbing in his knee. "I can feel it in my bones," Alban answered without slowing. "And I am going to free her."

Keanoff frowned, unsure what to think. The man had not even been human for more than a day, yet already carried himself with the stubborn weight of one. "You mean to rescue her? Alone?"

Alban's reply was calm, almost tired. "Come if you wish. Otherwise, that is my mission."

Keanoff narrowed his eyes. "But she told me not to find her." He hesitated. "To forget about her."

"That is because she has not seen the future yet." Alban's gaze flicked over him. "I saw my destiny when she created me, and it does not end by her hand. Now, I will go to Verdathos to free her from the mirror."

Keanoff stepped in close, refusing to be left behind. "What are you talking about?"

Alban exhaled slowly, as though the weight of truth had been pressing against his ribs. "Her powers are new, and she has not yet mastered them. When she made me, I saw what was to come, and it is not what Morwyn had told her."

Keanoff's voice dropped. "She spoke to Morwyn? Actually spoke to the goddess?"

Alban glanced at him, his eyes steady. "Yes, and the goddess was wrong."

Keanoff fell silent, struggling to grasp the enormity of it. Then he gave a sharp nod. "To Verdathos?"

Alban returned the nod, firm and final. "To Verdathos."

***

Demetra peeled off her tattered green gown, the rags slumping to the floor. She crossed to the wardrobe, its hinges creaking as she drew it open. A frown tugged at her lips when her eyes fell on the crimson robes. She turned toward Vallorith.

"My love, I wish to wear something else. Something fit for a queen." She pouted her lip as she walked to the desk, pushing Isrend's books and papers to the floor.

Vallorith arched a brow as he circled the desk. An hourglass rested at its corner, crimson sand trickling in steady measure. He reached for her, drawing her close, his touch warm against her bare skin. A smile ghosted across his face.

"Anything for you, my dear." He kissed her, hunger uncoiling after years of denial.

Twelve years they were apart. Twelve years were spent weaving the lie of a helpless cook shadowing the twin sister, following wherever she went. It had only happened by chance that the goddess in human form had entered the Axis cells. Chance and fortune had now given Vallorith and Demetra everything they needed for the priest to become a being with untapped potential, a god.

"When I ascend, I will give you everything you desire, and more, my queen." His whisper brushed her ear as he trailed kisses down her neck, his hands wandering her body like so many times before.

He picked her up and set her on the desk, the hourglass rocking back and forth from the force. Their mouths met again, hands devouring what they had long been denied. Demetra drew him closer, her fingers stripping away the red robe, revealing his burned arm and neck. She fluttered kisses along the damage, her eyes glowing as his skin mended under her touch.

Her gaze slid past his shoulder, and she watched the silver mirror that was now hung on the wall. The same mirror that now held a goddess. Her pupils flared with light, filling the priest with rapture, driving his hunger and need into a frenzy.

"Why wait for a god to grant me what I want?" Her voice was euphoric in his ear as she bit his lobe, sending a chill down his spine.

Vallorith suddenly inhaled shallowly, his chest flooding with unknown pressure and cold pulsing pain. He staggered back, lowering his wide-eyed gaze to a dagger buried deep in his flesh. Scarlet spilled down his skin, his hands useless to catch it all. He lifted his eyes to Demetra, whose smile glittered like broken glass. She slid the blade free, blood surging with each fading heartbeat.

"When I can become a goddess and take it all myself?"

Vallorith's hand groped for her, trembling, before his body crumpled to the floor. The last of his life drained into the stone.

Chapter Thirty-seven

Nemeah awoke in a world of silence, the dark pressing in on all sides. Her heart pounded in her chest, the memory of what had happened still raw, still swirling inside her mind. She stood and circled where she was, her eyes desperate for a flicker of light, anything she could be drawn to.

Time stretched into an eternity, with days, months, and years passing, yet her body never weakened, her legs never faltered. She drifted like a shadow across an endless void until, at last, a faint glow pierced the dark. A single candle burned atop the old dresser that had once stood in her childhood room, its flame quivering to the touch of an unseen breeze.

A voice stirred behind her. When she turned, the void melted away, and she was home. The hearth fire crackled warmly, filling the room with golden light. Her small bed was nestled against the wall, and across from it, Orla's tiny form rose and fell with gentle breaths, her sister fast asleep.

Nemeah's heart leapt. She slipped through the door and hurried down the narrow stairs. At the table, Maeve sliced bread in thick, generous cuts, while steam curled from bowls of fresh oatmeal.

"Ma? Oh, Ma! I have missed you so much." Nemeah rushed forward and threw her arms around her mother, only to fall straight through her.

She staggered back, staring at her hands in horror. Maeve did not notice, her knife still steady, her face unchanged. The door creaked open, and Eoghan limped inside, the slop bucket dangling from his hand.

"The pigs are restless today," he croaked, his voice older, wearier than she remembered.

Maeve only gave a curt nod and dusted crumbs from the table. Footsteps pattered above. Orla appeared on the stairs, dressed and neatly combed, her small face drowsy in the morning light. Nemeah's chest ached as she watched her sister move with practiced independence, with no sister's help to guide her.

Maeve ushered her to the table, setting down cups. Eoghan took his seat, Orla beside him. The fourth chair remained painfully, deliberately empty.

"Say grace," Maeve ordered.

Orla bowed her head, her tiny voice trembling as she whispered,

"May the gods bless this food and the crops we grow. Bless this day and the night to come. Bless our family, my momma and poppa," She hesitated, "and my sister."

Maeve's hand cracked against the table, making Orla flinch.

"How many times must I tell you? You have no sister." Maeve's tone cut like ice. She seized Orla's hand with crushing force. "Not anymore."

Nemeah's breath hitched, her heart tearing anew. Her eyes stung as she looked from her sweet sister to Maeve, who was now staring directly at her. Her mother's gaze brimmed with hatred. "I wish I had never borne you." Maeve's voice dripped with malice. "You are an abomination. A mistake I should have ended long ago."

A knife gleamed in her hand, appearing as if it had always been there. The room and its occupants faded into shadow, leaving only Maeve advancing, the blade poised. "I will finish it now."

Nemeah stumbled backward, eyes wide, until Maeve lunged. The knife slashed across her chest, burning like fire. She let out a feral scream, and in an instant, the vision shattered, dissolving into the void once more.

"Pathetic little girl."

The voice spun her around. Ismaara stood before her, one hand curled possessively against Keanoff's cheek. Nemeah froze as she watched Keanoff's fingers tangle in Ismaara's hair.

"Do not worry, little shadow rat," Ismaara taunted, her eyes gleaming. "I will take care of him."

Keanoff glanced at Nemeah, a cruel smirk twisting his lips. Then he turned and pressed his mouth hungrily to Ismaara's. Pain tore through Nemeah's chest. She clutched the wound, tears blurring her vision. She spun away, only to find Edna standing in the shadows, her gnarled hands weaving strange patterns in the air.

From the ground, a tombstone erupted, Jacob's name carved deep into the stone. The old woman's eyes lifted to Nemeah, burning with fury. "It is because of you he is dead. Because we tried to help you." Edna's fingers traced Jacob's name carved into the stone. Her gaze flicked up, sharp and unforgiving. "I have nothing now. Nothing because of you."

Nemeah's tears burned as they streaked down her cheeks, hot rivers of sorrow and shame. She stumbled backward, then turned and ran, her feet carrying her through the abyss. But there was no escape. More faces appeared, rising from the shadows, her friends, her allies, all of them accusing her, their voices a chorus of hatred.

Every word cut deep. Every accusation hollowed her out. Until no tears remained. Until her thoughts tangled into a snarl of blame and self-loathing. Until she feared her mind itself had shattered. She collapsed to the ground, her palms pressed to the cold black beneath her, her body trembling.

Then, through the storm of her torment, a voice stirred. Soft at first, gentle and coaxing, but stronger than the venom that filled her head.

"See past the lies."

Nemeah shook her head violently. "They are not lies. It is all true." Her whimpers echoed in the void as she clamped her hands over her ears, trying to silence the sound, silence herself.

Time became meaningless. Hunger never came, nor rest, only the gnawing ache of grief. She drifted in endless misery until a faint tapping disturbed the silence.

"Nemeah." The voice pierced the dark like a song on a sorrowful day, warm yet unfamiliar. "Are you in there?"

She lifted her head. Before her, a thin opening shimmered into existence. Beyond the glass lay a study of grey stone walls tangled with ivy, shelves of books, and crimson curtains heavy as blood. A face leaned into view. Recognition jolted her.

"Agnes?" she whispered, hope straining in her voice.

The woman laughed lightly, shaking her head. "No, no. Demetra, remember?"

The name struck her with unwelcome recognition. Nemeah gave a small, reluctant nod. Memory returned in fragments, the woman who had deceived them all.

"Come," Demetra coaxed, her voice singsong. "Come and see what I have done. I do hope you approve." She bounced with excitement, her pale skin flecked with dark stains. She now wore a golden dress, the neckline plunging and the material shimmering in the candlelight.

Nemeah edged closer to the opening. Only then did she notice the smear of blood across the stone floor. And the body. Her stomach lurched. Her hand flew to her mouth, muffling the scream that clawed its way out.

Vallorith lay sprawled in death, a deep gash carved through his chest. His blood had seeped into the mortar, staining the cracks of the stone.

"You, you killed him?" Her voice was a broken whisper. "Why?"

Demetra tilted her head like a curious child. "Is it not obvious?" She skipped toward Vallorith's corpse, grasped his slack jaw, and forced his lips to move beneath her hand. In a grotesque parody, she spoke through the dead: "Because I want to rule over all." Her shrill laughter rang in Nemeah's ears, shattering the view of the study, tearing her back into the abyss.

A vision ripped through her mind then, violent and unstoppable. She saw a future rewritten: Vallorith absent from the gods' thrones. In his place, a woman draped in golden finery, a ruby crown gleaming atop her brow. Demetra, a goddess, takes the others under her wing. Their new mother, a new Alune.

Nemeah watched her ascend as the world burned. Cities crumbled, forests withered, oceans boiled. Fire consumed the land while Demetra's voice rose in song, her words twisting into the ears of survivors like a cruel melody. A goddess born not of salvation, but of ruin. Worse than Dathmor himself.

The vision broke, and Nemeah reeled. She clutched at her skull as though it might split apart. Panic flooded her chest as her feet struggled to keep her upright. The abyss was cold under her hot skin, and her lungs never filled with the air she desired. She was drowning in her thoughts, in a world that was not real yet felt so.

Ash fell from nothing, coating everything around her in grey. She felt her body sink, and her will to escape leave. She struggled for breath, for purchase as she sank further and further down. The world closed up around her, leaving an echo beneath the ashes.

About the Author

Ripley Larrow is a firm believer that stories should take you somewhere new, preferably where dragons fly, castles loom, and heroes rise to meet their destiny. A lifelong reader turned writer, Ripley grew tired of reading the same fairy tales retold with different names and decided to craft fresh, original adventures that readers of all ages could enjoy.

Ripley is always dreaming up the next big quest. When not plotting epic journeys and quiet romances that bloom naturally amidst the chaos, she is hanging out with her family, navigating their own adventure through life. Ripley is on a mission: to write books the whole family can enjoy, stories that spark wonder, inspire courage, and leave readers eager for more.

Also, she was wrong about the dragons. Oops.

www.ingramcontent.com/pod-product-compliance
Lightning Source LLC
Chambersburg PA
CBHW022026110726
47901CB00006B/1659